"BEAUTIFULLY WRITTEN,
EMINENTLY READABLE.
A conundrum of reality and dreams
that will hold your attention while it
both entertains and instructs."

Marty Mann, author of
Primer on Alcoholism

"A DEVASTATING PICTURE
of the gradual descent into chronic—
and deadly—alcoholism."

Best Sellers

"A REVEALING
AND TOUCHING ACCOUNT
of a woman's battle with alcoholism
...a sensitive and perceptive
narrative voice with which she depicts
with horrifying realism the ravages
of drink upon the human psyche."

Chicago Tribune Book World

"STRONG NARRATIVE MOMENTUM
infuses a plot in which the heroine
recalls the vicissitudes of a once-
promising life...Mackay relates these
events...with style, compassion,
and tender sensitivity to her heroine's
emotional vulnerability."

Publishers Weekly

PRISMS

MARIANNE MACKAY

FAWCETT CREST • NEW YORK

A Fawcett Crest Book
Published by Ballantine Books
Copyright © 1981 by Marianne Mackay

Library of Congress Catalog Card Number: 80-52415

ISBN 0-449-20172-4

This edition published by arrangement with Seaview Books

Manufactured in the United States of America

First Ballantine Books Edition: August 1983

By some tearing awful might
eternity's road has reached a bend.
JOHN L. HEINS, August 1941

For men and women who share their experience, strength, and hope

Chapter One

"Hello, Courtney." I say it softly. The figure is motionless, unnaturally long and awkward amid the tumble of crisp white hospital sheets. Restraints slant down from each end of the bed, two at the shoulders of the straitjacket and two at the finely boned ankles. A white-on-white study of a flightless Peter Pan, flung aside and abandoned by a careless child. Wrong. It's all wrong. So is the metaphor, so is this place, so is the hastily scribbled non-name on the emergency-room wristband.

I look beyond the bed, through the window at the fine golden morning. There is a tang in the fresh breeze, a promise that Indian summer will soon be over. I shiver involuntarily. It's a good morning for riding out to Aspetuck to get freshly pressed cider, apples, jams, and honey. A good morning to walk along the beach or to sit on the seawall with Courtney, sharing coffee from a Thermos, watching the arrivals and departures of migrating birds in the salt marshes. Not a good morning to find

Courtney immobile, deathlike, trussed in a straitjacket, a Jane Doe tag circling her wrist.

My God, they don't even know her name. They don't know who she is.

I stand staring at the figure on the bed, absorbed by the emptiness of the room, until a wild, abrasive wail out in the main hall shatters the silence and sets my teeth on edge. It's a sound that would awaken the dead, yet Courtney remains immobile, unfazed by the piercing, awful sound.

"Mrs. Meridian is back with us," Connie sighs matter-of-factly as she crosses the freshly mopped floor and absently checks the knots on Courtney's wrists. Connie, an efficient, satisfied penguin in her starched white uniform and black cardigan sweater. No-nonsense head nurse Connie. "I had hoped this would be a quiet day. My feet hurt, I had too many piña coladas last night, and, to top it all off, both Raines and Francis are out sick." She pauses, her eyes scanning the room, then turns to me. "You're not supposed to be in here—this is Isolation." Her voice softens. "No need to bother with this one— she's going to be out of it for a while. Wish I could say the same for Meridian."

Isolation. Room 702. A room like any other on the ward, at first glance. I had always wondered where it was. Patients spoke of it from time to time and I had formed a mental picture of a windowless cell deep in the bowels of the hospital, next to the morgue or wherever the mysteries of pathology were worked. Instead, 702 is an ordinary room—no rubber walls, no heavy metal door, no wild-eyed lunatics raging to get out. If anything, it sounds as if Mrs. Meridian should be locked away in a soundproof cell. A closer look reveals the fine mesh on the window. Something else is different. What? There's an absence of furniture—only a bed, nothing else. No chairs for visitors, tables for flowers and cards. Subtle, very subtle. Everything about the unit is subtle; nothing screams *psycho ward*. I can feel the wryness of my own smile. Except the patients— once in a while *they* scream it. Even so, the straitjacket is rarely used.

"How long has she been in restraints?" I ask as matter-of-factly, I hope, as Dr. Baldridge would.

"Since last night. They probably should have taken her directly to Newtown, but Baldridge wants to run some tests first."

"What kind of tests?"

"Brain scan for one. He wants to see if it might be Alzheimer's disease."

"What's that?"

"Brain literally atrophies, dries up. It's very common among boozers and pill-heads." She rubs her temples wearily. "In plain language, premature senility. We had a kid in here before you started, twenty-four years old, he had it. Of course, she may just be a garden-variety psychotic."

"What do you do for it?"

"Nothing. Nothing we *can* do."

Isolate them, hide them, cart them off to Newtown, leave them to wander the halls in paper slippers.

"What's wrong with Mrs. Meridian?"

"She's angry again. Her son says it's been going on like this for ten days. Come on, help me get her to her room. Maybe we can get her quiet with some medication instead of waiting for her vocal cords to fall out. She hasn't responded to any of the previous therapy. I think Baldridge is going to have to resort to electro, and you know how he hates doing that. Sometimes there's no alternative."

"She can't keep on screaming forever."

"Tell that to her son. He can't stand it anymore. And I'm not sure I can either."

"What if shock treatment doesn't work?"

"Oh, it will, eventually."

Eventually, when they short-circuit that part of the brain, zap the rage out of her, burn the well dry. Will she remember? I look at the form on the bed, so quiet and still. "Why is this one still in restraints?"

"Poor woman was out of her tree last night—damn near maimed an orderly. After that episode last month with the

Simson woman swallowing Lysol in the broom closet, we can't take any chances. Some patients even ask for them."

I stare at her. "I find that hard to believe. Have you any idea what it's like to lie there and wonder when someone will come? Then, when no one does, wonder *if* anyone will come?"

"No, I can't say that I've had that experience. But in this case we haven't much choice, at least not until we find out who she is."

Why don't you tell her? "What if the restraints push her further over the edge? How will you find out who she is then?"

"We'll find out eventually."

"Eventually."

"Is this place beginning to get to you?" There is genuine concern in her voice.

"No, I guess seeing her like that brings back a lot of memories."

Connie peers at me thoughtfully; I can see the question forming in her eyes. "Come on," she commands cheerfully, "you can tell me all about it later. Let's get Mrs. Meridian to bed before she cranks herself up to full volume again."

I turn away from the bed and follow Connie obediently into the hall. Mrs. Meridian is shuffling and whining, the voice harsh with abuse. Connie takes her gently by the arm and signals me to take the other. "Come on, dear, it's time to lie down and rest. We have a nice clean bed for you, a nice pill to make everything all better."

We walk slowly to the room and place the screaming woman on the bed. Mrs. Meridian, her mouth wide with the awful sound, doesn't seem to notice as Connie deftly pops a pill down her throat. "That ought to do it." Connie motions for me to leave the room. I step into the hall. The boy who thinks he's being persecuted by the CIA has taken off his clothes again and is sitting, draped in a bedsheet, beneath the window at the opposite end of the hall, the sun highlighting his long golden hair.

"Jesus," Connie sighs behind me. I look at her. "Doesn't he look just like Jesus? Look at the light around his head. It gives me a start every time I see him there. It's okay for him to stay on the floor as long as he doesn't bother anybody. Oh, one other thing. If he should walk up to you and put his hand on your chest, don't be alarmed, he's just checking, making sure you're real. Come on, let's go get some coffee and relax while we can."

I follow her, adjusting the belt on my gym-tunic-blue uniform.

The staff room is bright with October sun; the freshly brewed coffee warms the hollow emptiness under my ribs. Connie takes a long swallow from her mug, then eases her feet out of her shoes and curls her toes over the rung of the chair. She pulls the patients' charts across the table, flips a folder open, and begins giving me terse one-liners about the people I will be working with. Alcoholics and pill addicts for the most part, housewives, businessmen and -women, writers, plumbers, and far too many children.

I make a list of names and room numbers on a slip of paper I'll keep in my pocket. My own name is engraved on a blue plastic volunteer badge. Even so, I always introduce myself.

In addition to filling me in on the clinical problems, Connie adds a few personal asides. "Mrs. Meridian gave the parish priest the finger a couple of Sundays ago, which has Baldridge thinking she might be on the road to recovery. Goggins, the self-made millionaire, is back, still unable to find the magic pill that will produce instant sobriety. Maude Greene, who has made a fortune writing paperback romances, is also back. Now she won't or can't speak—no one knows yet which. The pale little girl with the face of an angel is from a well-to-do family and has a three-hundred-dollar-a-day heroin habit. I give you one guess how she supports it." No mention is made of the woman in 702.

Connie refills her cup, then lights a Kool. She is telling me through blue puffs of smoke, in graphic detail, about the new man in her life. I nod and hmpf at appropriate moments. My mind is on the straitjacket.

"What about seven-oh-two?"

"The Jane Doe? You don't have to bother about her."

"How does someone come in as a Jane Doe? Who brings her in?"

"Police usually. This time it was a truck driver. He found her wandering down the thruway, totally disoriented, no ID, no sign of an abandoned car, nothing, so he brought her to the ER late last night. Being unintelligible isn't a crime, so we get to lock her up for the time being, or until we find out where she belongs."

"What if she comes to and realizes where she is? Won't it terrify her out of her mind? Couldn't that be what happened in the first place? What if she has a horror of loony bins?"

"The emergency room is not a loony bin, even though it may give that appearance on Saturday nights. But something about being there did set her off, no doubt about that. She bit an orderly while blood samples were being taken. When they tried to sedate her, she went wild and tore off Dr. Wang's glasses and even managed to hit the admitting nurse. You know how busy it can get down there. They had enough on their hands with the stab wounds and coronaries without getting into Marx Brothers chases. So they sent her up here to us."

"Okay, I'd better get going." I stand up abruptly, stuff the list of names in my pocket. The boy is still sitting under the window, in the lotus position. He really does look like Christ.

Mrs. James, held over from last week, shuffles out of her room, her thin hair wisping about a pale, vulnerable face. She has been wringing her hands continuously for six years and sneaking beers from under the kitchen sink. The family, at their wits' end, has brought her in for observation.

Dr. Baldridge is also in the hall. That's unusual, he rarely comes in on a Sunday. I wonder if he has been called because of the woman in 702. He smiles at Mrs. James. She asks him sweetly if she can go home. She has asked the same question every day for the last week and always receives the same answer.

"Mrs. James, you are an alcoholic. You are not suffering from any gastrointestinal or neurological disorder. You do have some liver damage and until you can accept the fact of your alcoholism, I'm afraid you'll have to stay here with us."

"But I can't be an alcoholic, I only drink beer."

"Nonetheless, you do have a disease, a terminal one. Until you understand that, I cannot, in good conscience, release you from this hospital. I don't want you to die, Mrs. James." His voice is devoid of any passion. "I'd like you to talk about it with Jinny, she'll be happy to answer any questions. You have time, don't you?"

"Yes, doctor." I wonder why he thinks I'll be able to get through when he can't.

Mrs. James is wringing her hands frantically. "But I really do only drink beer."

"I believe you, Mrs. James. Beer is alcohol and if you have alcoholism, it doesn't matter what you drink or how much. The results will be the same. Now why don't you go and talk with Jinny, she'll be happy to listen to you."

"I don't want to talk to anybody. I want to go home."

"I know you do. We'll let you go home as soon as you are well enough." He pats Mrs. James's hands. "You can get well, please try and believe that."

"I'll try. But can't I do it at home?"

"Eventually." He looks tired as he opens the door to the nurses' station. His sports jacket is baggy, the pockets bulge with notepads and lemon drops. Mrs. James smiles wanly as he nods to her and sits down at a desk.

I walk with her to the dayroom. Her hand-wringing has begun to subside; she's wearing down. She can be open about it here; no more sneaking off for hasty stolen wrings in the pantry. Wring away, Mrs. James, get it all out. We're on your side.

"Did you say something?" Mrs. James asks as she unclasps her hands and sits down at the table. The fingers are swollen and red from abuse.

"No."

"I thought you said something."

"No, I was just thinking. Would you like some coffee or juice?"

"It's all gone."

"I can make some more."

"No, I'm awfully tired. I'd really rather go to bed. Do you think it would be all right if I went to bed?"

"I'm sure it will be." I know Connie will be annoyed. The staff insists the patients be up and dressed during the day, no excuses.

"I'm so tired. I didn't get any sleep last night. First it was that poor woman in seven-oh-two, and soon as they got her quiet, the other one started with that awful crying. Does everyone in here have what he says?"

"Alcoholism? No, not everyone."

"Do you think I'll be going home today?"

"I don't think so, Mrs. James. I don't think it will be today."

"Then I guess I'll go to bed." She rises slowly; her shoulders are thin under her velour robe.

I stand up and push the chairs under the table and follow her into the hall. Her slippers brush in quiet rhythm along the floor; all the patients shuffle in here—male, female, young, old. None of them walk. Even the pacers shuffle. It must be the slippers. I wonder vaguely if that's why sneakers are recommended for those of us who work on the ward. Our steps, no matter how quick or defined, never intrude.

Mrs. James enters her room and I walk back to the dayroom. It's as I left it, the chairs in place at the table. The patients who are up are all gathered in the dark recesses of the TV room doing the *Times* crossword or staring blankly at a Bowery Boys movie. Blue shadows from the screen flicker and illuminate an occasional face. The images dance, marking off the seconds and minutes. There is no conversation, only the tinny sound of Leo Gorcey's voice and the rustle of newsprint as someone turns a page. It's Sunday. No tests today, no therapy, nothing to do but wait. Wait for lunch, wait for visiting hours, wait for tomorrow. I continue making a silent circuit of the halls; with the exception of the Christlike boy sitting under the window, they are empty. I am alone.

I stare at the door to 702. It is identical to all the others on the floor. It isn't locked. It can be opened, of course it can. This isn't Bellevue.

*   *   *

She hasn't moved.

"Hello, Courtney," I say it again. My voice echoes strangely. I stand facing the bed, my eyes adjusting slowly to the half-light after the fluorescence of the halls. The thick, boyish hair is tousled; the head is finely shaped, noble. No, not Peter Pan. My childhood friend, abandoned, forgotten, nameless. The nostrils are only slightly dilated; respiration has weakened. She is slipping further away, entering another world while Dr. Baldridge is making pronouncements and ordering medications at the nurses' station.

When had I seen Courtney last? Was it at my mother's funeral, when she had tried to tell me she wasn't as strong as people tended to think she was? No, it had been later. Much later, when she had come to New York to have a quick affair with one of her husband's colleagues. She had been angry with me for not getting drunk with her. She had not wanted to hear why I stopped drinking or about my trip to Bellevue in a straitjacket. I didn't blame her, no one liked hearing about it. She had laughed it off and told me to stop eating magic mushrooms. Yet it had happened. It had happened to me. It was happening to her now. How was it that I had come back? Would she?

I concentrate on the dust motes dancing across a ray of sun, reaching harder for a memory, an answer. Why *do* some of us survive? I approach the bed. All the familiar and ordered parts of the face are there. The absence of expression, the stillness, makes me hesitate and I realize that to touch Courtney's head would be an intrusion. Instead, I reach out. My hands linger on her ankles; they are smooth and cool. She stirs, then sighs softly and is gone again. My hands firm their touch slightly and I notice a change about the mouth, the return of something remembered. If I hold on, perhaps it will help her come back. Yes, hold on. What brought you here, Courtney? Or me, for that matter? My mind wanders away from the room, the fallen Peter Pan, the woman on the bed.

You have never asked, Courtney, but I will tell you about it. How it was at the beginning.

Chapter Two

Soaring freedom, that's what it seems to have been. There were butterflies so sated with nectar they could be lifted by a small hand for closer inspection, studied and absorbed before beginning their erratic flight to the next petal. The light was soft. Trade winds blew. There were land crabs and Fred, the cook who beheaded chickens in the backyard. Mango trees laden with luscious fruit shaded the sandpile where I played with my little tin trucks. Golden sweet tropical afternoons washed with gentle rains were all mine. Fred let me pick beans in the kitchen garden, and sometimes on Saturdays Alice, my governess, let me sit on the sagging bed in the back house where they all lived when not tending to our family. She'd give me rice and beans on a chipped enamel plate and I'd savor every mouthful while she pomaded her kinky black hair.

Were she and Fred married?

Lovers?

I never knew.

No one seemed to care enough to ever make mention of it.

Alice boiled the sheets in a big square tin over a wood fire in the yard where Fred killed the chickens. I can still smell the soap cooking and see her patiently poke the bellying linens with a smooth, bleached, square stick, her heavy-lidded eyes fixed on the endless West Indian sky.

There were honeybees behind the hangar where my father kept the plane. Sometimes he'd give me a honeycomb to eat while he tinkered with the engine. Chocks under the wheels, lines lashed to the wing struts and weighted with logs to keep the trade winds from blowing it away. A glistening, metallic blue bird straining for flight.

The hangar was made of corrugated tin and sat at the end of the company golf course, which doubled as the runway. There were no open sewers here. No herds of bare-assed children running among the rangy dogs and hectic chickens. Just honeybees and flowers, a wind sock ballooning, and an occasional gaggle of golfers, who had to be shooed away by a native boy of about fifteen whenever it was time for a takeoff or landing. The boy's name was Phillipe and he could play spectacular rhythms on a washboard while he sang haunting, anguished African melodies in a newly baritoned voice. When he thought he was alone, he would slip off his baggy trousers and fondle his long, uncircumcised penis.

My father. Reddish-gold moustache and gray-blue eyes, gabardine slacks, a jaunty cap, clean white shirt open at the tanned throat, marvelous crisscross lines on the back of his neck. Pouch pockets in his jackets filled with wonderful surprises; a good-smelling pipe to puff on before saying anything important. His voice rich and deep with an easy drawl that would have revealed his origins even if the nickname "Dallas" had not. I heard some grown-ups say he had shot a man back in the States, but I never believed them.

The plane— *aeroplane*, I was always told to say—navy blue with yellow stripes along the fuselage and a design that reminded me of flames painted on the cowling. A Beechcraft stagger wing with red morocco seats and a round U-Needa

Saltine tin just for me to throw up in. At four I was no Amelia Earhart.

Even so, I loved to fly with my father, especially when, as we soared above the clouds, he would sing about Barney Google and his goo-goo-googly eyes. I would join in the chorus and watch the needles flutter on the control-panel dials. When he had taxied the plane to a stop on the airfield, his eyes crinkling with laughter and kindness, we would sing a last chorus together as the propeller rocked to a halt. He would swing me down from the cockpit to the ground and open the compartment that held the big leather bags with shiny brass locks.

A man wearing a white suit and a panama hat would always be waiting when my father brought the bags. The man never smiled, and said very little, but stood and watched while two men in uniforms, with guns on their belts, loaded the pouches into a truck. I never knew what was in the bags, and when I asked, my father just said, "Important papers." Sometimes, after the bags had been taken away, we would go for lunch or visit people. Everyone knew and liked my father, and, because of that, they knew and liked me. Before leaving for Santo Domingo, we always stopped to buy a present for my mother, and once we even bought a tiny tea set for my dolls and a big floppy straw hat for me.

He called me Snooks because we listened to *Baby Snooks* on the big shortwave receiver in a room behind our house. I never understood why he called it a shack. It was a nice room, dominated by the towering black transmitter and receiver, and had cards with call numbers that had come from all over the world decorating the walls. When the workmen dug a huge pit behind the banana tree for a bigger antenna, Harry Murdoch, who lived three houses away and was almost exactly my age, toppled right to the bottom and cried so hard that mummy made me give him the chocolate rabbit that had been sitting on the top right-hand shelf of the icebox. It had been there for weeks, brought down by one of the Pan Am flying boats, to be eaten on Easter. A chocolate rabbit all the way from the States. Probably the only one in all of Santo Domingo. Maybe even the entire West Indies. Harry didn't care if it was the only one in the world. He took it and greedily devoured the whole thing, ears first, while I stared on in horror. Finally, unable to bear the sight, I ran and hid under the banana tree, weeping my frustration and rage. Later it occurred to me that Harry had thrown himself into the pit on purpose. He had done it to get the rabbit.

My mother sent me to my room without dinner for even suggesting such an idea. Disconsolate, I crawled under the bed and found Peter the dog happily chewing on a set of shark's jaws. Before the surprised animal could react, I snatched them away. He tilted his head and wagged his tail, eagerly awaiting the return of his "bone." Clutching the jaws, I explained that they were my last set and began to cry again. Why was it everyone wanted to eat my things? The dog inched his way toward me, wagging his tail and licking my face. My father's shoes and trouser cuffs appeared next to the bed, then his upside-down face as he held up the spread and encouraged me to come out from under the bed.

Still clutching the jaws, I crept out and sat next to the wonderful, strong body. Leaning my head against his chest, I sniffled, "*Harry* is the one that should be punished, not me."

"I know, *muchacha*. People do strange things when they're jealous. Harry could have hurt himself badly throwing himself into the pit like that. The wonder is that he didn't. I guess your mother was so relieved he was in one piece she didn't think twice when he asked for the rabbit."

"He *asked* her for it?"

My father nodded. "We can get another one, Snooks."

"I don't want another rabbit. I wanted that one, and it's gone!"

"I know how you feel. I remember flying a new aeroplane home to Texas after winning the Jackson race, and my brother and his gang of friends made a fireworks of it out by the barn. I was very angry and hurt because I had worked hard for a long time to get it."

"Why did he do that?"

"I guess he thought I was a show-off and he wanted to teach

me a lesson. Maybe that's what happened with Harry. Maybe he couldn't stand going to the icebox and looking at the rabbit with you every day."

"But I was going to share it with him."

"I know, but he couldn't stand it the same way your uncle Bart couldn't stand my aeroplane. It was too much for one person to have."

"I hate them all!"

"How about a story? Would you like me to read you a story?"

"Tell me a real story."

"Want to hear about the hobos or the sharks?"

"The sharks," I said breathlessly as I draped the jaws around my neck.

"Well, I was on my way home from Havana when the oil line in the Bellanca blew and I had to try for a forced landing and just couldn't make it to shore and down I went, right into the sea. I was all bunged up, my face cut and black with oil, when I saw two big dorsal fins heading my way. The cockpit was filling with water and I had no choice but to try to climb out and get up on the wing.

"Luckily, some fishermen had spotted me coming in and I could see them heading for me. That's when I drew my pistol and shot the big one. As the fishing boat got nearer, I shot the second one. The plane was sinking by that time and I didn't want to spend even a minute in the water with those two. The fishermen threw some lines and we towed the plane back to shore along with the two dead fish. Which one do you have?"

"The small one—the dog ate the big one. Look, he got some of the teeth on these." I showed him the gnawed shark jaws.

"Well, I'm not going to promise you another set. I'd rather bring you a chocolate rabbit."

"Weren't you afraid?" I studied the scars on his face; some-how they made him seem more beautiful.

"I sure was, Snooks. You want something to eat? Want some eggs?" He carried me in his arms to the kitchen, and then back to my room after I had eaten one egg, sunny-side up. As he tucked me in, he rested the tips of his fingers lightly on my face and suggested I might be more comfortable if I took the jaws off before going to sleep.

"Why?"

"Because they might bite you in the night."

He carefully lifted the jawbones over my head and placed them on top of the bookshelf next to The Camel with the Wrinkled Knees doll my mother had made for me. "Dog won't be able to get at them up here," he reassured me.

"Mummy doesn't like him sleeping on the bed. He might have fleas."

"He can just for tonight. Sweet dreams, Snooks."

"Thank you, daddy."

Harry, Max, and I were inseparable. We were the youngest children on the sugar estates. We all had tow hair, blue eyes, and could have been taken for triplets. We would soon start first grade together. The boys were obedient for the most part; they always took their naps and refused to join me when I escaped through the mosquito-netting marquee over my bed, out the window, across the lawns to see the Oriental bartender at the club swimming pool. It wasn't that they didn't enjoy Fong, it was just that they seemed to need the sleep more.

Fong would always greet me formally and then serve me a whole bottle of maraschino cherries, which I would eat one by one, spearing them from the bottle with a Johnny Walker toothpick he kept in a matchbox on the glass shelf behind the bar.

Sometimes the silence of the afternoon would be broken by the hum of the distant airplane engine and I would run pellmell for home, leaving the unfinished cherries on the bar. Whenever the plane buzzed low over the house, there was much excitement, for it meant there would be some new treasure in a pouch pocket or the Gladstone bag. If I jumped off the veranda and ran between the bamboo brakes and palm trees, I could see the tanned face grinning down at me. Then, a salute with the wings and he'd head for the golf course, the wheels barely clearing the treetops.

It was better than Santa Claus because it happened more often.

There was always laughter, tenderness, and time to play How Many Miles to Babylon? I would be me and ask if I could get there by candlelight, and he would be a big blue bear, telling me, "Yes, and back again," providing he didn't get me first. Then he'd jump out of the shadows with a big roar. I'd scream my best, most bloodcurdling scream, and then we'd both laugh while he swung me in his arms. In time, my mother would call to him from the veranda where she was waiting, smiling her quiet smile of welcome. He would set me down gently, hold my face in his hands, then kiss me lightly on the forehead and go to her. I followed and sat on the veranda steps, with my back to them, listening, absorbing the comfortable warmth of their voices.

Up the images bubble. Lacelike leaves rising to the surface of a serene pond. Leaves of memory disturbed, freed by some unseen turbulence, floating on the inky, smooth water. Memories never shared with Courtney, never shared with anyone. Was that why it was always so hard to tell people where I was from? Courtney had asked once, when we were in seventh grade. "Where are you from?"

"The West Indies."

"Really?"

"Really."

"Where in the West Indies?"

"Santo Domingo. The Dominican Republic."

"Is that anywhere near Sumatra?"

"No. Sumatra is in the East Indies."

"Oh well, I knew it was one or the other."

That had been it. She had gone on talking about her cousin in New Jersey, the one with all the good-looking boyfriends.

Driving back from San Pedro de Macoris, the capital city, in the Ford V-8 convertible, looking at the tanned neck and the crisscross lines from my position in the backseat, I listened to my father as he talked about the new gabardine suit he had just bought. My mother, remote, awesome, regal, sat in the front seat next to my father, her long, graceful neck indicating she was listening to him, too. I couldn't imagine myself ever being a lady and sighed, supposing that somehow, someday, it would all happen. On my lap sat the jack-in-the-box, wood covered with paper, a little hook of brass shaped like a question mark to hold him in. *Gabardine!* What a beautiful word.

"I'm naming my jack-in-the-box Gabardine," I announced. The darkness rushed by; they hadn't heard me. "Gabardine," I whispered as the white composition clown face with the bright red smile bobbed in silent acknowledgment.

Chapter Three

We made ice cream together, roasted peanuts, and made peanut butter that stuck to the roof of your mouth. Everybody laughed when I walked around the club veranda in my father's golf shoes; they said I looked just like Charlie Chaplin. They even took me to see Chaplin movies, and I couldn't understand why the grown-ups laughed so hard when he had to boil and eat his own shoes. My mother said the shoe was really made of licorice and that they weren't really in Alaska. It still made me cry.

The next morning, I told Harry and Max how sad Charlie was. They both had their flies open and were aiming their penises at the clubhouse wall, trying to see who could pee the farthest.

"I don't understand grown-ups," I said, after I had told them how everyone in the audience laughed. They didn't seem to care, and I didn't understand them, either; they were always doing silly things with their dicks.

"I don't think I'd like to eat a shoe," Max said as he shook the last drop off before tucking the pink bud back into his overalls.

"You know what Phillipe does?" I asked.

"What?"

"He sits by the beehive behind the hangar when my father's not around and plays with his thing."

They yawned, unimpressed.

"His is different from yours; it's longer and has droopy skin off the end. When he pulls the skin back and forth it gets huge," I announced dramatically. They were listening now.

"Huge!" Harry laughed derisively.

"Well, it gets very big. If you don't believe me, why don't you go and see?"

They liked that idea and began trotting across the lawns, through the bamboo brakes to the golf course.

The hangar was empty, no one appeared to be around; it was too hot for golf. We crept carefully around the hangar, and Harry peeked to see if Phillipe was where I had said he would be. Max and I crouched impatiently behind Harry. He looked back at us, his face red, and said in a whisper, "He's there all right!"

"Is he doing anything?" I asked.

"He's playing with it."

"Let *me* see," Max said, shoving Harry aside.

"Be very quiet," Harry cautioned. "He would kill us if he knew we were watching." As Max strained forward, I felt a sense of regret that I had brought them there.

"She's right—it *is* huge. It's almost as big as my dad's," Max said breathlessly.

"How big is that?" I wanted to know.

"Shh!" they both hissed, and we all began peeking around the corner of the building.

Phillipe sat leaning back against the beehive, legs akimbo, heels firmly braced in the grass, his trousers thrown carelessly aside. It was the best view to date: The chocolate testicles seemed to be bursting, and Phillipe appeared to be entranced by the sight of his own erection as it strained away from his groin. He wrapped his hand around his penis dreamily and began to fondle it lovingly; it was even bigger than I had remembered. "Maybe we'd better go," I whispered in panic as Phillipe began to stroke steadily. Harry was right, he might kill us. How would we explain that?

The boys hissed at me to be quiet and stared intently as Phillipe began making animal-like sounds, until, with one forceful thrust, he let his hand go and slumped against the hive, the swollen brown penis seeming to convulse with a life all its own.

It was at that moment we heard the approaching plane. Phillipe was motionless, his eyes closed, the once rodlike penis sagging, diminished, on the splayed testicles.

"Do you think he's dead?" I whispered as a bee investigated the limp brown sausage.

"No, he's not dead," Harry grunted as we scampered to the front of the hangar and watched the plane taxi toward us.

"He looks dead. He looks like he really hurt himself, like he pulled the bone right out."

"Bone? There's no bone," Harry assured me.

"Well, why did it shrink up like that?"

"They just do, mine even does," Max assured me.

"Not like that," I said, remembering the pink finger angling away from his body the day he had taken his shorts off in the baobab tree. "And icky-looking gooey stuff doesn't come out of yours, either. I'm sure he's broken it."

"It probably made him crazy. My mother says you'll go crazy if you do that, maybe even go blind," Max mused.

Phillipe had revived, and emerged from behind the hangar, adjusting his trousers as he approached. He didn't look crazy, just sleepy.

"Hey, Snooks, I see you got your gang with you," my father shouted as he swung down from the cockpit.

I held back for a moment when I saw there were people with him. Then, as Phillipe began placing the chocks under the wheels, I dashed to the outstretched arms.

Chapter Four

Christmas Eve was interminable. The house had been filled with merrymakers to the small hours of the morning, and I feared that Santa hadn't come.

In the morning I crept apprehensively into the living room. He *had* come. He hadn't passed the house by. There was a tree shimmering with a thousand glittering stars, something that had descended directly from heaven. It was the most beautiful tree I had ever seen. I ran to my parents' bedroom and informed the sleeping forms through the mosquito netting that *he, Santa,* had come!

My father stared up at me from the pillows around his head, blinked, and cleared his throat. "It's not morning yet, is it?"

"Yes, and Santa was *here*! Come and see the tree he left!" I said breathlessly.

He sat up and shook his head sleepily, then stepped through

the mosquito netting and stood up. "Let's go have a look, Snooks."

"But the tree is in the living room—it's this way." I tugged at his arm as he headed down the hall toward the kitchen.

"Okay, but I think I heard something out back. Let's go check while your mother gets her robe on."

Frustrated, I followed him impatiently through the kitchen—then stopped and stared through the door into the predawn mist at the shadowy form. Had Santa left one tiny reindeer behind?

"A pony! *He left me a pony!*" I gasped.

Standing in the mist was a small, fat, chestnut pony with a hand-tooled saddle. He appeared to be asleep. I rushed over and touched the velvet nose; the head bobbed in surprise as I stared lovingly into the wise brown eyes. My father lifted me into the saddle and handed me the reins, whereupon the pony promptly circled and began trotting across the lawn toward the DuMonts' house. I could hear the apprehension in my mother's voice as she called, "Oh, Dallas!"

The pony knew exactly where he was going and came to a halt at the canebrake next to the DuMonts' kitchen door. The DuMont girls always hitched their ponies there, and I began to suspect something. Could it be that there had been a mistake? That this was really a DuMont pony?

My father arrived, barefoot, still in his pajamas, and told me to give the animal a kick. I tried, but my legs were too short; all they did was stick straight out to the sides in the tiny stirrups.

"Kick him, Snooks—he'll move."

"I can't," I said, annoyed. "My feet don't reach."

He took the pony by the bridle and led him toward our house. "What do you think we should name him?"

"I think this pony belongs to the DuMonts," I answered.

My father looked at me and quietly asked, "What makes you think so?"

"He went right to the spot where Amalie's pony always waits. He even looks like Amalie's pony."

"I don't think so. Santa wouldn't give you someone else's pony."

That made sense. Santa wouldn't take Amalie's pony and then give him to me. "Doesn't he have a name?"

"Not yet. That's for you to decide."

The shaggy mane bobbed on the silky neck as we followed my father at a brisk trot across the lawns. I liked the sound of the sure little hooves as they clattered across the courtyard. "Then I think I'll name him Trit Trot."

Trit Trot persisted in going to the DuMonts for the next few weeks, but my mother kept reassuring me that he was indeed a gift from Santa and *not* Amalie's pony. She suggested that he might simply be lonesome for other horses and pointed out that Amalie still had a pony. That was true, except the pony seemed much larger and a darker brown than I had remembered, but it was always tied to the canebrake in the exact spot Trit Trot liked to go to.

All the children on the sugar estates rode their ponies to school and tied them to the hitching rails in front of the building. And although it wasn't allowed, we rode out to the canefields and sometimes to the bodega, where I liked to drink in the wonderful odors and sounds while watching the women carry their bundles of wares with weary ease on their heads. My favorite person at the bodega was the peanut-brittle lady. She was tall and thin with waxy yellow skin and wore a spectacular greasy turban under the flat wooden tray of brittle she carried on her head. When a visitor from the States got mad at her and called her a "damn nigger," she cackled uproariously and scared the woman half to death. She always gave me a piece of the crunchy candy, but only when I came alone. My mother would never buy any because, she said, flies walked all over it and left the candy covered with germs. I never saw any germs when I carefully checked each piece before popping it into my mouth.

Once, on the way home from the bodega, I passed a funeral procession, everyone, including the peanut-brittle lady, in immaculate white cotton and carrying a tiny white coffin on long smooth poles. There was an arresting eloquence in their grief as they marched silently down the dusty road in their bare feet, black umbrellas shading them from the sun.

Back in the cool house where there was always so much laughter, I thought about the coffin.

"Mummy?"

"Yes, my pet?" she answered as she put her tennis racket down on the veranda railing.

"Why was the coffin so small?"

"The small ones are for babies."

"Babies? You mean God lets babies die?"

"Sometimes."

"But why?"

"I don't know, my pet. Usually because they're very sick."

"Couldn't the doctor help?"

"Sometimes even the doctor can't help."

"Why not?"

"Well, some of the diseases don't have any cures, and down here they don't have that many doctors, or at least not that many who can help the natives."

"Why not?"

She frowned and I knew I was asking too many questions. I went to my room and curled up on the bed. How could God let a baby die?

Harry and Max appeared at the window and peeped at me through the jalousies. They called to me to come out. I refused.

"You should see what Phillipe is doing now!" Max gasped excitedly.

"He's there with the Schulzes' cook's daughter! Come on!" Harry urged.

"With Frieda?"

They nodded, and Max banged his head on a slat and began to cry.

"Okay, I'm coming."

I slid through the netting and padded outside through the back of the house. I could hear my mother and Mrs. Murdoch talking about the Polish Corridor and Czechoslovakia. How could grown-ups spend so much time talking about things like that when a baby had died? Why did the boys get so excited about Phillipe and his silly dick? Why didn't anyone ever have answers for my questions?

Harry and Max were waiting in the banana tree and jumped down as I approached. Soon we were all running full tilt to the golf course. As I trotted along, I tried to sort out the reasoning behind being born and then dying almost right away. Whose baby was it? Why was it no one ever knew these things? Maybe Alice or Fred would know; they knew all sorts of things.

When I reached the hangar, the boys had already flattened themselves on the ground, their heads concentrated on their folded arms as though they were studying an ant colony. I peered around the corner and saw Frieda kneeling before Phillipe's crotch. She was holding the large black penis in her hands, and then, much to our astonishment, took it in her mouth.

"Is this what they were doing?" I squeaked.

"No," Harry whispered. The boys' eyes were as big as blue saucers as we looked at each other. To our further amazement, she appeared to be enjoying it. We heard a car coming and darted into the bougainvillaea bushes bordering the road to the hangar. It was my father with a man I had never seen before. Leaving again, I thought sadly.

"Why did they do that?" Max asked. Harry shrugged his bare shoulders and adjusted his overall straps. "Why would anyone want to put a peepee part in their *mouth*?" Max continued queruously.

"Sometimes they do strange things," Harry whispered.

Phillipe had emerged from behind the hangar and was removing the chocks from the wheels of the plane. I could hear the whine of the engine as my father signaled to Phillipe to take the propeller. He reached up and pulled down on the blade with his body.

"Contact!" my father called as the blade caught and the engine began to sputter.

"Who does strange things?" Max whispered as we watched the plane turn away.

"The natives! They drink blood and cut people up and make them into voodoo drums and put their peepee parts in people's mouths!"

"But what about *her*?" I hissed.

"What *about* her?" Harry glared.

"*She's* not a native."

Harry pondered for a moment and then said, "She's a German and that's the same thing."

I crept out of the bushes; the plane was gone, so was Phillipe. I was sorrier than ever that I had told the boys about him. "I'm not going to do this anymore," I said.

"Why not?"

"I don't think we should."

"Then don't. But if you tell anybody, we'll . . ." Harry paused and glared at me.

"You'll what?" My voice was trembling.

"We'll never play with you again."

I turned and ran, following a flock of butterflies home.

My mother and Mrs. Murdoch were still on the veranda and I could hear her ask one of the houseboys to bring them two cuba libres.

In the kitchen, Fred was signing out orders to his son, Ti-Jacques, as they prepared dinner. That meant my father would be home soon, maybe with guests. I slipped through the French doors into the living room, which was dark and quiet, the shutters closed against the afternoon sun. Peter the dog was in my room, chewing on the shark jaws. I pulled them away. It was clear to me that less and less made sense; people came and people went; some disappeared altogether. I put the jaws on and wandered into the kitchen.

"Can I have rice and beans for dinner?"

"You can have what everybody eats," Fred answered in his musical voice. The cupboards were open and I stared at the emerald green of the crème de menthe bottle on the worktable. That meant we were going to have ice cream for dessert. I liked crème de menthe on ice cream. . . .

The bed was heaving and pitching as if we were in a storm at sea. I couldn't remember leaving for a ship. I drowsed and wondered if we were on our way to the States again. But was it a ship? I opened my eyes. It was my room. Then why was the bed spinning? I cried out for my mother, terrified; my bed was floating away.

Mummy explained that the house was not tossing and turning on the ocean, the bed was not spinning and swaying. It was because I was sick. I had drunk almost all of the crème de menthe. A terrified Fred had brought me unconscious to her. It was the alcohol, it had poisoned me.

"I can't imagine why you drank it, my pet," she soothed.

"I thought it was pretty."

"But I can't imagine your drinking so *much*."

"I liked the taste. It made me feel good."

She looked at me in surprise and brushed my hair away from my eyes with her beautiful hands.

They allowed me to get up and see the flag on the Schulzes' veranda. Everyone on the sugar estates was yelling about it, and someone had fired a gun. I tottered to the living-room window and looked out. It was a very big red flag with a white circle and, in the center, a black design just like the one on the Indian bracelet my grandmother had sent me from Texas.

"The design is a swastika and it's not at all the same as the one on your bracelet," my father said as he held me up to get a better look.

"It looks the same to me."

"It may look the same, Snooks, but it isn't. The swastika on the flag means the Schulzes are Nazis, that's what makes it bad. We don't want Nazis here."

"Are Nazis bad?"

"Very."

I thought about the Schulzes' cook's daughter and Phillipe. So, Harry was right about the Germans.

"How do you feel, *muchacha*?"

"Afraid."

"It's all right, your pappy's here, nothing will happen to you."

"And mummy, too?"

"And mummy, too."

* * *

When I was finally strong enough to play outside again, I told Harry and Max that I wasn't going back to the hangar with them and resumed my afternoon visits with Fong at the bar. The Schulzes, along with the cook and Frieda, went away. I never asked the boys about Phillipe. Fong consoled me with Chiclets in little yellow boxes when I told him that Amalie DuMont said Baby Snooks wasn't a real little girl. Fong suggested that Amalie might be mistaken.

"No," I sighed, chewing two of the white tablets, "my mother says it's true. Baby Snooks is really a grown-up named Fanny Brice. I don't know about Robespierre because he never talks. Maybe he's a real baby. Probably not. It's all pretend on the radio, except for Hitler."

Fong nodded, polishing a glass with his towel until it squeaked.

"I hate Amalie DuMont for telling me that. Now it will never the the same."

Amalie DuMont had five sisters, and everyone thought they were little saints. They were the ones who told me about "the curse." All six of them condemned me with their eyes when I said I didn't believe any of it and was going to ask my mother. The trouble was, I forgot by the time I got home, and when I remembered, there were guests on the veranda.

When we weren't in school, we all played in the baobab tree while our governesses fanned themselves with paper fans. Alice had one with a picture of Clark Gable on it; I thought it was beautiful, even with the fly specks, and told my mother she ought to get one.

All she said was, "Ummm-hmmm." She was studying Morse code, practicing dits and dots with her telegrapher's key.

"Why are you doing that?"

"It's important to know. I may need to send or read messages someday."

"Why? Is the transmitter broken?"

"These messages come on the transmitter, too."

"Messages from daddy?"

"Yes, and ships and other people."

"Can I have shorts like Amalie's?" I asked.

She umm-hmmed and put the earphone next to her ear and copied down dits and dots coming from the transmitter.

The DuMont sisters always wore navy blue shorts, white shirts, and white tennis hats, just like a team. The shorts had flap fronts with white buttons and white stripes down the sides and they looked very smart. It was quite a sight when all six of them would hang upside down like a litter of opossums on the parallel bars next to the schoolhouse. I had abandoned my overalls for a woolen, one-piece bathing suit, my cowboy boots, ten-gallon hat, scarf, and twin holster set. Grandma had sent the boots and hat from Texas for Christmas, along with red jodhpurs and a jacket I wore only on state occasions.

The grown-ups spent more time in the radio shack than they did on the veranda. My father would fly away for longer and longer periods of time, and my mother would sit with earphones on her head, listening.

Suddenly, one day, the DuMonts were packing and on their way to France: one day in the baobab tree watching dragonflies and talking about the second grade; the next, on their way to France.

"There's going to be a war, and they have to be there," my mother explained.

"What about the ponies? Will they take the ponies?"

"They can't, my pet. The ponies will be better off here, especially if there's a war." She clipped a silver barrette in my hair and I clamped on my sombrero and tottered out to the kitchen garden on the high-heeled, hand-tooled boots. Fred was sneaking up on a fat chicken with his machete.

It was far too quiet without the DuMonts, and I tried to imagine them in a war in their navy shorts, white shirts, and tennis hats. The ponies had been led away in a line by one of the natives who used to cut us sugarcane. I spent a good deal of time in the cool dark under the veranda; it was the best place to get the latest war bulletins from the grown-ups.

When he caught me creeping out, Fred told me to never go under the veranda.

"Why?"

"Because there are scorpions under there," he said as he flicked something off my neck.

Soon after the DuMonts left, we were packing and on our way to the States on a banana boat. I told my mother I hoped the nice man who smelled like rum would be on board.

"Why on earth a man like that?" she asked as she adjusted my beret.

"I'd like to see the shrunken head again," I answered as I studied the shine on my new party shoes. Going to the States was always a big event, and this time I had insisted on packing my boots, sombrero, and shark jaws.

"You'd like to see the what?"

"The little tiny head. He carried it around the deck in a pillowcase the last time. I hope I can see it again."

"My pet, you mustn't make up stories like that; it's not a good habit."

"He did have a shrunken head," my father said and then busied himself lighting his pipe.

"What a grisly thing to show a child! How disgusting! I certainly hope he's *not* on board!"

I had never seen my mother so angry, at least not since the night Poland fell. "It wasn't real, was it?" I asked in alarm.

My father picked me up and said, "No, Snooks, it wasn't real." I wondered why he winked at my mother as he carried me to the rail to watch the boys in the dugout canoes dive for pennies the passengers were tossing. My father gave me one and I hurled it with all my might into the emerald water for a beautiful laughing boy.

There was no way for me to know we'd never see Fred, Alice, Harry, Max, or the baobab tree again. Nor did I know, as the ship pulled slowly away from the concrete jetty, that my life was not a reality, that it would become real on a hot August afternoon in 1941.

Chapter Five

We didn't stay in the States; instead we went directly to the Cunard Line pier and boarded the *Queen Mary*.

"But I thought we were going to see our new house? I thought you said we were going to live in our new house?"

"Later, Snooks. Your mother wants to see her family while there's still time, before the war gets to England."

"Peter! We don't have Peter!" I remembered in panic.

"Peter will be fine. I'll take him to the house. Uncle Davey will look after him until you get back. Don't worry, *muchacha*, we'll all be together soon."

"Aren't you coming with us?"

"Later. I have to do some things first. Don't worry, I'll be there in time for your birthday. We'll have a nice party with your cousins."

"Do they know I'm going to be seven?"

He enfolded me in his arms. "Yes, they know." His voice

was low. "And now that you're getting to be such a big girl, I want you to promise to take good care of your mother. Will you do that for me?"

"Yes, daddy."

There was none of the gaiety that had marked our previous crossings; even the grown-ups' bridge games seemed more subdued. Mummy and I spent most of the time sitting in deck chairs, drinking bouillon. The steward would serve us the aromatic broth in cups and tuck tartan rugs around our legs and tell us when the next lifeboat drill could be expected. Sometimes we would stand at the rail watching the endless white wake as the great ship churned east across the Atlantic. But most of the time we would sit quietly in the deck chairs, staring across the endless ocean at the even more endless sky.

There weren't the usual throngs of children on board, just one little French boy, Henri, who spoke no English. Even so, we managed to communicate, much to the delight of the grown-ups. When the weather got too cold to stay on deck for very long, Henri and I would sit at a table in the lounge drawing ponies with my crayons. Every evening after dinner, our bedtime would be signaled by the ship's orchestra playing Brahms's "Lullabye." We would clap sadly and leave for our staterooms, and I would dream of galloping to the canefields on Trit Trot.

Two days before we were to take the train to Scotland to visit the rest of mummy's family, the air raids began. I brought my pillow to the cellar and snuggled against mummy's side while thunderous explosions filled the night. We never talked, but just sat waiting until the all clear was sounded. It was decided that it might be best if mummy went up to Scotland alone. I would stay with Uncle Alec and Aunt Madge because it would be safer, and, besides, my father might arrive any day.

"There's a brave lass," Aunt Madge said as she bathed the tears from my eyes with a warm cloth. "She'll be back soon and you'll be on your way to the States again. There, there, don't cry. No harm will come to her, you'll see," she crooned in her rich contralto.

* * *

I was in the garden, playing with cousin Elsa, when my father arrived. He looked strong and beautiful in his navy blue uniform. The jacket was belted and had the familiar pouch pockets. I liked the way the sun glinted on the gold thread in the emblem above the right-hand breast pocket. He had volunteered as a fighter pilot, and they had told him that, at twenty-nine, he was too old. So he volunteered for the British Air Transport Auxiliary and had been given the rank of flight captain. He had just piloted a bomber from Canada to England and would have two days' leave before he had to go back for another one.

We went to the station together to meet mummy at the train. I sensed her loneliness as she walked up the platform, then she saw us and smiled. My father picked me up and walked quickly to her and enfolded us in his arms.

The family in Scotland was fine, mummy reassured us. All the children had been sent to the country, where it was safer. She had boarded the train as soon as she got my father's message.

"Do you have to go back quite so soon?" she asked as we rode back to Uncle Alec's house.

"I'm afraid so. We know that the raids are going to become more frequent, and there might not be another ship available if we wait too much longer."

They discussed the plans in front of the cheery fire in Uncle Alec and Aunt Madge's living room. Mummy and I would live in the house on Long Island; it would almost be like old times. I fell asleep in my father's arms as he sat in the chair and talked on about the war and how much harder the times ahead would be. He didn't wake me when he carried me upstairs and tucked me into the big feather bed before leaving for the airfield.

The boat train was very crowded and the pier was jammed with people and luggage. Gangplanks led to every opening of the ship, including the cargo holds. I hung on to mummy's hand as we were pushed aboard by the crush of departing passengers. It was dark and rainy; the din, mingling with the odors of oil and salt water, made me wonder if we would ever awaken in the safety of the new house. There were no polite stewards or pursers greeting the people. Everyone was yelling, pushing, and milling about the deck. Our cabin was tiny, tinier than any we had ever been in. Mummy said we were lucky to have it at all. It felt more comfortable as soon as mummy laid out her silver vanity set on the little dressing table. I was thrilled when she said it would be all right for me to sleep in the top bunk and scrambled up the ladder to try it out.

There were very few walks on the promenade deck and no stewards serving bouillon. The ship pushed west laboriously, but once in a while I would be roused from sleep by the absence of the engines' throb.

"Why is it so quiet?" I whispered.

"Nothing to worry about, my pet. The captain stops the engines so the U-boats can't hear us."

"What are U-boats?"

Her crystal perfume bottles rattled on the dressing table and the bunk vibrated with the comforting thrum of the engines. "You see? If we dress right now we can go for a walk on the deck before breakfast. The air will do us both some good."

Uncle Davey, mummy's youngest brother, was waiting at the pier in New York with a shiny new black car my father had bought. The seats were plush and it was bigger than the Ford V-8 convertible we had in Santo Domingo. I loved the new smell and the solid sound of the rear door as it thunked shut. Uncle Davey asked mummy if she had heard that another ship had sailed from England at the same time as ours and had been torpedoed by a U-boat. She nodded, and stared through the windshield at the honking traffic in front of the pier. Uncle Davey put the car in first and we pulled away, the tires rumbling over the cobblestones.

The parkway to Long Island was serene. We turned off at the exit and drove past cornfields and potato farms to the new house, the one we had watched being built on our last trip to the States but had never lived in. Uncle Davey and Peter the dog had been staying there, getting it ready for our arrival.

"Do you think Peter will remember me?" I asked as we turned into the road that bore my father's name.

"Of course he will, my pet. We weren't gone that long."

Mummy was right—Peter turned himself inside out with joy, bounding into the air and then jumping like a stiff-legged mechanical dog, his tail whirring madly. I tripped and fell on the lawn while the excited animal bathed my face and ears with licks. When I tottered to my feet, the ground swayed and I fell again.

"It's all right, my pet. You still have your sea legs. You'll get used to being on solid ground again."

I reeled after mummy as she explored the house, Peter's nails clicking on the parquet floors. Mummy seemed pleased with everything and began making plans for the things we would need right away. I liked my room; it was bright and sunny with a window that overlooked the pond in back of the house, and, best of all, Uncle Davey had put my shark jaws and sombrero on the closet shelf.

In the center of the pond there was a small island where wild ducks nested. At the end that was on our property was a dam with a sluiceway which, Uncle Davey explained, could be raised to let the overflow out. On the far shore were woods with sandy paths that were perfect for riding my invisible pony. Peter and I would run to the corner of the back lawn that abutted the dam; tiptoe across, taking care not to fall in the brook below; and race off into the woods.

One day as I trotted farther along the path than I ever had been before, I saw a girl about my own age prancing toward me. She saw me at the same moment and stopped. We studied each other in silence until I asked her what color her horse was.

"Black," she smiled.

"Mine is brown."

"Does he jump?"

I nodded.

"Want to ride with me?"

I nodded again and followed her as she wheeled about and

galloped down the path, taking a fallen locust tree with room to spare. I followed her and soared over the tree in one of my best jumps ever. She laughed and we rode on until we came to a clearing and what appeared to be a small village of odd little houses.

"What is this place?"

"The Summer Grounds."

"Do gypsies live here?"

"Why?"

"The houses look like they might be gypsy houses. I don't think I've ever seen houses like these in real life."

The girl looked thoughtfully at the gingerbread trim and batt-and-board siding on a faded yellow house. "There might be some gypsies. Cookie Strumpowski's family might be gypsies."

"Really?"

"Yep, her mother wears big jangly earrings and lots of lipstick."

"Does she tell fortunes?"

"Cookie says she does horoscopes. Is that the same thing?"

"I don't know."

"I have a real pony," I said as we neared the pond.

"Where is it?"

"In Santo Domingo. His name is Trit Trot."

"Who's taking care of him?" I sobbed to mummy.

"He's just fine, my pet. Trit Trot is being well cared for. We'll go back as soon as the war is over, you'll see."

"But why do we have to wait? There's no war here."

"Your father says there might be. We have to wait. Where did you go this afternoon?" she asked, changing the subject.

"To the woods. I met a girl there named Annie and she showed me a place called the Summer Grounds. Have you ever seen it?"

"No, I haven't. Does Annie live there?"

"No, she lives on the other side of the woods. I don't think she believed me when I told her I had a real pony."

"You can always show her the pictures. Come help me shell some peas for dinner."

Mummy and I settled into a peaceful routine in the new house. We would sit by the fire every evening and I'd roll balls of wool for her while the ivory needles clicked, as if each knit, each purl, would bring the war to an early end. Heaps of woolen socks, hoods, scarves, sweaters, gloves—hundreds of each, it seemed. Bundles for Britain.

When my father came home on leave, we would drive to the village and shop for stockings, sugar, and jars of peanut butter for him to take back to the relatives in England and Scotland.

"Your cousin Elsa is crazy about peanut butter," he drawled as he carefully packed the jars in his bag. "Do you remember how good the peanut butter tasted that we used to make?"

I nodded, fighting back the tears.

Annie, Kenny, and I would walk to school together. The halls smelled of stale pencil shavings, chalk, and old books.

At recess, Annie and I often went to Jimmy's candy store to look at the comics and, if our budgets allowed, have an ice cream cone. One day as we neared the intersection, we saw a throng of children and walked over to see what they were looking at. A woman in a gray coat had pulled her car up on the grass and was weeping while everyone stared at my dog, Peter, as he lay panting in the road. His bright eyes stared at me in recognition and he struggled feebly. His stomach had been torn open. The children watched in silence as I picked him up and ran for home with the ruined body in my arms. I didn't believe he had died, even when mummy insisted I put him down.

Uncle Davey got the shovel and dug a grave next to the garden wall. Peter was lying on a piece of burlap, his eyes open, staring, no longer bright. I screamed when they began to lower him gently into the earth.

"He's alive! Can't you see? His eyes! Look at his eyes!"

Mummy took me aside while Uncle Davey finished the job.

She explained that the eyes stayed open, that Peter was dead, and, although his body was going into the ground, he would be with God. "God loves all living things—people, animals—and we all go to Him when we die."

"Where? Where do we go?"

"To heaven."

"Where's that?"

"In space, far above us."

"When will he go up?"

"You can't see it, my pet, but he will. He was a good dog." I sobbed bitterly in her arms.

That night I crept out, in the dark, onto the screened porch and stared at the garden wall until mummy found me and took me back to my room. The next morning I announced at breakfast that I had seen him go up.

"Who go up?"

"Peter. I saw him go up to heaven."

Mummy looked at me, her coffee cup poised, then she gradually took a sip.

"I sat in the dark and then I saw him go, a small golden light. It went straight up until I couldn't see it anymore. It was Peter, I know it was."

Chapter Six

A dog barked in the distance and I wondered what it would be like to touch the elephant. I was on a day-camp field trip to Frank Buck's zoo. My turn to ride the elephant was coming up next and my heart pounded with excitement as the great beast lumbered up to the boarding stand. I took my place in the *howdah* and reached down to touch the wrinkled gray back with my outstretched palm. It's prickly, I thought. An elephant is prickly like a brush. Funny bristles, not at all soft and smooth as I had imagined.

No sooner did my ride start, however, than the elephant was stopped. The counselor was pointing at me and telling the elephant man to get me down. I shaded my eyes with my hand——it was Miss Dorothy. Despite my outraged protests, I was lifted out of the *howdah* and put on the ground.

Miss Dorothy told the other counselors that she would drive me home; they were to wait until she returned. They all looked at me strangely as she led me to the station wagon, the kind with the real wooden panels.

"Why can't I have my ride?"

"They want you at home right away," Miss Dorothy said, holding the door open. I hopped into the front seat and slid under the wheel to the passenger side. "Make sure your door is locked," Miss Dorothy said as she jammed the key into the ignition and pushed the starter button.

She drove without saying a word while I told her about the war in England, the real bombs that blew whole buildings to bits. In silence, her eyes fixed on the road, we sped past potato-and cornfields to the house my father had built. Far from the twisted, still smoldering wreckage on an airfield near the Firth of Clyde, to the house that still smelled new.

There were men with cameras, too many strange people all talking at once. Mummy, remote, proud, in a beautiful black dress, her birthday pearls at her throat, her clear blue eyes looking through me.

"What is it?" Tears burned in my throat. What was happening?

A firm hand took me roughly aside: flashbulbs popping, strange shining particles in my eyes, one of the men insisting on getting a picture of me sitting with mummy.

Why couldn't I have stayed and ridden the elephant? Why did I always have to be singled out, different? "I never got my elephant ride!"

"Hush!" Another firm shake. "Hush, you'll make your mother cry. Your father is dead. He's been killed in a crash."

No.

Mustn't make mummy cry.

My father, killed?

A gull soared and swooped near the wreckage, crying his rusty anguish. The men with the shovels waited for the squall and the flames to subside.

Nothing was left.

"Did you see it happen, Gordie?"

The man nodded. "It hit the hill and split wide open; you could see all the bonny lads, then it burst into flames."

No, mustn't make mummy cry. We weren't supposed to cry?

No more laughing eyes, crisscross lines. No more gabardine. No more fat pony, no more waiting for the sugarcane train, the distant throb of the lone engine in the sky. No more happy landings.

And we weren't supposed to cry?

I looked at mummy. She was staring straight ahead.

The other man looked across the water at the waves rolling in. "The white horses are running."

"Aye," answered Gordie as they began to pick through the still smoking debris, looking for all the bonny lads.

Soon the house was empty. The men packed up their cameras, satisfied with their pictures, and drove away. I went to my room and sat on the newly waxed floor and stared at the Mother Goose wastebasket. She was astride her big white goose, nearly airborne. Geese never crashed.

The door opened; mummy paused, her face pale, before crossing quietly to me. She knelt beside me and touched me lightly on the shoulder. I could hear the wind in the cherry tree and without looking at her said, "Did you know elephants are *prickly*, like a brush?"

"No, my pet, I didn't know."

There was a constant flow of people in and out of the house; many of them brought newspapers that had bold headlines: YANK PILOT KILLED IN BRITAIN. LOCAL AVIATOR DIES IN FIERY CRASH. Some of the papers had pictures of my father in his uniform, the kind, clear eyes smiling off the page. There were pictures of mummy and me; one even said that I didn't know my father was dead. I shook my head in bewilderment.

Telegrams and phone calls poured in. There were too many flowers, and a man even sent a poem he had written. Newspaper people kept calling and trying to come into the house, and when they were turned away, they waited in cars, and those who didn't have cars waited on the front lawn. I wasn't allowed outside and watched the activity through the dining-room window. Annie and her brother were standing patiently on the sidewalk, holding bunches of flowers. When I told Uncle Davey, he let them in and we went to the kitchen.

"Can't you come out?" Annie asked.

"Not until all those people are gone, mummy says."

"Why?" Kenny asked.

"They keep wanting to take pictures."

"Did you see the one of you in the paper?"

I nodded and asked them if they'd like some Jell-O. "It's lemon."

Annie was peering at the newspapers on the kitchen table. "Look, here's one of your mother and father getting in a plane with writing all over it."

I handed her a spoon and looked at the page. There they were, looking happy and very young. On the plane someone had painted "Happy Landings!" "No Hits, No Runs!" "Just Married!" "Whoopee!" There were even some old shoes and tin cans tied to the tail skid.

"It says here they made headlines when they crashed taking off for an aerial honeymoon from Roosevelt Field."

I made a mental note to ask mummy about that, if we were ever alone again. "What else does it say?"

"It talks about the crash. It says it was the second one in six days where everyone on board was killed. The plane was rising clear on the takeoff when it suddenly began to lose altitude. At the edge of the airfield it struck a road which runs atop an embankment, crashed through a fence, and slid into a field. The plane was split open and immediately caught fire. The only man taken alive from the wreckage was First Officer Ronald Elliot from Oakland, California, but he died in the night."

Annie and I stared at Kenny while he paused to take a spoonful of Jell-O. Then Annie said, "Read us the rest. What else does it say?"

Kenny took another spoonful and continued reading. "It says your father had been working for the Allies for some time, but friends at Roosevelt Field were unaware of the fact until he wrote a letter to the newspaper in which he stated, 'The British will win the war and I'm staying here until they do!' Then it says he had been recently appointed leader of an air transport section, composed of American and Australian pilots. He was on leave of absence from the West Indian Sugar Company; the firm has large plantations in the Dominican Republic. That's where your pony still is, isn't it?" Kenny asked as he helped himself to more Jell-O.

I nodded, unable to speak.

"It says," Kenny continued, "that he had his own air service in Central and South America before that. Then it says your mother said, 'Had my husband been at the controls, I'm sure the accident would never have happened. He was an expert pilot.'"

"Let me see where it says that." I reached for the paper. Kenny shoved it toward me and finished scraping the last of the Jell-O out of the bowl.

"He wasn't flying the airplane?" Annie asked.

"No." I could feel the rage boiling. "He was just a passenger."

"That's awful," Annie mumbled; she was holding her spoon in her mouth. "This was terrific Jell-O. Who made it?"

"I did," I answered, wishing they would go home. I needed some time to think.

"Why do the newspapers want more pictures of your mother and you?"

"I don't know."

"Probably because he was famous," Kenny said as he studied another pile of papers.

"I don't think he was famous; he didn't fly around the world or anything like that," I said sadly.

"It says in this paper that he saved six people once. Listen to this: 'Like a scene from a movie thriller, the pilot of a Bellanca plane and an intoxicated passenger fought a hand-to-hand battle 1,400 feet above the ground, over Jackson Heights. He was Dallas Adams, slim young birdman from the Lone Star State, who died yesterday in the largest crash in aviation history. Adams steered the aircraft with the stick between his knees while he fought the inebriated passenger. For a moment it appeared as if the plane and everyone on board would be sent hurtling to their deaths as the craft rocked about the skies. Then a well-directed and sufficiently powered blow from Adams sent the man to the floor of the plane's cabin, unconscious.

"'The young Texan righted the plane and brought it back down to earth. After it had taxied to a stop, the belligerent passenger stepped down to the runway and, moving a few paces away, picked up a stone and hurled it at Adams before being hustled away by a policeman. Adams declined to make a formal charge, saying the poor devil was sick.'"

"What does inebriated mean?" Annie asked.

"It means drunk."

"He was famous," Annie declared.

Was?

After Annie and Kenny had gone home, I hung about the periphery of the grown-ups and was allowed to eat dinner with them in the dining room. Mummy wanted to go to Scotland for the burial, but Uncle Davey said the government had advised against it. She agreed finally to go to Canada, where a memorial service would be held. Her brother Alec would attend the graveside ceremonies since he was already there.

"May I go, too?" I asked.

"No, my pet. Children aren't allowed at funerals."

Chapter Seven

The nightmare began that night; it was to recur for years.

He wasn't dead. He had crawled out of the wreckage, burned, blind, unseen. He was wandering through the mountains and mists trying to find us, calling, calling. I kept trying to reach him but couldn't; he kept getting farther and farther away and my legs were too short for me to keep up with him.

"There, there, my pet." Mummy put on the light and straightened the tangled sheets.

"He's calling us. I hear him. We have to go, mummy. He can't see us, his eyes were burned, he can't find his way back. We have to help him."

She rocked me in her arms. "He's gone, my pet." She led me to her room and helped me into the big double bed and then climbed in herself and lay propped against the pillows, staring into space.

"Mummy?"

"Yes?"

"Do you think if we went looking we might find him?"

She sighed deeply and there was a quaver in her voice as she answered: "No, I don't think we can."

I could taste my tears as they rolled down silently past my mouth. Mummy stroked my head and I slowly drifted back to the dream where it was misty and dark. The world was a darker place now, darker than I had ever known. I said no more. He was gone.

The next morning Kenny said he had read in the paper that the authorities in Scotland were checking the crash to make sure it wasn't sabotage.

"What's that?"

"It's when someone makes a plane crash on purpose."

"Maybe the Germans did it," Annie said as she peered into the bread box.

Kenny pulled the clipping out of his pants pocket. "It also says that officials at the airdrome believe the crash was caused when one wing tip struck a hut at the edge of the runway."

Mummy left for Canada, and Uncle Davey said it would be all right for Annie to spend the night. We stayed up late listening to the radio and eating Fig Newtons in bed. My father was buried in a mass grave while bluejackets fired a last salute to the men who had believed so innocently in democracy. I still couldn't shake the nightmare.

In time, an envelope arrived with a photograph of the grave and a white sash with DALLAS printed in gold block letters.

"Uncle Alec sent this from Scotland; it was on the flowers they put on the casket and he thought you might like to have it." Mummy handed the sash to me. Uncle Alec had been at the graveside services "somewhere in Britain" while mummy had been at the cathedral in Canada.

"Is that all there is?" I asked, feeling sick to my stomach.

And still the dream persisted.

The summer drifted into autumn, the people who had been filling the house went back to their own lives. The war in

Europe raged on, and Mummy spent long hours playing the piano when she wasn't knitting.

"I got a letter from my father," I told Annie as we walked to school.

She stopped on the path and looked at me. "You did?"

"He's alive, he wants me to come to him. He's in Scotland."

"But why would he write to just you? Why wouldn't he write to your mother?"

"He did, but she won't believe him."

Annie said nothing more until recess. "Are you sure he wrote to you?"

I looked at my feet. It wasn't true and I knew it.

She told Kenny when he walked over with his gang of boys. Kenny looked at me thoughtfully for a moment, then said, "Maybe the letter is a trick. Maybe German spies sent it."

I could feel the flush in my face and the tears welling in my eyes. "It wasn't from spies. There wasn't any letter."

Annie frowned. "I didn't think so."

"What's the matter?" one of the boys asked.

"Her father was killed and she doesn't want to believe it," Kenny answered gruffly.

The dream still persisted, but I didn't mention it to anyone. I did check the mail daily, hoping there would be a letter. There never was.

Annie, Kenny, and I walked to Sunday school together and would stop at Jimmy's candy store on the way home to check the new comics. Once in a while we would buy one if we had any extra dimes. We were browsing through the racks when we heard about Pearl Harbor.

"War!" Jimmy was bellowing to people as they stopped in for their Sunday papers.

I went home and told mummy. She knew; she had heard it on the radio while we were at Sunday school. I asked her why everyone was so excited.

"It's only just the beginning for them," she answered.

We spent the rest of the day listening to reports on the radio:

The Japanese had bombed Pearl Harbor in a sneak attack; they still didn't know how many people had been killed.

I became a junior air-raid warden and was issued a ditty bag, one flashlight, and a World War I-type helmet. It was serious business and, even though I was still afraid of the dark, I faithfully made my rounds, saving Annie's house until last. Her mother would always invite me in for milk and cake. She would sweep aside the clutter on the table, make a space for my glass and plate, then sit down, folding her ample arms on the oilcloth, and ask if I'd come across any spies or saboteurs in the neighborhood.

Mummy had many suitors. At Christmas the one I liked best gave me an erector set. "I thought you might like this," he said as he showed me how to build a tower, "because you're your father's girl." I fell into his arms and he held me quietly until my sobs had subsided.

"Do you think she'll marry Uncle John?" Annie asked as we carefully cut out some new paper dolls.

"I hope so. I like him the best."

"I do too," Annie agreed as she neatly folded the tabs of a paper dress onto a doll. "He's not as handsome as some of the others, but he's the best."

We sang "Let's Remember Pearl Harbor" and dragged our wagons around, filling them with every bit of scrap metal we could find for the growing mountain in the school playground. It was taken away by big trucks to a place where they melted it all down so it could be made into tanks and bombs. Even the woods across the pond had been picked clean; there wasn't a can or bottle top to be found anywhere.

The pond froze the week before Valentine's Day and I brought out the new skates I had gotten for Christmas. Annie and Kenny were very patient as they taught me the nuances of staying perpendicular. Within a few days we were all engaged in hockey games, keeping well out of range of the bigger boys, who were too rough with their sticks.

While the older boys built a bonfire on the island, we skated like the wind over thin ice gathering up fallen branches to add to the pyre. Cookie Strumpowski, who didn't skate, joined us one dusky afternoon as we stood around the fire warming our hands and told us about the so-called facts of life, sparing no rococo embellishment, in grand four-letter words. She roared with laughter when I backed out onto the ice and said politely, "Well, all that may be true, but *my* mother never did that."

"Oh, yeah, kid?" one of the big boys rasped. "Where do you think you came from!"

The logic of his statement was irrefutable, even for a seven-year-old. I skated away from their raucous laughter and sniggers to the end of the pond and sat on the frozen sluiceway, wishing for spring, until I was called into the house for dinner.

"Maybe we should ask your mother if what Cookie said is true," I suggested to Annie as we laced up our skates the next afternoon.

She stopped and stared at me in amazement. "Oh, no, we *couldn't*. She'd whip us all! It's bad to talk about things like that with grown-ups."

"Why is it bad?"

"Those are bad words Cookie uses—my mother would have a fit. Who knows what *your* mother would do if she ever found out. She might even have a heart attack. No, don't say a word to anyone about it. Never let them know that you even know."

Although I was certain which words were the bad ones, I asked Annie anyway.

"'Fuck' is just about the worst word you can use. Never say it around a grown-up—they go crazy and might even kill you," she cautioned seriously as she stood up on the ice.

"But why is it a bad word?"

"I don't know, it just is."

Chapter Eight

Mummy didn't marry Uncle John. I wasn't sure where the one
she did decide to marry came from.

"Who is he? What's he like?" Annie asked as we tried to
catch polliwogs at the edge of the pond.

I scooped some water into a milk bottle and stared at the
wiggling black specks; they were all head and tail. "I don't
know what he's like. He doesn't say much to me, just hello
and goodbye."

"Maybe you should speak to your mother, tell her we think
it would be better if she married Uncle John."

"I can't do that." I sat staring disconsolately at the water
and then poured the polliwogs back.

"What did you do that for?"

"They should be with their mother."

"Polliwogs don't have mothers," Annie snorted.

"Of course they do. Everything has a mother."

"They have frogs, and the mother frog has probably for-gotten all about them. She just lays the eggs, she doesn't wait around to see what happens."

"But what if she does?"

Annie shook her head and pulled a pack of Walnettos out of her shorts pocket and offered me one. We sat chewing the candy, looking out at the water. Summer vacation would begin soon. Then what? I didn't know. There wasn't any talk of going back to Santo Domingo. Trit Trot had a new home. I wondered if he had any memory of me and our rides together.

"If we had a rope, we could swing from a tree just like Tarzan. Maybe your Uncle Davey could put up a rope in the tree that leans over the water. Do you think he would?"

"I'll ask him."

Mummy was busy planning for the wedding. She was having a gown designed and made in New York—probably with my father's money, Annie's mother had to go and say.

"Why is your mother always saying such mean things?"

"What mean things?"

"About my mother and the wedding."

"It isn't just my mother."

"What do you mean?"

"I've heard people talking in Bohack's grocery store, they say the same thing. They say he's after her for your father's money."

"The only person I've heard say that, besides you, is Cookie Strumpowski, and she's always saying mean things about everybody."

"Well, I heard people in Bohack's talking. They say he's after her money and that she's fallen for his good-looks."

"The people in Bohack's think he's good-looking?"

"Don't you?"

"I guess so."

"He doesn't look anything like your father. He looks like a movie star."

"Which one?"

"I can't think of his name—the one with the black hair and the white teeth."

"All movie stars look like that."

"What do you mean?"

"What does he do for a living? My mother says as far as she knows, he doesn't have much of a job. He's not at all like your father."

"I know he's not. He works in New York City—he goes there every day. That's all I know."

"Why don't you ask your mother? She must know what he does."

"I will when I see her."

"Is she away?"

"No. She's just very busy getting ready for the wedding."

I asked mummy if I had to go to the wedding. No one I knew had ever been to a wedding, much less their own mother's. Her eyes widened in surprise and she looked up from the invitation list. "Why? Don't you want to be there?"

"Do you want me to come?"

"Of course I do. I'd be very upset if you didn't."

"You'll have a new name, Annie says. We won't be Adamses anymore."

"You'll always be an Adams, my pet."

I had the nightmare again that night. My father still wandering, crying out our names, searching the mists with his blank eyes. How would he find us now?

"Are you going to be a flower girl?" Annie asked as we peeked at the gown. It had arrived that morning, packed in tons of tissue paper.

"No, I'll be in the audience."

"Are they going on a honeymoon?"

"I guess so."

"Will you be going away too?"

"No, I'll stay here with Uncle Davey."

"Is he going to live with you after they come back?"

"No, he's going in the coast guard. Is your father going in anything?"

Annie was making me uncomfortable and I knew she didn't like it when anyone asked her if her father was going to the war. She looked at me sadly and turned away from the closet. "No, he can't."

"Why not?"

"He just can't."

It was a beautiful wedding. Mummy looked like a queen in her gown, and I tried not to cry when they drove off for the honeymoon after the reception. Uncle Davey and I went back to the house and changed into old clothes. He got some good rope and tied it to the tree so Annie and I could swing over the water. Then we went to the upstairs bathroom he used as a darkroom and developed the pictures he had taken at the wedding. I sat on the toilet-seat lid staring down at the pans in the tub, watching mummy's image slowly emerge in the liquid.

"Do you have to go to the coast guard?" I asked.

Uncle Davey jiggled the picture with his wooden tongs, then lifted it out of the pan and set in another. "Everyone is going into the service, you know that."

"Not everyone."

"Well, most of the men are unless they're too old or have something wrong with them."

I wondered what could be wrong with Annie's father. He never seemed to be home much, and, when he was, he just sat in his big overstuffed chair, puffing on a pipe and reading the paper.

Uncle Davey tousled my hair. "It will be all right, I'm sure it will."

On the day they were supposed to return from the honeymoon, I played in the woods across from the house, at a spot where I would be able to see the car come up the road. But they didn't arrive until it was nearly dark. Mummy had brought presents for everyone, even Annie. As she started for the living room with the packages, I saw my stepfather open the hall closet and toss his hat on the shelf. "Well," he said, "that's that." Then he reached down and picked the shark jaws up off the closet floor. "What the hell are these?"

I cringed at his tone. "They're shark jaws that my . . ." I stopped.

"Shark jaws, eh?" He burped. "Well, they don't belong in here. Go and put them away somewhere." He handed me the yellowing bones and I dashed up the stairs to my room and hid them in my bottom bureau drawer, under my pajamas.

Mummy called to me from the bottom of the stairs. "What are you doing up there? Don't you want to see your present?"

I ran down to the living room, the one that had been crowded with reporters less than a year before. She was wearing a pretty silk floral-print dress, no more black crepe, yet there was a sadness in her eyes as she handed me the package.

She had brought me navy blue shorts with white stripes down the sides and a white shirt, just like the DuMonts used to wear. "I couldn't find the right hat," she smiled. "We can look for one in the village."

I buried my head in her arms.

"I thought you'd like them," she said gently. "You see? I didn't forget."

"Those are nice shorts," Annie said as we met on the path. "Where did you get them?"

"My mother got them at Best and Company, when she was on her honeymoon."

"Well, how is he? Can you tell what he's like yet? Does he make you call him daddy?"

I shrugged. "He told me to call him by his first name, Jim."

"Why his first name?"

"I don't know, maybe it's because he's not my father. Look, there's a box turtle. Let's see where he's going."

Annie sat down on a fallen log and gazed at the turtle. "That might take all day. There's something about him that scares me."

"About Jim?"

"Yes. It's a feeling I get, especially when he looks at you."

"Why? What does he do?"

She shrugged. "Nothing, he just seems dangerous."

I nodded slowly, wondering if I should tell Annie that he had punched me in the nose. I knew she would tell her mother, and I didn't want people in Bohack's talking about it. "I know what you mean." I wiped my eyes, hoping Annie hadn't noticed the tears.

"Do you think they'll have babies? My mother says she bets they will."

The thought delighted me. "Oh, I hope so."

"Even though you know what they have to do to get a baby?"

I leaned over and picked up the turtle and watched the chubby dragon legs flail the air. "Annie, I don't care what Cookie says, it can't be bad if our mothers did it." The turtle tucked himself in and I set the shell carefully on the path and waited for the gnarly head to poke out.

Annie's mother was sitting at the kitchen table stirring her coffee. "Just in time, the cake is cooling. Have yourself some if you can find a clean dish." She brushed some crumbs off the oilcloth. "I hear your new father is going into the navy."

"Who told you that?"

"I heard it at Bohack's."

Bohack's grocery store seemed to be the center of information, the way our radio shack in Santo Domingo had been. I wondered if that's where Annie's mother had heard about Poland falling.

"He's going to boot camp next week."

"Well, let's hope nothing happens to this one, for your mother's sake."

"Mrs. Reynolds?"

"What?" She glared, stirring her coffee vigorously.

"He's not my *new* father. He's not my father at all."

"Ah, true, true. I shall try to keep that in mind, Your Ladyship." She groaned to her feet and went out to the backyard. The kitchen seemed strangely empty without her; she was always in the kitchen, at her post at the table. Annie sliced me a chunk of cake and handed it to me. It was superb.

"Why doesn't your mother like me?"

"She likes you," Annie said as she cut herself a piece.

"No, she doesn't. Why does she always call me the baroness?"

"I guess because she thinks you exaggerate."

"About what?"

"Everything. Your father, writing to you when everybody knew he was dead. All those stories about the pony and the shrunken head and all that stuff."

"But I didn't make that up."

"You made the letter up."

I blushed with shame.

All Jim ever seemed to talk about was shoes. He had mentioned them at least once a day since he had married mummy. Now he was worrying about the shoes the navy would make him wear.

"Why does he talk about shoes all the time?" I asked as I carefully set the kitchen table for supper. We never ate in the dining room anymore.

Mummy frowned and then adjusted the flame under the double boiler on the stove. "I imagine it's because his feet bother him a lot."

"Why do they bother him?"

"Because he has to stand all day on a cement floor."

"Is that why he's crabby all the time?"

"What do you mean?"

"He always gets mad at everything when he's here. He gets mad at me."

"He doesn't get mad at you."

"If he wasn't mad, why did he make my nose bleed?"

"I spoke to him about that. He didn't know that you had never cleared the table before. He didn't mean to hit you so hard."

"If he didn't mean it, why did he do it?"

She wouldn't look at me. "He just lost his temper."

"But he punched me. He punched me in the face and made my nose bleed. My father never hit anybody when he lost his temper."

"I told you, I've spoken to Jim about it. It won't happen again."

I didn't quite believe her. "Why does he have to stand all day? Why can't he sit down?"

"He works a press, a big printing press. He can't sit down."

"Why doesn't he do something else?"

"He doesn't know how."

"Well, he can learn, can't he?"

She flashed me a look that meant I had gone too far. "I don't want to discuss this anymore."

"He's not at all like daddy. My father wouldn't do anything he didn't like. My father wouldn't punch children. Jim doesn't laugh unless someone has hurt themselves."

"What a thing to say!"

"Well, it's true. The only time I heard him laugh was when I fell over the rake and hit my head. I don't think that was funny. Why did he laugh?"

"I don't know. Not everyone can be like your father."

"Why not?"

"I don't know why not. They just can't." Then she brightened. "But he's really hoping to learn how to do something else in the navy."

"Like what?"

"Maybe go to sea."

"On a ship?"

She nodded.

I liked that idea the best of all.

When my stepfather came back from boot camp, he looked different. His thick dark hair had been shaved off and he wore a sailor suit. He smiled a lot and seemed happy to be home. Maybe doing something else would make everything better. It was something to look forward to.

When his orders came, he was very upset. The navy had decided to have him do the same thing he had been doing in civilian life. Mummy tried to calm him down and suggested that maybe he could apply for officer candidate school, and they got into an argument. He kept saying he couldn't do it and to just stop talking about it anymore. Then he left for Washington, where he was going to be stationed.

"As soon as he can find a place for us to live, we'll rent the house and go down there so we can all be together."

"I don't want to leave," I wailed.

"Well, we have to. The war is far from over."

Jim found a place for us to live just outside of Washington, and mummy rented the house. All the things we weren't taking were locked in the attic for safekeeping. Jim came home to help and drive us to our new quarters.

It was dark when we pulled out of the driveway, because they wanted to get an early start and beat the traffic on Route 1. They had packed the back of the car so tightly with suitcases, boxes, and odd pieces of furniture that there wasn't any room for me to sit up. Mummy spread some blankets across the pile so I could lie across the boxes and luggage comfortably. "Just like an upper berth," she smiled as I crept in. "You can come up front with us after a while, but I thought you might like to sleep awhile now since it's so early." She handed me a pillow and I used it to brace my elbows and glumly watched the house recede in the darkness as we drove away.

We were going to live in a barracks, mummy explained as we headed toward New York City on the Northern State Parkway. I put my head on the pillow, closed my eyes, and tried to go to sleep.

Dawn broke in New Jersey as we rolled down Route 1 behind a convoy of army trucks. I counted telephone poles and watched for Burma Shave signs in the fields and shifted my position awkwardly from time to time. They never did remember to ask if I'd like to climb into the front seat.

As we crossed the Delaware River, I turned on my side, shielding my eyes from the sunlight with my arm and feeling a dull ache as I remembered the sturdy, reassuring warmth of

Peter the dog's body when he'd nestle close in the back seat of the plane. Everything was gone. I closed my eyes and dreamed of the blacksmith and the crunchy good taste of peanut brittle thin as a butterfly's wing.

Chapter Nine

"Here we are," Jim said as he swung the car to the curb in front of a building with a sign in the window that simply said, "Office."

I stretched and peeked through the rear window. It didn't look too bad—rows of oblong white buildings with nice lawns; children and flowers everywhere.

"Which one is ours?" I asked, anxious to be free of my cramped quarters.

"I don't know, but it shouldn't take long. I'll go get the keys," he said as he opened the car door and stepped out.

Mummy looked up at me from the front seat. "Are you starved?"

I nodded and then said, "Here he comes." Jim was marching toward the car, his sailor hat clamped squarely on his head. He looked mad.

"What is it?" mummy asked as he slammed the car door shut.

"They've given our place to someone else."

"But why?"

"Some damn officer pulled rank and got our place."

"Do you want me to go in and talk to them?"

"No! I don't!"

"What will we do?"

"Oh, they have quarters for us in one of the newer barracks."

"What's wrong with that?" I piped.

"You'll see when we get there," he said.

He threw the car into gear and we bounced over a dirt road to a barren complex of shingled barracks. They didn't look anything like the nice buildings we had just left. There were no expanses of green lawn, nothing but red clay and open trenches for pipes as even more buildings were being hurled up.

"This is it," Jim announced gruffly as the car lurched to a stop. My legs were numb and I had to be helped to the ground. The three of us stood for a long moment staring at the bleak facade, then mummy straightened her shoulders, smiled, and said, "Well, shall we go in and have a look?"

The quarters were a compact duplex with a living/dining room, storage closet, and kitchen downstairs, three small bedrooms and a bath upstairs. It didn't take long to set up the few small pieces of furniture we had brought in the car. Mummy sat at the folding bridge table on a folding chair and made lists of things we would need right away, then prepared a delicious supper with the groceries she had packed in the trunk of the car, while I helped Jim set up cots in the bedrooms.

"It won't be so bad once we get some furniture and drapes," mummy said as she swept the floor.

"May I go outside? I hear children," I said.

"Yes, but don't stray too far. It will be dark soon."

Everyone else in the barracks was new and just as disoriented as we were. Best of all, there were lots of children and the first ones I met were Bertie Green and his little sister, Josie, who had driven all the way from California and had even less furniture than we did.

When school began, it was pandemonium. There were too many children and too few teachers crammed into what had been intended as an extremely modern building. I began third grade sitting on a small chair in the back of the gymnasium, which was being used temporarily as classrooms for grades three through six. It was wonderful being anonymous. No one knew my father had been killed or that I had once had a pony of my own and lived among the clouds. It would be two more years before I would confide any of it to Bertie.

I couldn't sit on mummy's lap anymore while she did my braids in the morning. It wouldn't be too much longer now before the baby came. Intrigued with the process, I asked, "How is the baby formed? What's happening to it now?"

Immediately I sensed her discomfort as she paused and then said, "You're not old enough yet." I gathered my books and left for school remembering Annie's admonition about what could or could not be discussed with grown-ups. Someone had scrawled "fuck you" in white chalk in the concrete gully that bordered the sidewalk and I wondered what mummy would say if she ever saw *that*.

When I got to school we had a substitute teacher, and at recess Bertie told me that they had taken the fourth-grade teacher away for good.

"Why?"

"They say she was a German spy."

"In the fourth grade?"

"A lot of the kids' fathers work at the Pentagon," he answered mysteriously.

I told mummy after school and she said she doubted the teacher was a spy. I was inclined to agree with her; it was hard to imagine Miss Calam a spy, not with all that bright red lipstick that ran up and down the cracks in her mouth and those lumpy blue veins in her legs.

* * *

Mummy was taken to the hospital to have the baby the day before school let out for summer vacation, and an awful woman named Mrs. Maggerly came in to take care of the house and cook our meals. She had horrible breath and sat around all day listening to soap operas on the radio and drinking beer. Her skirt would ride up and the garters she rolled her stockings up with showed. She said if I told anyone she had made me wash the dishes and dust every day, she would break my neck. I believed her and hurried through her chores as best I could.

On the day mummy and the baby were due home from the hospital, Mrs. Maggerly decided to give the house a good cleaning and suggested that it would be better if I got out from underfoot and went to the movies. I was so excited about the baby that I didn't want to go, even though I had become thoroughly addicted to the fantasies that unreeled every week on the screen. Mrs. Maggerly assured me that *Gone With the Wind* was the biggest and best movie ever made; she had seen it three times the first time it was out.

"I'd rather wait and go on Saturday when a really good movie will be playing."

"And what would that be?"

"Cobra Woman."

Having none of it, she showed me to the screen door and pressed a sweaty quarter into my hand. It was too great a temptation, and I knew Bertie and the others were going.

Walking back from the matinee, subdued by the horrors of the Civil War and Scarlett's foolishness, I lingered at the fence surrounding the community swimming pool. What would happen when I got home? What if mummy didn't want me anymore? The impact of the new baby had not hit me until that moment.

Prolonging the walk, I stopped at all my favorite haunts: the playground, the co-op for a Dr Pepper, the woods where all the children from the compound had reenacted so many savage Pacific battles, the trenches where we had fought hairraising versions of the European front. I was afraid to go home.

When I reached the barracks, Mrs. Maggerly was gone and mummy and the baby were upstairs, waiting.

Sick with fear, I began to climb the narrow stairs. The bedroom was dark; the shades had been drawn against the fading June light. Mummy was lying on the double bed, pale and frail under the thin coverlet. Mrs. Maggerly had told me it had not been an easy birth.

I stood in the doorway for such a long time that I began to wonder if my wish had been granted—if I had finally somehow become invisible. Then, in her most memorable gesture of tenderness, saying nothing, she saw me and stretched out her arms. I hurled myself toward the bed, buried my head in her arms, and wept my grief for all that had been and never would be again.

"There, there, my pet. It's all right, it's all right. I'm home now."

I looked up shyly, then asked where the baby was. She gestured toward the wall. I had rushed right by the bassinet, not even noticing the sleeping infant. I tiptoed over and peeked down. How tiny and sweet she was, one small hand daintily tucked under her chin.

"Have you named her yet?" I whispered.

"Yes. We've named her Kirstin."

Mummy's name. They had given her mummy's name.

"How do you like her?" mummy asked softly from the bed.

"Oh, she's beautiful! Do you think I could hold her sometime?"

"Later, when I give her a bottle."

I looked back down at the sleeping form and saw the mass of dark hair. They all had dark hair. Mine had been tow color, almost white. Now it was turning to a reddish straw blond, like my father's. Their skin was clear; mine was covered with armies of loathsome freckles. I stared at the baby and then, in horror, I knew.

I didn't belong. I was finally truly invisible.

Chapter Ten

The war dragged on. Kirstin grew from an infant to a roly-poly toddler we called Kirsty. Try as I did, I couldn't quite develop a taste for Spam. Bertie Green and I broke the routine of the war games with forays to the Community Theater. Saturdays were westerns or Tarzan movies; Sundays offered rich, Technicolor fare. Bertie liked the Betty Grable musicals best, my preference was for Gene Kelly.

Mummy called me in from the trenches one day and announced that John Lyons was in Washington and would be dropping by for a brief visit. John Lyons, the man I had hoped mummy would marry. The man Annie and I had called "Uncle John." I willingly scrubbed my face and changed into clean clothes. I had just emerged from the bathroom when an official gray navy car pulled up in front of the barracks. Uncle John stepped out of the rear door looking magnificent in the dress summer whites of a lieutenant commander. The brass buttons

gleamed, his chest was proud with multicolored campaign ribbons. He had been in all kinds of combat in the Pacific. At
dinner we listened raptly as he told wonderful stories of great
ships, jungles, atolls, and marsupials in Australia.

After dinner, he pulled out an envelope of photographs that
had been taken of him during his travels.

"What is that?" I asked as he showed one of himself holding
a small, fluffy, bearlike creature on his hip. It was unlike
anything I had ever seen before.

"That's a koala bear. See how he holds on just like a baby?"

"Is it tame?"

"No, but they're very shy creatures and can be pretty nasty,
but if you have the patience, they'll eventually let you pick
them up."

My stepfather let out an awful belch and didn't excuse
himself. Uncle John went on talking as if he hadn't noticed.
Mummy looked embarrassed.

"Why didn't you bring one back?"

"I don't think it would survive in this part of the world."

"Why?"

"Why?" He grinned, his blue eyes dancing. "You know,
your father called you Snooks because it was always *why* this,
why that, '*Why*, daddy?' Remember Snooks?"

I bit my lip and nodded. He drew me to the crisp whiteness
of his chest. The clean, good, man-smell of his bay rum was
familiar and comforting. I found myself listening for the thrum
of the lone engine in the sky.

When it was time for him to leave, we saw him to the
waiting car and he gave us a salute before he slid into the back
and the driver closed the door for him. We stood watching as
the car pulled away.

"Was that your father's C.O.?" Bertie asked as the navy
car disappeared around the curve.

"No. Just an old friend."

"He sure must have seen some action; did you see all his
campaign ribbons? Did he tell you how he was wounded?"

"I didn't know he was wounded—he never said anything
about it. What makes you think that?"

"Well, maybe he wasn't wounded, but he's won the Navy Cross. Usually you get that for something pretty big. You sure he didn't say anything about it?"

"No, he just talked about the war. He thinks it's going to be over soon. He didn't say much about himself, just that he saw a lot of battles."

"I think he must have done more than just see them."

The next day, while helping mummy fold the wash, I asked her if she had known Uncle John had been wounded.

"No, what makes you think so?"

"Bertie says he was wearing a citation. He knows about all those things."

"He didn't mention it. But that doesn't surprise me."

"It doesn't? Why not?"

"He's not the sort of man to brag about his accomplishments."

When Jim came home from the naval base where he worked at the printing plant, he went directly upstairs and changed into his old khaki pants and a plaid shirt. He hated his uniform and took it off whenever he could. He never wore dungarees the way some of the other men did. Mummy removed an ice tray from the refrigerator and set the metal cocktail shaker and two martini glasses on the drainboard. The evening ritual was in progress. I didn't have to look to know she was reaching in the cupboard above the sink for the gin and vermouth. I spread the newspaper Jim always brought every night on the living room rug and scanned the funnies as I listened to the last few minutes of Jack Armstrong on the radio. As soon as the martinis had been mixed I knew I would have to turn the radio off and set the table for dinner. Macaroni and cheese again with fresh sliced tomatoes from the plants that flourished near the doorstep.

As Jim poured the martinis, mummy asked him if he had noticed Uncle John's citation.

"No, I can't say that I did. I wasn't aware that you were familiar with that sort of thing."

"I'm not. Bertie Green noticed it and mentioned it to Virginia."

"What citation did Bertie Green think he saw?"

"The Navy Cross."

Jim settled into an armchair with his martini and rattled the newspaper open. I had folded it back up carefully and laid it on the end table for him. "Wonder what he would have gotten the Navy Cross for?"

"Well, he did seem to have been through quite a lot of combat."

Jim wasn't listening, he was studying the stock market listings and frowning.

I was in the kitchen washing the dishes when Bertie tapped on the screen on the window. "Jinny, are you coming out?"

"I have to do these first," I groaned.

"Well, hurry up. Can't you leave them on the drainboard to dry?"

"No, I have to wipe each one and put it away. He always checks. If they're not all absolutely clean, I have to do every dish over again."

"Well, hurry up. All the kids are up in the big woods behind the hill."

I scrubbed the plates, rinsed them, and stacked them in the dish rack, and then put the casserole to soak. The macaroni and cheese had already dried and hardened like concrete around the sides. I hoped the hot soapy water would soften everything while I dried the silver and china. Finally, as I was drying the casserole, Jim stepped in to check on my progress. He didn't like it when I took too long; I didn't either.

"What the hell is this? Look at this! Macaroni and burned cheese stuck all over it. What are you trying to do, poison us!" He was livid and I backed away; something dreadful was going to happen. I wouldn't be able to play with the other kids in the woods on the hill. My mouth went dry and I closed my eyes before I felt the blow. "Now wash it properly! You are a slob, you really are. When you're done, go straight to your room."

I turned to the sink, my hands were palsied and the Pyrex dish clattered ominously on the bottom of the sink like an old hubcap. I couldn't grasp what had happened and stared at the offending dish. There was a tiny spot of charred cheese under the rim. "Damn slob, you could have given us ptomaine," he muttered as he returned to the living room. I held on to the faucets and tried to keep from crying before applying the Brillo to the small black spot. It wouldn't come off, I scrubbed until the pad disintegrated and then finally chipped it off with the point of the vegetable knife.

I didn't know how long I had been standing there rinsing the clear glass dish when mummy said over my shoulder, "That's perfectly clean, let me dry it for you." She took the bowl and wiped it with a tea towel and I ducked around the corner, through the living room and up the stairs. I didn't turn on the light, but knelt before the window with my elbows on the sill and gingerly cupped my chin in my hands.

"Star light, star bright, first star I see tonight," I whispered through silvery tears. "I wish I may, I wish I might, have the wish I wish tonight." What wish, what wish? "If wishes were horses, beggars would ride. That's what mummy always says." Now I'm talking to myself. Had I said that aloud? I scanned the sky, it was midnight blue, the color of mummy's Parker ink. No stars anywhere. It wasn't any use. It wasn't any use at all. There wasn't any way for me to go home, go back to Santo Domingo. It was gone. I would never again feel the velvet touch of Trit Trot's nose searching my hands.

I could hear Bertie asking for me at the screen door, and mummy telling him that I was being punished. I pressed my nose against the screen and watched him walk back to the hill where the others were playing hide-and-seek in the dark, their voices tweetling and echoing in the distance.

July had moved into August and we had been fighting our own version of the battle of Iwo Jima for three days in the woods on the hill. I had relinquished my command to Warren Townsend because I was always being held prisoner in my room and had missed too many of the war games in the past few weeks.

Bertie Green and I had paired off; he said he liked having me with him because I was little and quiet. "You do sneak attack better than any of the boys." I blushed and adjusted my junior air-raid warden's helmet. It had never fit right after Jim backed the car over it, but even so it was good protection whenever the enemy tried to bean us with clay clods. I handed Bertie a branch and he draped it over the realistic-looking machine gun his father had made for him out of old tomato cans. We were setting up a machine-gun nest to ambush George Chilkes, a hulking eleven-year-old with a petulant lower lip and continuously running nose which he refused to blow.

When we had begun the war games, George was informed that he could play on the condition that he would always be the enemy. (After V-E Day, the enemy was always the Japanese.) He agreed, and gave himself the rank of general and conscripted his troops by promising to treat them to popsicles when the Good Humor man came.

We had already ambushed the better part of George's army, and the rules of the game were that the dead had to lie where they had fallen until they were called in to dinner.

I sprang at George as he came lumbering through the underbrush and punched him squarely in the face. He made a lunge for my braids as he toppled forward, blood running from his mucus-laden nose. Bertie and I stared at him as he sat in a blubbering heap in a pricker bush. I bent over and rubbed the back of my hand in the red dust in order to clean the nasty mess off my knuckles. "Ugh!" I shuddered. "You are really horrible."

Bertie turned and listened as a boy came running toward the woods. I watched, fascinated; his arms were pumping like windmills and I expected him to propel himself into the air. As he approached, the other children, including the fallen troops on both sides, jumped up and began cheering wildly. Snipers tumbled down from their trees, leaves and twigs tangled in their hair and T-shirts. George looked around in bewilderment as we heard the shouts. *It was over. The war was all over. President Truman had said so on the radio.*

"It's all over, George," Bertie said as he put down his tomato-can machine gun and started walking out of the woods. *It was all over. We could go home now.*

I looked down at George; he was rubbing his eyes with his porcine fists. "Is your nose still bleeding?" I asked.

He nodded miserably.

"Come on, I'll walk you home. Maybe it'll feel better if you put a nice cold facecloth on it." I helped him to his feet and rubbed my hands clean again.

Major Chilkes opened the screen door and demanded to know who had given George the nosebleed.

"Tell me, dammit!" he bellowed, his face very red.

George pointed at me.

"A girl?"

"She did. Socked me right in the nose," George whimpered.

My eyes met the major's for a moment. Then he turned to George, his hand smartly whacking the stunned boy across the mouth. "A girl! A lousy little girl half your size! Get in the house, you fat little bastard!"

I beat a hasty retreat to the sidewalk in front of the Greens' kitchen, where Josie was methodically bouncing a pink rubber ball. It had once been a hand grenade in our rendition of the Battle of Stalingrad. "Major Chilkes sure was mad," Josie piped before launching into the litany, "A, my name is Alice and my husband's name is Alphonse. . . ."

"Alphonse?"

". . . and we sell apricots." Bounce, bounce. "I wonder if the major will tell your mother," she said without breaking the rhythm of the ball.

"Probably." I was dismayed. It would mean more solitary confinement in my room and I'd miss all the excitement. "Maybe he'll forget to tell her, now that the war is over. I hope he does."

Josie suspended the ball in her hand midbounce. "Why, will your mother hit you?"

"My mother never hits me, but my stepfather might."

"Does he hit you a lot?"

"No, just when I'm bad."

Mummy was not pleased. The major had indeed made a point of lodging a complaint. "I will not have you punching little boys," she sighed in her where-have-I-gone-wrong voice. "You'll soon be a young lady, and young ladies simply do not beat up little boys."

"He's not a little boy, he's bigger than I am."

"That's even worse."

"Why?"

"Because it just is. I didn't raise you to be a hooligan." She mixed a fresh highball and tasted it. "Now that the war is over," she sighed, "maybe we can get back to normal."

My mother's words rang in my ears as I sat in the bathtub scrubbing off the battle grime. The house was filled with grown-ups who were clattering in and out, laughing and shouting about the victory. *Soon you'll be a young lady.* I looked at the wart on my right index finger, the scabs on my knees, and then at my thin body, and thought: *Soon you'll have a bosom. You'll have to wear a bra. You'll never see your ribs or stomach again.* I peered closely at my chest for some sign. It was as flat as Bertie Green's. Then, in a gesture of enormous optimism, I said aloud, "Goodbye, ribs. Goodbye, stomach."

"It's really over, no doubt about it," Jim said as he poured somebody a drink.

"Let's hope so," a man answered.

"How can they go on? A bomb of that magnitude—they don't have a chance; we can wipe them all off the face of the earth. Mark my words, it's over, they'll go through with an unconditional surrender."

I walked outside and found Bertie sitting on the curb waiting for the Good Humor man. "I thought you said the war was over?"

"It is."

"The Japanese haven't surrendered, so how can it be over?"

"We dropped a new kind of bomb on them and it destroyed a whole city. It may still be burning now."

"What kind of bomb?"

"They call it an atomic bomb."

"I've never heard of that."

"It was secret until now. My dad says there'll never be a war again because of the bomb. It would mean the end of the world."

I stared across the compound. There were lights blazing in all the barracks windows; everyone was having a party, it seemed, voices laughing in tempo to the rattle of ice cubes and soft squeak of corks being wrung from bottles.

One bomb had flattened a whole city.

"How could one bomb do all that?"

"I don't know, but the radio says it's true. Look how crazy all the grown-ups are acting."

"A whole city burning. That means all the people, too?"

"I guess so."

"Mothers and children?"

Bertie inspected a scab on his knee. "I guess so."

"It must be an awfully big bomb. Do you think they're right about it?"

"Who?"

"The grown-ups, the radio."

"They're right. My dad says there'll be newsreels of it soon. He heard that they have newsreels of it hitting."

I stared at him. "Are you going to see it?"

"Sure."

"What was the name of the city?"

He paused and picked at the scab. "Hiroshima, I think."

"Not Tokyo? Is Hiroshima big?"

"I don't know if it was. I just heard that after the bomb hit it was burning for miles and miles. The Good Humor man is coming. You want a popsicle?"

I shook my head no. "I wonder where Hiroshima was. The only city in Japan I ever heard of was Tokyo."

"You sure you don't want a popsicle?"

"I'm sure."

"I'll get you one anyway. The war is over, we should all be happy. We can all go home now. What's the matter with you?"

"I don't know if we should be so happy. You might understand better if you had ever seen a bomb fall."

"Of course we should be happy. You might even get to go back to the East Indies again."

"West, not East. West Indies."

"Well, wherever it is. I wonder what happened to the pony?"

"I don't know."

"What was his name?"

"Trit Trot."

"Maybe you should ask your mother."

"About what?"

"Going back."

"I don't think it would do any good."

When the white truck pulled into the compound, bells jingling jubilantly, Bertie rushed over, and smiled happily as he returned brandishing two orange popsicles.

Chapter Eleven

"Is the war over now?" I asked the next morning as I helped mummy wash the glasses and ashtrays from the night before.

"No, the Japanese refuse to accept our terms. They don't seem to believe the bomb. But Truman says if they don't surrender they can expect a rain of ruin from the air, the likes of which has never been seen on this earth."

"What does that mean?"

"It means we're going to drop another atomic bomb."

"More people will die?"

"I'm afraid so, my pet. I'm afraid the world will never be the same after this."

Mummy was right. The war was really over, and soon we would be going home. Home. Home to Annie, to school, to the pond and polliwogs in the spring. We began packing almost immediately. This time the car wouldn't be jammed; the navy was going to ship everything for us.

As I walked along the gully that bordered the road to the Center, I thought of the thousands of steps, back and forth, that I had taken. Steps to the school, the library, the movies, the co-op, the swimming pool, and the playground. Falls, winters, springs, and summers of steps, usually carrying books and usually alone. Always walking further and further away, with longer and longer strides, from the perfumed afternoons that had been my childhood.

"Hi," Bertie said as he trotted up alongside. "Where are you going?"

"To the library. I have to return these books before we go."

"You doing that for your mom?"

"No, they're my books."

"You read even when you don't have to, don't you?" He sounded genuinely perplexed.

"I like to read."

"I wonder why that is?"

"If you read more, you'd know."

"Want to play Tarzan when we get home?"

"It's no fun without vines to swing on," I sighed. "Get Josie and we can play Cobra Woman. Josie can be Sabu."

The librarian thanked me for remembering to return the books, and I blinked at the unexpected wetness filling my eyes. Going home meant never seeing her shelves, never reading all the books she had suggested. She reached across the desk and shook my hand. "Goodbye, dear. I want you to know I've enjoyed knowing you. Did you like *The Microbe Hunters*?"

"Very much." I could barely speak.

"What is it? Is something wrong?"

"I guess I won't be able to finish all the books we talked about."

"Of course you will. Would you like me to make you a list?"

I nodded, wiping my eyes with the knuckles of my index

fingers. She filled a slip of paper with a list of titles in her precise hand and gave it to me.

"Thank you." I put it in my pocket.

"Well, goodbye then."

"Goodbye, Miss Petrie."

"You cried when you said goodbye to her?" Bertie was surprised.

"It's too bad you never got to know her. She's really very nice."

"I'm not a very good reader even when I do read."

"Maybe if you read more you would be good."

"Do you think so?"

"Of course."

Bertie stopped at the co-op and bought two Dr Peppers. He dusted off the wooden step and we both sat and guzzled in silence.

"Don't forget to get the deposit back."

"I won't," Bertie said as he sucked the remaining drops out of his straw.

"We're going to leave in the morning."

"I know."

"I wonder if we'll ever see each other again."

"Maybe. If you come to California, we might."

I handed the empty bottle to him. He returned with a small bag of candy root-beer barrels which we ate as we continued the walk back to the barracks.

Josie didn't want to be Sabu until Bertie pointed out that it was the Farewell Game, the very last time we would ever play Cobra Woman together.

"I guess we won't see you anymore," Bertie said gruffly after his mother had called them to come in.

"After dinner?"

"No, we're going to the Hot Shoppe in Hyattsville for supper, and then to the movies to see *The Road to Morocco*."

"It's a good movie, you'll like it."

"I really don't want to say goodbye," he mumbled.

"Then don't."

"I'll miss you," he said shyly.

I nodded my head in thanks and wiped my nose with my sleeve. "Have a good life, Bertie," I called after him.

He turned, smiled widely, and shouted, "You too!"

"I'll never forget you, Bertie Green," I said softly as he disappeared behind the screen door.

Mummy looked tired but happy as she organized the luggage and few boxes we were taking in the car. As usual, we were leaving at the crack of dawn. I settled back in the seat. Kirsty was stretched out beside me, too small and too sleepy to know that we were leaving to live in a house she had never seen. I gazed out the window, watching the shadowy landmarks drift by in a dreamlike procession. We were going home, to Cold Spring Harbor. At last.

The tenants had left the house a shambles; a downstairs window was broken and trash littered all the rooms. Mummy couldn't believe her eyes and almost broke down and cried. Then she gathered herself once again and set about tidying up. Jim made a temporary pane for the window out of some cardboard and began to scrub out the refrigerator. "I don't think they cleaned it once the whole time they were here!" he snorted as he applied boiling water to the smelly mess.

"I'm going to Annie's first thing in the morning," I announced to mummy as I helped her put fresh sheets on Kirsty's crib.

"Not too early, my pet."

When I awoke, the house was still. I dressed in shorts and ran to the pond: It was still there, although it didn't look as big as I had remembered. Then to the fields next to the house, the ones with the abandoned well that Annie and I had almost fallen into. The fields that lay on the other side of the garden wall, where Peter the dog was buried. I lay on my back in the soft meadow grass, feeling the earth turn on its axis, measuring the movement by the clouds. My body felt longer, older, and I wondered with a sense of alarm if Annie was still my friend.

A screen door slammed in the distance and I realized that mummy was up. That meant it was no longer too early to go to Annie's. I rose and brushed my shorts, then climbed over the wall and ran across the top of the sluiceway. The foliage along the footpath through the woods seemed thicker, the trees larger. Of course, I was too. Years had passed. "Hello, trees," I shouted as I ran along the path and through the fields to Annie's.

Mrs. Reynolds was putting the garbage out on the back step as I approached. "Well," she said with her hands on her hips, "if it isn't the baroness, in person. We've been expecting you."

I flung myself at her and she engulfed me in her generous arms.

"Come in, come in," she said, holding the screen door open. "Annie!" she bellowed. "Get the lead out! The baroness has returned!"

I pulled out a chair and sat at the kitchen table while she poured herself a cup of coffee. "What will it be, Your Ladyship, toast or cereal?"

"Cereal, please."

"Class," she sighed. "You always had class. It will be nice hearing pleases and thank-yous again."

Annie was taller, taller than I was, and Kenny's voice had begun to change. We spent the morning resuming our acquaintance at the kitchen table.

"Wow!" Annie gasped when she came over to help launch the flat-bottomed boat Jim had bought. "Did *he* get this for you? Are you sure it's all right for us to use? Maybe it's really his."

"I'm sure it's for us. He's too big—it would sink if he got in. It's for us, all right."

Annie laughed nervously and looked toward the house as if expecting someone to tell us to leave the boat alone. "Have you tried it yet?"

"Yes. He took me out in it when it first came. That's how come I know he's too big for it—we sank right to the bottom when he sat down."

Annie laughed. "I wish I could have seen that. Was he mad?"

"Not too. He laughed."

"That's nice, that's a really nice present, isn't it?"

I nodded. It was the nicest present I had gotten in a long time. We shoved the boat into the water and I held the line while Annie gingerly took a seat, then I threw the line in and stepped into the bow and poled away from the shore.

"Maybe he's sorry he punched you and made your nose bleed. Maybe things will be better now."

"Who told you he made my nose bleed?"

She looked at me curiously. "No one told me, I saw it happen. I *saw* him do it. Don't you remember? It was when I spent the night and he got mad because we were making so much noise listening to the radio. How do you make the boat go? There aren't any oar things."

"You don't need oarlocks with a kayak paddle," I said as I paddled to the far end of the pond.

When the navy delivered the rest of our belongings, I asked mummy if I could have one of the big wooden packing crates.

"What for?"

"We can put it on the boat—it'll make a great cabin."

"Ask your father," she said as she carefully removed excelsior from the crate.

My *father*?

Kenny didn't like being called Kenny anymore; he asked us to call him Ken. Then he nailed an old baby-carriage wheel next to the off-kilter door we had cut in the crate, to use as a helm. He drilled a hole in the roof and stuck a broom handle in the top of the box to serve as a mainmast; bamboo curtain rods held the sail, made of an old sheet, in place. Even my stepfather appeared delighted with the results. I crayoned a Jolly Roger on a smaller piece of sheeting, and the three of us—Ken, Annie, and I—sailed off to conquer imaginary armadas with stores of ginger ale, Walnettos, and a box of Ken's father's condoms.

"What are they for?" I asked when he pulled the box out of his pocket.

He looked around cautiously and made certain no grown-ups were within earshot. "Men put them over their things. It keeps the woman from getting pregnant."

"What do *we* want with them?"

"They'll make great bombs. We'll fill them with water and blast the enemy when they come alongside," he said, unrolling one and dipping it over the side. Then he whacked me to demonstrate.

"That's great, but wouldn't balloons be just as good?" I asked, wiping the water from my eyes.

"Balloons break too easily. These can take quite a beating."

"That's fine, but we're the only boat on the pond. Who's going to come alongside?"

On the Saturday before school. Annie announced that she had important news.

"What is it?" I grunted as we prepared to shove off on another of our voyages.

"Wait until we get out in the middle," Ken said, poling the boat away from shore. Satisfied that no one could hear us, he nodded to Annie. "Okay, you can tell her now."

"Ken has a hair," Annie said happily.

"A hair?"

"On his you know what." She was beaming. "Show her, Ken."

We huddled inside the piny-smelling box, the boat rocking precariously, as Ken slowly unbuttoned his fly to display a lone pubic hair. We all peered at it closely.

"Do you have any yet?" I asked Annie.

"No."

"Me either. I wonder when we'll get ours."

"See how big his dick is getting," Annie said admiringly.

"Why is it blue like that?" I asked.

"That's the color they are," Ken said, fondling himself absently.

"Show her how big it gets when it's hard."

"Well—" Ken hesitated. "I don't know if I should."

"Go on," Annie encouraged.

Ken began working his hand, and when the erection was complete, he proudly stretched a condom over it.

"That's very nice," I said.

"He's even fucked with it," Annie exclaimed proudly. "Isn't it terrific?"

"Uh-huh," Ken corroborated. "I fucked Cookie Strumpowski."

"She likes Ken the best, because his dick is so nice and big."

"You mean she does it with more boys?"

"Oh, sure, everybody, even that icky Arthur Perkins. Even Howard Chaney, but he said he couldn't feel a thing and so he stuck his up Arthur's ass and now all Arthur wants is to get fucked by Howard."

"Ugh!"

"It's true, isn't it, Ken?"

He nodded. His face was very red, and he continued holding his swollen penis. It looked like a sausage about to explode through the condom.

"Take the bag off so she can see it when you come. Make it really spurt."

"I don't really need to see." I coughed.

Ken had rolled the condom off and said in a tight voice, "It's okay, I don't mind showing you."

Annie beamed as Ken came in his own hand. "Isn't that terrific!"

We saw less and less of Ken after that; he preferred spending his time with Cookie. Annie and I built a tree house in the woods and used the balance of our condom supply to bombard the unsuspecting Arthur Perkins as he walked home from his trombone lesson. He told his mother and gave her a condom as evidence.

"I don't know what we're going to do with you," mummy said angrily when I explained what we used the condoms for. "Where did you get it?" she demanded.

"We found it in the woods. Is it something bad?"

Mummy said nothing, and I told Annie we had better go back to balloons.

Private-school catalogs began arriving in the mail. Houses began to spring up in the meadows down the road, and I learned that we were going to look at property in Connecticut.

"But why? Why do we have to move?"

"You'll like Connecticut, my pet. We've even found a wonderful school for you. You'll be able to go riding every week."

"Will you be taking the boat?" Annie asked as we trudged home from the candy store.

I removed the bright red wax lips from my mouth. "No. No pond. They say there's a brook in the woods with lots of rocks in it and a waterfall. They'll sell the boat with the house."

"But I thought it was your boat? How could they do that?"

"I don't know, but that's what they say."

"He's an Indian giver," Annie muttered through the wax buckteeth she had stuck in her mouth.

I clamped down hard on the red wax lips and nodded in agreement.

Chapter Twelve

Miss Tyneside's School for Girls, in Westport, was situated in
a dilapidated Victorian house that had seen better days. It was
a college-preparatory school founded and run by two English-
women who, although they were sisters, acted as if they de-
spised each other with a vengeance. They addressed each other
by their surnames—Miss Tyneside, who had never married,
and Mrs. Claxton, who had been a widow for years. They only
spoke when they had to, and usually only to criticize something
the other had done. These conversations took place across the
long table in the gloomy dining room where we assembled with
the teachers for dinner at six o'clock every evening.

I had been installed in a small upstairs bedroom at Miss
Tyneside's house the Sunday before the fall term began. I
would live there until our new house in Weston was finished.
As soon as mummy and Jim had pulled out of the driveway,
Miss Tyneside had stopped smiling and suggested that I might

like to go upstairs and unpack. Taking the cue, I obediently
climbed the stairs, my shoes echoing hollowly on the uncar-
peted wood. The room reeked of emptiness and I sat soundless
and alone on the small single bed. My school clothes were
hanging neatly in the closet where mummy and I had put them
before she left. I lay back on the bed; tomorrow school would
begin and I would be "the new girl" again. I took the writing
pad from the bedside table and began a letter to Annie.

Courtney and Evie were new that term, too, and we clung
together while waiting to pass muster with the "old girls," who
had been a close-knit unit since kindergarten. Courtney had an
acerbic wit, brilliance of mind, and the biggest boobs of anyone
in the middle school. I didn't have any sign of a bosom, even
though I was several months older, and would grow faint in
the locker room when it was time to change into gym clothes.
The others all had bras. I had an undershirt with a little bow
in the front. Courtney, sensing my discomfort and embarrassment, claimed to have been born with boobs. In her best blasé
voice, she assured me that mine would appear eventually and
told me to enjoy my flat chest while I still could.

"When will your house be finished? It must be awful having
to live at Tynzie's. I don't know how you stand it."

"It *is* awful. She really doesn't like having anyone around.
The only time I'm really comfortable there is when she goes
to her bridge game."

"Do you go to Cold Spring Harbor on the weekends?"

"No, my parents come up here sometimes and we go and
see how the house is coming along. Sometimes I go and stay
with the Bouchards. They're friends of my stepfather's and
they're very nice, but I'm not too crazy about their daughter."

"Paulette? Ah, yes, I could see where you'd find her a strain.
Very infantile."

"You know her?"

"Let's say I've observed her. How would you like to come
to my house some weekend?"

"I'd *love* to. I'll ask my mother to tell Tynzie it's all right
when they come this weekend."

"Good. Father likes to discuss current events at dinner. He's a staunch Republican, so if you have anything like a Democrat lurking in your family, I suggest you keep it quiet. You might start taking a look at the *Times* so you won't feel foolish if he asks you something."

"I will. I'll ask Tynzie to let me borrow hers."

"Not that I think you're illiterate, I just know how sensitive you are to things like that. I wouldn't want you to suffer any embarrassment at my expense."

Courtney's secret vice, I was to learn on our first weekend, was reading movie magazines and eating Mars Bars.

"I'll strangle you and never speak to you again if you ever tell any of those empty-headed twits at school," she announced before reading aloud the latest in the life of Doris Day.

Even after the house had been completed and we had finally moved in, Courtney and I continued to weekend together, taking turns at each other's house. We packed our pajamas and toothbrushes in our portable typewriters; she had an Underwood and I an ancient Royal. No matter the season—rain or shine—we'd sit by the hour hunched over the typewriters, pounding out novels about great dynasties, heavily laden with sex, about which we had very little firsthand knowledge.

"How is it you come to know so much about the male genitalia?" Courtney asked as she read my most recent batch of pages. I told her of Phillipe, Max, Harry, Ken, Arthur, and Howard. She took a drag on the rumpled Pall Mall she had filched from her mother, her graceful dark eyebrows arching in amazement. "My dear, you are a gem! And to think you haven't begun puberty yet!"

"That's why," I snorted, "I'm titling my memoirs *I Was a Failure at Twelve*."

She liked that so much she fell over laughing. I liked making Courtney laugh.

"Tell me," she said, sitting up again and rescuing her cigarette from the floor where it had fallen. "Did you and the magnificent Ken ever . . ."

"Ever what?"

"You know."

"Oh, no." I flushed with embarrassment. "He was busy with Cookie Strumpowski. In fact, he wanted very little to do with Annie and me—I think he was afraid we might let something slip in front of his mother."

"I don't imagine Cookie, for all her aplomb, was too crazy about having their activities being broadcast either. How old were they?"

"Ken was fourteen and she was fifteen. He was very mature for his age."

"Needless to say. Did you ever witness them in action, as it were?"

"Not Cookie and Ken. I did see Howard and Arthur once, quite by accident. They were having at each other in the woods and evidently didn't hear me coming."

"Indeed? I've often wondered, how is it done?"

"Up the poop."

"Up the poop! *How* déclassé. Who was up who? Whom? I always forget which is which."

"Howard was up Arthur."

"Mmm. Perhaps I should have Laurence and Tim have a scene like that, instead of the other-woman business."

"You could—it would certainly be different—but I don't think *Seventeen* magazine would publish it."

"Are you kidding? They won't publish it anyway."

Although our peers, or fellow twits, as Courtney called them, talked of "necking," "petting," and "doing it" with the pimply assortment of preppies available to us, we fancied ourselves far beyond their mundane naïveté and referred to "going all the way" as *la pénétration*.

"Yes, I think I'll have Laurence and Tim get to the 'up the poop' business when they're out sailing, instead of having Alison and David perform *la pénétration* under the stage in the theater." Courtney had abandoned her epic about the West for a monumental and lurid Gothic about incest, lust, and insanity in Fairfield County.

"Actually, I liked Alison and David under the stage the

best," I said laconically through the bent Chesterfield I was smoking.

"Under the stage it is," she said crisply, her bony fingers flying across the Underwood keys.

Where Courtney was gregarious, brittle, and bright, Evie was deliberate, quiet, and profound. She loved to play chess and showed no embarrassment over her addiction to "Kukla, Fran and Ollie." Neither Courtney nor I had a television set, and we always welcomed invitations to Evie's. Evie's father was an architect and he was always dressed impeccably in his fabulous wardrobe. He loved to shop for clothes, especially for Evie's mother.

"Can you just see my father or your stepfather shopping for women's clothes!" Courtney was shocked. "The only thing my father ever buys for my mother is stocks or golf clubs." Courtney's father was president of a bank. "What does your stepfather buy?"

I thought long and hard. "He bought her a shovel for Christmas."

Courtney and Evie both roared with laughter.

"Well, he did."

"Oh, come on," Courtney snorted, "be serious." Then she frowned and looked at Evie. "A *shovel*? Do you know what my mother would do if my father ever dared to do something like that? She'd hit him with it."

"I think he meant it to be funny."

"Some sense of humor," Evie said, popping open a fresh bag of potato chips and offering us some.

"He's a brute," Courtney said. "Do you know that he actually attacked her in front of me? He hit her so hard her nose started to bleed."

"What did he hit you for?" Evie asked as she took a handful of chips from the bag.

"No reason." Courtney helped herself from the bag in Evie's hand. "We were making too much noise in her room, laughing. That's all we were doing, laughing. He came in, and the language and look he gave us were enough to curl your hair. All

I could think of was what he would have done if he had caught us smoking! We probably wouldn't have survived."

Evie looked at me quizzically, then at Courtney. "Does he do that often?"

"Only when he's angry," I mumbled.

"And that appears to be most of the time," said Courtney.

"What does your mother say? Doesn't she try to stop him?" There was concern in Evie's voice.

"Sometimes she tries, but most of the time she doesn't do anything."

"Because he'd hit her, too," Courtney said through a mouthful of potato chips.

"Is that true?" Evie asked.

I stared at the floor and didn't answer.

Courtney was going to one of the top Ivy League women's colleges when she graduated. It didn't matter which one, as long as it was one of the Seven Sisters. "Father says it's an absolute must if I'm to marry well."

Evie was going to be a doctor or a nun or both. Her father didn't like the idea. "He hopes I'll grow out of it," she sighed.

"What does he want you to do?"

"He wants me to be like Courtney, to marry well. The problem is, I don't think I'll ever get married." Evie carefully marked her place in *Gray's Anatomy* with a trading card.

"Well, don't let my father ever hear you say that." Courtney picked up the book and flipped it open. "Any good pictures in here?"

"Not the kind you're interested in." Evie retrieved the book from Courtney. "You'll get it greasy and it doesn't belong to me."

"Where did you get it?"

"Dr. Martin loaned it to me."

"Ask him if he has any good sex manuals."

"I can't do that," Evie said impatiently. It was clear that Courtney was getting on her nerves.

"Well, if you can read Darwin and be a nun, the least you could do is get us some books *we* can learn from."

"Why don't you think you'll get married?" I asked, hoping to change the subject.

"It's just a feeling I have. Men don't like women with minds. They never want to discuss anything important unless it has to do with themselves."

"My father talks about important things with me and my mother," Courtney said.

"Your father talks *at* you; he's training you to think a certain way. You don't have conversations, you have lectures and quizzes."

I was surprised at the vehemence in Evie's voice. "All my stepfather talks about is money—how we don't have enough."

Evie's voice softened as she said, "I didn't mean to offend you, Courtney. It's just that there's more to life than sex."

"I can't imagine what it would be."

We all laughed.

Although Courtney never would have admitted it, she shared Evie's and my fondness for three of the teachers: Miss Whitney, Mam'selle, and Miss Mann—English, French, and physics were their respective specialties. They had perceived our loneliness at not being accepted by the "old girls" and had handled us with thoughtful patience.

They lived in tiny, cell-like rooms in what was the attic of the Victorian house that served as the main school building. Their quarters had always been referred to as "the cubicles." Miss Tyneside's office, under the main staircase on the second floor, was the dreaded "cubby." No one liked being summoned to the cubby, and few students had ever been invited to the cubicles.

We were always made to feel welcome in the teachers' parlor and would pass the hours after school discussing theater, music, theology, literature, and Ezio Pinza over cheese and cheap red wine.

Courtney's father didn't like her socializing with the teachers. "'They're just a bunch of old maids who can't get jobs where they can earn some real money.' That's what he says. Can you imagine what he would do if he ever found out that

Whitney is a Socialist! You must promise to never let it slip. He'd go absolutely berserk."

"Don't be a dimwit, I'd never do a thing like that. He might turn her over to Senator McCarthy."

"Or at the very least have her pilloried in the middle of the quadrangle," Evie added.

"Ha-ha, you're both very funny. I don't as rule disobey him, but in this instance he's wrong about the teachers, and what he doesn't know, won't hurt."

"Well," Evie smiled, "there may be hope for you yet."

"More ha-ha, Evie," Courtney snapped as she stomped up the narrow staircase to the attic.

In the spring, Evie and I began working on the squat, ugly sailboat that belonged to her older brother. He had taken a job at a summer theater in Maine and had turned the boat over to Evie on the condition that she maintain it properly. We scraped and sanded for weeks, caulked and painted, until he gave his approval and helped us launch the boat officially.

We would pack the sails in a duffel bag and pedal on our bikes to the Pequot Yacht Club, where the boat was moored. In minutes we would have it rigged and would tack slowly out of the harbor while sleek, aristocratic Atlantics sliced through the channel, leaving us in their wake with our thin brown legs and bony, callused hands, our hair stiff with salt. We would sail along the Gold Coast, where the last bastion of the Jazz Age lived. The money was so old in those great shore palaces that no one, not even the tradespeople in town, could remember where it had come from.

"It reminds me of *The Great Gatsby*," Evie remarked as we sailed toward Westport one day to pick up Courtney.

"Gatsby was on Long Island."

"I know. But he could have combined Connecticut with Long Island. Writers do that, you know."

"Did Courtney say she was bringing lobsters?" I asked, changing the subject.

"Lobsters, tomatoes, and something to drink."

We tacked carefully into Cedar Point, where Courtney was waiting on the dock with a large cardboard carton.

"Why didn't you tell me this place was crawling with men? I'd have come sailing with you sooner if I'd known!" She stepped cautiously into the boat, trying to maintain her composure as she smiled at a group of bronzed boys who had been watching us.

We sailed east again, and I lay on the bow and stared at the houses. Imagining the gay parties with shiny, talented people in elegant clothes, I was vaguely stirred into memories of life as it had once been. An oyster scow churned by and a heavyset man yelled at us and waved his beer can in salute.

"I wonder if he'd give us some oysters," Courtney said as she waved back.

"If you flash a bit of thigh, he might," I chuckled.

We found a good spot and Evie neatly beached the boat.

I hoisted the cooking pot out of the boat and lugged it to the rocks where Evie was making the fire. Courtney dropped the lobsters in the sand. "Poor buggers." Then she pulled a bottle of her father's gin out of her beach bag. "Here's the *pièce de résistance!*"

"Where did you get that?"

"I pinched it from my father's liquor closet."

"Won't he miss it? Won't you get in trouble?"

"He won't notice, he's got a whole closetful." She poured us each a paper cupful.

Evie took a sip, winced, and daintily spat it out. "It tastes like gasoline," she said, wiping her mouth on the back of her hand.

"I rather like it," Courtney said as she poured herself another.

"I don't think you're supposed to drink it so fast," I said as I held out my cup for another.

"Warms the cockles of the heart, doesn't it?"

I nodded. "I like the way it makes me feel, although I must say I don't like the smell." The smell reminded me of my mother.

Evie methodically cracked the lobster shells for us. Courtney toasted her surgical skills and we ate and drank watching the sun follow the tide beyond the horizon. I sighed and sipped some gin. "Don't you wish life could always be like this?"

"Why shouldn't it be?" Courtney burped.

Evie looked at me briefly, then reached for her guitar and began strumming. I sat staring at the adolescent moon as it slowly climbed above the water, listening to Evie's plaintive song, aware that we were all on the eve of life.

Chapter Thirteen

Mummy almost said no when I told her that I had gotten a job as an usher at the Westport Country Playhouse. I could tell by the frown that fleeted across her face as she poured herself a martini in the kitchen.

"I can ride my bike down and back, and you won't have to give me any allowance, because they'll be paying me eight dollars a week."

She tasted her drink, then added some more gin to the shaker and whirled it around gently with the ice. "We'll see."

"But I told the manager I could do it—I didn't think you'd mind. It gives me something to do. Everyone I know is doing something for the summer."

"When do they want you to start?"

"Tomorrow."

"I suppose it will be all right. If it's all right with your father, you may do it."

"I wish you wouldn't always call him my father."

"What else am I supposed to call him? He's the man of the house, the head of the family. I *know* he's not your father."

"I'm sorry," I mumbled. "But what if he says no?"

"Why would he say that?"

"He's always saying no to everything."

"Not everything, just the things we can't afford."

"This won't cost, they'll pay me. When will he be home?"

"I don't know, whenever the 5:02 gets in." She poured another martini.

The train was late and the dinner ruined. Jim was tired and in a bad mood when he finally arrived. The Playhouse still hadn't been discussed when I went to bed; they were in a heated argument about money. Things were slow at the printing plant. I lay staring in the darkness, listening to the sounds of the night and the muted angry voices drifting up the stairwell.

The next evening, mummy told me to take my shorts off and put on a dress.

"Why?"

"Aren't you going to the Playhouse?"

"I didn't think you'd let me do it."

"It's all right."

"You asked him?"

"No, but it will be all right. He won't mind."

"Are you sure?"

"I'm sure, my pet. I'm sorry about the arguing last night, but things have been getting me down lately. There never seems to be any end to the bills. It gets us both down."

"What happened to the money?"

"What money?"

"Our money. What happened to it? We never used to have to worry. You never had to build walls yourself, spread tons of topsoil, work like a dog."

"I enjoy gardening."

"Mummy! What you're doing isn't *gardening*! It's hard labor, it's too much for you."

"Well, it has to be done and I don't mind."

I didn't believe her. "It's because we can't afford to have someone do it, isn't it?"

"That's part of it, but I also like doing it."

"You're killing yourself. It's too much for one person."

"He works hard, too. Look at all the trees he's planted. Hurry and dress—you don't want to be late, do you?"

I felt helpless. I turned and ran upstairs and pulled a dress from the closet. When was the last time she had had a new dress? I couldn't remember. I would simply have to do it—get a job, make a lot of money, so things could be the way they were. Even though I was only fourteen years old, I would simply have to find a way.

During the opening-night performance of the third week, I saw him. He was the most beautiful creature I had ever seen, standing there, leaning against the rear wall of the theater, the soft light emphasizing the heart-stopping cheekbones, the clean profile. He had slipped in during the performance. It was a new Noel Coward play, starring Claudette Colbert, and even all the bad seats had sold out. I stood in the shadows, riveted. If I looked like that, I thought, I'd stand that way too, with a golden light bathing my face. Even though he wasn't very tall, his body was beautifully articulated, like a dancer's. His hair was long and thick; I assumed he was an actor or somehow involved with the production. All of his attention was directed at the actors on the stage.

Everyone on the staff was enthralled by the parade of living legends who came that week to pay homage to the master and the movie star. The apprentices lurked in the shadows at intermission and marveled at the sight of Dietrich shimmering in gold lamé, or Gertrude Lawrence with her husband, asking directions to the Green Room. I watched them all from my post in the shadows as they watched the play. And most of all, I watched the young man as he stood in the same place, under the same light, every night.

"Who is he? Is he with the production?" I asked Flo Kendall, the assistant to the producer, after the third consecutive appearance. She always checked with me after the house lights went down to see if anyone important was in the audience.

"Him? He isn't anybody. I think he's from around here. He does know Miss Colbert and comes to see her every night."

On the fourth night, I approached him slowly, hoping to get a better look.

"I don't have a ticket," he whispered sheepishly.

"I know."

"You mean it's all right?"

"Sure." I tried to sound casual.

On the fifth night, he waited on the veranda while I finished calling the audience back from intermission with a cowbell.

"Would you like a cigarette?" he asked, after I had closed the last of the barn doors.

"Uh—yes. Yes, I would."

His name was Jonas Barton and he lived in Westport. His family had known Miss Colbert for years. He laughed, delighted, when I told him I'd thought he was an actor. I was even more delighted when he continued to come to the theater after Miss Colbert and Noel Coward had taken the play to Kennebunkport.

I never talked to Courtney about Jonas; the risk of her barbed ripostes was too great. Besides, she was completely absorbed in her social life and would call only occasionally, to tell me that she and her new boyfriend, Clay, had advanced from tennis and golf games to the rarefied atmosphere of country-club dances and pool parties. When she asked how things were at the theater, I was offhand in my reply. It had occurred to me that Jonas might find her more attractive and certainly more sophisticated. I knew if I told her I had met a boy who drove an MG, she would have wasted no time in flying down for a look.

Chapter Fourteen

Summer in Connecticut is always the best time. The air is redolent, sensuous with promise. Even the rain has a diffuse, magical quality. On the night Jonas asked if I'd like to have a ride in his shiny red MG, I felt my eyes fill with tears. It was too much, more than I had hoped for. His sure, easy command of the little car overwhelmed me, as did the enchantment of the moonlit beach, the sweet scent of new-mown grass mingling with the warm fragrance of his tanned skin.

"Want to row out to Cockenoe Island?" he asked, his voice catching huskily. "I know where there's a boat."

Of course he did; he was obviously experienced and had probably gotten those terrific shoulders rowing thousands of girls out to the island. "Sure," I answered, "great idea."

Phosphorous glowed in the water and the steady creak of the oars kept tempo with the singing sweetness of anticipation. I wondered, could it be that he felt it, too?

We walked through the island scrub, the rusting beer cans and decaying condoms clearly visible in the light of the moon. Surprisingly, in view of the debris, we were alone. My breath caught as I wondered if any of that debris was his.

Jonas sat down in the sand and motioned for me to join him, then fished in his pocket for a pack of cigarettes and lit two. Wow. Just like Paul Henreid in *Now Voyager*. I accepted the cigarette and he said, "I saw a guy do that in a movie."

"Now Voyager."

"What?"

"That was the movie. *Now Voyager* with Bette Davis and Paul Henreid. He lit two cigarettes. I think it was the first time it was ever done."

"Now everyone does it. Is that the one where Bette Davis is the dowdy old maid with bushy eyebrows and a domineering mother? She has a nervous breakdown or something and goes away on a cruise that her cousin sets up?"

"That's the one. I love it when she puts on her cousin's clothes and is suddenly transformed into a gorgeous creature. Even her eyebrows are transformed," I said, taking a drag on the cigarette, wondering which version of Bette Davis I was in his eyes, pre- or postbreakdown.

He smoked in silence, staring out across the water, then said, "Want to go to a movie sometime?"

"I'd love to." God, I sound too earnest.

"What about the Playhouse—don't you have to be there every night?"

"Yes, but I can get a friend to cover for me." Maybe he had asked because he knew I couldn't go. I closed my eyes and held my breath.

"Good. How about Friday? There's a new Swedish film at the Beverly. Want me to pick you up at home?"

"No, the Playhouse will be fine. I'll have to get the ushers started, make sure my friend knows what she's doing."

We both stared across the water; small whitecaps were scudding across the surface, and the wind seemed to be building in force. Shivering, he doused the cigarette and said, "It looks like a blow coming up. We'd better get back."

I stood up, said nothing, and followed Jonas back to the boat. The dumplike aspect of the island had shattered the delicacy of the moment. He sat at the oars and I gave the boat a running shove into the oncoming wavelets. We didn't say anything; all of his concentration seemed to be directed at keeping the boat headed toward the mainland. I wondered how it had been with all the others he had brought to the island.

"We don't seem to be making any headway—the current is pretty strong." A light tone of panic had entered his voice.

"It does seem to be taking longer. We're headed into the wind, that's probably why."

"I think there's a storm brewing. I guess this wasn't such a hot idea. I'm not sure I can get us back. I have a heart murmur, that's why I'm not very good at things like this." He sounded as though he were going to cry.

"Well, it's not so far now. We could take turns. I could row for a while."

He sagged on the oars, his eyes downcast. I stared at his fine brown ankles, then changed places with him and managed to row us back to shore. Once at the beach, we dragged the boat up on the sand and sat leaning against it, trying to catch our breath.

"I guess you think I'm pretty stupid," he said finally.

"Why?" The despair in his voice had startled me.

"For not being able to get us back. I hope no one saw us."

"I don't think anyone did."

"I didn't realize it was so far away. The guys made it sound much easier."

"You've never been out there before?"

"No. Have you?"

"No."

"I didn't know a storm could come up that fast—I mean, the moon was so bright."

"Well, there were only a few clouds. It's probably just a passing storm."

The rain began pelting us and we dashed to the little red car and struggled to get the top up. As soon as we had climbed inside, we looked at each other and burst out laughing. I loved the way he looked with his dark hair slicked down around his face. To my astonishment, he leaned over and planted a full, wet, salty kiss on my mouth. He flipped on the ignition before I could recover and backed the car out onto the road. I sat transfixed by the wondrous sensation on my lips; it traveled all the way to my toes. Wait until Courtney heard about this.

"Let's go to Smitty's for coffee," Jonas suggested as he shifted the car deftly around a hairpin curve.

"My dear, you've got a man!" Courtney bugled over the phone.

"No. I simply have an invitation to a movie. Now, are you going to be able to cover for me on Friday or not? I'll give you eight dollars." It was my entire week's wages.

"Wait while I check my engagement calendar—"

"Courtney," I interrupted, exasperated, "just say yes or no. If you can't do it, I'll have to find somebody else."

"Well, I can't then."

An apprentice agreed to do it if I loaned her a dress and paid her five dollars.

Jonas arrived ten minutes early and smoked impatiently as I explained the routine to the apprentice. "You said you'd wash your feet," I groaned in dismay at the sight of her purple ankles.

"Relax, I did the best I could. It's paint from the scene shop and it won't come off any more than that. Besides, the box office says Montgomery Clift is coming tonight, and if he's not enough for people to stare at, Liz Taylor and Mike Todd ought to take their minds off me."

"Gee, I've never seen Monty in real life."

"Would you rather skip the movie?" Jonas asked as he flipped his cigarette over the veranda rail.

"No, of course not."

"Well, how was your evening?" Courtney asked the next morning on the phone.

"We went to the movie and then back to the theater and saw Monty Clift and Liz Taylor."

"*Monty* was there? Rats! I wish I'd known. What movie did you see?"

"*One Summer of Happiness.*"

She whistled and then asked, "Are you still, as they say, intactus?"

"Oh, for God's sake, Courtney, I'm not an acrobat. Besides, you know how crummy and rickety the seats are in the Beverly. We just watched the movie."

"Is it as sexy as they say? Are they really stark-staring-naked?"

"Yes."

"Any frontal stuff?"

"No, more profile than front."

"Aren't you going to tell me about it?" she demanded.

"There's not much to tell. It's just a long shot of them going into the lake."

"God! Don't be blasé. I'm sitting here going berserk and you're acting as though it's the most natural thing in the world to see a naked man. I mean, was it long and skinny, short and fat, limp or hard?"

"You couldn't really tell. Their bodies were silhouetted against the sun."

"Oh, nuts, I'm never going to find out what they're like with nothing on. You don't care whether or not I die without ever seeing a nude man."

"I don't think that's too likely," I sighed wearily. "But from the little you could see, I would say it was long and thick."

"You don't say! I wonder if I can get Clay to take me to see it. Probably not. He'd be horrified. How about a hamburger before you go to the matinee?"

"Meet me at Klein's at eleven-thirty. I have to get some more paper."

"You mean with all you're doing, you're still working on your novel?"

"When I have time."

Mr. Klein greeted us warmly and said that he was having a special on rag bond. Courtney said she preferred Corrasable, but I didn't like it because it smudged. Mr. Klein pointed out that Edna Ferber was partial to the rag bond and what was good enough for Miss Ferber should be good enough for fourteen-year-old novelists.

"I can't afford the paper and lunch, too," I said as I checked my wallet.

"Don't worry, all my authors charge, they never pay with money. Why should you be any different." It was a statement, not a question.

A charge account, my first. "But I don't have a checking account," I said apologetically.

"You can open one," Courtney suggested.

"That's right," Mr. Klein agreed. "By the time the bill comes, you'll have your checks. And if you don't—well, the worst thing that can happen is you'll pay with money."

I hesitated. "I'm not sure I should."

"You'll probably be needing some new ribbon, too," he said, reaching for a roll. "You use a Royal portable, am I right?"

I was amazed. Imagine Mr. Klein remembering my brand of typewriter ribbon. "Thank you," Courtney said, taking the box of paper from him. "She certainly appreciates it."

"Courtney, wait—"

"If you don't charge it, you won't have enough money for lunch," she hissed as we followed Mr. Klein to the counter.

"All right, then," Mr. Klein said as he wrote up the sales slip. "It's settled. Now you can have lunch."

I loved the stacks of pads and paper of every description on Mr. Klein's shelves. There was something comforting in the creak of the old wooden floorboards and the idea that some of the best and most successful writers in the country bought their supplies from this man. Mr. Klein had been attentive and sensitive to the difficulties of our work ever since Courtney had blurted to him that we were novelists. When he asked how the books were coming, I told him I had been stuck on the same page for three months.

"Ah, writer's block. Everyone has them. Why should you

be any exception." He smiled as he handed me the bag with my purchases.

"He never asks us what we're writing," I said, cradling the package in my arm. I liked its heft.

"Just as well. He'd probably tell our mothers if he knew," Courtney said as she selected a Tootsie pop from a bucket on the counter. "Should we charge these, too?"

"No, pay for it. Mr. Klein wouldn't tell our mothers."

"Then why don't you let him read your manuscript?" she said as she stuck the Tootsie pop in her mouth and handed a dime to the saleswoman who had been observing us out of the corner of her eye.

"I'll wait until I'm done and send him an autographed copy."

"He'll be senile by then. I've written three books to your one."

That was true, and, what was worse, they were all very good.

Hurricane-force winds and a driving rain spoiled the last days of summer as a nor'easter raged down the coast. I stood in the door of the scene dock watching a muddy river of water rush by. The season was over; only a few of the older apprentices had stayed on to help batten everything down for the winter. I shivered and watched a figure dash from the parking lot. The water was sluicing down his clothes, soaking through to the skin. "Jonas? Is that you?" I called, squinting through the downpour.

"Yep," he gasped as he bounded through the doorway. "I called your house. Your mother said you were down here. I told her I'd bring you home."

"You're soaked through."

"The car top leaks," he panted as he peeled off his shirt and wrung it out. The water spattered the dusty floor, his white duck pants clung to his legs, water rained from the cuffs. "You don't have a dry towel by any chance?" he asked as he dumped the water from his moccasins.

"No, we have something better."

"Oh?"

"Up there"—I indicated the loft—"is the wardrobe room. You can put something on if you promise to bring it back."

"You mean a costume?"

I nodded.

"Let's go." His teeth were chattering.

We climbed the ladder and pushed through the trapdoor. The rain drummed on the rotting cedar shingles, occasionally leaking through onto the racks of costumes shrouded in dusty muslin.

"What do you want?"

"Anything that's dry, nothing too formal," he shuddered. His chest and arms were covered with goosebumps.

"I think there are sailor pants in that trunk. I'll look for something to wear on top."

"Make it warm."

I checked through the racks and found a bright red jacket with gold braid and elaborate epaulets that must have been worn in something to do with Strauss waltzes. "How's this?" I blushed. He was stepping into a pair of white sailor pants. His penis looked defenseless and small as he dropped it into the trousers. "Oh, excuse me."

"I'm so cold, I'm shriveling up. My balls are climbing back into my body. Oh, God, forget I said that." His voice was trembling.

I pretended not to notice. "This will get you warm."

He reached for the jacket and slipped into it. "What's this from?"

"I don't know—something they did on Broadway years ago, probably before we were born. It smells of mothballs."

"I don't care, it's warm." He closed the jacket around his bare chest and rubbed his hands. "I feel like someone in *The Student Prince*," he laughed.

"You look like the prince." He looked magnificent, his wet hair hanging down over his forehead, his tanned face shining in the half-light.

He pushed a rack away from a leak and sat down on the trunk filled with sailor pants. "Now if we only had some cigarettes. Mine got wet in the rain."

"I have some down on the table. I'll get them."

"No, you sit. I'll be right back. Is there an ashtray? We wouldn't want to burn this beautiful barn down."

"On the table." My heart was pounding. I watched his head disappear through the trapdoor and emerge again a few minutes later. He sat down next to the trunk and patted the floor for me to join him.

"Here," he said, putting a derby hat on my head, "I brought you this. Got one for me, too." He placed the hat at a rakish angle over one eyebrow and lit two cigarettes as he had always done since our night on the island. "Now we can be twins."

I love you, Jonas. I love you in that ridiculous outfit. I puffed on the cigarette in silence as he leaned back and looked at me with great intensity. "What are you thinking?" I asked.

He smiled sadly. "I was thinking about all the good times we had this summer, about how hard it is to say goodbye." He inhaled slowly. "My folks are moving to Switzerland, so they're driving me up to Andover early."

"How early?"

"Tomorrow."

"Oh." My heart sank and I flicked an ash unsteadily into the ashtray. "You'll be home for Thanksgiving?"

"I don't know. They've decided to put the house on the market. My mother wants me to transfer to a school over there."

"Where over there?"

"Geneva. That's where they'll be living. I don't want to go."

"Do you have to?"

"I suppose I could stay here, find a job, but I really should finish school and go to college so I can do something decent with my life."

"Yes, well, you have to do that."

"Will you write to me, no matter where I am?"

"Of course."

"Will you do something else?"

"Yes, if I can."

"Would you just hold me for a while?" He leaned into my

arms, the derby shading his eyes. His mouth looked vulnerable and sad as he sighed softly. "I always feel safe with you."

"You do?" I was amazed.

"I suppose the girl is supposed to say that. But I do, you're so strong."

"No, I'm not. I'm scared to death all the time."

"You may think you are, but you're the strongest person I've ever known. I wish we could just stay here like this always."

I sat holding the sleeping boy as the rain began to subside. He felt comfortable, peaceful, and stirred slowly. "It's stopped raining?"

"Yes."

"Then I guess I'd better take you home."

"Yes."

He leaned over and kissed me slowly. I knew it was for the last time, that I would never tell Courtney.

Chapter Fifteen

"What do you hear from Jonas?" Courtney asked as she adjusted her mother's cast-off mink coat. We were browsing through the bookracks at Klein's while waiting for the matinee to begin at the Fine Arts movie theater.

"Not much. His grades have been going down so he doesn't have much time for letters."

"Is he coming to Westport for Thanksgiving?"

"No, his parents finally sold the house. He guesses he'll go to his aunt's in Boston."

"Oh, that's too bad. What about Christmas? If he comes for Christmas, he can take you to the County Assembly."

"He didn't mention Christmas."

"Oh—well, there's plenty of time. Tell me, how do you like it?" She swirled the coat from side to side in the narrow aisle. She had plucked her eyebrows, beaded her lashes with mascara, and had fire-engine-red lipstick on her mouth.

I shrugged, not quite knowing what to say, hoping no one would see us. "Uh—it has a certain *je ne sais quoi.*"

"Très soigné?"

"Oh, *très.*"

"You hate it, I can tell."

"No, honestly I don't. It's just that I'm surprised. I thought your father wouldn't let you wear makeup."

"He doesn't. I stopped at the drive-in and put it on in their powder room."

"Powder room?" I couldn't help laughing. "I don't think powder rooms have phone numbers and obscenities scrawled all over the walls, or smell of pine disinfectant. I'm surprised you could see anything in the mirror, it's always so dirty."

"Actually, I *couldn't* see too well. You don't think it's too much, do you?"

"Maybe a little too much lipstick."

She pulled a used Kleenex from her pocket and nervously blotted her lips on it. "That better?"

"Much."

She picked up a book and thumbed through it distractedly, trying to regain her composure. "Tell me, what do you make of the new art teacher? A bit *outrée*, wouldn't you say?"

"Madame Sexton-Poole? I think she's terrific."

"A bit eccentric, *n'est ce pas*?"

Look who's talking, I thought.

Mme Sexton-Poole had piercing blue eyes, an ample bosom, and a breathy, vital voice. She never walked, she sailed across the quadrangle, usually on her way to her cubicle for a "small nip of the sacramental grape before dealing with the next on-slaught of teen-age cretins."

Her classes had become the high point of the new term. As we sketched or painted, her majestic voice would transport us through her past. She had crossed the African veldt on a mo-torcycle, given birth to a daughter during a typhoon on the Indian Ocean, studied art in Paris, taught English in China, contemplated with Taoist monks, and was currently writing her memoirs. No one, not even Miss Whitney, Miss Mann, or

Mam'selle, could figure out what she was doing in Miss Tyneside's School.

"You don't really believe that claptrap she hands us in class!" Courtney exclaimed. "How can you read *Thus Spake Zarathustra* and believe all her nonsense!"

"Nietzche, in case you're interested, didn't believe in the emancipation of women. He thought it would make them feebleminded."

"Well, that proves my point. The woman is totally feeble and practically makes no sense at all."

"I think she makes a lot of sense."

When Courtney squinted, she looked exactly like her mother, with the exception of the Tootsie pop. "Well, I don't believe any of it. I'm not as gullible as you. She should leave all the crap about God for chapel; I don't appreciate her proselytizing in art class. It isn't right. As for those ridiculous stories, one or two episodes I might have bought, but she doesn't know when to stop. It was the business of the birth in the typhoon that got me. Father says she's either a lush or shot her mind on hashish while she was in the Orient."

"At least you believe the stories about the Orient."

"Father says her husband had something to do with the State Department. I can't imagine what she's doing at Miss Tyneside's."

"Maybe she needs the job while she finishes her book. You'd look a whole lot better in that getup if you didn't eat Tootsie pops."

Courtney wrapped the coat tightly around her thin body and glared at me. "You really do believe the woman, don't you?"

"I do."

"Sometimes I fear for you—you're too incredibly naïve and trusting. The wonder is that you are, with the life you've led."

"Maybe I'm like Madame Sexton-Poole, maybe your father thinks I'm a lush too!" I was angry.

"If he ever saw the way you swig scotch, he might. I don't know how you can stand drinking it first thing in the morning. Doesn't it taste horrible? Just the thought of it makes me nauseous."

I was sorry that I had ever confided in Courtney, or let her see me sneak a drink in the pantry. "It makes me feel wonderful. How else can I get through Tynzie's Latin class?"

"I don't know, but I should think being tiddly won't help. What made you think of doing it?"

"First of all, I'm not tiddly in class. It makes me calm. If she picked on you the way she picks on me, you'd need something, too."

"Perhaps. But what made you think of a drink?"

"A cocktail seems to calm my stepfather when he gets home from that stupid job of his. I saw the bottle on the shelf one morning when I was getting some jam for breakfast, and I just tried a little taste. It worked, and I've been doing it ever since."

"What will you do if they ever change Latin from first period?"

"I don't know," I mumbled as I pulled *Point Counter Point* off the shelf.

"Ordinarily I would say you're not a weak person. It has always mystified me that you fall apart in front of her."

"She was convinced that I was hopelessly stupid from the first day we met. No matter how hard I try, I can't seem to change that."

"You're not stupid. A little backward at times, but definitely not stupid."

"Gee, thanks, Courtney."

"Why don't you get extra help? Cicero isn't bad. You'd do well in that."

"Madame Sexton-Poole is going to help me."

"Ah, no wonder you feel the way you do about her. Is she qualified to teach Latin?"

"Probably. And with all due respect for your father, I think she's done all those things, plus things you and I have never dreamed of."

"No doubt. Come on, we'll be late for the movie. And, please, try and look as though we belong at *Forever Amber*. I'll never forgive you if they don't let us in."

"It's really that bad?"

"Really bad. Come on."

I followed her obediently as she marched regally out of Klein's.

I raced to the studio. Mme Sexton-Poole was tidying the paintpots. She looked tired and suddenly very old. "Are you all right?" I asked.

"It will pass."

"What will?"

"Nothing—everything. What wretched business brings you here? Won't you be late for your bus?"

"I just wanted to let you know that Tynzie says if I keep up the good work I'll be moved into Cicero next semester."

"That's wonderful," she smiled.

"It's because of your help. How can I ever thank you?"

"You don't have to. It is giving me great personal satisfaction to get you out of Tynzie's clutches. Did you tell her I was the one tutoring you?"

"No. I never will."

"Fine. Now run along, you'll miss your bus."

"Tomorrow at the usual time?"

She nodded. *"A demain."*

The house was eerily quiet, empty. "Mummy?" There was no answer. I set my books down on the hall table "Mummy? I'm home!" I called a little louder.

"Up here," Kirsty called in a small voice from the landing on the stairs. "She's up here, she's hurt. Hurry."

"Where!"

"At the top of the stairs. She's bleeding. I can't get her up."

I dashed up, taking two steps at a time. Mummy was sprawled on the carpet, blood oozing from her nose and mouth, her face a ghostly white. I knelt down beside the crumpled body, my heart thumping with terror. Kirsty watched, her tearstained face pale.

"Tell me what happened. How long has she been lying here?"

"I don't know. I was watching TV and then I heard her fall. She kept bumping around on the floor, it was horrible."

"Okay, okay, she's going to be okay. Didn't you try to call anybody?"

"I tried the Davises and the MacDonalds, nobody's home."

"Mummy, mummy, can you hear me?" I fought nausea at the overpowering odor of gin on her breath and placed my ear over her chest. Her heart was beating. She was alive! I dashed to the bedroom and dialed information. "A number, please"— I was losing control of my voice—"for Dr. Sidney Joseph in Westport."

Dr. Joseph's nurse put him right on the phone when I described mummy's condition. "I'm on my way. If the ambulance arrives before I do, have them take her immediately. If she comes to before any of us get there, don't let her move." He hung up and I raced back to the hall. She hadn't moved; the blood around her nose and mouth had become thick and dark.

As the ambulance attendants carefully carried the stretcher out the front door, Dr. Joseph asked, "When will your father be home?"

"Whenever the 5:02 gets in."

"I guess there's no point in trying to reach him, then; he's probably already on the train. Here's my home number"—he scrawled it on a piece of prescription paper and handed it to me. "Have him try me there as soon as he gets in."

"What's wrong with her?"

"She's had a seizure."

I looked at him blankly. "A seizure?"

"Yes, convulsions. She's bitten her tongue quite severely, but I think we can save it. The question is whether any other damage has occurred."

"What sort of damage?"

He hesitated, then said, "I won't know until we run some tests."

"What kind of tests?"

His eyes were kind as he looked at me. "To see if there's been any brain damage. We'll know in a day or two. Now I really must go. Try not to worry."

"What would cause that?"

He drew his car keys from his jacket pocket. "Alcohol."

"Alcohol?"

"Yes."

"You mean drinking?"

He looked at me sadly, nodded, and stepped out the front door as the ambulance gunned out of the driveway, lights blinking wildly in the dusk. As the siren faded down the hill, I walked slowly to the kitchen and looked numbly around. Dinner. I'd better get something on for dinner. I took a glass from the cupboard shelf and walked to the pantry. Mummy's gin was behind the jars of jelly she had worked so hard to make a few weeks before. The smell was revolting as I filled the glass. I closed my eyes, gulped it down and waited for the fiery warmth to spread through my body.

Chapter Sixteen

"Where were you yesterday?" Miss Mann asked. *"Violet waited* for an hour and a half; she was quite miffed when you didn't appear."

I hesitated in the doorway of the teachers' sitting room, flushing and feeling awkward. "I had to go right home and stay with my little sister. My mother is in the hospital."

"Oh. Nothing serious, I hope," she said without looking at me.

"We don't know yet."

"Come in, come in." She extinguished her cigarette and rose. "I'll tell Violet you're here. Have a seat." She padded down the long dark corridor to Mme Sexton-Poole's cubicle. I sat carefully on the sagging sofa and waited.

"She wants to see you in her room," Miss Mann announced from the sitting-room door. "Stop by on your way out. Evie and Courtney are coming for tea."

"Thank you, I will."

"Her room is the last door on the right."

The floorboards creaked under the frayed carpet as I walked the length of the hall. Mme Sexton-Poole sat at a tiny desk under the eaves, a gooseneck lamp spilling a pool of light on the smallest typewriter I had ever seen. Piles of typed pages were scattered around the desk and on the bed. I wondered if it was her manuscript. She looked up and gestured to a small overstuffed chair with a frayed chintz cover. "Well, what happened to you yesterday?"

"I had to stay home with my little sister, there was an emergency."

"So Margaret said. What seems to be the trouble?"

"My mother is in the hospital and there's no one else to stay with Kirsty, make her do her homework, and get dinner."

"Nothing serious, I hope?"

"The doctor isn't sure yet. He has to run some more tests."

"I see." She rose from her chair at the desk and reached over to the window, raised the sash, and brought in a bottle of white wine from the ledge. "I prefer it with a slight chill. Would you like some?"

I nodded gratefully. She poured a glass and handed it to me. "Thank you." I was trembling.

"*Pas de quoi.* Now, tell me all about it. Have no fear, whatever you say will be treated with the utmost confidence. I guessed it must be something serious if you missed your lesson."

"You did?"

"*Certainement.*" She smiled. "I know how desperately you want to get out of Tynzie's clutches. Now, what is it?"

"I don't know what to tell you." I took a careful sip of the wine. My hand was shaking wildly.

"Try, *chérie.* It can't be as bad as all that."

I took another, larger swallow of the wine and waited a moment for the warm glow to take hold. "When I came home from school the day before yesterday, I found my mother on the floor. She was bleeding at the nose and mouth."

"How frightening."

"It was. I was terrified."

"She struck her head when she fell?"

"No. The doctor thinks she must have had a seizure. The blood was from biting her tongue. She almost bit it off."

"By 'seizure,'" she asked gently, "I take it you mean a convulsion?"

I nodded. "She was unconscious—at first I thought she was dead. Poor Kirsty was there when it happened. She was scared to death. I called the doctor right away. He ordered an ambulance and they took her to the hospital."

"Where was your father during all this?"

"My father is dead. He was killed in the war."

"Yes, I knew that. I meant your stepfather."

"You knew about my father?" I was really surprised.

"Certainly. It's in your school records. Your real name is Adams."

"Muir adopted me," I answered dully.

"From your tone, I gather you aren't too pleased about that."

"I'm not."

"Why did you let him?"

"They didn't ask me, they just went ahead and did it. Mummy told me to put on my best dress one morning; she said I wouldn't be going to school that day. She said we were going to court so Jim could adopt me."

"When was this?"

"The year before we moved to Connecticut."

"They didn't consult you? Didn't prepare you at all?"

I nodded and cleared my throat. I didn't want to cry. "Mummy said it was important that we all be one family, with the same name."

"You're saying that they just marched you off to court with no warning?"

"Mummy seemed so happy about it, and I was so surprised I didn't know what to do. I told her I wanted to stay an Adams, but she said the arrangements had all been made. She said we had to go; it would be better this way—people wouldn't ask so many questions. I didn't know what to do and I didn't want to make her angry."

"Why? What would she have done?"

"I don't know. But there would have been a lot of trouble, I think."

"So you went, being the obedient girl you are?"

I nodded. My eyes were filled with tears. "I was so proud of my name. It was all I had."

"Of your father?" she mused, not expecting an answer.

"Next to my mother, that was all that was left of our old life." The tears were sluicing down my cheeks. "I'm sorry," I sniffed.

"Whatever for?" She handed me a Kleenex.

"For feeling sorry for myself, for crying."

"There's nothing wrong with crying when you feel grief. Have you thought about changing your name back?"

"I used to think I would when I grew up, but now I don't care anymore. It's as though that person I used to be never really existed, as though she were only something out of a book or a dream."

"She exists. They may have dressed you all up and taken away your name, but they can't take your life away from you."

I was startled by the vehemence in her voice. "I don't know—life is so different now. It can never be the same again. I realize that now."

"That may be true. Nothing ever remains the same," she said wistfully as she slowly turned the wineglass in her hand. "And now your mother is ill. Has she ever had a seizure before?"

"No, at least not that I know of."

"Does the doctor know what brought it on?"

I hesitated, too ashamed to tell her.

"No matter, how is she now?"

"Better." I paused, not sure whether I should continue. "The doctor is afraid there might be some brain damage." I stared down at my loafers—the pennies were no longer shiny. New pennies mummy had given me the day we bought the shoes at the Bootery. Now they were a muted brown. All the kids wore pennies in their loafers.

Mme Sexton-Poole finished the last bit of her wine and

wiped out the glass with a wad of Kleenex. "I know this is a difficult time for you. You must pray, ask God for the strength to go on. Pray for your mother, too."

"I'm not sure I believe in God. If there is a God at all, He isn't very fair. My mother is a good person; she deserves better than she's getting."

"No," she smiled, a faraway look in her eyes, "He isn't very fair by our standards. He tests some of us more than others, but He never gives us more than we can handle. One day you will understand. Now go, and let me know when we can resume the Latin."

"Your mother will be coming home on Friday," my step-father said as he hung his coat in the hall closet. "Have you eaten yet?"

"No, we waited for you. What does Dr. Joseph say?"

"I just told you. She's coming home."

"No, I mean about . . ." I couldn't go on.

He turned and looked at me wearily. "He says there is brain damage, if that's what you're getting at. She still has trouble talking, but he thinks once her tongue has healed it won't be so noticeable."

"But what if it is?"

"Don't be so negative. We'll know when the time comes. I'm going up to change. What's for dinner?"

"Meat loaf."

"Do I have time for a drink?"

"Yes, I can turn the oven down."

"Fine, do that. God, what a day," he sighed as he lumbered up the stairs.

Chapter Seventeen

Courtney was accepted at Vassar, Wellesley, Radcliffe, and Smith. She wanted to go to Radcliffe. "But," she sighed, "father is adamant. He says he's damned if he'll invest his hard-earned savings in having some pinko commie-symps ruining my mind for four years. Not after he's devoted so much time and energy to giving me every intellectual advantage."

Miss Whitney almost choked on her Camembert. "Well, can we assume it's Wellesley then?" she asked as she dabbed at the corners of her mouth with a paper napkin.

"That's what *he* would like. But I don't want to give in to him totally, and, since I'm not the Smith type, I've decided on Vassar."

"What in the world is a 'Smith type'?" Miss Mann asked as she opened a fresh box of crackers.

"You know, straight blond hair, matching sweater sets and tweed skirts from Peck & Peck."

"Will your father allow you to go to Vassar? After all, it is his money," said Evie.

Courtney glared at her. "Oh, he'll carry on for a bit, but I think he'll give in. Anything but Radcliffe—he gets rabid whenever the subject comes up."

"I envy you having so many choices," Evie said as she carefully sipped some wine.

"Why? You've always known what you want to do and you've got the college of your choice. Your father isn't frothing at the mouth, pressuring you to go to a school he wants."

"Sure he is. He simply hates the idea of my going into medicine. He thinks it's unfeminine."

"What would he like you to do?" Miss Whitney asked quietly.

"God only knows. Be pretty, have a coming-out party, get married and have two children. Be perfect, all the things I'm not."

"Well, is he going to let you go to the University of Chicago?"

"Yes. I think he's secretly convinced that I'll change my mind, or, better yet, fail."

"I think he's just got your best interests at heart." Courtney burped as she spread some cheese on a cracker and gobbled it down. "And what about you?" she asked, looking at me.

"I haven't decided yet."

"Don't you think it's time you got on the stick? We graduate in four months."

Icy rain beat relentlessly on the eaves; we all sat in silence listening to the desolate February sound. The wall lamp glowed warmly through the nicotine-stained paper shade. Miss Whitney lit a cigarette and made a soft, satisfied sound. Mme Sexton-Poole sat quietly in the corner chair, her glasses perched on the end of her nose as she concentrated on the mending in her lap. She looked up over the rims of her glasses. "Have you given any more thought to art?"

"You mean the Art Students League?" Courtney asked, her face aglow with too much wine.

"That or something better." Mme Sexton-Poole set her sewing down. "Why not think big? Why not the capital of it all? Why not Paris?" She paused dramatically and reached for her wineglass as we gazed at her.

Why not Paris?

After a moment, Miss Whitney exclaimed, "What a positively splendid idea!"

"Do you really think I could?" My heart was knocking against my ribs. It was a great idea.

"If you mean do you have the talent, I would say most emphatically yes. There are many fine ateliers to choose from that are not too expensive. It would do you good to get away, be in a new environment."

"Yes," Courtney breathed, "Paris!"

"I've decided to go to Paris after I graduate," I announced at the dinner table.

"Assuming you even graduate," my stepfather mumbled through a mouthful of food.

"To study art," I continued lamely.

"Pass the potatoes." My stepfather held out his hand.

I handed him the bowl and looked at mummy. Her eyes were vacant; I wondered if she had heard me.

"Paris, France?" Kirsty piped.

"Yes."

"Isn't that far away?"

"Very far away," mummy answered softly.

"How did your family react?" Mme Sexton-Poole asked as the rest of the class filed out of the studio.

"I'm not sure. They didn't seem to think much of the idea either way."

"Did they say no?"

"They didn't say yes or no. But even if they say they can't afford to send me, I'm going anyway. I have a little money saved and I can earn more between now and next fall."

"Your own father left nothing in trust for you? Nothing for your education?"

"Not that I know of."

She frowned. "That wasn't very responsible of him."

"I don't think he was expecting to die. He wasn't very old when he was killed."

She looked at me skeptically. "How old isn't 'very old'?"

"He wasn't even thirty yet."

"*Mon Dieu*, he was young. Well, he's forgiven then." She smiled weakly.

A few days later mummy said, as she pried the cork out of a new gallon of Gallo red wine, that it had all been arranged. I would stay with Bernard Bouchard's mother, who had a big apartment at the Port d'Orléans.

"Where is that?"

"In Paris," she answered as she poured some wine into a highball glass. Ever since the hospital, she had switched from martinis to wine.

"May I have some too?" I asked, indicating the jug of wine.

"I suppose you're old enough."

As I poured, I wondered what she would think if she knew I had been helping myself to her scotch every morning since eighth grade. It had allowed me to pass for normal. It had made life possible. "To Paris!" I said happily, holding out my glass toward her in a toast.

"What? Oh—yes. To Paris." She clinked her half-empty glass against mine and we drank.

Now that I was going to Paris, Courtney suggested that I'd do well to abandon my writing and concentrate on art.

"I guess you're right. Random House turned my book down."

"You sent them your book?" She was astonished.

"Well, I have to get money from somewhere—my parents really can't afford the whole thing and Random House seemed a good place to start. They make a beautiful book."

"My God, what did they say?"

"Not much. They thanked me for submitting the manuscript and sent it back."

"Do you think they actually read it? They must get thousands."

"They sent me a letter."

"Did it mention the fifty-three-page run-on sentence?"

"No." I flushed with anger.

"They probably didn't read it; you couldn't miss that if you were blind. What did the letter say?"

"It was probably just a form letter. Why don't you send them yours? It's really good."

"I'm not ready yet. In due time I will."

"You shouldn't be afraid."

"Who says I'm afraid? I just don't feel that I'm ready to be published yet. I read Françoise Sagan's book and it has convinced me that people our age have absolutely nothing to say. Besides, I have to finish school yet. Have you found out where you'll be studying?"

"The Bouchards have written to their family in Paris asking for suggestions. I'll be living at Mr. Bouchard's mother's place."

"How divine! I really do envy you." She began humming "La Seine," spinning in waltz turns across the quadrangle. I quickened my step to keep up with her as she blithely spun, her long, skinny arms flailing the air. She looked like an out-of-control Olive Oyl, oblivious to the laughter she was provoking. "Paulette Bouchard!" she panted, careening to a halt. "Ye gods, she's such a twit, definitely *de trop*."

"She's all right once you get to know her."

"Perhaps. Let's hope the French branch is more interesting than their American counterparts."

Genevieve Bouchard, Paulette's mother, Bernard's wife, was a superb cook. She invited us all to dinner to discuss the letter she had received from her sister in Paris. There were a number of art studios that I could enroll in; she wanted to explain the variety of choices.

During the meal she filled me with wistful descriptions of the fourteenth arrondissement and the life that would be awaiting me there. Mummy smiled happily and Bernard nodded from time to time in approval. My stepfather asked for seconds. The fact that a world war and an enemy occupation had occurred since Genevieve's own student days eluded us all. Even my stepfather seemed pleased with the decision, especially since it was going to cost a good deal less than any college.

I collected sailing schedules from steamship companies, worked after school and on weekends, and made sure that I would have a job at the Playhouse during the summer. I also submitted short stories to the *Atlantic Monthly* and the *Saturday Review*, just in case. They were all rejected, and I began to believe there might be something to Courtney's statement— maybe people our age really didn't have anything to say.

"Ah, Paris," Courtney sighed, twirling her wineglass. We were in the sitting room with the teachers, listening to a new recording of *Les Pecheurs des Perls* that Mam'selle had found in New York. "I wonder if you'll meet some gorgeous expatriate who'll dance you through Montmartre, the way Gene Kelly did with Leslie Caron in *An American in Paris.*" We had seen the movie sixteen times, following it all over Fairfield County.

"I don't think Paris is going to be like an MGM musical, not really."

"Yes, but it could happen. You could meet someone, and everyone knows it's the most beautiful city in the world. That's why they do so many movies there—even Hollywood couldn't dream up Paris." She sighed. "Just think, you'll be sipping aperitifs in some café while Evie and I are going blind in academe. God, you're lucky!"

"I have written to Marcel and told him that you are coming," Mam'selle said in her lush accent. "He will take you to Montmartre on his Vespa."

"Ah, Marcel! He's even better than Gene Kelly, who, let's face it, is probably old enough to be our fathers. Marcel is so—" she halted, reaching for the right word—"so *French*!" Courtney was getting tiddly from the bad red wine we were drinking. "May we see him again? We promise not to slobber."

Mam'selle rose and went to her cubicle and brought us the dog-eared snapshot, cautioning us to handle it with care.

"*Magnifique!*" Courtney crooned.

"*C'est vrai,*" Evie sighed. "*Quel homme!*"

Marcel was Mam'selle's godson, and there was no doubt that he was dutiful; he wrote to her constantly. I dreaded meeting him and hoped that he would be too busy to follow Mam'selle's directive to look me up.

Courtney leaned over and whispered, "Now *he'd* be someone to get to *la pénétration* with, you've got to admit that."

"He's all right, Courtney."

"He's better than all right. Don't forget, you've promised to let me know the moment it happens. I'll do the same for you, although I can't imagine Poughkeepsie being the same as Paris."

"Courtney, he's probably got plenty of women; what's he going to want with me?"

"You never know. Will you promise?"

"Okay, okay." I wanted to drop the subject and held my glass out for more of the terrible wine. Try as I might, I couldn't imagine myself being ravaged by anyone, let alone Marcel. I simply wasn't the type—my stepfather had made that clear over and over again: I was unattractive, very unattractive; no one would ever want me.

Chapter Eighteen

"You haven't changed your mind about Paris, have you?" mummy asked as I dropped two slices of bread in the toaster.

"No, of course not. Why?"

"You've been so subdued ever since the Playhouse closed. I thought you might be having second thoughts now that it's almost time to go."

"I haven't changed my mind. It was hard saying goodbye to everyone this time. I can't help but wonder if I'll ever see any of them again."

"You might, you never know. Well," she sighed, "I guess we'd better start packing the trunk. Genevieve Bouchard is bringing over some things she wants you to take to her mother-in-law and the rest of the family." She rose slowly from the kitchen table and took her cup and saucer to the sink. "We still have to get you a good winter coat. I understand it can get very cold in Paris."

"Can't I use my old one?"

"I think it's probably too small—you've grown quite a bit since last winter."

"I'll go try it on."

"Don't bother. I'd like you to have a new coat, my pet."

My pet. She hadn't called me that in years. I tried to remember the last time she had bought herself a new coat and couldn't. "I'm sure the one I've got will be fine—it's practically new. You need a new coat more than I do." What had happened to her fur coat? I hadn't seen it for a long time. "Mummy?"

"Yes?"

"What happened to your fur coat?"

"What do you mean?"

"Where is it? Why don't you ever wear it?"

She looked away, and I knew. It was gone. Sold. Along with all the good silver that had disappeared piece by piece over the last few years. "I didn't need it anymore," she shrugged.

"You loved that coat. You sold it, didn't you?" She didn't answer. "You sold it, just like you've been selling the silver. Why?" What else had she sold?

"To pay bills," she answered wearily. "There never seems to be any end to them."

"I don't understand *what* bills. You never go anywhere, you never buy anything for yourself. What happened to all our money?"

"The money?" She looked at me blankly.

"Yes, what happened to it?" I looked back at her. She was speaking, making the motions, but something was missing. Something had been missing ever since she had gotten home from the hospital.

"The money is gone, all gone."

"Where did it go?"

"The house. Your school. The stock market. It's gone."

"You've been selling your things to pay for my school?" I was horrified.

She nodded slowly. "I wanted you to have a chance to catch

up. It wasn't good to move around so much, change schools. I wanted you to have a decent chance."

"But I didn't have to go to Miss Tyneside's if we couldn't afford it."

"Gone, everything is gone."

"Maybe I'd better stay home, get a job. I don't need to go to Paris." She wasn't well, she wasn't herself, she needed someone to take care of her.

"But your art? What about your art?"

"I can draw anywhere, I don't have to go to Paris. I'd like to stay, be here with you."

"No, you must go. You may never have the chance again." Some of the animation had returned to her voice; she sounded almost like her old self. Then she lapsed into silence. The lapses were occurring more frequently. Sometimes she'd start a sentence and never finish it. She was functioning, but something was missing, something was gone that would never come back. She stirred in her chair, as if she had awakened from a light sleep. "Well," she repeated, "we'd better get started on packing the trunk."

The ship loomed over the pier. My trunk had been sent the week before by Railway Express and was probably already somewhere in the hold. "Have you got everything?" mummy asked, her voice catching as we approached the barrier at the passengers' gangplank. I nodded. "All right, get your boarding card. We'll see you in the Cabin Class dining room."

I walked forward and presented my ticket and passport.

"Have you been to your cabin yet?" mummy asked nervously as the dining room began to fill with more people.

"Not yet."

"Shall we go and see it while there's still time?"

I set my champagne glass down and we both headed for the staircase to the Grand Foyer.

My luggage had already been set against a wall by the steward, leaving little or no room to turn around in the tiny cabin.

"It's small, but you should be comfortable," mummy smiled as she tested the mattress on the bunk.

"Not like we used to get when we sailed, is it?"

"No," she sighed wistfully, "it's not. But once you've un-packed, it should be fine. Here..."—she reached into her purse and withdrew an envelope—"this is something extra. Don't forget to give your steward a little something before you leave the ship in Le Havre. Uncle Davey has taken care of the waiters in the dining room, so you don't have to worry about that."

I opened the envelope. It contained three hundred dollars. A fortune. "I don't need this much."

"I want you to have it. Keep it in a safe place. Please," she smiled.

"All right." I pushed the envelope to the bottom of my purse, wondering what she had sold. There was so little left.

"We'd better get back to the others. I just wanted to make sure everything was all right here. You'll write to me, won't you?"

My heart ached at the thought of leaving her, she seemed so lost and defenseless. "I'll write, of course I'll write. You will too, won't you?"

"Of course, my pet. Of course I shall."

I reached out and embraced her, my eyes filling with tears. "Will you be all right?"

"I'll be all right."

"Mummy?"

"Yes?" She had started to open the door to the passageway.

"I love you, mummy," I said awkwardly.

"I know. I know you do. Come, we'd better hurry, they'll be calling the all ashore soon."

There was no hint of apprehension or fear as I stood at the rail and watched the group reassemble on the observation deck of the terminal. Courtney had had a few drinks too many and had been flirting outrageously with one of the waiters in the dining room. Even Evie had thrown caution to the winds and had cried when we said goodbye. "Don't forget to write, don't forget to let us know if Marcel is as beautiful in the flesh as he is in the picture!"

They were waving and jabbering with each other as the ship began to glide slowly into the river. I leaned on the rail and watched them diminish into the golden haze as the *Liberté* headed out of the harbor. Even after the lunch gong had been rung for the last time, I remained at the rail, watching the skyline grow smaller and smaller. Without conscious effort, I followed the sight until I was standing at the stern rail. The island stood on the horizon, a sand castle, with carefully dripped spires reaching for the sun. Somewhere back there, they'd all formed into separate groups and were going to lunch or back to Connecticut with their stolen swizzle sticks and French Line ashtrays.

Only a few passengers had remained on deck staring back at land as I had; the rest had all obeyed the summons to lunch. The passageways were quiet, no boisterous visitors toasting or cheering their departing friends and loved ones on. I made my way back to my cabin, slowly familiarizing myself with the ship.

Baskets of fruit and champagne had been delivered during my absence. There were even some radiograms with last-minute messages, including one from Courtney: *N'oubliez pas la pénétration!* On the bunk, a small, beautifully wrapped package. I opened it carefully and found a delicate gold Saint Christopher's medal with a note from Evie. Leave it to Evie.

I stretched out on the bunk, fingering the medal on its chain, feeling the power of the great engines somewhere below. We had passed the Ambrose Lightship and were heading east, to Europe, away from all that was familiar. I closed my eyes. At last, I was on my way.

The ship was jammed with students, most of whom were traveling alone. When I arrived in the dining room for the evening meal, the maître d' accosted me with a grand flourish. "Ah, Mademoiselle Muir! We have been expecting you!" He led me to the center table and held a chair at a table for six. "This will be your table for the rest of the voyage." He smiled.

"We have chosen a group we think you will enjoy as your partners."

One by one, my five tablemates arrived. An attractive group of young men and women, with the exception of Gaston Jaures, a young Frenchman with horrible teeth. Paul Clarke, from New Jersey, was headed for the Sorbonne, as were Fran Shaw and Deirdre Pearson. Fran was from Michigan and had little use for Deirdre, who was, as she put it, "a professional southern belle. I can't bear it when she bats her lashes at Paul and Larry." Larry Fulton was joining his family in Paris.

Fran, Paul, Larry, and I formed an immediate quartet and spent the better part of the voyage with one another. Deirdre had fastened herself to an older man who was traveling to France on business. We only saw Gaston at mealtimes.

"Wonder what he does with himself between meals? We never see him," Larry said as he watched Gaston march from the dining room.

"It's a big ship, he could be almost anywhere without our running into him." Frannie folded her napkin carefully and rose from the table.

Paul looked around to make sure no one was within listening range. "I understand he's a professional gambler and has gotten a poker game going with incredibly high stakes."

"Is he winning?"

"According to the guy in the cabin across from me, he is."

"Sounds like something out of a movie. He sure doesn't look the part," I said, accepting a cigarette from Larry.

"No doubt that's the key to his success."

"Tomorrow's our last night. Are we going to have a party?" Frannie asked, changing the subject.

"We should. I have some champagne in my cabin," Paul said.

"I do, too," I said.

"Who has the biggest cabin?"

"Gaston probably does." Paul pulled his jacket around him. There was a chill in the air.

"Yours would be best, Paul," Fran suggested.

"Okay, my cabin, everybody bring something. Tomorrow, after dancing?"

Gaston seemed pleased when Paul invited him to drop by the cabin for a farewell drink. "What time?"

"We'll probably rendezvous at about one A.M. Anytime after that."

We all exchanged addresses and promised to look each other up in Paris, even people we had invited on the spur of the moment and had nothing but nodding acquaintances with. Frannie was drunk. "We'll never do it," she sobbed. "We'll never see each other again once we leave the ship!"

"Sure we will."

"No, we won't." She was weeping profusely.

I hung on to the rail, squinting in the bright sun, as the ship maneuvered into Le Havre. There was no sign of the others and I wondered if they were feeling as rotten as I was. I turned and watched the porters on the quay below as they began carrying the hand luggage on straps slung over their shoulders. Red tile roofs stood out brightly in the sun amid gaping, bombed-out holes and twisted wreckage that stood as mute reminders of the war. I tried to shake the disturbing memory of my visit to Gaston's stateroom for a nightcap.

"Did you get any sleep?" Larry croaked.

I looked at him; his normally ruddy skin was a livid white. "No. I was afraid I wouldn't be able to get up out of the bunk if I did."

"Where did you go, then?"

"Gaston invited me for a drink and I didn't know how to refuse, he was so pitiful."

"God! I hope nothing happened. Are you all right?"

"Nothing happened—he was too drunk, thank God." I didn't tell Larry that Gaston had greeted me at his stateroom door, brandishing a bottle of Courvoisier, in nothing but a pair of black lace panties. "I had a slug of his brandy and then went to my cabin and packed."

"You get your landing card yet?"

"No. Where do I go?"

"Over there." He indicated a group of people waiting in line. "If I miss you, I'll see you on the train."

I turned and walked to the line.

Gaston was waiting on the platform, signaling for me to hurry. He had another bottle in his hand and I wondered vaguely if he still had the lingerie on under the baggy tweed suit. "The others are holding a table in the wagon-lit, come on."

I struggled onto the train and sank into the seat. Larry looked even worse and ordered a Perrier.

"You should have some of this," Gaston said, offering him the Courvoisier bottle.

"It'll make me sick."

"No, ask Fran, she's already looking better."

It was true, the color had come back into Fran's ashen cheeks. We drank our way to Paris, Gaston producing another bottle when the first had been depleted. Promises were again made to get together once we were settled.

In the hubbub of the arrival at the Gare St.-Lazare, I lost Gaston and the others and started walking through the clouds of steam belching from the arriving/engines, wondering if the French Bouchards would resemble the American ones. I had never seen them and had no idea whom I was looking for.

A small group of anxious people stood at the head of the platform. They looked my way, and, after a hurried conference, a man approached and said, "*Pardon*, but are you Virginia Muir?"

Never having heard my name spoken so musically, I stood for a moment savoring the sound, and then nodded, "I am. I am Virginia Adams Muir."

"Pierre Bouchard—welcome to Paris!"

Chapter Nineteen

Pierre took my luggage checks while the rest of the family piloted me too quickly across the station in a flying-wedge formation. Before I could catch my breath, we were in the street and piling into an ancient Citroën taxi. A soft rain had begun to fall, washing away the memory of Gaston, Paul, Fran, and Larry, the boat train, the ship, my life until that moment.

I had arrived at last. The streets of Paris were as exotic as Baghdad; I was absorbed in the sounds and scents, unaware of the Bouchard family crushed around me as the car hurtled and bounced madly toward the Port d'Orléans. It was as alien and wonderful as the bodega had been the first time I'd gone there alone. The falling rain had transformed the pavements into inky mirrors reflecting kiosks and warm yellow lights. We seemed to ebb and flow through an extraordinary wash of color. It was no longer a dream. It was happening, and I would never be the same again. I gulped in the new aromas and felt the excitement of the Klaxons as we spun across Paris to the four-teenth arrondissement. Genevieve Bouchard had not prepared me for this!

Mme Bouchard, it was explained as we mounted the spiral staircase to the third floor, would not be at the apartment to greet me. She had been called away at the last moment to attend a funeral, but would return in the morning. Cousin Flore, however, was there and would see that I was made comfortable.

Flore, her narrow face white with anxiety and dominated by large moist eyes, stared at me in terror. She proceeded to serve me a cold supper in silence. I noticed she still had her battered felt hat on; beneath it, her wispy hair clung in thin tendrils to her forehead. The rest of the Bouchards had all left the moment my bags had been deposited in the little rear bed-room that was to be mine. They would return when the steamer trunk packed with gifts from Bernard and Genevieve was ready to be picked up.

As soon as the supper dishes were cleared away, Flore made soft guttural sounds, buttoned her gray wool coat to the top, and lurked out the door.

I was alone. Alone in Paris, I walked to the dining-room window. It had a balcony. Of course, Paris was full of bal-conies. I carefully drew the windows apart and smiled. *French* windows. What else? A soft breeze stirred the gossamer white of the curtains and I leaned forward and stared up and down the avenue, fully expecting to see Gene Kelly and Leslie Caron jeté around a corner.

I turned back, my eyes taking in the furnishings—the large round table, the buffet, the china stove that stood on the hearth of an ornate marble fireplace. I stepped down from the window and walked through the dining-room doors to the narrow kitchen. It was dominated by a huge black cast-iron stove and a small sink with a single faucet. Cold water. On a narrow shelf was a bottle of clear liquid. It had no label. I pulled the cork and inhaled. It smelled wonderful.

I told myself that Mme Bouchard wouldn't object if I had some. I carried the bottle back to the dining room and found a wineglass. At the first sip a golden fire crept through my veins; it was unlike anything I had ever felt before. I carried the bottle and the glass to the balcony and settled with my back against the window frame to drink and watch the dawn break over the chimney pots.

I was awakened by the sound of a key in the front-door latch and hastily closed the windows. Mme Bouchard looked magnificent in her funeral clothes. Her pastime, I would learn, was attending funerals. Any funeral. It didn't matter whether she had known the deceased or not. She liked the pomp and panoply of the march and the funeral mass.

She greeted me warmly, not seeming to notice my disheveled state. As she unpinned her hat and packed it away in a beautifully carved armoire in the main hall, she asked in carefully spoken French if I would like to begin my orientation right away.

I explained that I was still tired from my journey and would rather stay in, if it was all right. I'd had very little sleep in the past forty-eight hours and had begun to feel light-headed.

Mme Bouchard nodded and went to the kitchen and checked the kettle on the stove. She brought an ancient Peugeot coffee mill down from the shelf, filled it with beans, and methodically ground the beans with a steady motion. She pulled the little wooden drawer at the bottom of the mill and spooned out coffee into a small espresso pot. As the water filtered through, she opened the kitchen window and brought in a pot of butter and a small bottle of milk from the ledge. It was then that I realized there was no refrigerator in the kitchen. I rubbed my eyes; they felt raw from lack of sleep.

When the coffee was ready, she neatly filled two cups to the halfway point, topped them both with milk. "Café au lait," she said as she handed me my cup. I wobbled to the dining room and sat at the table; she followed with her own coffee, a baguette, the butter, and a jar of preserves. I watched her as she broke off a piece of the bread, sliced it in half lengthwise, and slathered it with butter and preserves. I followed suit and savored the first bite. The bitter chicory coffee was palatable

with the milk and two cubes of beet sugar. The ritual of breakfast at Mme Bouchard's had begun.

Mme Bouchard said she was going out to do her shopping
for lunch and would be gone most of the morning. I nodded
and went to the small bedroom, undressed, and fell into the
rich softness of the feather bed.

During the first week, Mme Bouchard showed me around
the *quartier*. Since she had no refrigerator, she shopped daily,
and she spent long hours in the kitchen preparing sumptuous
meals. She explained that the clear liquid I had enjoyed on the
balcony my first night was calvados, homemade by her brother
in Normandy. She wrote and asked him to send some more.

One day a note arrived from Marcel, delivered by *pneumatique* since no one in the building had a telephone.

> I shall be delighted to see you. May I take you in Mme
> Bouchard's apartment Saturday night at 8:30 P.M. about? If
> you agree, don't answer me. If not, send me a word 5 rue
> de Veronese. I hope you are settled nicely and have not too
> much the sick home.

It was signed, in the same cramped formal hand, *M. Marcel
Vigier*.

Delighted by the syntax, I immediately sat down at the
dining-room table and wrote to Courtney, telling her I would
be taken by Marcel the following Saturday at about 8:30 P.M.
in Mme Bouchard's apartment. Marcel, I said, was obviously
not one to waste time.

As Saturday approached, however, my apprehension grew.
What if he decided not to "take" me? What if he found me a
dreadful disappointment? What would I tell Courtney in that
event? What would *he* tell Mam'selle?

Marcel arrived at exactly 8:20. I followed Mme Bouchard
from the dining room and heard her gasp with delight as she
opened the door. I stood rooted to the carpet. This can't be
real, I thought. The young man standing in the doorway looked

as if he had stepped off a Hollywood-musical sound stage. He was dressed in a navy blue uniform with a scarlet-lined cape. I wasn't sure, but I thought I saw the glint of a sword handle as he reached up to remove his kepi politely. No doubt about it, he was magnificent. Much more magnificent than the rumpled, dog-eared photograph fondled by so many eager hands had led me to expect. He would have been magnificent even without the costume.

While Mme Bouchard asked Marcel in and offered him an aperitif, I darted into the kitchen and bolted down an enormous gulp of calvados. I stared down in dismay at my plain wool dress—what to do, what to do. I didn't have any dressy clothes; somehow they hadn't seemed necessary. Why hadn't he mentioned a fancy-dress ball in his note? I took another gulp of calvados, then poured an aperitif for Marcel. I could hear him explaining to Mme Bouchard that he was taking me to a dance at his school. I broke into a cold sweat as Mme Bouchard called to me. Oh, God, don't let me get sick now.

Marcel sipped his aperitif, then set the glass carefully on the table and explained that we had better be going, he had a taxi waiting. As we descended the spiral staircase, I could feel eyes upon us: Everyone in the building was peeping through quietly opened doors, alerted in some way that a fine young man had come to call on *l'Américaine*.

As the taxi tore off at a breakneck rate to an unfamiliar quarter, I tried to summon enough courage to tell Marcel I didn't really know how to dance. But the glow from the calvados was wrapping me in a comfortable warmth and I settled back on the seat and shrugged. He'd find out soon enough; meanwhile, I would enjoy everything as best I could since I'd probably never see him again.

Marcel chatted amiably and pointed out the sights as we swerved into the boulevard St. Michel. When the taxi made a sudden stop, he announced that we had arrived. I stood stupidly on the sidewalk while he paid the driver. There were throngs of young men, in uniforms similar to Marcel's, and sensuous laughing girls, all of whom seemed to know Marcel. I had no idea where I was.

*   *   *

He danced beautifully and seemed unaware of my initial clumsiness, and after a few glasses of wine I found that I was having no problem following his lead. I can't believe I'm actually doing this, I thought, as we sank breathlessly into chairs at the tiny table we had commandeered. I can't believe I actually danced a rhumba.

"Are you tired?" Marcel asked as he poured more wine.

Now it comes, the truth. He wants to get rid of me; his duty to Mam'selle has been performed. "A little."

He looked disappointed. "Oh, I'm so sorry."

"You are?"

He nodded, and took another sip of wine. He had beautiful hands. "I thought perhaps we could go to Montmartre. But then, you have seen it already?"

"No. No, I haven't."

"Would you like to go?"

"Now?"

"Right now," he smiled.

It was quiet and dark at Sacre Coeur. The night was crystalline, with a hint of autumn in the air. I could feel my head slowly begin to clear, my heart decelerate to a more normal beat. There, stretching into infinity, more beautiful than any MGM process shot, shimmering and alive, the whole of Paris. Overcome, I sighed and drank it all in. "It's all right, I can die now," I said as I gazed out at the city.

"Ah, Jinny, you love it as I do. But dying," he smiled, "that would be a little extreme."

Jinny—he had called me by my nickname; it rolled like a delicate white foam on an incoming wave. His smile and the gentle velvet of the night made me aware of all the possibilities life could hold. He was right, dying now would be extreme.

Chapter Twenty

Two days before my eighteenth birthday, a letter arrived from Mme Sexton-Poole. The postmark was Dallas, Texas.

On the Friday after commencement, I had driven her to the Greyhound bus stop in front of Muriel's Diner on the Post Road. I had loaned her the only remaining possession of my father's, a battered suitcase, which was loaded, along with a motley assortment of boxes, into the baggage bay of the bus. She assured me she would parcel-post the suitcase back to me once she had reached her destination in Texas.

Her parting gift, which she pressed into my hand, was a crucifix. "Remember me with this, *chérie*. Treasure it, for it was given to me by someone in China many long years ago, a saintly soul if ever there was one. It may be that you, too, will one day consider the contemplative life." With that, and without looking back, she vanished into the bus.

In disbelief, I picked up the letter from the dining-room table and read it again.

Dear and Glorious Wretch,

I have been receiving your letters and am enthralled by your obvious delight in, and your vivid descriptions of, Paris. My reasons for not answering you sooner than this, I will get to anon. But first, for you, rather than return to the States for so paltry a reason as no cash, why not drop into the American Embassy, Consulate, Express and/or what not? There are always odd joblets going that will keep thy loathsome body and glorious soul joined together. Of course, France may have changed since my day, so long ago in the eighteenth century, but I'd bet I'd find the wherewithal to live without having to take constitutionals all up and down *les avenues*!

I still have your father's suitcase with me, not even unpacked. The thing of it is, I have renounced the worldly coil and have become a nun, and only wear a habit (underthings, idiot, of course). Now don't broadcast this at Tyneside's. In fact, don't let it leak past your own ears, if you please. Anyway, all my worldly garments of glorious shame are squashed into all the many cases which you so nobly helped me stow on the Greyhound. . . .

I put the letter down and reached for the calvados. It was unbelievable, incredible in fact! I poured a generous glass and drank it down. There was more to the letter. Her good-for-nothing publishers still had her book in their beastly editorial department and not yet in print. Why wouldn't she tell me what it was about? "Or the title, at least," I said aloud to the bottle. I would not hear from her again, she said, although she would always welcome news. She would be taking her final vows in a few days. That meant she had taken them already; it had taken the letter five days to reach Paris. Final vows. I hadn't even known she was a Catholic.

Be sure to go to the Parc Monceau for me, and blow the trees a kiss. Walk up and down les Jardins de l'Observatoire, sit on an iron chair (and put your feet on the grass, if you dare), and flirt with any tall, dark-eyed, handsome young medical student you see, on my behalf. Sketch and paint like mad, day and night. *Ne parles que le français, et priez pour moi.*

> Lovingly in Him,
> Luke of Jesus, Nov., O.P.

I finished the calvados and closed my eyes, trying to envision her sailing through the southwestern sun in a nun's habit. It was no good; she was too colorful, I couldn't get the image. I took the letter to my bedroom and put it with the rest of the mail, then went down to the café on the corner to wait for Marcel. He was late. I bought a pack of Gauloise *bleu*, ordered a cup of coffee, and sat at the little marble-topped table pondering Mme Sexton-Poole's bizarre choice. Why was becoming a nun bizarre? I didn't know—it just didn't seem to fit. Not for Mme Sexton-Poole.

Marcel's reaction, when I told him, was thoughtful. "It *is* strange, I suppose. Especially if she was all you say she was. But then," he shrugged, "if she has been everywhere and done everything, why not?"

I laughed. "Oh, Marcel. Sometimes you're so French."

"Is that bad?"

"No, it's wonderful. I feel better about it now."

"Why should such a thing upset you?"

"I guess because I admired her so. I wanted to be like her— vital, alive, so much a part of life. It's very hard for me to picture her on her knees mumbling over some beads. That kind of life has always struck me as being a form of hiding, as being out of everything."

"Not always."

Pam Ellis was from Shaker Heights, Ohio. She had been asked to look me up by relatives of hers who lived up the hill from our house in Connecticut. I accepted her invitation to meet at the little hotel she was living in on the rue Bonaparte. Her note had said she had a package for me from my mother and that she was in Paris to spend a year at the Sorbonne. Her relatives had suggested that I might be able to help her meet other young people.

She turned out to be equally purposeful in person. Everything she did was clearly defined, even if it only amounted to pursing her lips, which she did often. She didn't like Paris: It was filthy; there was too much poverty; she was appalled by the number of men and women who slept on the gratings above the Métro. "It's a disgrace. Why won't they do something for them?"

I was uncomfortable. "I don't know. I guess the war has ruined the economy."

"And the streetwalkers—my God, they're on every corner. If my parents ever saw this place, they'd have a fit."

"I think it's a very nice room. Here, I brought you something," I said as I handed her a bottle of *vin ordinaire*.

She thanked me and placed it on the chest of drawers, then opened a drawer and lifted out a package wrapped in brown paper. The box contained a pair of walking shoes that would make the long walks to the studio on the rue de Vaugirard, where I was studying, much less painful.

"Leave it to mothers to pick out the worst-looking shoes," she commented as I showed her the soft leather oxfords.

"It just so happens," I said testily, "that I *asked* my mother for exactly those shoes."

"Well, so be it."

I eyed the wine bottle restlessly, wondering whether she was going to leave it on the chest of drawers or open it. "It's just *vin ordinaire*," I said, nodding toward the bottle, "everyday wine. Nothing special or worth saving."

"That was very thoughtful. Shall we have some?"

"That might be nice."

"I don't have a corkscrew."

"I do." I fished one out of my bag. "Will it bother you if I smoke?"

"No, go ahead," she said, tugging the cork out of the bottle and pouring two small glasses. Miss Priss, I thought. "I must say"—she smiled crookedly—"my liver's having a time getting used to all the wine. I'm afraid I'm going to have to start cutting back before I get yellow eyeballs."

"I couldn't cut back even if I wanted to."

"Oh, really? Why's that?"

"The water is so bad at Madame Bouchard's, it's not safe to drink. We have to put wine in it to brush our teeth."

"I'd think that would discolor them."

"It's white wine."

"Couldn't you use mineral water?"

"I never thought of that." I spied a small wooden stand in the corner with a random-shaped, shallow china bowl resting in it and said that I had one just like it. "It's handy for rinsing out lingerie."

Startled, she smiled. "Don't you *know* what that is?"

I shook my head, sensing I had made a bad faux pas.

"It's a bidet."

"What's a bidet?"

"It's a . . ." She stopped and looked at me curiously. "You must be kidding."

"No, I really don't know what a bidet is."

She got up and laughed as I squirmed in embarrassment. "This," she said, just as Betty Furness would have indicated a Westinghouse refrigerator, in cool, precise tones, "is to wash one's muff in."

"Oh."

"You do know what a muff is?"

"Of course I do. Everyone knows what a muff is, for God's sake."

"Not necessarily," she said, crossing back to the wine and refilling my glass. "This is fun, to hell with our livers! We're here, that's what counts. So what if we get yellow eyeballs!"

"I'll drink to that." I hoisted my glass in a toast.

She smiled and sipped her wine. She's shy too, in her own way, I thought. "Would you like to come to Madame Bouchard's for dinner sometime? She's a superb cook."

"I'd love to. If it weren't for Bruno, I'd probably have gone berserk weeks ago. This room may seem charming, but it's awfully small; it can get to you after a while. You're lucky to be staying with a French family."

I agreed. She went to the armoire and brought out another bottle. "I've been saving this for a special occasion. What do you say we have it?"

"Do you think we should? Maybe Bruno will want a drink sometime."

"Bruno isn't fussy about what he drinks. That's why I wanted to save this for something special."

I couldn't imagine what was so special about my visit and said so.

"Why, speaking English, being with someone from home. That's special." She handed me the bottle to uncork and began rummaging in a drawer for some cheese.

"You're right, this is an occasion. I hadn't realized how much I've missed speaking English."

"You have no trouble with French?"

"Sometimes, but usually I can make myself understood. Of course, it is hard to communicate in any kind of real depth, but it's coming along. Marcel isn't much of a talker."

She smiled knowingly. "Marcel, I take it, is your lover?"

"Oh, no. Nothing like that. He just takes me out a couple of times a week. I'm sure he has a real girl friend somewhere."

She snorted. "I doubt that. He wouldn't be wasting his time on you if that were true."

"He's doing it because his godmother told him to."

"How long has he been taking you out?"

"About four months—no, six."

"You must be joking. A man doesn't take a woman out two or three times a week for six months if he isn't interested in her. What made you think he had someone else?"

"I just assumed he did. Sometimes he disappears for a week or two."

She shook her head. "Hasn't it occurred to you that he might be conserving his money during the times he's not around?"

"I never thought about it that way. It's true he always takes me somewhere, to a dance or the movies."

"That could be putting a big dent in his budget. Sounds to me as if he's got more than a passing interest in you."

"Tell me about Bruno."

"I met him at the Sorbonne. He's not much to look at, but he's tremendous in bed. In fact," she chuckled, "he's tremendous, if you get my meaning."

I blushed. "Ah, yes."

"He's everything I imagined a French lover to be. Except he's Italian." We both laughed. "So why haven't you and Marcel consummated it yet? Is he impotent?"

"Not that I know of. It's very hard when you have someone as old-school as Madame Bouchard around all the time. Since Marcel has been on the scene, she's *always* around. He shares a room with another student, so that's out."

Pam poured herself some more wine. Her cheeks were flushed and her eyes were glassy. "When my parents were here last month, I had the same problem, but we managed." She smiled wryly.

I was fascinated. Could this be the same bland girl that had greeted me a few hours before? It was difficult to imagine her in bed with anyone, much less a passionate, well-endowed Italian.

"You want to know how?" Without waiting for me to answer, she gazed dreamily at her wineglass and said, "I jerked him off under the table, right in the middle of the Tour d'Argent, and my parents never suspected a thing. It was absolutely fantastic. Now Bruno wants it that way all the time. He likes having to fight for control. Last time we were having dinner in a café in Montparnasse, before I knew what he was doing, he had his cock out. We were in full view of everybody and he kept right on talking as if nothing unusual was happening."

"Wow," I said, impressed.

"It was exciting that first time. There was daddy, yakking about all his farty business deals, buying factories or whatever the hell it is he does. Bruno was getting bored and I'd heard it all a thousand times before, so I reached very calmly under the tablecloth, undid his fly, and pulled that marvelous dong of his out. Don't you love how soft and smooth they are when they're not hard?" She assumed that I did and continued. "Daddy kept yakking, I kept doing Bruno, and sat there looking daddy right in the eye with Bruno exploding twenty-five million little Italians in my hand."

"But Bruno must have reacted in some way. Couldn't they tell by looking at him? What would have happened if they had found out?"

"His face did get quite flushed, but he has absolutely unbelievable control, like no one I've ever known. I may even have an orgasm with him someday. At least with any luck I will. You should try it sometime."

I smiled and tried to imagine Marcel's reaction if I reached under the damask cloth and undid his fly while he conversed with Mme Bouchard. "But what if they *had* caught you?"

"Oh, all mummy would have probably said is 'Don't you think you're a little out of line, dear?'"

"You're kidding!"

"Unfortunately I'm not. For all I know, they did notice and just didn't bother mentioning it."

"Pam, I'm really sorry, but it's getting late and I've got to go. I promised Marcel I'd meet him at the movies. Would you like to come?"

"No, I'm meeting Bruno for dinner. But I'll walk you to the Métro—I've got to clear my head. You could always try it with Marcel in the movies, or does Madame Bouchard follow you there?"

"I wouldn't be surprised."

During the film I allowed myself to lean closer to Marcel. Were those his fingers tracing a delicate pattern on my thigh? They were. We sat through the movie twice.

"The moment may be at hand," I wrote to Courtney, later that night. "Marcel has finally begun making what have to be the opening moves. In fact, it could easily have all been *fait accompli* as I write this were it not for the cold rain and the fact that I didn't want to be deflowered standing in a doorway in the place du 25 Août 1944. Yes, that is indeed the name of a little corner in Paris. A liberation battle was fought there.

You can still see the bullet holes in some of the buildings. And what about you? Any luck yet?"

I posted the letter in the morning on my way to class at the studio. Courtney's letters were becoming less frequent and I wondered if she was finally living out her torrid fantasies in Poughkeepsie.

Chapter Twenty-one

Pam took to dropping by the rue de Vaugirard studio regularly after I introduced her to Augusta one chill afternoon. Augusta would have preferred to spend her time painting in North Africa, where the sun was bright and she never had to worry about staying warm. Her money had run out and she had taken on some students who weren't much better off than she was.

There was a hole in the skylight that had been packed with rags. The place was a clutter of easels, paint-encrusted worktables, canvases that had gone unsold and were collecting dust in the dark corners of the cavernous room.

"How in the world did you ever find her?" Pam whispered while Augusta walked to the small alcove that served as her kitchen.

"One of Madame Bouchard's sons told me about her. Even though she's dead broke, she doesn't take on many students."

"Why not?"

"The vibrations have to be right."

"Vibrations?"

I nodded. Augusta had walked to the big iron stove that dominated one corner of the studio and removed the kettle. "Yours must be okay, because she's making tea. If she doesn't like your vibrations, out you go."

"Strange."

"She is strange. But she's a wonderful artist and apparently was doing really well before the war. That's how she got this big studio. Then I guess the Occupation was too much for her—at least that's what they say. She hardly sells anything anymore; she lives on what the students pay, and half of them barely pay anything at all."

"I'm not an artist, but I'd love to learn how to watercolor. Do you think she'd take me on?"

"Ask her."

"Ask her what?" Augusta demanded in her thick accent. She rarely spoke English.

"Pam was wondering if she could take some watercolor classes."

Augusta studied Pam, then carefully poured the tea. She sank back into the piles of faded pillows and cushions on the divan, which I suspected also served as her bed. Then she closed her eyes and seemed to sink into a trance.

Pam looked at me curiously. I shrugged, and motioned for her to be quiet. "She's reading you," I whispered.

"What the hell does that mean?"

"Shhh, you'll see."

Augusta's voice seemed to come from a great distance. "I will take you, even though it will only be for a short time—"

"But I'll be here for at least another year," Pam interrupted.

"No, it will be for a short while."

"Is something going to happen?" I asked.

"Something is going to happen," she sighed sadly.

"What? What's going to happen?" Pam asked in alarm.

Augusta had sunk back into her trance and didn't reply. We finished our tea, waiting for her to revive.

"How long does she stay like that?" Pam asked nervously.

"Once she didn't come out of it for over an hour."

"I've got to get to a class. Will you tell her that I'm really interested?" Pam slipped into her coat and walked softly to the door. "Maybe she's just asleep."

"She might be. Don't worry—if she said you could study here, then you can."

"Is she gone?" Augusta's voice startled me.

"Yes."

"Ah," she sighed. "It's tragic, such a nice young woman, too."

"What is?"

"I'm not certain, but I read something in her vibrations. She carries a great burden. It will affect her life."

"What kind of burden?"

Augusta shrugged, and patted the side of the teapot before pouring some into her cup. "It's not very warm, but it will do. Can this one pay?"

"I think so. Money doesn't seem to be a problem for her."

"That will be a welcome change. Now, show me what you have done this afternoon."

Pam began private classes with Augusta, and while it was true that she couldn't draw, she did have a nice sense of color.

"What are you doing New Year's Eve?" Pam asked as we walked to the Métro.

"Marcel says there's going to be a dance on the Boul Mich. We'll probably go."

"You see, he doesn't have anyone else."

"What makes you think that?"

"If he did, he'd be busy New Year's Eve."

"Maybe that's not such a big deal here."

"Sure it is."

"Do you and Bruno want to come?"

"Maybe. How are you progressing with Marcel? Have you made it with him yet?"

I flushed. "Not yet."

"I'm surprised he's still around. I don't care how sensitive and sweet they may be, they're all alike. They only want one thing."

"Who? What?"

"Men. Sex. That's their main motivating force, mark my words, you'll find out. They think of it all the time."

"All the time?"

"Morning, noon, and night. If you gave them a chance, they'd be at you constantly."

"Marcel's not like that."

"Is he a fag?"

"Pam, what a thing to say!"

"Well, he sure doesn't seem to be too motivated, if you ask me."

"I didn't ask you."

"So you didn't."

"Actually, Nizu told Marcel that she and Jean-Claude use the storage room in the basement at Madame Bouchard's."

"Neezoo? What kind of name is that?"

"It's short for Denise. She lives in the apartment above Madame Bouchard's. We were all in the café last week and she was telling us about it. She says they have a mattress down there and she offered it to Marcel. I almost died of embarrassment."

"Well, what did Marcel think? Are you going to use the cellar?"

"The whole thing seems so crass."

"Crass?"

"Yes, setting an appointment, planning it days in advance. It's crass."

"That's sweet. You're a romantic. Let me tell you something, it ties in with what I was saying earlier: It's *never* spontaneous with them; they're always maneuvering, calculating. Most of them will go to bed with anything that moves. Some even like it better if the object is inanimate. Romance is something that happens in movies and novels, not in real life."

"You'd go to the cellar?"

"Sure, why not? It may not be a cozy boudoir, but it can't be any worse than the back seat of a car, which is where most of us get it. If you don't come across soon, Marcel's going to start getting bored or restless and start looking around for someone who will."

"Maybe you're right."

"I know I'm right."

We descended the stairs to the Métro and stood on the platform in silence.

"Isn't it dark and dirty down there?" I asked Nizu as we walked to the charcuterie. I had run into her just as she was leaving the building on an errand for her mother.

"It's not too bad. We have candles, of course."

"But what about the coal?"

"It's in a bin, with a cover. I keep everything swept up and the mattress is quite comfortable."

"What if your mother comes down for some coal?"

"She gets it in the morning, she never goes down at night, never."

"You're certain of that?"

"Absolutely. Why, are you thinking of using the cellar?" She smiled slowly; I watched with a horrible sort of fascination as the pits and craters in her awful, colorless skin shifted. Maybe Pam was right, men didn't care what they slept with. Not that Jean-Claude was much to look at either. He was a frizzy-haired Marxist who looked and smelled as if he rarely, if ever, used soap and water.

"I have the key," Marcel said softly as we climbed to our seats under the rafters at the Comédie Française. "Nizu and Jean-Claude won't be using the cellar tomorrow."

Tomorrow.

I didn't go to Augusta's but stayed in the apartment and struggled with the fear clutching the pit of my stomach. Trying to shrug it off, I took my writing materials to the dining room and began a letter to Courtney.

"By the time this reaches you, I will no longer be *intactus.* Tonight, as they say, is the night."

I stared out the window. The whole thing was crazy, I didn't care what Pam said. It just didn't seem that this sort of event should be on a level with an appointment for a tooth extraction. Would I want to read about this on the front page of *The New York Times*? AMERICAN WOMAN FOUND DEFLOWERED IN PARIS COAL BIN.

The afternoon light was beginning to fade, dry terror was hanging in the back of my throat. If only we had a phone, I could call Marcel and cancel the whole thing. *What will I do? What will I do?* It kept repeating inanely in my mind. The fact was, for all my bravado, I didn't know what to do, what was expected. Fortifying myself with an enormous tumbler of calvados, I took the unfinished letter, crumpled it up, and dropped it in the stove in the kitchen. I filled the glass again and gulped the calvados down. It felt as though all the enamel had come off my teeth. I took another drink. He won't want me if I haven't any enamel on my teeth.

Marcel arrived and made his usual polite conversation with Mme Bouchard. She asked what we were going to be doing for the evening. Why was she asking that? She'd never asked before. I was sure she suspected. Marcel told her we were going to see *Gone With the Wind*.

"At the Gaumont Palace?" She beamed.

Marcel nodded, unable to speak; he knew what was coming and I felt the muscles in my throat begin to relax.

"Oh, I loved that film. I saw it before the war. I'd go with you, but"—she rubbed her leg—"my phlebitis is very bad today."

"I'm so sorry," Marcel consoled. He wasn't sorry at all, I could tell by the lights dancing in his eyes.

"You have seen the film, I hope?" he said as we slowly descended the staircase. I nodded dumbly.

We froze on the landing. Nizu's mother was conversing with someone in the hall. Satisfied that we had time to slip by unnoticed, Marcel beckoned for me to follow him quickly. When we reached the cellar, he lit the candle he had stuffed

in his coat pocket. Each apartment had its own coal-storage
unit; some were closed off with sturdy wooden doors, others
with rusting iron grillwork.

"This place always reminds me of a catacomb," I shuddered,
"of what the Château d'If must have looked like." My voice
cracked. Lord, my throat was dry.

"Shhh!" Marcel had stopped. He relaxed and started holding
the candle to the doors, looking for the Millets' number.

"What was it?" I whispered hoarsely.

"Nothing. I thought I heard something. It was probably just
a rat."

"Rats?" Somehow this wasn't what I had envisioned. "Marcel?"

"Come," he beckoned. He had found the right door. It
creaked as he pushed it open. I was sure the sound had echoed
throughout the entire building. He held the candle high and
studied the room. "See? No rats in here."

The room was damp and reeked sourly, but it was relatively
neat. The coal bin had a lid on it. Old furniture was piled along
one wall, a sheet covered most of it. The sheet glowed whitely
in the candlelight; Nizu had said we might want to throw it
across the mattress, otherwise we might find ourselves covered
with coal dust. No wonder she always looked gray.

Marcel set the candle in some tallow on the trunk and removed his topcoat and cap, then took mine and carefully laid
them over the corner of an old steamer trunk. Then he fished
in his jacket pocket for his cigarettes. "It's not very elegant,"
he said as he offered me a cigarette. The flare of the match
illuminated his face: His cheeks were flushed, his wonderful
eyes seemed brighter than usual. I wanted to tell him I had
changed my mind, that I couldn't go through with it. No sound
came from my throat. I ran my tongue over my teeth and was
grateful for the semidarkness. The enamel was definitely gone.

Marcel had taken off his jacket and lain it across the coats.
He beckoned for me to sit with him on the mattress. It looked
very crummy. Nizu and Jean-Claude's battlefield, playground.
I shuddered. God knew what had gone on on this thing. I had
to force myself to sit down on it.

"It crackles," I said nervously.

"That's because it's filled with straw."

What would Courtney have to say about that? What would she do if she were here instead of me? Maybe it wouldn't matter to her.

"You've done this before?" he asked conversationally.

My throat was still parched. I tried to clear it. He was studying me, waiting for an answer. I couldn't find my voice and shook my head no. Maybe eighteen wasn't too young for other girls, I knew it was for me.

He seemed pleased, really pleased. "I just assumed that you were like most American girls."

What did he mean by that?

He read my thoughts. "You know, experienced."

This wasn't going at all the way I had imagined it would, or had written it, in those feverish scenes when Courtney and I were twelve on our weekends at the typewriters. The French lover fit. The dark cellar, straw pallet, soft scampering noises didn't. It was like a bad scene in a grainy black-and-white Italian movie. I wanted the director to yell, "Cut! Lunch!" I looked at Marcel; he seemed strangely defenseless sitting in the shadows in his baggy sweater.

"What are you thinking?" His voice was soft, gentle.

I sighed and was surprised at the clarity and sadness in my voice. "I was remembering how I felt one spring at home. Everything was beginning to bloom, the trees were touched with delicate pinks, greens, and yellows, and I had a sense of my own beginning, of something wonderful just ahead, and at the same time a terrible feeling of sadness and loss."

"You feel that way now?"

My eyes were smarting with tears. "Yes. I knew I would never have that moment again, even as I was having it. There would be other springs, but never one like that one."

"There's nothing to be frightened of, you'll see." His fingers caressed my face with surprising tenderness, then traveled to the nape of my neck, sending my nervous system into spirals of shock. If this was calculated, as Pam said, then it certainly was working. His kisses were long and lingering and I slowly began to relax. I ran my fingers along the soft, nubby wool of his sweater. *I have to remember this. Every little detail.* He leaned forward and gracefully pulled the sweater over his head. He had on a sleeveless undershirt and looked like a sleepy boy with his dark hair tousled about his face. Then he undid his belt and slipped out of his pants and undershorts and reached for the sheet draped over the pile of chairs.

I think I screamed.

Nizu and Jean-Claude were crouching there, eerie and white, the candlelight flickering on their nude gargoyle bodies. Marcel was immobile, the muscles in his back carved marble. Jean-Claude moved forward and in one rapid motion hit Marcel on the base of the neck. He crumpled to the floor with a small *oof*!

Hands tore at me; something was stuffed in my mouth—a filthy rag; they grunted orders back and forth to each other. Nizu was holding me down, her weight crushing my sternum; rough hands were prying my legs apart. I fought, unable to breathe, while Nizu methodically slapped my face, hissing over and over again, "Dirty American!" I kept thinking, Why do you hate me so? We fought for you. My father died for you. Something long and hard smashed across my knees; they jerked apart in reflex and Nizu released an enormous glob of spit in my face. Jean-Claude was ready; Nizu ordered him to "*va t'en.*" My body shattered at the same moment Nizu kicked the side of my head. Slowly I began to drown in my own nausea and blood, and then there was nothing.

Marcel was crouching over me. I gagged and began to panic.

"No, no, no," he crooned. His face was wet through the haze and I wondered if it was because he was crying. "Jinny? Jinny?" I tried to reach him with an answer, but my voice was lost somewhere beneath a sour, brackish weight in my throat. "Jinnneeee!" I blinked my eyes. One for yes, two for no. That was the way they always did it in the movies. Why didn't he see? He was crying. I blinked my eyes once; the pain was blinding.

"Who am I?" he kept asking over and over again. Didn't

he know, for God's sake! What had they done to him? Then, very softly, he said he was going to try to help me sit up and began raising my shoulders. I stared in surprise at the vomit as it cascaded down my body.

"I'm going to get some water. Don't move. I'll be right back." He had put on his pants and sweater and he struggled to jam his arms into his jacket. "Stay there, don't move."

Don't move—okay, Marcel.

When he returned, he had three bottles of mineral water and a bar towel. He must have gone to the café on the corner. He slowly began wiping the mess from my face and neck, the cool towel soothing gently down my ruined body. *It wasn't supposed to be like this. It really wasn't supposed to be like this.* Marcel hadn't stopped talking, his voice kept catching with rage as he cursed Nizu and Jean-Claude. "Filthy pigs." Over and over again, pigs.

"Marcel?"

He began to cry again and touched my cheeks lightly with his fingertips. Rockets of pain shot through my head. "Yes, Jinny, yes."

"I'm sorry," I croaked. Yes, I thought as I tried to swallow, the enamel on my teeth is definitely gone.

Chapter Twenty-two

"Nizu is here to see you," Mme Bouchard chirped from the bedroom door. Before I could say anything, Nizu had entered the room and was approaching the bed. My body recoiled instantly. I knew she had noticed. She was carrying a small bouquet of flowers, which Mme Bouchard took to the kitchen for a vase. As soon as we were alone, Nizu leaned over, her face practically touching mine, her fetid breath hot on my face. "You've told her?"

I shook my head no.

"You will say nothing!" she hissed. "Do you understand? Nothing!"

I blinked my eyes, wishing her away. She stared me down until I nodded my head.

"You will not believe the consequences if you say anything to anyone." She stepped back as Mme Bouchard entered and placed the vase of flowers on the bureau. "Poor thing, she seems very tired. Let me know if there is anything I can do."

"You are very kind, Nizu." Mme Bouchard smiled. "The doctor says no bones are broken, she will be fine once the bruises and scratches heal. We thank you for your concern, don't we, Jinny?"

I turned my face to the wall.

I slept fitfully for the rest of the afternoon; gargoyle faces kept leering horribly, awakening me. I stared at the ceiling. Why had they done it? Nizu had hissed something in my face before the pain had shattered my memory. Something about dirty Americans. Something about teaching me a lesson. What lesson? Something about Americans—stupid, dirty Americans. Yankee Go Home. All right, I'll go home. There was nowhere else to go.

"What the hell is this?" Pam's voice jarred me. I hadn't heard the doorbell ring. I stared at her, trying to make sure I wasn't still dreaming. "You look terrible! Did Marcel do this?" She entered the room and sat gingerly on the side of the bed and fussed with the down comforter. "Madame Bouchard tells me you fell off the Vespa. Is that true? You went to the cellar, didn't you?"

I couldn't look at her. "No."

"When Augusta told me you hadn't been at the studio for four days, I knew something must have happened. That's why I came right over. I hope you don't mind. Madame Bouchard says she can't get you to get up—she wants to change the bed. Come on, we'll sit in the dining room. You can walk, can't you?"

I struggled to my feet and crept slowly to the dining room, hanging on to Pam's arm. Mme Bouchard smiled happily as she set the teapot on the table. "Here's some tea." She fussed like a mother hen, setting out cups and saucers.

"I'll pour," Pam said, and Mme Bouchard nodded and went off to change the linen.

I took a careful sip. "It's very good."

Pam gazed at me, her blue eyes were moist. "I could kill myself for encouraging you to go to the cellar," she whispered.

"I'll be all right, Pam. I'm just a little shaky. I appreciate your coming."

She blew her nose daintily and cleared her throat. "I have a great idea. My visa's about to expire and I have to get out of the country. I thought I'd go up to Holland in a couple of weeks. Why don't you come, too? Get away from Paris for a bit."

"I don't think I can afford it."

"It won't cost much. We can get Eurail tickets, and I already spoke to Madame Bouchard—she won't charge rent, so you can use that money for the trip."

"I don't know . . ."

"Come on, I don't want to go alone. We both need the change, you'd be doing me a big favor."

And to think I called you Miss Priss, I thought. "Maybe. My visa will be up in a while, too."

"Then it's settled. You don't have to do a thing, I'll make all the arrangements."

Mme Bouchard returned a moment later. She eased her ample body into a chair and accepted a cup of tea from Pam. "The bed is changed."

"Thank you, you didn't have to do it."

"It's all right, I don't mind. Are you going to Holland with Pam?"

"If you're sure you don't mind."

"Not at all, you will like it. I will write my friend in the Hague—she has a beautiful big house on a canal and I'm sure she will be glad to receive my little Americans. Maybe you can go to Scheveningen—the sea air will do you good."

I drank a second cup of tea while Mme Bouchard discussed the itinerary. It did sound good. It would be a nice change, certainly better than hiding in the little bedroom.

Pam and I left on the nineteenth of April. As the train pulled out of the Gare du Nord, I eyed two nuns in shabby habits on the seat facing us and wondered about Mme Sexton-Poole. "Remind me to go to the Parc Monceau when we get back."

Pam looked up from her newspaper. "Why there? It's so out of the way."

"I promised someone I'd go."

As we crossed the Belgian border, one of the nuns reached into the folds of her habit, pulled out a pigeon, and released it through the compartment window. Her companion seemed unfazed and continued to stare at a point just above my head. The uniformed immigration officers inspected our passports, stamped them, and moved down the train. As we picked up speed again, I stared through the grimy window and thought of all the newsreels I had seen of weary infantrymen inching their way through the German defenses, fighting and dying for every mile.

"What's the matter? You look so sad," Pam said as she folded her newspaper carefully.

"I was thinking of the war and how we're sitting here zooming along as if none of it ever happened."

"You're getting too serious. Come on, let's go see if we can find a dining car or something. Those nuns smell awful and the fumes are beginning to get to me."

"Probably comes from keeping pigeons in their habits," I whispered as Pam slid the compartment door shut.

After we arrived at Roosendaal Station, we looked for lodging. Pam said, "I'll pay for the room. I'll register with the bags, and then you can sneak up later. That way we'll still have enough money to get up to Delft and I can get some more cash from my father's office there."

"How will I know what room you're in?"

"Wait for me outside. I'll come out and tell you."

I felt like a criminal as I lurked on the sidewalk in front of the hotel. Pam finally emerged and we walked up the street as she explained that the room was tiny with a small single bed. "We can put the mattress on the floor—it certainly beats sleeping on a park bench."

"Does the room have a bathtub?" I asked.

"No, it doesn't. There's a toilet down the hall. A bathroom is extra."

"Oh, well. It's just that I haven't had a bath for ten months. I was really looking forward to a good long soak."

"Maybe there'll be one in Delft."

In the morning, Pam and I marched to the consulate, bags in hand and a little lighter from having eaten some of the food Mme Bouchard had packed. The consulate arranged for us to stay with a family named Vosser that was participating in an exchange-student program. The Vossers opened a small attic room for us and lent us bicycles to tour the Hague.

On the day before we were to leave for Delft, the Vossers suggested we ride out to Scheveningen on the bicycles. Vrouw Vosser packed fruit and homemade bread in a small hamper and pointed us in the right direction.

When we'd arrived and parked the bicycles, we bought some herring from a vendor and sat on the beach drinking wine, gazing at a vast sea of dunes sealed off with barbed wire. The dunes were off-limits, the herring vendor had explained in halting English, because they were still filled with German land mines.

"Looks serene enough," I said, munching some herring and a chunk of Vrouw Vosser's bread.

"Deceptive, like people. The old still-water-runs-deep stuff. Jinny, if I ask you something, will you tell me?"

"I'll try. What is it?"

"Did Marcel rape you?"

My heart clutched with fear and I stared at her speechless with surprise.

"It would be better if you talked about it. It's not healthy to hold things in."

Unable to speak, I stared at the waves as they rolled in steady rhythm toward us.

"I don't believe that falling-off-the-Vespa story for a minute. I knew you were going to the cellar. Why can't you tell me what really happened?"

"Marcel didn't do anything to me."

"Well, somebody did something," she said sadly. "Sons of bitches, that's what they all are!"

"Who?"

"Men! Did I tell you that mummy's coming in a couple of weeks, after we get back to Paris? We're going to Switzerland for a while, then I guess we'll be going home."

"Home? But you're not finished at the Sorbonne."

She smoothed the sand with the palm of her hand. "Oh, yes I am. I'm finished with everything." There was enormous weariness in her voice. "Daddy took care of all that when I was ten."

"Your father? How?"

"We're going to Switzerland, good old mummy and me, because she's arranged for me to have an abortion in a clinic there."

"An abortion!" I was aghast.

"I don't have any choice," she mumbled. "I've been afraid to tell you that I'm pregnant, afraid of what you'd think."

"I think abortions are dangerous. How pregnant are you?"

"Three months."

"Won't Bruno marry you? He's just going to let you go through with it?"

"Oh, he'd love to marry me—he wants to come to America. Daddy won't allow it."

"But if you love each other—"

"Love!" The word exploded. "What has *love* got to do with anything! I love *you*, and you don't even trust me enough to tell me what happened to you that night. And Bruno, if you must know, doesn't believe it's his baby." The careful veneer was gone, her face was contorted with rage. "The funny thing is, he may be right. It might not be his baby."

"But if not Bruno, who? You haven't gone out with anyone else."

In a deadly, dreadful voice she said, "Jinny, I'm my daddy's girl. Don't you get it? Daddy has to *have* his girl. He has since I was ten."

Her father? I stared at her blankly.

"You," she choked as she stood up, "don't really know what I'm talking about, do you?"

"Don't tell me. I don't want to hear it!"

"He screwed me, dummy, two or three times a week, right up until I came to Paris. That's *why* I chose the Sorbonne, to get away from him. But it didn't do much good—he followed me there." She turned and dashed toward the water and threw herself headlong into the rush of an oncoming wave.

I raced after her. "Pam! Come back!"

She disappeared under the foamy turbulence, then bobbed to the surface. I stumbled into the water and dragged her back to the sand.

"Now look what I've gone and done," she said bitterly. "We're both drenched."

"We'll dry off in the sun. We'll be all right," I said, helping her back to the small blanket the Vossers had loaned us. I pulled the cork from the wine bottle and offered the bottle to her.

"To us," she said through chattering teeth. She took a long swig from the bottle and handed it back to me.

"To you." I was shivering.

"You're a nice kid, Jinny. I hope no one ever hurts you again."

I began to weep.

"We'll be all right," she said with great bravado. "You'll see. Somehow, we'll be all right."

Our clothes were stiff with salt when we got up to leave. "What will we tell the Vossers?" I asked, trying to smooth away the wrinkles.

"We'll tell them we couldn't resist an opportunity to swim in the North Sea."

"They're not going to believe that."

"Sure they will. They think all Americans are crazy."

We didn't go on to Delft. Pam became quite ill as a result of her plunge, and Vrouw Vosser insisted that she remain in bed until she was well enough to travel back to Paris.

We sat quietly in the compartment, watching the fields of pink piglets and the neatly drawn canals recede before we sped through the charred ruins of Rotterdam, then into Belgium and France.

"Remember the smelly nun with the pigeon?" Pam asked as we crossed into France.

"That seems so long ago."

"A hundred years, at least. Did you notice that her friend had nicotine stains on the fingers of her right hand? I wonder if they were really nuns."

"They probably weren't. I don't think nuns are allowed to smoke."

"What do you suppose they were?"

"Diamond smugglers probably."

"You know," she said, looking out the window again, "I wonder if my father would have done it if I had been a boy."

I didn't know what to say.

"You're lucky, you can express your feelings visually. I can't do anything, unless you count screwing, and I don't really enjoy that." She slumped back against the seat and stared at her fingernails.

"Jesus, Pam—"

"My mother hates me for it, as if it were my fault, as if I had asked for him to mess around."

"Your mother *knows* about your father and you?" I was astonished.

"Of course," she answered bitterly.

"Don't go to Switzerland."

"What else can I do? I can't have the baby; it would probably be an idiot or deformed."

"I don't think you should go. We'll think of something. There's got to be a better solution."

Pam and I were seldom apart during the days before Mrs. Ellis arrived. I saw them off at the train and handed Pam a small nosegay of flowers as she climbed into the first-class compartment. She turned to me, ignoring her mother's order to hurry, and put her hand on my arm.

"I don't think I've ever known anyone who feels other people's pain so intensely. It's going to give you a lot of anguish in your life, you know that, don't you?"

I nodded.

"We had fun, didn't we?"

"Yes, Pam."

She brushed my tears away with her hand. "Don't do that, your cheeks will get chapped. I meant what I said in Holland— you really are nice. More than that, you're the best."

"You are, too," I sniffled as her mother fussed nastily at her to close the compartment door.

Bruno was standing at the fishmonger's stall. I hadn't seen him since Pam had left. We performed the solemn ritual of shaking hands, once, firmly. He reached into a basket of opened oysters, selected one, and popped it into his mouth. "The news of Pam is sad, no?"

"What news?"

"You have not heard?" He seemed surprised.

"No, Bruno, for God's sake, heard *what* news?"

Selecting another oyster, he carefully squeezed some lemon on the meat. His voice was flat. "Her mother wrote to ask me to get her things from the concierge at the hotel. After Pam got out of the clinic, she went climbing with some students from Germany. She fell. She fell off the mountain." He gulped the oyster down.

"What do you mean? Is she all right? Was she hurt?"

"It was three days before they could recover the body."

He paid the fishmonger, picked up his string shopping bag, and walked on to the next stall. I stared dumbly after him.

"Marcel?" He was leaning the Vespa against its stand.

"Yes?"

"People don't just fall off mountains, do they?"

His eyes filled with sadness. "Some do, some do."

Chapter Twenty-three

Staring through the balcony window, the same one I had sat on on my first night in Paris, I let my mind soar away from the pain of Pam's absence. In the warm glow of the June afternoon, there was a feeling of languid promise, an affirmation of life. I had been sitting with Mme Bouchard and her wiry sister from Neuilly, listening to them as they talked in low, liquid tones. Survivors, wheezing and whistling tea through sugar cubes in their teeth. Pam's bones would never know the fatigue of too many winters, and I wondered absently whether mine would either.

They said nothing when I rose and left the apartment. On the street, I hesitated, then walked up the avenue and into l'église St. Pierre. The facade of the church was still pock-marked with bullet holes; there had been a desperate liberation battle there, too. Three old women in black were on their knees doing the fourteen stations of the cross. Everyone was old in

Paris, even the young people, even the children. Not knowing how to genuflect, or cross myself, I slipped furtively into a chair and stared at the floor, listening to the wispy murmurings, feeling nauseous.

Why did she do it? The votive candles flickered enigmatically in their blood-red glass holders. I left the church feeling emptier than when I had entered. I didn't know how to pray. I didn't know what to pray to, what to pray for.

After I left the church, I decided to write to my mother's family in Scotland and see if it would be all right if I came for a visit.

Marcel took me to Orly on the Vespa and saw me to the Air France gate. My two small suitcases were filled with a minimum of clothes and lots of butter, cheese, sugar, and wine.

"You are not frightened to fly?" he asked as we waited for the flight to be called.

"No, I grew up in airplanes. I haven't been in anything that big, though," I said, looking through the window at the enormous tail section. "In fact, I've never been in a commercial plane before."

"I have never been in a plane at all. You are still going back to America? It's all over for you here, isn't it?"

"I guess so. I'm sorry."

"I am, too. Who knows what might have been?" He paused and stared out at the runway. "Maybe someday I will be able to come to America."

"I hope so."

He kissed me lightly on the cheek when the flight was called, and waved as I turned for a last look before boarding the plane.

I splurged and bought two cartons of American cigarettes during the flight, in case any of the relatives in Scotland smoked. If they didn't, Marcel would enjoy them.

The weather wasn't good; we seemed to be coming in dangerously low over the water. I had never felt uncomfortable in the air before and couldn't wait for touchdown. Before the night was over, I would have my first bath—if we didn't crash.

London Airport was crowded with passengers waiting for delayed flights and my senses were heightened by the novelty of hearing English spoken all around me.

The hotel reeked of stale cabbage and seemed to be a residence for the aged. It didn't matter; upstairs there was a room for me with a bath. That had been my only stipulation to the travel agent in Montparnasse when I arranged the trip. Uncle Alec and Aunt Madge had moved to Cornwall when their home in London was destroyed in the blitz. If I had enough money, after going up to Scotland, I planned on taking a train or bus down to see them.

As the water thundered into the tub, I unpacked some of my provisions and placed a chunk of cheese, a baguette of bread, wine, cigarettes, matches, and an ashtray on a chair I'd put next to the tub. It was going to be a long, luxurious soak. Tomorrow I'd be in Scotland and with people who knew my mother when she was a girl.

I slipped into the water; it was deliciously hot, and as I leaned back I sighed. It was pure ecstasy; every fiber in my body relaxed as I soaked, sipping some wine and letting my mind go completely blank. This was living!

The next morning, I went down to the dining room and was shown to a small table for two next to a fluted pillar and a potted palm. After ordering breakfast, I looked around the room, fully expecting to see Alec Guinness or Margaret Rutherford at the next table.

At the small registration desk in the lobby, the clerk checked bus and train schedules for me and, when I decided on the bus, phoned ahead to make a reservation. He then put through a call for me to mummy's cousin, who said she would meet the bus when it arrived in Glasgow. I went back up to the room and took another long bath. I hadn't enjoyed anything more in my life. I could imagine Courtney's expression when I told her I'd spent my day in London soaking in a bath. Maybe I wouldn't tell her.

Late in the afternoon, after a delicious tea in the lounge, I checked out and headed for Victoria Station and the all-night bus ride to Scotland.

As we proceeded along the Carlisle Road, the other passengers settled in and went to sleep. I stayed awake, staring vainly into the blackness, hoping for a glimpse of the villages and countryside. There were many tea breaks along the way, and the driver assured me during the last one that we wouldn't be crossing into Scotland until about dawn and he would awaken me if I fell asleep.

"Here it is," the driver said. He had leaned across the aisle and shaken me lightly. I sat forward and peered through the windshield. The first light of morning was breaking through the low-lying mist. The engine strained as we began climbing the hills. It looked like Connecticut, stone walls covered with thick bramble, and I imagined that the fields they bordered were lush and green. What had appeared to be white clouds in the distance were flocks of sheep spreading down the hills in random, rippling patterns.

I turned to the driver and asked, "Is this the high or the low road?"

"This is the Carlisle Road," he answered, and then laughed. "Is this your first trip to Scotland?"

I told him that it was, that my mother had been born here and my father had been killed here in 1941.

"Was he a Scot, too?"

"No, he was from Texas."

"That's strange. How did he come to die here?"

I told him about the crash.

"At Prestwick. I remember it well—too well."

"How can that be?"

"I was at the aerodrome the day it happened. The plane never left the ground. It hit a fence or a building, I think, and then split wide open." He paused and navigated the lumbering machine around a curve. "You could see all the bonny lads inside."

My cousin Robina was waiting at the bus station. She explained that we would have to take the tram, but would be home in plenty of time for dinner. She appeared to have great difficulty in walking and apologized when she saw that I had noticed. "Och, it's an old ailment that affects my hands and feet." Her burr was throaty and musical. Adjusting her battered hat, she insisted I take the window seat and we rattled along Clydeside to a little town called Renfrew. "All the great ships were built here," she said, indicating the river. "The Queens— the *Mary* and the *Elizabeth*—you've sailed on them, I know."

"The *Queen Mary* only," I answered as I gazed at the forest of cranes and sheds.

I told Robina that I had brought simple gifts of butter, sugar, cheese, cigarettes, and wine.

"Och, they're not simple. My mother and father will welcome them." She seemed genuinely pleased, and then after a moment of silence asked if I would mind not mentioning the wine or cigarettes to her parents. Her father disapproved strongly of women who smoked or drank. However, she and her sister Mae did like to have a puff or two along with a wee dram or two before bed.

I looked at Robina. She was my mother's first cousin, and had to be at least thirty-five. Her father, my great-uncle, had gone to sea as a lad, spent many years in Singapore, and, as I was soon to learn, ran the little row house and his crew of women like a tight ship. I agreed not to mention the wine and cigarettes.

"Well, then, that's settled," she sighed with relief.

Great-aunt Jeannie, my grandmother's sister, was a tiny woman with bright blue eyes and an almost indecipherable burr. She reminded me of Dame May Whitty. She didn't have the "Glesca" accent, even though she had lived in Glasgow for years. I never knew my grandmother; she had died before I was born.

"She was a good, strong woman with a mind of her own. Aye, a mind of her own," Great-aunt Jeannie mused. Mother of eleven, seven of whom had survived infancy; divorced her drunken husband when those things simply weren't done, and then sailed away to America with her three youngest to start a new life.

"Aye, I loaned her the money," Great-uncle Robbie said from his overstuffed chair. "She was a strong woman with a will. She even smoked in public," he concluded, with a tinge of disgust.

I knew some of the story. Mummy never liked talking about her childhood, no matter how hard I pressed. But once, after too many martinis, she had told me that my grandmother had gone back to Scotland on some family business, leaving the three of them in the care of a minister. On the way back, her ankle had been injured boarding the train and she had waited until the ship was well past the point of no return before seeing the doctor. When the boat docked in New York, the three children were waiting to meet her. They were loading her onto a stretcher when my mother forced her way up the gangplank. "Go away, Kirstin," were the last words she ever spoke. It was an abandonment my mother never recovered from.

"Do you know how she hurt her ankle?" I asked.

"Aye," Uncle Robbie said, puffing on his pipe and staring into the fire. I waited, but that was all he was going to say.

Later, as Bina, Mae, and I sat on the beds in their room having our nightly smoke, Mae said, "I know what happened to your grandmother."

"Do you think you should tell?" Bina asked, checking to make sure the door was closed.

"Why not?"

"All right then."

"Your grandmother stayed with us that time she came back. She was waiting to get money from America so she could return. When it didn't come, my father loaned her what she needed for her passage. We saw her off at the train for Liverpool."

"Is that when she hurt her ankle?"

"No. What we didn't know was that she had been in touch with your grandfather and, instead of going on to Liverpool, she stopped in Coventry. That's where he was. It was there she got the injury, and it was very bad—she should never have gone on with the journey. The doctor at the railway station wanted her to go to hospital, but she refused. That's why she waited so long to see the ship's doctor. She knew he would have her put ashore when he saw the wound. I guess by the time she did go to him, it was too late—blood poisoning had set in. And then I guess it's as your mother told you, she died on the deck of the ship."

"I wonder if my mother knew this part of the story. How did you find out?"

Mae sighed. "I guess our mother must have contacted your grandfather after it happened. She received a cable from another cousin who was over there in America at the time. All it said was 'Mrs. MacPherson died today. Details to follow.'"

"Your mother may not have known," Bina said as she filled her teacup with wine.

We sat up until quite late, and they told me of the poverty my mother had lived in. My grandmother had let her go to work as a scullery maid for a well-to-do family in Paisley, while she and the other two stayed here in the row house. "There wasn't room for them all," Mae said.

Scotland is a hard country. How many times had I heard mummy say that?

"Aye, she sent Kirstin to work. She was a lovely girl—everyone felt she would do well."

Do well? What did that mean? She couldn't have been more than twelve at the time.

"It was one of the best families, they were quite well-off," Mae concluded. Yes, and she had observed well. She had learned all the nuances of running a fine home. No one would ever have guessed, at those elegant dinner parties in Santo Domingo, that she hadn't been born with a golden spoon in her mouth.

I accepted a cup of wine and mourned for that quiet, lonely child who had become my mother. Her most treasured possession as a child, she had once told me, was a porridge bowl with blue forget-me-nots painted on it. I had to get home, I had to take care of her, I had to make everything up to her somehow.

They were also the last people to see my father before he

was killed. They told me how he would arrive, pounding on the door in the wee, small hours. "Och, he looked so handsome in his uniform. Such a fine young man. Aye, they were right about your mother, she did do well," Mae sighed.

"Ironic. It was ironic," Robina said as she waved cigarette smoke away from her face.

"Would you like another wee dram of the wine?" Mae asked. I nodded and she carefully poured a few drops into the teacup.

"Did you know he had a premonition that something would happen with the plane?" Robina held her teacup with incredible grace despite the twisted state of her hands.

Mae nodded solemnly. "Aye, he had a feeling the plane was meant to crash, so he changed his flight. He decided to get a ride on a later one. And to be sure, the first plane blew apart. Then, six days later, he took one thinking all would be well, and that one exploded, too."

"Did I tell you the man who drove the bus up from London was at Prestwick when it happened? That he actually saw it?"

"Did he now?" Mae lit another cigarette. She made up for not smoking in public by chain-smoking in the bedroom.

"Yes, he described it exactly."

"Aye," Robina said sadly, "he was a bonny man. We'll not see the likes of him again soon."

They gave me lemon marmalade and Robina finally allowed me to walk to the pharmacy for her prescriptions. Her terrible "ailment" affected her hands and feet, and every morning she would sit before the coal fire and apply salves and bandages to the crusty remains of her fingers and toes. Great-uncle Robbie puffed on his pipe and stared into the flames, his rheumy eyes far from his daughter's agony. Was the ailment an unexpected gift he had brought back from the mysterious Orient? I never knew. In Scotland it's not good form to ask.

They took me to Davidson's Bar for some more wee drams when the wine bottles ran dry. The owner, Molly Davidson, lived next door. She was a florid, jolly woman with iron-gray curls that bobbled comically through her snood. She had snoods for every occasion in an incredible variety of colors.

"I didn't know you could still buy snoods," I said as Molly went to fetch another round of whiskies from the barman.

"They can't be bought. She crochets them herself." Mae squinted through a cloud of blue cigarette smoke.

"'Snood.' What a great word," I said.

"Aye, it has merit," Robina agreed as Molly set the tray of glasses down on the table.

I loved it. I had never been in a bar before. Cafés were different; we ate at them as much as we drank. Here, everyone just *drank*.

We embraced and wept openly at the parting in the Glasgow bus station. At the last moment, Great-uncle Robbie had clamped his tweed cap on his head and marched off to the tram with us. It was the first time he had left the helm of the house unattended since the war. "A truly great occasion," Robina whispered, rolling the "r" majestically.

I blinked at them through the sooty window. Great-uncle Robbie and his women, erect and proud, descendants of fierce Highland warriors and Viking raiders, oddly out of place in the dreary grime of the Glasgow morning.

One day I'll come back. I'll buy a ruin in the North, overlooking the sea. It will be filled with sturdy red-cheeked children and there'll be horses and sheep and good warm tea before the fire.

Chapter Twenty-four

The plane banked slowly as we made the approach to Orly Airport. Below, the lights of Paris, a giddy, shimmering sea of golden stars. Somewhere, down there amid it all, dancing with a languid, almond-eyed Russian woman, was Marcel. That was it! He *must* have someone somewhere. That would explain the long absences, the unexplained disappearances. He probably had had her all along.

He was standing at the gate, waiting, his collar up, the breeze playing with his fine dark hair. He cradled my face in his hands and kissed my eyes. *He's actually happy to see me.* The thought took its time settling in my mind. "Marcel! How did you know what flight I was coming on?"

"Madame Bouchard sent me a *pneumatique* when she got your cable. I had been checking with her for the last week— I was worried."

"You were? Why?"

He shrugged his wonderful Gallic shrug. "I thought you might go home without seeing me."

"I brought you this," I lied, and handed him the jar of lemon marmalade Robina had given me.

He smiled happily and stuffed it in his jacket pocket, then set about strapping my bags on the back of the Vespa.

"Can we all fit?" I asked dubiously as the airport bus for Paris roared off.

"Of course," he grunted, straining to hold the scooter upright while I eased slowly onto the seat behind him.

The only way to enter Paris, really, is on a motor scooter.

Mme Bouchard was filled with news. She had received a new shipment of calvados from her brother in Normandy and it was the best batch yet. "This was made before the war. He buried it when the Boches came, and forgot all about it until one of the bottles in the cache exploded and wounded his best truffle pig!"

We sampled the clear white liquid and agreed that the long aging process had definitely added an extra something. Pouring another round, she went on in dramatic tones to say that Jean-Claude had been arrested for kicking an American tourist on the boulevard Raspail. But it was Nizu who was the biggest news of all. She had run off to Israel with a lesbian she had met in Montparnasse. By day they were picking grapefruit on a kibbutz, by night they patrolled the borders with machine guns. I made a mental note never to go to Israel; I was sure Nizu would shoot me on sight. Mme Millet had gone into deep mourning and resigned from the Communist party. As if all that weren't bad enough, Mme Millet had found, under Nizu's bed, enough ingredients to blow up the entire Left Bank. Mme Millet was afraid to tell the police and had an awful time trying to dispose of it.

I gaped at Mme Bouchard; I had never seen her this animated before. She insisted that Marcel and I accompany her while she made her nightly call on her distraught neighbor.

"I can't say that I ever really liked the woman, but I feel

sorry for her having to go through all that," I said as Marcel and I descended afterward to the street.

"Madame Bouchard has been sedating her, I think."

"What would she sedate her with?"

"Cocaine." He said it nonchalantly.

"Where in the world would she get that?"

"At the pharmacy. All the old people use it."

"You mean you can just buy it at the pharmacy?"

"Certainly."

No wonder I had slept so well all that time I had hidden in the little bedroom. She had probably been slipping me some.

I was stunned when Marcel told me at the café that his military service had come up. "Unless I am very mistaken, I will be going to Indo-China before the summer is over."

"Why there?"

"Because there is a war there. Two friends I trained with have left already for Saigon. Yes, I'm certain that's where they'll be sending me."

I didn't know anything about a war in Indo-China, or why the French were involved. Saigon. It had always been just another mythical movie place: Alan Ladd and Veronica Lake starring in a plot filled with smuggling, tough non sequiturs, drinking, offscreen sex. Not a place where Marcel would go to be in a war.

We sat silently at the table. The old man who played the accordion in the doorway of the building next door was running through his repertoire of tragic love songs. No. Nothing would ever be the same again; one of us would always be fused in the memory of the nightmare—one in a way that neither of us had ever imagined possible.

"I wonder," he mused quietly, "if we will ever see an end to wars. For as long as I can remember, someone in our family has been going to and sometimes not coming back from a war."

I looked at him; his eyes were moist. "When do you have to go?"

"I don't know. Soon. And you? You have definitely decided to go back to America?"

"I don't see how I can stay."

He nodded, his index finger traced the base of his glass absently. "Ever since that night, I have been expecting it. I want you to know that I blame myself."

"Oh, Marcel! You mustn't, it wasn't your fault!"

"Yes, it was. I should have realized that Nizu and Jean-Claude were planning something. In fact, it even occurred to me that they were going to do something—I didn't know what. All that mattered were my own motives."

I stared at him. What motives? "How could you have known what they would do?"

"It's idiotic, I know, but you always seemed so contained, so hard to reach. I thought I could be the one . . ." He stopped and shrugged. "How like a man, eh?"

Was it? Was it like a man? "You mean I was interesting to you because I was a challenge?"

"I suppose you could say that."

I just *had* said that. Was that why everyone was always so eager to teach me something—I was a challenge? Why? What was it that made them feel that way? What did I do? I didn't know.

"And now"—again the shrug—"nothing can be the same."

That's right, I thought. Now I'm damaged goods, and no one wants that, God knows.

"Nothing can be what it might have been. I can feel you thinking, but I don't know what you are thinking. We have become strangers and I am like so many French people now, I am very tired. I hope someday you will be able to forgive me."

I searched his eyes for the fine golden light that had always been there. It was gone. His eyes were expressionless, dark pools. I stared at the dust motes floating like fallen stars on my wine.

In the morning I walked to the travel agent in Montparnasse and learned that the only space available on any ship for the next five months was a bunk in an inside cabin for four on the *Queen Elizabeth*, departing Cherbourg in two weeks. I booked passage and then walked to Augusta's studio and told her I was leaving.

"Ah, *chérie*, I am so sorry to see you go. You know that, of course."

"It's time—time for me to get on with my life."

"And you have not been experiencing life here?" she asked wryly.

"I mean at home."

"I understand."

"I need a favor."

"Anything, name it."

"Do you think you could sell some of my paintings? It would take care of what I owe you—"

"You owe me nothing. You must take them with you, show them to your family."

"—and I could use part of the money to pay for my passage and buy some gifts."

"For your passage, yes. That I can see. But there are so many, so many that are good, can't they be the gifts?"

I doubted it. The last painting I had given mummy had ended up in a corner of the attic. "I can't come back empty-handed."

"Taking your paintings would not be going back empty-handed."

I shrugged. She rested her hand gently on my shoulder. "Never mind. I will see what I can do. But you must promise me that you will continue your work at home, yes?"

"Yes, I promise."

"Good! Come back on Friday, I will have some money for you then."

Augusta was as good as her word. She had more than enough money, and most of my paintings were gone. She refused any payment for her classes.

"But at least take a commission—there's more here than I'll need."

"No. I told you before, you owe me nothing."

I folded five ten-thousand-franc notes and tucked them under one of the pillows on the divan while she fetched the kettle from the stove. She would be angry, but by the time she found the money, I would be on my way to Cherbourg. Now maybe she could have the skylight fixed.

The concierge's son and I hauled my bags down to the street. He had gone looking for a taxi while I went back up to the apartment to say goodbye to Mme Bouchard and her sister from Neuilly. Marcel arrived, calling my name as he entered the apartment without knocking or ringing the bell. "I was afraid you had gone."

"Almost," I said shakily, and then turned and put my arms around Mme Bouchard, then Tante Nini. I didn't want to leave any of them.

As Marcel loaded the luggage into the taxi, I turned and looked up at the apartment windows. The two old women were on the balcony looking over the railing, smiling and waving. It was time to go. I slowly climbed into the taxi and watched them through the rear window as we careened up the avenue. When they were out of sight, I fell against Marcel's shoulder and wept. They had probably helped each other back into the dining room and were sitting at the table, their arthritic knuckles resting on the good damask cloth, the one that was used only for special occasions. They would talk from time to time about their little American, in the gentle sad way reserved for their dead. I knew I would never see either of them again.

The platform was crowded, farewells were in progress on all sides. Marcel rushed to the compartment and placed my bags in the overhead rack. As the engine began to bleat its departure signal, he pushed his way back to the platform. The window wouldn't open, it was jammed shut. I pressed my hands against the glass and tried to call to him. His lips were moving, but I couldn't distinguish the words. He made a helpless gesture and stood, smiling weakly, his hands in his pockets, until I could see him no more.

* * *

The crossing was miserable—heavy seas, cold and wet. We pitched, heaved, and rolled west through the angry Atlantic. I eased my own turmoil with calvados in the bunk, ignoring the trio of schoolteachers from Ohio who had been delighted, then dismayed, to find me in their cabin.

Four days had passed. I had not moved from the bunk. The calvados was gone, so were the Ohio ladies. One of them had left a stale cheese sandwich on my chest; the bread had begun to curl before rigor mortis had set in. The sandwich clunked when it hit the floor. I tried to sit up, knowing that I would die if I didn't get abovedecks and get some air.

The sun felt warm and the fresh air began to clear the cobwebs in my brain. I sat on the deck itself, trying to figure out what had happened from the time I had boarded the ship.

"Feeling better?"

I looked up at the open, kind face, and nodded.

"You were mighty sick. You gave us quite a scare with all that ranting and raving and jumping around."

I didn't know what she was talking about.

"Mildred said it was dt's, but I told her you were much too young for that." She looked around. "Mildred's late husband drank!"

"I don't know who Mildred is," I said lamely. I didn't know who this woman was, either.

"She's in the cabin with us. We're all coming back from our tour abroad. Remember, we're from Ohio?"

"Now I remember," I lied.

"I'm Betty Collins. How about a cup of tea or broth? I know you must be hungry, you haven't been in the dining room for four days."

"Four days?" *Four days! How could I have lost four whole days?* It just didn't seem possible, but something told me the woman wasn't being facetious.

Betty Collins ignored my pleas to go back to the cabin; instead she walked me around the deck and took me to tea, then to dinner. Her companions were leery at first, which led me to believe that I really *must* have ranted, raved, jumped around. Why couldn't I remember any of it?

"Well, we dock tomorrow," Betty sighed.

"Then the long train ride home," Mildred added. "Lord, it will be good to be home again."

"How long were you gone?" I asked timidly.

"Two weeks. How about you?"

"A year."

"A *year*! My! Isn't that something! A whole year. It must have been quite an adventure. I imagine you'll remember it for a long time."

"Yes, a long time."

Some triumphal return, I thought, as I leaned on the railing and watched the lacy foam of the waves. The sea never stopped moving, shifting. I understood now why it was used to describe emotions. Color had begun to return to my cheeks; the face that confronted me in the bathroom mirror no longer reminded me of a raccoon. The shakes had begun to subside a little. I was feeling almost human. Yes, some return. You're a failure. You gave no thought to anything but getting to Paris. And when the time came for you to become a woman, all you could think of was another drink and what you would tell Courtney. And what about Marcel? What had he been? An attractive, enigmatic French figment, and when you could have told him how you really felt, you said nothing. What a loser. What a waste.

I saw a gull. It wheeled and executed an exquisite sequence of aerobatics. I wondered how far he could see. It wouldn't be long now, I could begin again, I could do better this time.

Chapter Twenty-five

I stared down at the bile-green water, an ugly broth of garbage roiling against the steel of the ship and the battered wooden pilings of the pier. Yellow cabs and noisy trucks swarmed. There were no porters in blue smocks, no expanse of quay, no acrobatic native boys diving for pennies. This was New York, too complex for such primitive nonsense. I have come home, I thought, an unwashed, overweight, rumpled mess. For the first time since leaving Paris, I wondered if mummy had received my cable, if anyone had come to meet me.

Then I saw them. They were waiting at the foot of the gangplank, mummy's pale blue eyes glistening, Kirsty smiling shyly, my stepfather standing beside them looking tired.

I rushed down the gangplank and embraced mummy fiercely.

"You look so French!" She was smiling.

"How did you get on the pier?"

"We got a pass. We didn't want to have to wait while you

cleared customs." She hooked her arm in mine as we walked
to the letter "M" and waited for the baggage to arrive. It was
all behind me—Marcel, Pam, Nizu and Jean-Claude. Perhaps
someday I would understand it all; the only thing that mattered
now was being home.

As soon as all the baggage had been inspected, we carried
the bags to the car and made a sweeping U-turn away from the
pier. Heading up the West Side Highway, I gazed out the
window. It was as though I were seeing everyone and everything with new eyes, for the first time. How beautiful and alien
it all seemed.

"Dad built those shelves for you," mummy said as we all
tumbled into my bedroom with the motley assortment of baggage. "He even made spaces for you to store your paintings."

"When did you do all this?"

"We started as soon as we got your cable."

"I helped paint," Kirsty beamed.

Less than a week ago. The room had been transformed—
they must have worked day and night.

"Did you do a lot of paintings?" Kirsty asked as I opened
the suitcase with the gifts.

"Not too many. They're in the trunk."

"You don't have many paintings?" Mummy sounded disappointed.

"Just a few. I sold most of them so I could bring you some
presents." I handed her the box of Guerlain perfume. "I wanted
you to have something special, something you'd never buy for
yourself."

She opened the box carefully and smiled. "Shalimar!"

"I hope you still like it." It hadn't occurred to me that
perhaps the reason she no longer wore it was because she didn't
like it.

"Of course I like it. I haven't had this since before the war."
She dabbed some perfume on her wrists and ears; the delicate
fragrance filled the room, evoking memories of languid afternoons and evenings on the veranda.

* * *

Courtney suggested we meet in front of Muriel's Diner since she would be coming from the dentist's. As I approached the corner, I saw her standing like an obelisk in a pair of Bermuda shorts and a pink oxford shirt. She looked the same—everything looked the same, nothing had changed. The same limp chintz curtains hung in the windows of Muriel's, the same people ambled along the sidewalks, the same leathery-faced woman who pedaled everywhere on a three-speed bike headed down Main Street on another unknown, urgent errand.

"My God, it's you! How I've looked forward to this!" Courtney beamed as she slid into the seat in the booth. "I'm so tired of all the human amoebae—that's nominative plural, first declension—that I've had to frit my time with since you left. What say we get together for a good cathartic cry one night this week? There's so much to tell!"

"What's wrong with right now?"

"Nothing, other than my mother is picking me up in forty-five minutes. We're teeing off at two."

Courtney had lost her virginity—not up in Poughkeepsie, but in the back seat of a 1949 Chevrolet convertible after a country-club dance. "Academe is not all they would have you believe. Intellectual men, I'm now convinced, have no balls. Ergo, Ernie. He's the golf pro at the club. Besides, it was one of those balmy spring nights and I thought, what the hell, I'm not getting any younger. I mean, it wasn't as though I'd ever have to take him home to father."

I couldn't help smiling.

"I must admit, it did smart a bit at first, and I did give the poor bugger the fright of his life."

"Really? How?"

"At the moment of climax, I fainted! Can you imagine? He thought I had died from the shock. What a way to go," she chuckled. "How was he to know? I was his first virgin—and thanks to him, I'm now rid of *that* millstone. And you? Tell me, was it absolutely divine with Marcel? Gad, it makes me horny just imagining him. So, it was fantastic, eh?"

"Well, I—"

"Say no more, there's really no need. I can tell by looking in your eyes that it was a profound experience."

"Courtney—"

"More coffee, please," she said to the vacant-eyed waitress as she passed the booth. "What this town needs," she sighed, "is a sidewalk café. Not that we'd be allowed to sit and sip aperitifs, what with the arcane blue laws, but it would be fun to watch the passing parade. Especially once the annual summer influx begins. They're getting more and more outrageous, you simply will not believe your eyes. Damn New Yorkers! Why don't they go somewhere else? They're ruining the town, you can tell; the character of the shops is beginning to change."

"Change?"

"Yes, getting so gaudy, cheap. Well, what are you going to do now that you're back?"

"I'm not sure," I said slowly as the waitress set two fresh mugs of coffee down on the table. "I hadn't really planned anything beyond Paris."

"How curious. Do you mean you intended to stay there forever?"

"I don't think I was that clear—I don't know what I intended."

"Of course you know, you went there to study art."

"I mean beyond that. I guess I'll just keep on trying to get my bearings, look for a job."

"Well, I still want to hear about it all. Especially Marcel." She shivered with delight. "Sad to say, I can't stay and hear it now."

"It's only one-thirty. I thought you were teeing off at two?"

"I am, but I have to trundle off to the doctor first. He's— ah, how shall I say it?—agreed to fit me for my teeny tiny trampoline. One can't be too careful, can one?"

I looked at her quizzically as she gulped down her coffee. I hadn't remembered the staccato speech pattern; it was disorienting. "I'm afraid I don't understand."

"If I didn't know you better, I'd think you were being affected. You're changed, you're different somehow. A trampoline, a diaphragm. My first. Want to come along? Maybe we could get two at a discount. That's what *they're* always asking for."

"They?"

"The New Yorkers! For heaven's sake, Jinny, get with it."

"Some other time perhaps." My God, I hadn't been gone all that long, yet she had turned into her mother. I could see her in twenty years snapping her way through sportswear at Saks, being rude to the saleswomen before dashing off to the Palm Court at the Plaza for martinis with another matron. I squinted: Would the other matron be me? Courtney would have her not-so-tiny trampoline tucked safely in her handbag. "One never knows," she might say as she and the friend, who would not be me, powdered their noses before going their separate ways.

Gordon Llewellyn was shuffling contracts in the Playhouse office above the scene shop. I rapped on the wall lightly to let him know I was there.

"Well," he said slowly, rolling the word across the flat desert of his voice, "you're back. I must say, I didn't expect it to be so soon."

"I ran out of money—you know how it is." Of course he didn't. He was to the theater born, scion of a great producing family. It was all there for him, all he had to do was reach out and take it.

"There isn't much left. The only opening we have is in the box office, and that might be a bit boring for you. You could help keep an eye on the apprentices; we have too many, as usual, and if you can keep them unscathed by drugs, sex, the usual, I'll see that there's a handsome bonus for you at the end of the season."

"Gordon, I've worked here almost as long as you have and no one's been scathed yet."

"Times, you will find, have changed. They're messing themselves up much earlier now. I'd like you to begin tomorrow, if that's okay."

I felt relieved and left him fumbling his papers in the musty little cubicle that smelled of empty winters and latex paint.

Soon the scene shop below would be humming. This was where it all happened, where fantasies were made real. It would be safe here.

Driving home through the warmth of the early summer afternoon, I thought of Marcel. It would only be a matter of time before his letters stopped. He had gone to Saigon, and it was an even greater abomination than he had imagined. I parked the car at the beach and stared across the water. The tide was rolling in across the clam beds. If there's time later, I thought, I'll come back and dig some.

"You're *not* going back to that place," mummy groaned when I told her of my conversation with Gordon. We were in the kitchen, shelling peas for dinner. Her hands, still slender and eloquent, were rough and callused from building another stone wall.

I shifted uneasily in the chair and reached for more pea pods. "It's not Sodom and Gomorrah, and it's better than nothing. At least I'll be earning some money."

"Well," she sighed, "I should think you'd be able to find something better to do. After all, you *have* been to Paris. You speak French beautifully, according to Genevieve and Bernard." She poured herself another glass from her gallon of Gallo. "Would you like some?"

"Yes, please." I went to the cupboard and brought down another glass. "How can you stand that stuff? It's worse than the rotgut cheap wine we used to get in Paris and costs twice as much."

"It's only two-fifty a gallon."

"It tastes it. In Paris, you take your empties to the wine store and the man fills them right from the barrel."

"I wonder why we don't do that here. Do they have half-gallons?"

"No—at least not that I ever saw." I tasted the wine and grimaced. "This stuff needed more time in the barrel." Aching frustration was building in my throat at the sight of the once proud head and shoulders now slumped in defeat over the fresh peas.

I hate your weariness, your defeat, the fact that you guzzle too much cheap wine, that the life has gone out of your eyes. I want you to be the way you were. I want to hear the sound of your laughter and see you preside again in a home filled with light, music, and love. If pleasing you will make you that way once more, then I will please you. But how?

"Tell me something?" I said.

"Yes?"

"Just exactly what sort of future do you see for me?"

She finished rinsing the peas and set them to drain, then slowly dried her hands on a tea towel. "Virginia"—she pronounced each syllable—"you are your father's daughter. Once he made up his mind to do something, he did it, and he did it well. I know you have more of him in you; that whatever you set your mind to, you will do. I don't want you to be like me."

I felt her humiliation and wanted to comfort her. "Mummy, I'm not trying to be perverse. I really do want to know on more specific terms. Saying I'm like my father isn't enough."

"From the time he was a small boy on the farm in Texas, he wanted to fly. That's all he dreamed of and worked for. He did it in spite of opposition from his family. Did you know that his own brother set fire to the plane he had brought home to show them?"

"I remember him telling me that story. I was never sure if it was just a story."

"Nothing he told you was ever just a story. Texas is a raw land, especially so when he was a boy. I guess the family thought his flying was crazy and frivolous. Later, of course, they were very proud of it."

"Then *his* parents didn't like what *he* chose to do, either?"

"I see your point," she smiled wanly.

"How did you meet him, anyway?"

"How did we meet?" She seemed startled by the question.

"Most people know things like that about their parents. You never talk about your past. How can I know whether I'm like either of you or not?"

"That's all over and done with."

"I know, but unless you don't want to tell me, I'd really like to know." I poured more wine into her glass.

She lit a cigarette and puffed on it thoughtfully. "It was during the Depression. I was working as a waitress at the Roosevelt Field Inn after my mother died. He and some of the other pilots came in for dinner one night. Aviators were always coming in and out. Most of them you never saw again. At any rate, the group he was with ordered an enormous meal and then left without paying the check. The manager was very angry at me for not collecting the money, so he took it out of my salary, which wasn't much anyway.

"A few weeks later your father flew back to the field, and apparently someone said something to him about my having been stuck with their check. He came to the inn immediately and insisted upon giving me the money. I refused. I doubt that he had known the check hadn't been paid. He was adamant that I take the money, I was adamant that I wouldn't. Then he said, 'Well, at least let me buy *you* dinner.' There was something about him. He wasn't like the others—I sensed it while he was talking. I *knew* he was different. The others were all outrageous womanizers.

"I gave in finally and did have dinner. We went out every night for ten days, and then, in the rumble seat of Uncle Davey's car, he said he was leaving for a job in the West Indies in the morning and he wanted me to marry him." She was smiling. "I told him I couldn't possibly, that we didn't know anything about each other. He said that was all well and good, but since he was leaving the next day there wouldn't be time for that, and furthermore he didn't know how long he would be gone. He had to have a yes or no answer by morning. In those days you didn't have to wait to get married.

"I lived in a boardinghouse, the telephone was on the wall in the hall. Everyone in the house knew about the proposal, so when the phone rang they were all waiting around to hear the outcome. I said hello, and he said, 'Well, which is it? Yes or no?' Then I laughed and finally said, 'Yes.'"

I loved the story and could see her as she must have looked

that morning. "Is that when you took off on the aerial honeymoon and crashed?"

"It wasn't an *aerial* honeymoon. That's what the newspapers
said when we cracked the plane up. We were on our way to
Santo Domingo and he was so excited and nervous that we
didn't make it off the runway."

"Had you ever flown before?"

"Not really, just a spin or two with other aviators."

"It must have been frightening to crash."

"No, it was quite funny actually. The other pilots had tied
old shoes and tin cans on the tail skid and written 'Just Married'
and 'Happy Landings' and 'Whoopee' all over the sides of the
plane. My hat had fallen down over my eyes, so I didn't really
see what happened. Even if I had, I doubt I would have been
frightened. I was never afraid when he was at the controls. It
was almost as if something metaphysical existed between him
and a plane. I don't think the one he was killed in would have
crashed if he had been the one flying it."

She tapped the cigarette out gently. "You remind me of him
in a great many ways. That's why I expect so much from you."

"Didn't being different bother him?"

"If it did, he never showed it. He loved everything in life.
And even though we never spoke about it, each time he left
there was always the element of risk that he might not come
back."

"It gave you a sense of urgency?"

"Yes. We tried to make all our moments together count."

"It was a good way to live."

"I wonder if he would still want me to fly away with him
if he could see me now."

"If he had lived, you would be different."

"Perhaps."

"You would." I finished my wine, remembering the Hattie
Carnegie clothes, the aromatic perfumes, the delicate silk lingerie. *You would be different. You wouldn't be killing yourself
building stone walls, drinking Gallo, and doing without—that
I'm sure of.*

As if she had read my mind, she said, "I guess I *would* be

different. Even when we didn't have any money, he always managed somehow. It was never something he was obsessed with. I guess I'd better get dinner on." She refilled her glass and carried it over to the counter.

"Mummy?"

"Yes?"

"I don't want to be a disappointment to you."

"I know, my pet."

Chapter Twenty-six

As the apprentices arrived, Gordon passed them on to me for duty assignments. It was becoming clear that I wouldn't be spending much time in the box office.

"How about a beer?" Gordon suggested as we walked to the tavern.

"I'd love one." Actually I didn't really like beer, but it was all that anyone drank during the day at the theater.

"We have a problem," he said as he settled into his chair.

"Really?"

"Yes, Caitlin Cole."

"The name is vaguely familiar."

"Margaret Cole's daughter."

Margaret Cole had dominated the box office in films since the 1930s. She was still on top; everyone knew who Margaret Cole was. "Yikes."

"'Yikes' is hardly the word, 'catastrophic' would be better.

From what little I've been told, she is being sent to us because of some sort of problem at school. Jesus, you'd think we were running a summer camp for the wayward instead of a theater. You're not to let her out of your sight."

"Gordon, you've got to be kidding. How can I work and keep an eye on somebody all the time?"

"I don't know, that's what I'm paying you for. But I want no trouble while she's here. If there's any scandal, it will be"— he made a throat-slitting gesture—"for all of us. The Cole dame is someone I'd rather not tangle with."

The next morning the longest limousine I had ever seen slid into the lane bordering the scene shop. All the would-be actors, writers, and directors paused in their mowing, painting, and hammering to watch the procession.

"Jesus," Gordon muttered under his breath, "she's tiny, practically a midget! I've always thought of her as being at least six feet tall."

Margaret Cole had emerged from the padded interior of the car. She was followed by a distinguished-looking man in a business suit—her most recent husband—and a very pale blond girl in a shirtdress with at least six petticoats.

"Is *that* her kid?" Evan Windsor asked as he stood beside me. Gordon had rushed toward the group in welcome.

"I guess so," I answered, wiping my dirty hands on my jeans as the group turned and looked at us.

By evening the full complement of staff and apprentices had arrived and Caitlin Cole's fingernails had all been broken to the nub. She had scrubbed and put a coat of paint on the lavatories. Even Evan was impressed. "She did that like a pro. Wonder where she learned?"

"I don't know. But she seems like a nice kid."

"She's sure got some set of knockers," Evan grinned.

"Hands off, Evan. Gordon will personally have you tarred and feathered if anything happens to her while she's here."

"Probably wants her all to himself," Evan sighed as he wandered off to the lighting booth.

*   *   *

Four days later, the theater treasurer was brutally beaten and hospitalized. "A young man he tried to solicit in a bar," Gordon sighed. He unscrewed the cap from an aspirin bottle he spied poking its neck through the pile of papers on his desk, threw a handful of tablets down his throat, and rubbed his head. "We have suggested he take a protracted leave until the publicity blows over and his eyes heal up."

"I can't imagine *The Town Crier* printing a story like that. Where would they ever find out about it?"

"It was a local bar—the nincompoop must have been off his rocker. They'll get it from the police report, and I don't need irate trustees on my back."

"Do you think he really did something like that?"

"A bad habit, what can I say? Usually he goes a little farther afield."

"Maybe he had car trouble."

"Ha-ha! Very funny. He probably was drunk. In any event, a replacement will be coming up in time for this evening's performance. I'd like you to meet him at the train and show him the box-office receipts and whatever else he needs to see."

"What does he look like?"

"I haven't any idea, but he comes highly recommended. Take the wagon, he'll be looking for that."

"Are you going to town?" Evan asked as I descended the stairs from Gordon's office.

"No, to the station. Why?"

"I thought you might take Caitlin with you if you were going to town. Now she wants some sneakers. She wouldn't listen when I suggested she get some while we were buying the Levi's, and I can't be bothered with shopping right now."

"It's okay, we can stop on the way to the train."

The train wheezed in twenty minutes late, and it was Caitlin who spotted the new treasurer first. "That must be him," she said, pointing to a figure in the wilted-looking stream of commuters fanning across the parking lot. "And, if it is, I want to be assigned to the box office. He looks like something from Central Casting."

I followed her gaze. She was right, he didn't look real. He was ambling easily along in white pants, a faded work shirt, and loafers without socks. "A bit too actory, if you ask me. He might as well be wearing a neon sign."

"He doesn't need a neon sign. I've seen some gorgeous men in my day, but this is something else!" She opened the station wagon door and waved her arms. "Over here!"

"Hi," he drawled as he approached. The voice had a nice pitch, not too deep, just right. He swung his bag onto the back seat and motioned for Caitlin to sit in the middle. "Mind if I drive?"

I was nonplussed, then reluctantly got out from behind the wheel and walked to the passenger side of the wagon. Just like any commuter wife. Really!

"Which way?" he asked as the engine puffed into action.

"Left, under the bridge, then right. The clutch slips."

"I can handle it."

Yes, I thought, I bet you can.

His name was Ted Aristes, he was an actor between shows, and, yes, he was Greek. I marveled at the ease with which he introduced himself and gratuitously offered the information that he had slept with a man but he wasn't a fag. "Just a pervert."

Caitlin roared with laughter. I turned my head and stared out the window, hoping he hadn't noticed my blush. He hadn't been in Westport for ten minutes and he was clearly in charge.

I was surprised and pleased a week later when Ted suggested we have a beer one night after we finished counting up the receipts. Then I remembered it was strike night and all the apprentices were occupied taking down the set on the stage and wouldn't be available for hours.

"What a week," Ted sighed after taking a deep swig of his beer directly from the bottle.

"So I gather."

"What's that supposed to mean?" His brows were knit in a

frown. I wondered if his adoring fans had noticed that his hair had begun to thin.

"To quote: 'Deflowered three virgins in as many days.'"

He had a delightful laugh. "Absolute bullshit! Besides, I doubt there are three virgins within ten miles of this place. I've never seen such a bunch of little baggages! Don't tell me you believed the little twats? I've got better sense than that. Although I must say I wouldn't mind having a go at the Cole girl—she's something else. Don't worry, Gordon's given me my orders." He took another gulp of beer and burped contentedly. "Besides, she's about as messed up as they come, although I'm sure it's no fault of hers."

"She's not bad."

"She's not good, either. Be careful. People like that, young or old, are emotional cannibals. They'll devour you alive before you even know it's happened."

"Don't you think you're being a little judgmental?"

"Maybe. Let's get out of here, I'm hungry and could do with a burger or something. Is there anyplace open at this hour that we can walk to?"

"Just Barney's. Smitty's and the drive-in are closed at this hour."

He made a face. "Barney's is too far. It's raining, or hadn't you noticed?"

Actually I hadn't. "Of course I noticed. I have a car, unless the walk to the parking lot is too much for you."

"That I can handle. Let's go!" He pulled up the collar of his shirt, jammed his hands in his pockets, and waltz-clogged through a puddle. "Quick! Who am I?"

"Gene Kelly, *Singin' in the Rain*."

"Riggght!" He spread his arms and tour-jetéd into another puddle. "Now, if we only had some garbage-can lids, I could do the number from—"

"It had Dan Dailey and Frank Sinatra—I can't think of the title."

"Dan Dailey and Michael Kidd. The movie was *It's Always Fair Weather*. Come on, dance with me." Before I could tell him I really didn't know how to dance, he hooked my elbow with his and said, "You're not going to be the impartial observer anymore. I've been watching you."

I marveled at how he had found the time, then he grabbed my hands and swept me in a breathtaking tango through the puddles to the car.

"You are a certifiable maniac," I laughed. "I can't dance."

"Ridiculous, you just did." He reached out with his cool wet hands and pulled my face to his. His mouth was warm and soft. "Get in the car," he murmured.

I slid into the seat and he followed me with another kiss. "Now you're getting into the spirit of things."

"I am?" I squirmed nervously.

"You have a wonderful mouth."

"I do?" I was amazed, too amazed to realize he probably said that to everyone.

He laughed. "You do. Mouths are my hobby, I know. Look—" He had somehow unzipped his fly, exposing the erect penis. My God, he must keep the zipper oiled; I hadn't even heard it open. I didn't know what to do: look, not look. "Go ahead," he murmured.

I looked at him in bewilderment.

"Touch it."

"Touch it?" Jesus, had I said that aloud? Had he heard me? What a boob he must think I am.

He took my hand and moved it to the warm flesh. His mouth covered mine and I felt myself being drawn to the sweet warmth of his body. How spicy and clean he smelled. I felt him guide my hand further into the yawning maw of his fly. Not sure of myself, I let my fingers tentatively explore his body. It was enormous—not that I had that many to compare it with, but I was sure this was the largest penis in the entire Northeast, possibly the world. He buried his head in my neck, his tongue leaving delicate white shocks at each point of contact.

"Relax," he whispered. "You're doing just fine."

Chapter Twenty-seven

"*Dog days. Now I understand what they mean by that expression.*" Courtney dabbed the perspiration off her face. "How about a Tom Collins or something?"

"Won't your parents mind?"

"I doubt it, but if they do, I'll tell them we used the gin for medical reasons—to keep us from going rabid in the heat. Besides, father is always saying he wants me to learn to drink like a lady, and what better place to start than in the home?" She walked to her father's bar and deftly mixed the drinks in tall frosted glasses. "Sorry, I don't have any cherries." She laughed. "No pun intended, of course."

"Of course."

"Well, here's to us and another of our farewells. Let's go out on the terrace, it might be cooler there." She had on one of her father's white shirts, the crisp tails hiding all but an inch of her always unwrinkled Bermuda shorts. The air on the terrace was just as heavy and humid as it was in the house, my own clothes were rumpled and damp. Courtney smiled as she tasted her Tom Collins. "Ah, this is living."

I sat on the rough stone of the terrace wall and sipped my drink. It was good. "Delicious. Nice and strong."

She lit a cigarette and leaned back on the chaise, drink in hand. "I shall certainly miss this up at school. There's no doubt of it, dorms do lack all the amenities, although I suppose I could always stash a bottle or two in my footlocker."

"You could. When do you have to go back?"

"Week after next." She smiled, gesturing with her glass.

I ached with envy. College had validated Courtney—not that she needed any validation. I gazed out at her father's acres of perfect green lawn. The trees, the shrubs, and running brook had all been installed to act in perfect harmony with each other. It never seemed to need weeding, pruning, or trimming, it just was, all the time. Not a leaf or bird stirred. My breath caught in an unexpected spasm of sadness.

"What's wrong? You seem so melancholy." She tapped her cigarette ashes neatly into a little beanbag ashtray she had set on the arm of the chaise. She was neat about everything, meticulous in fact. It came naturally with the house, the family. Everything just so. Perfect. I wondered if they ever argued, committed thoughtless, messy acts. I doubted it. Everything had always been polished—the rooms, the conversations.

"I guess I am," I admitted.

"Are you having problems with Ted?"

"Not problems *per se*, but it's the end of the season and I can't help but wonder what will happen after the theater closes."

"Aren't you going to New York with him?"

"Well, it isn't definite yet."

"I thought you were going to share a sublet?"

"He hasn't mentioned it recently."

"Has he said he's changed his mind?"

"No."

"What are you worried about then?"

"He could have forgotten to tell me he's changed his mind."

"Oh, Jinny, don't be so dense. If it's worrying you, why

not ask him what the story is? I'd be more worried about your mother's reaction. What does she think of all this?"

"I didn't tell her I was going to share an apartment with Ted."

"What did you tell her?"

"That I was going to be sharing with someone from the theater."

"Won't she find out eventually? What if she comes in and sees his things in the closet, the bathroom?"

"She won't come in."

"What makes you think that?"

"She rarely, if ever, goes to New York anymore."

"What if he answers the phone?"

"I'll think of something to tell her."

"Has she met Ted?"

"Yes, she doesn't like him. I didn't think she would."

"God, I envy you!"

"You *envy* me? Whatever for?"

"Going to New York, living with a man. You're out there in the world, doing everything, while I'm stuck away up there in that school."

We had one for the road, and then I left. I could see her from the driveway; she was stretched out on the chaise again, her head back, the glass dangling in her hand. She's become a stranger, I thought as I put the car in reverse and headed down the drive.

Evie was leaning against the seawall, strumming her guitar. "Where's Courtney?" she asked as I dropped down on the sand.

"I didn't ask her to come."

"Just as well, she's become very fatiguing, never stops pontificating. I think it helps her keep her shell intact. There's something even worse."

"What?"

"She's turning into her mother. Even as we sit here, it's happening."

"Yes, I suppose it is. Her fate is sealed. Charge accounts at Best's, Saks. Volunteer at the Red Cross. Women's Club, mediocre golf, bridge on Thursdays, the right husband, and two ideal children."

"And she'll vote straight Republican all her life." I sighed, feeling some of the tension go out of my body.

"What a waste." Evie stared out across the water. "She has a potentially fine mind, she could do anything if she'd just try."

"You think she won't try?"

Evie shook her head slowly. "No. And I've thought about it, too. I've envied Courtney her mind. But she'll do what's expected of her. If she were a boy, it would be different—she would be able to do something with her talent and brain."

"Don't you think she'll do something with her writing?"

"No, I don't."

"I think we'll be reading her engagement announcement in the next year or two. She's going to be the first one of us to get married."

"I don't think she wants to get married right away."

"She'll do it to please her parents. She'll graduate with honors and then she'll marry some upstanding young man from the right sort of family."

"I can't imagine her doing that—not yet, anyway."

"Courtney will marry. College is going to enable her to meet the right man. Why do you think her father was so set on Wellesley? He doesn't care that you need top grades to get in, that Courtney is brilliant and could really do something with her life. College has been a good investment for her parents; even at Vassar she ought to be able to make a good alliance, one that will please her family."

"I have a horrible feeling you're right. She isn't like you or me, having to work so hard to find our niches. I wonder if we ever will."

"You will, I'm sure of that. My grades are so bad, I'm afraid I'll never get into a good medical school. It's ironic, isn't it?"

"What is?"

"That I have to work so hard, that you never got the chance

to go, and Courtney is just breezing through a pretty tough academic program, knowing full well that she'll never use it."

"Maybe she will."

"I don't think so. I don't think she'll have the courage."

We sat staring at the outgoing tide as the light faded, Evie's fingers absently picking out a melody on the guitar.

Chapter Twenty-eight

The last three Sundays of the season were spent driving to New York with a well-marked real estate section of the *Times*. Ted had simply announced that he felt it would be more practical if we shared an apartment, and the problem of keeping up appearances could be solved simply. We would each have our own telephone in the event my mother should call.

We settled on a large one-and-a-half-room walk-up in a restored tenement building at York Avenue and 69th Street. Ted had no furniture, which struck me as odd. He explained that he had always been a firm believer in "traveling light." Everything he owned fit into one large suitcase, which we stowed in the Playhouse wagon with an old bed we bought at the Goodwill. Mummy contributed sheets and a blanket and six cans of Campbell's tomato soup. Ted's contribution to the household was a beer can opener and a plank of wood he had

had the foresight to take from the scene shop. Set upon the suitcase, it served as a coffee table.

"It's not much, but it's home," Ted said as he stood back and admired the spartan room. "We'll get more stuff once we're working, but I think you might consider borrowing a saucepan and some dishes from the prop room when we return the station wagon to the Playhouse."

"I don't want to steal their stuff, I'll see if my mother can spare anything."

"Whatever." He flipped off the overhead light and held the door for me.

What little cash we had soon ran out. Ted crept out early and stole a morning paper from the doormat of the neighbor across the hall, copied information from the want ads, and returned the paper before the owner was any wiser. He walked daily to the theater district and haunted producers' offices in hopes of landing a stage manager's job.

Disgust was written all over Ted's face. I tried to lighten my voice as I asked, "Any luck?"

"Nah, same old thing. Don't-call-us-we'll-call-you crap." He sagged into the wicker armchair we had bought for four dollars in Macy's basement. "Walked my cotton-pickin' feet off. How about you?"

"Gordon sent me to see a guy who writes for television and occasionally produces plays."

"What's his name?"

"Clive Weymouth."

"Never heard of him. What's he done?"

"The all-star revival of *Uncle Vanya* last season."

"Oh, *that* Clive Weymouth. It was a pretty good production. Did he hire you?"

"Yes, he wants me to start tonight."

"Tonight? What kind of craziness is that?"

"He has to turn in a script by Friday. As he says, he writes by night, produces by day."

"What does he want you to do?"

"Type the script."

"I thought you said you didn't know how to type."

"I don't, not really. I type hunt-and-peck, not touch. Gordon told him that and he said it didn't matter."

"He must be desperate, although I can't think why. There must be dozens of typists out there who would give their arms to work with someone like him."

"I know, but he's decided on me."

"What are you going to do?"

"Type his script the best I can. I don't think we can afford to be choosy."

"I wanted to go hear Mabel Mercer," he said.

"You can still go."

"I don't want to go alone."

"You could always call Caitlin."

"Christ, are you going to start riding me about her again? Just because I said she had great tits!"

I hated him when he talked that way. "You could take Sam."

"Sam?"

"You remember her—we met her at Gordon's party. She's very nice, good-hearted and generous."

"The southern chick? Yeah, I remember her now. All those southern twats are good-hearted and generous. They also never stop talking. I'd rather hear Mabel alone," he muttered as he pried the cap off a beer bottle. "What does she do?"

"She studies at the American School of Ballet."

"A dancer?"

"Yes, at least that's what she's trying to be."

"Is she any good?"

"I don't know, I've never seen her dance. From what she tells me, she works very hard at it."

"A dancer, huh? I love their crazy muscles. You just lie there and they do all the work. Did I ever tell you about that dancer I knew in Toledo?"

"Yes, you did."

"Wild, she was just wild. Look, it's giving me a hard-on just thinking about it."

"Is there any more beer?"

"Yeah, in the fridge. Get yourself a blast and we'll have a little quickie before you go to Weymouth's."

I stood in front of the refrigerator, staring numbly at the empty shelves.

"Hurry up," Ted called.

I reached in and pulled out an amber bottle. I was going to have to get something stronger; beer wasn't enough to get me through anymore.

Ted insisted on taking me to the theater district and Clive Weymouth's office. "You might get mugged on the subway," he explained as I waited for him to finish combing his hair.

As we rang the night bell at the building on 44th Street, he asked, "Are you sure this guy's legit? What time should I pick you up?"

"I don't know. I'll just come back to the apartment whenever I'm finished."

"Okay, I hope it's not too late. See you, good luck."

Clive Weymouth splayed his lips in what I thought was a smile. It give him a strangely Oriental look. "Welcome aboard," he boomed as I stood helplessly in the doorway to his office. "Come on in, have a seat." He gestured to a sagging sofa facing his massive desk. "First thing you can do is call the Stage Deli and order up some supplies. The number's on the wheel on my desk under 'S' for Stage or 'D' for Deli—I forget which. Get some turkey legs, three—no, four sour dills, potato salad, four six-packs of Heineken's, and a couple of packs of Kools. You can order something for yourself. Do you have any money on you?"

I wasn't sure he was serious. "No, not enough for all that."

He fished in his baggy trousers and pulled out some mangled bills. "Okay, this ought to be enough. You make yourself comfortable, I'll be back in a minute—I have to go pee." He shuffled quickly through the door to the hall.

I looked around the office in wonderment. The walls were hung with photographs, a literal gallery of theater greats. Each was inscribed with a personal message to either dear or darling

Clive. Half the ceiling was a skylight, grimy with soot and pigeon droppings. The desk was strewn with sheets of yellow legal-pad paper, turkey bones, and what looked like bounced-check notices from a bank. I dialed the Stage Deli, placed the order, and gave the address.

"Is this Weymouth's office?"

I said that it was.

"We can't send it, not until he pays his bills. No more charges. I told him that yesterday."

I assured the voice on the phone that it was a cash delivery.

"Cash? American?"

"Yes, of course." I looked down at the rumpled bills to make doubly sure.

"Okay, we'll be right up. Tell him we want the balance paid by the end of the week. Otherwise don't call here anymore."

"Yes. Thank you."

Weymouth shuffled back in as I hung up; he was struggling with a safety pin holding the trousers shut. "I think it's gotten rusty." He squinted at me through greasy lenses and grunted as he finally got the pin shut. "I don't know where the button went, it's probably around here somewhere. Let me know if you find it."

"Yes, sir."

"Clive—call me Clive." He straightened the waist of his trousers; pee dribbles stained the left leg. "Food here yet?"

I shook my head no.

"How about a blow job before we start work?" he asked hopefully.

I stared dumbly at him, not knowing what to say. He couldn't be serious. But what if he was?

"No? Okay, let's get to it then. You sit at the desk and I'll read the script to you. How about some scotch?"

I nodded.

"There's some paper cups in the outer office somewhere. Double them—this stuff eats right through the paper."

I trotted dutifully to the outer office, found the cups, doubled them, and brought them back to Clive. He filled the cups to the brim and then began pacing the office with a fistful of the yellow paper. I noticed one of his shoes was missing a lace, the leather was cracking and splitting, the toes were pointed and curled up. He shuffled the papers, squinted, chewed his lower lip, hobbled out of the room and back again, the ancient shoes squeaking as he moved. I waited, fingers poised above the typewriter keys. His voice startled me, it was sepulchral. "Okay. Title page. *Queens Boulevard*." He fished a handful of pills out of his pocket and washed them down with some scotch. "An original screenplay by Clive T. Weymouth."

I typed out the title and credit with two fingers. So far, so good. He was staring off into space, thinking. I drank some scotch.

"H-and-P school, eh?"

"Pardon?"

"Hunt-and-peck. That's how all the great journalists type."

"I thought Gordon told you." My voice was cracking.

"He did, that he did. It's not a problem. Now, where was I? Oh, yes, tonight we are going to create a great film. Don't type that. New page."

I rolled a fresh sheet of paper into the typewriter. "Ah," he breathed, "Stage has arrived with sustenance." He paid the delivery man and set the bag of food reverently on the desk. "I hope you ordered something for yourself," he said as he hauled a turkey leg out of the bag.

Three hours later he was still pacing, gesturing with the remains of the third turkey leg. There were eight pages beside the typewriter, my back was beginning to ache. "Do you mind if I go to the ladies' room?" I asked, not sure my knees would unlock.

"By all means. We'll take a pee break—that's allowed."

I sloshed rusty cold water on my face and neck and went back to the office. Clive was swigging from a beer bottle; he had refilled my cup of scotch. "It's going to be a long night. Have one of these—it'll help you stay awake." He dropped a handful of pills on the typed pages.

"What are they?"

"Dexedrine. Try one, they're great." He popped another pill in his mouth.

"Maybe later." I drank some scotch and resumed my position over the typewriter keyboard. The strain was easing out of my back. I was beginning to enjoy Clive.

Daylight began filtering through the skylight. Clive paused and squinted up at the glare, then snapped off the floor lamp. The warmth of the sun through the dirty glass felt good on my shoulder blades. I reached for a pill.

"How many pages do we have now?" he croaked.

"We're on seventy-three."

"Good, almost done now. Another thirty or forty ought to do it and it's a wrap. That's movie talk."

I nodded. My head felt like it was going to fall off and roll across the floor. I tried to stop it, keep it in position on my neck.

"Read me back what we've got, I forgot where we were." He had long since run out of his scrawled notes and had been dictating the material to me.

"The whole thing?" I was hoarse.

"Yep, helps me get the rhythm of the dialogue."

The scotch was gone. I was on my third pill and eleventh beer when the phone rang. Clive had gone out to get more supplies and try to clear his head in the air. I struggled to get the receiver to my ear; my reflexes had stopped functioning. "Jinny?" It was Ted.

"Yes," I whispered.

"What the hell is going on over there? You haven't been home all night! Do you know what time it is?"

"No."

"It's two goddamn thirty in the afternoon! When are you coming home?"

"I don't know. Soon. Please don't yell at me, I'm very tired."

"Yeah, I'll bet," he snarled, and slammed down the phone.

"Bill collector?" Clive asked as he entered clutching a grocery bag to his chest.

"No, it was personal."

"Your roomie?" he grunted as he unpacked four scotch bottles.

I nodded my head, even though I knew it was going to fall off, roll across the desk, and break open on the floor. "Tell her/him/them we're almost done."

"He hung up."

"He hung up?"

"He hung up." My tongue was thick, my teeth felt like they were encased in angora.

"What does he do?"

"Do?"

"Besides calling you and hanging up, what does he do? Does he work, what?"

"He's an actor, or is when he works."

"Then he should understand. Read me back that last scene and then order up some coffee and danish—you look like you could use something."

"You were there for fifty-six hours!" Ted snarled. "Fifty-six fucking hours! What the hell were you doing?"

"Working, believe me. He wrote the whole script, rewrote it, it's finished. I typed it clean and he's on his way to California with it."

"Didn't he have it written when you got there?"

"Only about ten pages."

"How the hell does he do it?"

"Pills. He takes Dexedrines and booze. It's great stuff, keeps you going, you don't even feel tired." I yawned. "But now I am, now I'm going to fall apart. I'm filthy, but I'm too tired to even take a shower—I'll fall down."

"Didn't you get any sleep at all?"

"Little tiny naps, tiny fast naps on the typewriter while he was thinking."

"I'll run you a tub."

"Ted, I don't have the strength to get in it."

He undressed me and helped me into the tub and held me up when I dozed off. "You'll sleep better if you're clean. Come on, sit up." He soaped me down, rinsed, then wrapped me in a towel and led me to the bed. I was asleep before my head hit the pillow.

Ted was gone when I awoke—a note was propped against an empty beer bottle on the counter next to the sink. I was dying of thirst, my eyes wouldn't focus. I opened a beer, drank deeply from the bottle two or three times, and peered at the note. He had found a job, he would be home at eight and give me the details then. I finished the beer, trying to slake my parched throat. . . .

"Christ," Ted muttered, "you still sleeping?"

"What time is it?"

"Eight-fifteen."

"At night?"

"No, morning."

"What's that white stuff in your hair?"

He put his hand to his head and looked at the white powder on the tips of his fingers. "It's flour."

"Flour?"

"Flour, from a bakery. I took a job in a bakery."

"How was Mabel Mercer? Did you go? I never asked you if you went. Did she sing 'Walk Up' for you?"

"Yah, she sang it."

"Did you take Sam?"

He nodded as he lit a cigarette.

"She's not so bad, is she?"

"She never shuts up—blah, blah, blah. Southern dames talk too much, they act as if they all thought Scarlett O'Hara really existed."

"Gordon says she was raised to be Scarlett. He says the house looks like something in the movie, that there are pictures of Sam in every room done up in full regalia."

"You don't mean hoopskirts and all that junk?"

"I do."

"God, she needs a keeper, that's what she needs."

"What makes you say that?"

"She's crazy. I mean *crazy*. How about a drink? Or haven't you had breakfast yet?"

"A drink would be fine."

Chapter Twenty-nine

Clive picked absently at the filthy callus on his third finger. It was, he had once explained, his "writing lump," although he seemed to use it more as a talisman. In the five years I had been working for him, I'd rarely, if ever, seen him actually hold a pen or pencil and write. We usually worked directly into the typewriter; sometimes he would sketch the idea verbally and disappear for days while I tried to adapt it to the written word.

His hair still hung in limp, oily ringlets around his ears, and I still wondered vaguely what he had against soap and water. No amount of subtlety or bluntness had any effect on him; he had steadfastly refused to follow any suggestions that he shower or bathe.

"Saunders will be here any moment and I don't want to be disturbed, no matter what. He's not going to be an easy nut to crack, so keep the world away while I work on him. He's the only man alive who knows where to get two-watt light bulbs with twenty percent off for cash."

Clive had farfetched hopes of getting the front money for his all-star production of *King Lear* from Winston Saunders, a moderately talented actor with a reedy voice who also happened to be enormously wealthy.

"The little turd has always wanted to play Lear. Who knows, with a strong director we might be able to pull it off. For a mere ten thousand up front, I, Clive Weymouth, will make his dream come true. Oh, and if the bank calls about the overdraft, tell them I'm out of town and you don't know where to reach me, okay?"

I nodded as Clive hobbled into his office on the ugly old shoes. It mystified me whenever I wondered what he did with his money. Not that he had ever made that much consistently, but what had been made had certainly never been spent on clothes.

As soon as Saunders arrived Clive rushed toward him, both hands extended in welcome. The actor was an immaculate little man; he frowned and wrinkled his nose as he quickly withdrew his hand from Clive's outstretched paw. Clive smiled at me as he closed the door to his office. Within moments I heard Clive's majestic voice quoting passages from *Lear*. Saunders didn't have a chance; Clive would have his guarantee of the front money within the hour. There was no way Saunders would be able to resist the hypnotic voice and the panorama unfolding. I had seen it happen time and time again with everyone from city marshals to theater-party ladies.

I tried to type the scrawled casting notes Clive had written on what seemed to be a used delicatessen bag. I picked up the phone on the first ring. "Jinny?" Ted sounded out of breath.

"Yes, I'm here."

"Did I get you at a bad moment?"

"No, Clive's in his meeting with Saunders. What's wrong?"

"I was going to tell you tonight, but it can't wait."

I caught my breath. We had never discussed marriage, but we had certainly been living in a good approximation of one for the last five years. How much easier everything would be if we did make it official, if he did suggest it. It would be better if he entered into it willingly, not because he had to. "Tell me what?"

"I'm leaving. Moving out."

"You can't!"

"I've done it already. It's better this way, believe me. I know you won't mind. Let's face it, you don't dig sex that much."

"I *what*?"

"Anyone who has to get tanked up before they can perform has a problem. I've tried to be patient, Jinny, I really have. It just isn't working."

I was speechless. This must be a hallucination—yes, that's all it is. I heard his voice, firmly saying it was his final decision, he didn't want to discuss it anymore; I would find a month's rent under the quart of beer in the fridge.

"Ted?. . . Ted?" He had hung up.

I dialed the apartment. There was no answer. I let the phone ring and ring, staring stupidly at the closed door to Clive's office. I had to see Ted—he wouldn't do this if he knew. I started to scribble a note to Clive; my hand was shaking, I couldn't form the words. My stepfather's words of ten years ago mocked in my mind: *Who the hell would ever want to marry you!* He had sneered it when I had been chattering with mummy about what I would do when I grew up. Mummy had tried to console me, tried to explain that Jim hadn't really meant it. "Sometimes he says things he doesn't mean when he's worried about money. You know that. You're really quite attractive." I hadn't believed her then, I certainly didn't believe it now.

The door to the inner office opened. Clive was beaming as he showed Saunders to the outer door. He turned back and flung a check down in front of me. "How about that!" I looked dumbly at the check; it was made out to Clive Weymouth, for twenty-five thousand dollars. "We can pay the rent, get rid of the city marshal for a while, and even have lunch. You think Houlihan's Bar will cash this?"

I knew my expression was glazed.

"Come on, kid, this calls for a celebration! We're back on the track again, like when we were doing those stupid television scripts. We'll even buy you a new dress. Want Chinese? I want Chinese. Come on, Ho-Ho will let us sign when they see this." He folded the check and stuck it in the breast pocket of his shirt. "What's the matter? Aren't you hungry? You need a drink, that's what you need. Come on, let's go."

"I can't."

"Of course you can. I'm the boss and I say you can."

At first the hostess didn't want to seat us, but Clive showed her the check. Even after he had flourished it under her nose, she didn't look happy.

"How about some Anna May Wong Tong Soup to start?"

I didn't answer.

"Jeez, you're a real drag today. What is it? Something wrong?"

"Ted has moved out."

"Good. I never liked him anyway. I hope you gave him his walking papers."

"He did it by himself."

"Well, that hurts. Especially from a turd like him. I never could figure out what you were doing with him—he hardly seems your type."

"I used to think that, too. That's why I was so surprised."

"I don't follow." Clive held his martini daintily in his grimy paw.

"Surprised that he made such an effort to convince me that he was really interested in me."

"Why should that be a surprise? You're interesting. Got those wonderful ladder legs that don't stop, that pristine body. I could see where that would be a turn-on."

"But he could have had anybody at the Playhouse. They all wanted him."

"And you didn't?"

"I didn't think about it. I don't know how to play those games, I never have."

"You don't need to. That probably turned him on, too."

"You think so?"

"Sure. Men like that love challenges and you probably fascinated the hell out of him."

"I didn't do anything."

"That's precisely it. Look at it from his point of view. There you are—this aloof, tawny, coltish girl, probably a virgin . . ." Clive sipped his martini and closed his eyes. "Yes, it probably gave him wet dreams."

After the fourth martini, Clive bolted up from the table and rushed to a forgotten appointment at William Morris. I paid for the drinks with the last of my cash and started walking uptown. Maybe Clive was right. Maybe my aloofness had been the big fascination for Ted. My first instincts had been right: Once he knew me, he would lose interest. Never again. Never again. I walked slowly—it didn't matter anymore; I knew Ted would be gone when I reached the apartment.

I didn't return to the office until three days later. Clive took one look at me when I walked in and he hit the ceiling.

"What the hell is wrong with you? You look worse than when you left! Are you sick or something?"

I began to cry.

"Christ! Don't do that, I didn't mean to yell on you. Come on, come sit down. Take this, it will calm you down." He handed me a white pill and poured me a scotch. "Do as the doctor says."

"What is it?" I asked dully, accepting the pill.

"Miltown. Take it, you'll feel better. Then we can talk. Don't cry, it makes me crazy."

He was right, the pill did make me feel better. So did the scotch. We spent the rest of the morning in his office, talking about Ted.

"I never liked that guy, not from the first time I saw him. He was using you—that's why I wouldn't ever hire him for a show. I figured as long as he thought there was some hope of your getting him a part, he'd stick around. What happened? He finally get a job?"

"He found someone else, someone with lots of money. *Lots* of money."

"Everyone's dream, sometimes not worth the price. Someday you'll wonder what you ever saw in him—it always happens that way. You don't need him, you're destined for great things. He was holding you back, you'll see that eventually."

"No, he wasn't. He was holding me together."

"Before I forget, while you were out"—he handed me a slip of paper with a phone number scrawled on it—"some dame named Courtney Wilson called from Connecticut. She said she was coming to town today and wanted to take you to lunch. You can call her at this number before eleven if you can make it."

Courtney suggested the Palm Court at one; she was leaving in a few minutes for the train.

"Will your mother be with you?"

"No. Just me and you. Be there and wait—I'll be coming directly from Grand Central. I have a lot to tell you." She hung up before I could say a word.

"Old friend?" Clive asked, leaning in the doorway, clicking his lump.

"We went to school together."

"What does she do?"

"She just graduated from Vassar."

"Can she type?"

"Probably. Courtney can do anything."

"Good. Go wash your face, you can have the rest of the day off."

"Thanks," I said, starting out to the ladies' room.

"Kid?"

"Yes?"

"I meant what I said: I think you are destined for great things."

"What great things?"

"I'm not sure. Something. You'll see when it happens, mark my words."

* * *

Courtney was waiting at a table for two. She looked very chic; I almost didn't recognize her.

"Ye gods, you look like you've been through the mill. Has that maniac been working you too hard?"

I sat down and accepted a menu while she ordered two double martinis. She chatted amiably as she lit a cigarette: Everyone in Westport sent their regards and she had absolutely wonderful news to tell. "Or hadn't you noticed?" She flashed a beautifully cut diamond ring at me.

I hadn't noticed. "It's beautiful." It took me a moment to realize what it was.

"You bet your kazoo it is. You are looking at the future Mrs. Cornelius Martin the Fourth."

I didn't know who Cornelius Martin the Fourth was.

"Don't look concerned, I haven't mentioned him to you. He's not that Colgate man I was sleeping with—father would never tolerate a Colgate man. This one is Princeton. I met him at my sainted cousin Sue's wedding. We've been corresponding and got together last spring. He popped the question last week, and I, of course, said yes. Want to see his picture?"

I nodded. She fished in her purse, her gold bracelet jangling richly, and handed me a black-and-white snapshot of a very handsome, square-jawed young man.

"He looks like Steve Canyon."

She leaned across the table and looked at the face. "Yes, he does, sort of. My parents are out of their minds with joy. It will be a small wedding, very small, just family. You don't mind, do you?"

"That you're getting married?"

"No, that it's just going to be the two families. He loathes spectacles and wants to keep it *très intime*. By this time next week we'll be off to Bermuda on our honeymoon. Ah, here they are," she sighed happily as the martinis were placed before us. She sipped daintily and looked right into my eyes. "You look like absolute hell. What's going on?"

"Ted left me three days ago."

"He left? I thought you said it looked like marriage?"

"That's what I thought."

"What happened?"

"I'm still not sure. He called me at Clive's and said that it was all over, that he was leaving, that it was his final decision, that it had been coming on a long time."

"How bizarre."

"Yes. To think I misread him so completely—it's pathetic. How dumb can you get."

"So tell me what happened."

"Clive dragged me out for lunch the day it happened and then left me with the tab—he's always doing that. I started walking home and I really didn't want to go to the apartment— I couldn't bear the idea—so on the way I decided to stop off and see Sam. She's that girl from Georgia I wrote you about."

"The professional southern belle?"

"That's the one."

"I rang the bell to her apartment and she opened the door. Don't ask me why, but the minute I saw her face, I *knew*."

"Knew what?"

"That she was the reason Ted had left me."

"How could you know that?"

"I could just tell. Her eyes dilated, her face went white as a sheet. All that stuff you read, that you think is just rhetoric— it happened. I saw her and I *knew*. Before she could close the door, I pushed her into the apartment, I walked right in. I was in a rage—I think I would have maimed or killed her if her mother hadn't been there."

"What did she do?"

"She kept staring at me as though I were a monster. Maybe I was, I don't know. All she kept saying was she couldn't help it, that I didn't really care for Ted, not the way she did."

"How the hell would she know that?"

"He probably told her."

Courtney shook her head and sipped her drink. "Where was her mother during all this dialogue?"

"Right there, clucking around like a chicken, offering me a lamb chop. Can you believe it? Sam took me into the bedroom and closed the door. She said she loved Ted, that she was going to marry him and that was that."

"Tacky. Tacky, tacky. How did she happen to meet Ted?"

"I introduced them. I even suggested he take her out when I was working late. He didn't like her, or so he said. You should have heard the things he said about her. Never in a million years did I suspect anything."

Courtney burped as she speared the olive out of her martini. "You may decide, once and for all, that I am an unfeeling clod after I say what I have to say. Anytime I ever asked you how *you* felt about Ted, you always came back with a nebulous answer. Now"—she signaled briskly to the waiter for another round—"we find that he is enamored of Sam, and she of him. No one enjoys the shaft, I realize, but you've been thinking of it purely from your own point of view. If Ted and Sam both feel this is 'right,' might it not be?"

I stared at her. How brittle she had become. Her diamond refracted the afternoon light as she accepted the fresh martini, sipped it, and leaned over the glass. "You know what I said to Cornelius the other night?"

"What?" I asked.

"I told him I would never fight for someone I love, because if they wanted to leave, they might be right, and much happier elsewhere."

"What did he say to that?"

She looked surprised, then thoughtful. "Now that you mention it, I don't think he said anything either way. They make a great martini here."

I nodded. "Courtney, I'm not fighting to get Ted back. I always expected him to leave, right from the beginning. I'm fighting for my sanity. I have been all my life."

"I wish you'd come up to Cambridge with us. Cornelius is going to grad school at Harvard and we've found a darling little apartment. Maybe in September you'll come? There'll be vino under the sink, we're buying a Castro for the living room. We could talk day and night, work this whole thing out. We'll be there right after the honeymoon. Think about it. It might make you feel better, although I realize Shakespeare was right when he said, 'Everyone can cure grief but him that has it.' I guess you'll just have to give it time. Time changes everything."

"Time changes nothing. *We* change."

She arched her eyebrows. "Very good, I'll have to write that down. But I think you'll find that sometimes time alone can change everything, even if *we* don't change; news events occur with the passage which alter the picture. Of course if nothing ever occurs and we don't change then you're right. Time changes nothing. Do try and come and see us in September."

"Courtney, I know you're doing all you can to make me feel better. You want to know why Ted left me?"

She gazed at me; her green eyes were bloodshot; she looked tired, hurt.

"He left me because I stank in bed."

"He said that?"

"Yes."

"Just like that? 'Jinny, you stink in bed'? Do you think he would have lived with you as long as he did if that were true? You think it took him all that time to come to that conclusion?"

"Yes. You're forgetting it took him no time at all to break my resistance down. Once the challenge was gone, ennui set in and, bingo, bye-bye."

"I don't believe that. I've known you longer than he has. You are a complex, very contained, but passionate person. It shows in everything you do. Don't you know that men are cowards? Insensate cowards? They have to say cruel things, hit you where you're most vulnerable, especially if they feel inadequate."

"I don't think he felt inadequate. I don't think he knows how."

She looked around the room, then back at me. "Don't be so sure of that. You really have no idea of the effect you have on people. If I were a man, I would ask you to marry me."

I couldn't help laughing. "He's probably right about me. He ought to know, he's an authority. It's been a lifetime study from the day his father took him for his initiation in the neighborhood bordello."

"His father took him?"

"An old Greek custom, or so Ted said. His father took him when he was fourteen."

"Must have been a bit precocious for the old man to do that. But before you come to any negative conclusions about yourself, best you bed some more men, then decide."

"They're getting married, did I tell you that? Sam has even invited me to the wedding."

"Now that *is* crass."

"Well, actually it was her mother who invited me."

"It's a bit sudden, even for them."

"She's pregnant."

"Ah, well, there you have it. He *has* to marry her."

"No, he doesn't have to. He likes her trust fund."

"Now *you're* being crass."

"Perhaps. There's something else you should know. *I'm* pregnant, too."

She whistled under her breath.

"Ted is the only man I've ever slept with, he knows that. He also knows Sam sleeps around a lot and has for years. Did I tell you that Gordon boffed her one night in the doorway to Bonwit Teller?"

"Fifth Avenue or Fifty-sixth Street side?"

I laughed wearily. "Fifth Avenue—she's a debutante."

Courtney sagged dejectedly over her martini glass. "I take back what I said about your being melodramatic."

"You never actually said it, but thank you for taking it back."

"How can you sit there so calmly? I'd be splatting off the walls!" She signaled furiously to the waiter.

"I thought that's what I was doing. I got so drunk that night that I lost two whole days out of my life. I don't even know if I left the apartment. Drinking helps, it takes the edges off everything. I told Sam I'm pregnant. You know what she said?"

Courtney bit her lip and frowned. "I'm not sure I want to hear this."

"She called me a liar."

"That bitch! That southern bitch! What are you going to do? Have you told Ted?"

"I don't know where he is—she won't tell me. I'm pretty sure he's moved in with her."

"He was sleeping with both of you simultaneously, as it were?"

"As it were. For all I know, it happened that first night, the night I suggested he take her to hear Mabel Mercer. It didn't occur to me that there'd be any hanky-panky. She knew he was living with me. I wouldn't have tried anything if he had been living with *her*."

"No, you wouldn't have. That's one of your more endearing qualities. Jinny, *were* you in love with him?"

I stared at the potted palms. "I think so. Maybe I don't know what love is."

"Don't be an idiot, of course you know what love is. You know it better than anyone."

"I can safely say I know what hatred is. The night I went to Sam's I would have killed her. I've never hated anyone so much in my life. It's a good thing her mother was there, fussing around the way she was. Do you know, I think she knew. I think she heard me call Sam a cunt."

Courtney shuddered. "Gad, how wonderfully outrageous! Imagine being able to say that word out loud right here in the middle of the Plaza. Four years at Vassar and I'm still too inhibited to say anything more than damn, in public anyway. What I think is something else, it would put a deckhand to shame."

"It wasn't funny."

"I'm not suggesting that it was. What are you going to do?"

"I don't know. There aren't too many alternatives, especially since I'll never know Ted's thoughts on the subject. Got any ideas?"

"Should we order some lunch, or have we eaten already?"

"I don't feel very hungry. You have something."

"You have to eat, you have to keep your strength up. We could call Margie Berman—she'll know what to do. She lived in my dorm and had an abortion over the Christmas vacation one year. You remember, I wrote you all about it. If my memory serves me, Margie lives here, right here in New York. We'll call her. She works for a magazine now."

"What if her doctor isn't in business anymore? What if he's been arrested?"

"Not to worry. Margie is so thoroughly debauched, she probably has a whole address book filled with names. C'mon, we'll go try her now."

"We haven't paid the check."

"You get it, I'll go phone."

My head was spinning. "Courtney," I said with difficulty, "I don't have enough money. You said this was going to be your treat."

"Oh, so I did." She waved to the waiter and made a signing motion in the air.

Chapter Thirty

Margie Berman did indeed have the name of a doctor. He was in Perth Amboy, New Jersey.

"I don't even know where that is," I trembled.

"Not to worry, we'll get directions," Courtney insisted as she deposited coins in the pay phone.

"Courtney," I whispered as a quarter boinged, "I don't want to go to Perth Amboy. I don't believe in abortions."

"Jinny," she snorted, "this is no time to moralize. You can't have a baby—how would you support it? You can't go home—your mother is in no condition to deal with an infant, and God knows what your stepfather would do. Really, what choices have you got?"

I swallowed hard; she was right. Expensively dressed women marched in and out of the powder room chatting amiably about a world that had expelled me, a world that I could never be a part of again.

Courtney briskly made the appointment, using the code as Margie had directed. Then she suggested we go back to my apartment, where she would call Cornelius and her mother.

"I appreciate your coming back with me," I said as I closed the apartment door.

"Those stairs are incredible, I don't know how you stand climbing them." She sank into the wicker chair. "Here—" She held out the paper bag with two quarts of scotch she'd bought on the way. "Fix me a drink so I can get my heart pumping normally."

I looked in the fridge; the ice trays had never been refilled. "There isn't any ice," I apologized.

"That's okay, let's just have it straight, it's better that way. I'll call home and get that out of the way. Is it all right if I tell them that you're ill?"

"It's not exactly a lie."

"True. My God, who did that painting of Ted?"

"I did."

"It's fantastic. You really must keep up your painting, old girl." She dialed her call and I rinsed out two glasses for our drinks.

"It's all set," she smiled as she accepted the tumbler of scotch.

"They don't mind?"

"No. Cornelius has his sainted mum with him, he won't even miss me. Someday, when you have the time and the patience, we'll lurk off to a nice dark bar and I'll tell you my innermost secret thoughts on the subject of Cornelius and his mother."

"Do you love him?"

"He's attractive, comes from a good family, has a good future charted, and I'm fond of him."

"Is that enough reason to marry him?"

"Well, I have to do something with my life. I might as well get started now, before any more time runs out, and I couldn't do much better than Cornelius. Both families are ecstatic, of course." She paused and lit a cigarette; her hand was trembling.

"But how do you feel about it?"

She didn't answer. She went to the sink, where the scotch bottles were standing on the counter, and poured herself another. With her back to me, she asked, "You want the truth?"

"Of course."

"I'd rather have been down here, living in whiskey-sodden profligacy. I'd live within walking distance of the theater, see everything, and maybe eventually write."

"Why don't you do it?"

"I can't."

"Why can't you?"

"I don't know why the hell I can't, I just can't. It's not realistic, I don't know where it would take me."

"What's wrong with that?"

"Everything. There has to be order and purpose. Cornelius will give me that."

We sat up until dawn, trying to find the order and purpose. Courtney was lying on the floor with an ashtray on her stomach when the phone rang.

"It's for you," I said groggily. "I'll make some coffee."

She nodded and took the receiver. After a few mumbled words, she hung up. "Cornelius is having a crisis. I know that in view of what you have to go through today, it isn't much, but men are so helpless, and he seems more so than most. Margie says there's nothing to it—zip, zip, and you'll be in and out in no time. You'll probably even be able to go to work."

"I'm not Margie Berman."

"No, thank God. But you are strong. You're a survivor, I know you'll be all right. It's not as if this were a kitchen-table operation, he's a real doctor."

"I've never been to Perth Amboy." I couldn't look at her. I had known all along that she wouldn't go with me.

"And let's hope you never have to go there again."

"We're doing this without anesthesia; I want you on your feet and out of here as quickly as possible. I don't like this business, I never have," the doctor had said as he snapped on a pair of surgical gloves. "Put your feet in the stirrups."

I concentrated on the cracks in the nicotine-stained ceiling. Kitchen tables don't have stirrups.

"This is going to hurt. If you think you can't take it, leave now. I can't afford any trouble."

"I understand," I whispered numbly.

"Good," he nodded, and inserted the icy, impersonal metal. My body lurched and was consumed by spasms of pain. I hadn't yelled.

"No—oh, no," I whispered.

"It's too late now," the voice wheezed. "Just a few more seconds and you'll be out of here. Now I'm going to do it once more."

No. The death sign of the small, defenseless life. Acid rose in my throat; I gargled on it and swallowed.

He was pleased; it had taken a little over ten minutes. Good old Margie Berman—zip, zip.

"Now get up, I want you to walk out of here. Save your tears for later." He handed me a Kleenex; I wiped my eyes and shakily began to dress. "Change the sanitary napkin as needed and take these as prescribed."

"What are they?"

"Antibiotics, and I suggest you wait a month before you resume."

"Resume?"

"Intercourse."

"Oh, of course." I couldn't look at him and turned toward the door.

The bus trip back had been interminable. Harsh white lights winked like evil stars on the refinery rigs; noxious clouds of steam and smoke billowed across the chemical flats. I retched dryly into my hand as the bus plowed indifferently past the sulfurous hell.

* * *

I looked at the scotch. It was all right to get numb; Clive had said to take the day off. Good old Clive. When Courtney calls, if she calls, I'll tell her what I know. The speed of light— zip, zip—is transcended only by the speed of love.

Chapter Thirty-one

"Now that's gall!" Clive boomed. *"Gall and complete lack of taste. You're not going, are you?"* He tossed the invitation onto the rumpled pile of unpaid bills on his desk.

"I don't know," I said.

"Do you want to go?"

I shrugged. "Maybe. Maybe it would help me realize that it's really happening. That it's really final."

"I thought I was a masochist, but you've got me beat. Why can't you forget them?"

"I'd like to, Clive. I really would. It's hard."

"I know it is." His voice softened. "Of course they probably don't expect you to show up. Maybe you should go—it would serve them right. Where is the wedding?"

"At the Plaza. Actually, I think her mother is responsible for the invitation. She mentioned it to me that night. They might not even know about it."

"When is it?"

"The twenty-fifth of August."

He checked his calendar. "We'll be rehearsing *Lear* at the Morosco, you could run up and run back. It might be interesting. Do you think you can handle it?"

"I don't know. I feel as though I'm damned if I go, damned if I don't."

"Well, there are always these little beauties." He held out a palmful of Seconals. "They'll get you through anything. They'll keep you nice and mellow. Go ahead, take them."

The ceremony had already begun. Sam looked ethereal in her white dress, Ted was subdued and serious in his new dark suit. They made a handsome couple, little figures topping a cake.

"So glad you could make it, sugar." Sam's mother pumped my hand frenziedly. She had deep circles under her eyes, her smile was a grimace. Our eyes met and I knew that she knew. She wasn't any happier about it than I was. I was sorry I had come. I hovered near the door, not quite knowing how to make an exit, and became aware of a tall, angular man studying me thoughtfully. He approached and in a pleasant, well-modulated baritone introduced himself.

"Tom Cavendish. We met last winter, at Ted's workshop production. You were, I believe, wearing a polo coat. I've loved you from the moment I saw you. What say we fly to Rome and get married?"

I laughed in spite of myself.

"How about a drink at the Sherry Netherland while you think it over?"

"Think it over?"

"My proposal. Come on, the bride and groom show no signs of leaving this tawdry affair. I simply loathe tomato aspic."

"The reception hasn't even started."

"Precisely." He offered me his arm and swept me away from the Plaza.

* * *

They knew him at the Sherry Netherland bar. We were immediately ushered to a corner table and Tom ordered two stingers. "I may be wrong," he said as he offered me a cigarette from an elegant gold case, "but the bride didn't look too thrilled when she saw us leave together."

"I didn't notice."

"She's probably wondering if we're going to compare notes."

"Compare notes? About Sam?"

"Weren't you two a thing?"

"Me and *Sam*?" I almost choked on my stinger.

"She once told me she had a female lover. When I saw you looking so stricken at the door, I assumed that was the reason."

"I lived with Ted, I never knew Sam that well."

"A thousand pardons, I didn't mean to be offensive. The fact of the matter is, I've known Sam for quite a while. She's a hedonist—I doubt she has any sexual orientation; she'll try anything if it suits her, and probably has."

"I guess you could say the same thing about Ted."

"Then they deserve each other. Shall we drink to them?" He held his glass toward me; his fingers were slender, well shaped.

"So you knew Sam?"

"In a manner of speaking. She's a phase one goes through the way some people do acne. I suspect it was the same for you with Ted. He scarcely seems your type."

"Actually"—I flushed; what was I doing having this strange conversation with a man I didn't know?—"I always felt it was the other way around."

"Same difference. It never would have worked—she's done you an enormous favor. Mark my words, at forty he'll have a paunch, little or no hair, a bloated face, and will be one of those tedious types who dedicates himself to the pursuit of unsuspecting virgins."

All of Ted's relatives at the wedding had fit Tom's description, the men and the women. They all might have been young gods and goddesses once.

"Now that I've dispatched the newlyweds to their seedy future, tell me about you."

I told him about Clive, Saunders, and the production of *King Lear*.

"I'm not sure I see Saunders as Lear. He's so Clifton Webbish. Too lightweight."

"But it's such a great role, and Charles Aaronson is such a strong director."

"Perhaps. Lear is my favorite character in all of Shakespeare. He is all humanity, flawed and magnificent. It's exciting to me to discover majesty and dignity in the elemental, pared-down shape of things. Look at Lear." He ordered another round of stingers. I felt completely relaxed. "There he is, utterly stripped of his splendor, power, and strength. Instead of becoming weak, he becomes stronger and grander as he discovers his ultimate resources. Those are the people who interest me the most, not the Teds, not the Sams, the opportunists. It's the people without trimmings or accessories, with life glowing from the core. They are the ones who are real, who count. You," he smiled, "interest me."

"Why?"

"There's something in your eyes, the way you hold your head when you listen. I know you know exactly what I'm talking about."

I didn't know if it was the stingers or Clive's assortment of pills, but I had to agree with him about Ted and Sam. They were gone and I didn't care. No matter that I might go mad tomorrow, now was all that counted. "My father had life glowing from the core. He was one of those people."

"Was? What happened to him?"

"He was killed in the war."

"You grew up without a father?"

"I have a stepfather. It's not as if there weren't someone."

"Was he wicked and cruel? Did he stuff you up the chimney?"

I laughed; it was so extraordinary to be sitting in an elegant bar with this outrageous man. "No, he didn't stuff me up the chimney."

"Ah, then he was kind and loving?"

"Not that either."

"What then?"

"He wasn't anything. He was just there."

Our eyes locked, and I was taken aback by the intensity and openness in his gaze. An electrical shock—he had caught me unawares and he knew it. I tore my eyes away and looked down at my hands.

"Don't worry," he said softly. "It will be all right."

"I really have to be going, I have to be at work."

"At this hour? You haven't eaten anything."

"What time is it?"

"Six o'clock."

"Oh, my God, Clive will be furious. He hates it when I'm late, says it's unprofessional."

"Don't worry, I'll take you. If he says anything, he can answer to me."

"Jeez!" Clive breathed. "Tom Cavendish! How did you bag him? You are truly a wonderment. I was about to send out a search party, thinking you had flung yourself into the Plaza fountain, and you walk in with him!"

"You know him?"

Clive looked at me strangely. "You don't know who he is?"

"I met him at the wedding."

Clive grinned and rubbed his paws. "Kid, you have just sent the heir to one of the greatest fortunes in this country to the corner for cheeseburgers and coffee. I love it!"

"Are you serious?"

"Quite. Didn't you see the way Saunders perked up when he walked in? The old fart knows real money when he sees it. Maybe now he'll shape up and get to work. Better yet, maybe Cavendish will come in as a partner and we can fire Saunders."

Tom returned with a cardboard box filled with cheeseburgers and coffee containers. We sat munching eighth row center, watching Saunders.

"You know, maybe the old coot can do it," Tom whispered. "It's a very interesting characterization."

That was for sure. No one in the theater could believe their eyes or ears.

* * *

We broke rehearsal at midnight. "See you Monday?" Clive asked as Tom held the stage door.

"Yes, of course."

"Have a good weekend!"

Tom held up his hand and a cab materialized in the darkness. "Where to?"

"You don't have to take me home." I felt ridiculous, awkward.

"I know. Where do you live?"

I gave him the address and we sped past the ghostly faces of the night people who fed off the theater district.

"What are you doing on the weekend?" Tom asked as he tapped a cigarette on his gold case.

"I'm going home, to Connecticut. I haven't seen my mother for a couple of months."

"Do you have to?"

"Why?"

"I thought perhaps we could do something."

"No, I have to go, I promised. I'm always disappointing her."

"I somehow doubt that."

"It's the truth."

"I'll see you Monday then. How about lunch? They do let you out for lunch?"

"Sometimes," I smiled.

"You'll still be at the Morosco?"

"As far as I know." The cab halted in front of my building; even in the darkness it looked dingy and gray. "Well, here I am. You don't have to get out."

"Nonsense, I'll see you in." He slid gracefully through the door and paid the driver. I fumbled for my keys and he held the door to the tenement for me as if it were the door to a palace. "I can see these stairs are going to do me good," he panted when we had reached the sixth floor.

I didn't know what to say.

"Sleep well, and have a good weekend—I'll see you Monday." He stepped back. I caught my breath; I had never seen such sadness in a mouth before. He composed himself, smiled, and turned back down the stairs.

My stepfather was waiting at the station. I felt my heart clutch with fear: Something was wrong—mummy always picked me up. "What's the matter?" I asked as I climbed into the passenger seat.

He cleared his throat self-consciously. "She's not off again, if that's what you're thinking."

"What is it, then?"

"She's having a problem with one of her eyes." He was staring straight ahead at the road.

My skin crawled with dread. "What kind of problem?"

"Her eye has turned."

"Turned? I don't understand—what do you mean?"

"It's hard to describe. Her left eye has turned, crossed."

"Has she been to a doctor?"

"Of course." Now he was annoyed.

"Well, what did he say?" God, was I going to have to drag it out of him.

"He doesn't really know, he thinks the muscle has given out."

"Can it be fixed?"

He didn't answer.

She smiled weakly, her hand shading the bad eye. "Let me see," I asked. It was terrible, worse than I had even imagined. "When did it happen?"

"A few weeks ago."

"And you didn't call me?"

"I didn't want to worry you."

"Does it hurt?"

She bowed her head and nodded like a little girl. I knelt before her chair and put my arms around her: How small she was, how defenseless. I felt her hand patting me gently on the back, comforting me. I can't bear any more, I thought. She's had enough. I've got to do something!

"What doctor did you go to?"

"She's been to them all," Jim said, hitching up his pants nervously.

"What do they think is causing it?"

"They aren't sure."

"None of them?"

She shook her head. What was she thinking, feeling? "I've made some coffee, it's on the stove. I'd love a cup," she said.

"Of course." I stumbled to the kitchen, fighting back panic. Jim had gone out back to prune a tree. I slammed the cupboard closed and tried to steady my hands as the cups clattered on the saucers. Milk, two sugars, that's how she liked it.

She sipped her coffee carefully. "Tell me about the play. How is it coming? I want to hear all about it."

I struggled to find anecdotes; she listened with her head back, her eyes closed, smiling occasionally.

"What's going on?" I knew I sounded angry, but I didn't care.

"They really are baffled," Jim said wearily as he set the pruning shears down on a wall. "She's been to I don't know how many doctors—eye specialist, neurologist, the works. None of them can figure out what's wrong."

"She's in a lot of pain, isn't she?"

He didn't look at me. "Where is she now?"

"She's upstairs, lying down."

"Good. She didn't get much sleep last night, she was worried about how you would take it."

"I guess I'm not taking it very well."

"It isn't easy."

"There must be something we can do. What about a doctor in New York?"

"I suppose we could try that. She doesn't want to go to any more doctors."

"She's probably terrified. Wouldn't you be? Eyes just don't do that. Something is wrong, really wrong."

He didn't say anything, just studied the tree. I turned away and walked up the hill, climbed over the wall, and ran through the fields until I tripped in a woodchuck hole. The katydids were singing; there would be frost in six weeks. I wept helplessly.

Chapter Thirty-two

I lay on the narrow single bed in the guest room, my mind wandering the night, like a terrified child. Something awakened me—but then, I hadn't really been asleep. I opened my eyes and stared at the ceiling, waiting. Waiting for what? I heard the sound. A whimper. It's my mother searching like a small wounded creature for a place without pain. Something had to be done.

I slipped out of the bed and padded to the foot of the stairs. There was no sound. I walked to the kitchen and carefully opened the cupboards, like a thief, until I found a bottle. I didn't even look to see what it was—anything would do. I carried the bottle and a glass to the living room and sat in the darkness watching the stairs. How many times had I found my mother doing this very thing? Now I understood. I understood the futility, my own helplessness. The answer was in the bottle;

only *it* could anesthetize me from the sounds at the top of the stairs. . . .

Jim was in the kitchen scrambling eggs. Bacon sizzled in the pan. He said nothing, he looked very tired. He must have heard her, too. I dropped some bread into the toaster and poured a glass of orange juice. My teeth were in their angora sweaters again. "Is she awake?"

"No. She's sleeping." His voice was dull.

"Where's Kirsty?"

"She went to the Stevenses'." Betsy Stevens was Kirsty's best friend. They weren't at all like Courtney and me; they pored over fashion magazines and experimented with makeup and hairstyles. Thank God for that, I thought as I buttered the toast.

"I called John Wallace yesterday while you were out walking. He's a doctor in New York. He wants your mother put in the hospital this afternoon. She's furious, she says she won't go. Maybe you can talk to her."

"I will. Does he have any idea what might be wrong?"

"No. He says he won't be able to tell until he runs some tests. I took her in two weeks ago to see him and he wanted her to go in then."

"You brought mummy to New York without telling me?"

"She didn't want you to know. She didn't want to worry you." He spooned some eggs onto a plate and handed it to me.

"What kinds of tests will he run?"

"Everything, head to toe. A brain X ray."

"Does she know?"

"She's been in enough hospitals to know what goes on."

"What time does she have to be there?"

"Five o'clock this afternoon."

When mummy came down, she was dressed in her gardening clothes. "What are you doing?" I asked as she opened and closed the kitchen drawers.

"I'm looking for my gardening gloves."

"Don't you want something to eat?"

"No, I'm not hungry. I have to do the weeding."

"At least have some coffee. You want some coffee, don't you?"

She refused to look at me and kept searching for the gloves. I took the pot from the stove and filled a cup for her. "I know they're here somewhere. I always keep them in the tool drawer."

"I'll find them for you. Why don't we have some coffee on the porch? Come on, I'll find the gloves. We can weed together, the way we used to. Okay?"

She nodded and obediently walked to the screened porch; I followed, carrying the coffee cups. After she had settled comfortably in her chair, I handed her her coffee.

"I'm not going."

"Why not?"

"I don't want to. I'm fed up with the whole thing. I'm not going to the hospital." She looked away, but I had caught the quiver in her chin.

"It's probably something very simple—maybe just a pinched nerve. I'll come every day while you're there. You'll probably be home by this time next week."

"You really think so?"

"Sure."

"But the doctors up here can't find out what's causing it."

"Down there they have all kinds of specialists, they'll know what to do. You want to feel better, don't you?" It was like talking to a child.

She nodded and sipped her coffee. "This is good. Who made it?"

"Dad did."

"It's good. Where's Kirsty?"

"She's at Betsy's."

"I never see her anymore."

"You know how it is when you're that age."

"I guess so. Will she be home before I have to go?"

"Sure she will."

"Who will be here with her? Who will make sure she doesn't stay out until all hours?"

"I'm sure dad has made some arrangement."

"What if he hasn't?"

"I can stay with her."

"See that she does her homework?"

I looked at her. She was gazing at me, her hand covering the bad eye. "Mummy," I said gently, "it's summer, she doesn't have any homework."

"That's right, I forgot. Don't let her stay out too late. What about work? Don't you have to be at work?"

"Don't worry, I don't have to be there until ten tomorrow morning. I can take the train in with dad. You'll see, everything will be fine."

"May I have some more?" She held out her cup and saucer.

"Of course."

We weeded the garden together and then she said she would go up and pack her bag for the hospital. I went to the garage and found my stepfather. "She's getting ready. What time do you have to leave?"

"Three-thirty, to be on the safe side."

"I'll stay here with Kirsty, and take the train in in the morning."

"Could you? I don't trust that boy, Bill, that she's been seeing."

"Kirsty can handle herself."

"I guess she can."

"I'll go and help mummy pack."

She was sitting at her vanity. The small overnight case was on the bed. She had put in one nightgown and a jar of cold cream. "What else do you want to take?" I asked.

"I guess my slippers."

"How about a robe?"

"Yes, a robe."

"Something else to wear? Something to wear home?"

"No, I'll wear what I have on." She was hanging on to the seat of the vanity bench, her knuckles were white.

"Do you have a headache?"

She nodded slowly.

"Do you want me to rub your neck?"

"Could you?"

I rubbed her shoulders and neck, gently but firmly. She let out a long sigh. "I'm not hurting you, am I?"

"No, that feels so much better. You will come and see me while I'm there?"

"Every day."

Jim had backed the car out into the driveway when we came downstairs. I set mummy's overnight case down in the living room. She walked slowly to the chair my stepfather always sat in and sank back. I lifted her legs and placed them on the ottoman. All the resistance had gone out of her. Fear clutched me—she was desperately ill.

"I'll go up and change," Jim said. "There's a fresh pot of coffee, if you'd like some."

I looked at mummy; she had closed her eyes, her head propped on her hand. I walked to the kitchen and hung on to the counter. *Please, God, let it be something simple.*

I carried two cups of coffee to the living room. Tears sparkled like diamonds on the lush dark lashes. She never wore mascara, she never had to; her pale eyes had always been startling, framed by the natural darkness. I set her cup and saucer down, trying to keep my hand steady. "Please," she whispered, "don't make me go."

My eyes were stinging.

"We want you to be well. Do it for me—please? I love you so."

"All right," she sighed.

I couldn't bear watching her walk from the house; she hung on Jim's arm, each step an effort. He placed the case in the back seat after she had settled in the front, her purse beside her. I leaned through the window and kissed her on the cheek. "I'll see you tomorrow. I'll call you as soon as I get to the office."

"Take good care of Kirsty."

"I will."

"Don't forget to feed Lassie."

"I won't."

"All right."

I watched the car until I couldn't see it anymore. She had looked so small, her shoulders bravely squared as they turned out of the driveway.

Kirsty took the news quietly, then asked, "Will she be all right?"

"I hope so. I'm sure she will." *Will she? Will she?* It repeated in my mind, over and over again, as I made hamburgers for supper.

I called the hospital as soon as I reached the office the next morning. There was no answer in the room. I called back and asked for the nurses' station. "Mrs. Muir is in X ray," a weary voice explained after putting me on hold for an eternity.

"Do you know when she'll be back?"

"No, I can't say for sure. Call back later."

"At lunchtime?"

"No, later than that. Try about three."

"Thank you." Three o'clock? That's an awfully long X ray.

"Any news?" Clive asked as he packed his briefcase with yellow legal pads.

"No, the nurse says she's in X ray and won't be back in her room until three."

"Well, you know how hospitals are—they run a million tests, haul you from pillar to post. Don't worry, I'm sure everything will be fine. Is your stepfather with her?"

"No, he's at the plant."

"You see? If it were anything serious, I'm sure the doctor would have had him there. Can you sharpen some pencils? We'd better get over to the theater."

"Sure." I madly fed about twenty chewed pencils into the sharpener and stuffed them into my purse.

"Here," Clive said as we waited for the rickety elevator, "I got you these—they'll help settle your nerves."

"What are they?"

"Librium, marvelous stuff. Better than Miltown."

I stuffed the pills into my dress pocket and stepped into the elevator.

"You look zonked," Tom said as we waited for Jimmy to seat us at Sardi's.

"I'm just tired. It was an awful weekend, we had to get my mother to the hospital."

"Oh? Nothing serious, I hope."

"I don't know, I'm afraid it might be. I think she is, too. I think that's why she wouldn't go on her own."

I told him about the headaches, the eye. He looked concerned. "What hospital is she in?"

"Flower Fifth Avenue."

He frowned, and poked at his chef's salad with his fork.

"Isn't it any good?" I asked nervously.

"I don't know. Columbia-Presbyterian has an excellent neurological department. It might be better if she were there."

"You think it's something neurological?"

"Sure sounds it. Don't get panicky—they've made tremendous advances in the last few years, brain surgery isn't anything to be frightened of anymore."

Brain surgery. The words screamed through my mind. *Brain surgery?* Of course, she knew. She knew. That's why she was afraid to go.

"Tom, I can't go back to rehearsal. I'm going up to the hospital right now. She shouldn't be alone. Tell Clive I don't care if he fires me."

"He won't fire you."

"I don't care if he does."

"Calm down, finish your lunch. You aren't going to do her much good if you're falling apart. You haven't even finished your martini."

I gulped it down and he ordered another.

She had been unconscious when I arrived at the hospital. When I asked how she was, the nurse simply said she was resting. Tubes and wires had been strung from the bed to a life-support system; plasma and saline were being pumped into her intravenously. Her head had been partially shaved across the crown; two purple-ringed holes, livid and horrible, were clearly visible on the top of the cranium. I had collapsed into a chair, careful not to jar anything. I had been there trying to compose myself when my stepfather and the neurosurgeon came in.

The spinal had been unsuccessful; there had been some sort of blockage and the dye wouldn't travel to the brain. They had had to drill into the skull and flush the dye directly through the brain for the X rays.

The man was chatting as though he were discussing an aphid problem in his vegetable garden. I struggled to my feet and interrupted him. "Could we have this conversation in the hall?"

The doctor looked at me, then at the bed. "She's unconscious, Miss Muir. She can't hear anything."

"Do you know that for sure?"

"All right, let's go into the hall."

Outside the room, he continued his discussion of the tests, then said that he felt a craniotomy was in order.

"What is a craniotomy?" I asked. I knew my stepfather didn't know either, and wouldn't ask.

"We'll open the cranium on the right side. The X rays indicate a mass in that area, and we must determine what it is."

"What do you think it is?"

I knew he didn't like me; he was becoming impatient, but I didn't care. He sucked in his breath and tried to smile. "If I knew, I wouldn't have to operate."

"When will you do it?"

"She's got to recover from the tests first. Depending on her condition, anytime within the next two weeks. The sooner the better."

"When will she be awake?"

"Probably not until morning. Why don't you come back then?"

"Will they let me in?"

"Yes, I'll see that the nurses are notified. You can come and go whenever you please."

"Is that usual?"

"In cases like this it is."

Tom took me home early so I could get a good night's rest. In the morning, I went to the hospital, hurrying to her room so I could see her before going to work.

I stared in horror at the empty bed. Sunlight streamed across the stripped mattress, everything was gone. "Oh, mummy," I whispered, and then rushed to the hall. I nearly collided with a nurse.

"What is it?" she asked anxiously.

"Mrs. Muir—"

"She's been moved to room three-eleven. Go back to the reception area and turn right."

"Thank you," I whispered gratefully, and rushed back to the reception and turned right as directed. Mummy was sitting up, propped against the pillows, smoking a cigarette. She looked wan and small, a see-through plastic bandage over the drill holes in the top of her skull, both eyes black. I tried not to react. "Hi!" I smiled.

"Hi!" She sounded really pleased.

I sat down in a chair and fumbled in my purse for my cigarettes. "How do you feel?"

"Well, I have a headache, of course. I nearly had a heart attack when I saw myself in the mirror. I guess it looks worse than it really is, although I do remember hearing one doctor say he thought they were losing me while they were drilling."

"You were awake?" I was appalled.

"As far as I know, I was. At least I was for most of it."

My God, what must she have thought! "It must have been terrifying."

"I don't want to ever go through anything like that again. As soon as I feel better, I want to go home and forget all about this. I'm tired of being poked, prodded, and X rayed and I don't think they really know what's wrong."

I was inclined to agree with her. "Your eye looks fine." My voice cracked.

She smiled wryly. "If you discount the bruises and the stitches, I suppose it does."

Chapter Thirty-three

"You know that Cavendish is married, don't you?" Clive said as we walked from the office to the Morosco.

"I know."

"I thought you said you'd never mess with a married man, that there were no percentages in that."

"I'm not messing with him. He's been a good friend, that's all."

"Ha! Where's his wife?"

"Out in the Hamptons."

"Probably having a fine time, too. I guess they have what you would call an 'arrangement.'"

"She wants a divorce. He won't give it to her. He knows she married him for his money and he's damned if he'll give it to her. He doesn't care what she does."

"Where does that leave you?"

"Right where I am."

"How's your mother? Is she out of the hospital yet?"

"No, she's scheduled for more surgery tomorrow."

"I guess you'll be going up there again tonight."

"That's right."

"Do they know what it is?"

"Not yet. The tests show there's pressure on the brain. They can't seem to locate the mass that showed up on the X ray."

"Jeez, it gives me the creeps. I'm sorry, Jinny, I know it must be terrible."

"It is," I said, and walked through the stage door.

She was surprised and pleased when I tiptoed into the room at ten o'clock that night. "I thought you weren't coming." Her voice was small.

"Rehearsals were a fiasco. Saunders has a hate on the director—he got the rest of the cast to sign a petition to have him fired. Clive went berserk and scared them all into submission."

"Was the director fired?"

"No. But he won't speak to Saunders, and Saunders won't speak to him."

"How can they work that way?"

"Clive is going to be the intermediary."

"Why does the director stay if no one wants him?"

"He doesn't want to, but Clive says it will be bad publicity for the show if he leaves now."

"How did you get in here? Visiting hours are over."

"I just walked in."

"They'll make you leave."

"No, they won't." I excused myself and went to the bathroom. I had a quart of scotch in my handbag; I opened it carefully and took a long swallow, then brushed my hair without looking in the mirror. I didn't like what I saw when I did look.

Mummy was lying on her side when I stepped back into the room. I pulled a chair closer to the bed and sat down. "I'm not asleep," she said softly, "just resting."

"Are you afraid?"

Her shoulders raised slightly.

"Dr. Hughes is very positive, he thinks everything is going to be all right."

"All surgeons talk that way," she said, turning to look at me. "Otherwise they wouldn't operate."

"He's supposed to be a very good neurosurgeon."

"I hope so."

"Want me to rub your back?"

"Would you? It really makes me feel better."

I rose from the chair and leaned over and rubbed her shoulders. Her flesh was warm and smooth. All the lotion, I thought. All the lotion I've been rubbing in. I could feel the tension slipping out of her muscles.

"You should go home, get some sleep. You'll be exhausted. You can't come here every night and work all day."

"I feel better when I'm here. In fact, I was thinking of staying with you until you're well again."

"You mean here? At the hospital?"

"No, afterward, when you go home. I'll come home and take care of you."

"You can't do that. What about your job? The play?"

"I'm not essential, Clive can replace me."

"Of course you're essential. Why is it you never see that?"

"I guess for the same reason you don't." I saw her smile.

"Well, I think you should stay with your job. Besides, I've never seen *King Lear* and, after hearing all that's been going on behind the scenes, I can't wait. Maybe dad and I will come when it gets to New York."

"I've already put away a pair of opening-night seats for you."

"When is it?"

"Not until October twenty-fifth. It's already sold out."

"We'll be there," she smiled.

Sirens wailed in the night. I watched her as she sank deeper into the safe warmth of sleep. Oh, God, I thought, let her be all right. There's so much we have to do yet. She's still young. Let her grow old gracefully, let her live.

* * *

"Going now?" the nurse rasped from her desk, where she had been reading a cheap paperback.

"Yes, thank you very much."

"Well, see you tomorrow."

"Yes." I walked the empty hall to the elevator, and as I waited for the door to open wondered numbly if I'd be able to find a cab. Tomorrow. I was afraid of tomorrow, afraid of what it would bring.

Tom was sleeping in a chair in the lobby. I walked over to him; how long had he been there? "Tom? What are you doing here? Do you know what time it is?"

He opened his eyes and looked at me blankly for a long moment. "Oh, you ready to go?"

"What are you doing here?"

"Waiting for you. I missed you at the theater—Clive said you had already left for here. Thought I'd bring you home." He rose and we walked out to the empty avenue. A lone taxi was parked at the curb without any lights on. The driver was asleep.

I tugged at Tom's sleeve. "I think he's off-duty."

"No, he's ours." He tapped on the window and the driver shook himself awake. Once we were settled in the seat and the driver had finished his coughing spell, Tom asked, "Are you hungry?"

I was. "But is anything open at this hour? It's practically morning."

"We can go to Riker's on Fifty-seventh Street, they're open all night. I could use a burger."

We sat hunched over our plates and mugs of coffee, eating wearily with all the other night people. I wondered why they were there and kept my handbag with the scotch bottle carefully braced between my ankles. I would have to get more in the morning—I was running out.

"What time is the surgery?" Tom asked as he saw me to the apartment door.

"Early. Seven o'clock, I think."

"In two hours. Do you think you can sleep?"

"I don't know."

"Try, lovey, it's going to be a long day." He kissed me lightly.

My lips were numb; I felt nothing.

I made rehearsal on time. Clive looked surprised; he had already bought the coffee. I set my box of containers down on the seat next to him. "I didn't expect you today," he whispered.

"I couldn't sleep. I'd rather be here than alone."

He nodded. "We'll never drink all these."

I opened a container and gulped it down. "Yes, we will."

"When will she be out of surgery?" Clive asked as he rose to walk toward the stage and give Saunders a direction note.

"The doctor thought about eleven."

"You can use the phone in the manager's office, it's open."

I looked at him gratefully and when he had neared the stage and I was sure no one could see, I opened the bottle in my purse and filled my coffee container.

At eleven I was told that Mrs. Muir had still not returned to her room.

At noon I spoke with Dr. Hughes's secretary and was told that he was still in surgery.

"Isn't it taking awfully long?"

"Sometimes these things do. Be patient."

Be patient.

"Any word?" Clive asked when I returned to my seat.

"No, it's still going on."

He didn't remove his eyes from the stage. "If you need anything, a pill, I've got some." I heard the bottle rattle in his pocket.

"I'm afraid I'll pass out."

"Might not be a bad idea. You can go lie down in the lounge. I'll wake you up when we break for lunch."

I accepted a pill and forced my body out of the seat. I could barely make it up the aisle. Maybe a little nap would be good. . . .

"Wake up, kid, it's three o'clock!" Clive was shaking me.

For a moment I didn't know where I was. I stared at Clive uncomprehendingly. "Three o'clock?"

"In the afternoon. We're breaking for lunch. Are you all right?"

Thousands of roaches were running around the floor! How could he stand there? They were swarming over his ugly shoes, eating the turned-up cracked toes. I recoiled in horror.

"Come on, you need a drink." He reached for my hand; roaches fell out of his shirt cuff and spilled down on the floor. I began to scream.

"Christ, it was awful." Clive's voice was shaking. He was leaning on the bar at Sardi's. "You kept saying there were roaches everywhere. There wasn't anything, so help me God." He held a martini on the rocks toward my lips. "Just sip it slowly. How many Libriums did you take?"

"Just one."

"Maybe you'd better not take any more—not until you get some sleep and food. When did you eat last?"

"This morning."

"Maybe you're coming down with something. Want me to call the hospital for you?"

"Could you?"

"Sure. Be back in a minute."

My hands were steadier and I finished the martini quietly, watching roaches advance across the bar. I looked at the bartender; he was polishing a glass, just the way Fong used to. He must see the bugs. I watched him as they crawled up his arms—and then I knew. There weren't any bugs.

"Ready for another?" he asked cheerfully.

I nodded, afraid to speak.

"She's in the recovery room." Clive was beaming as he climbed back onto his stool. "Are you all right? You look like you've seen a ghost."

"I'm okay," I mumbled.

"Why don't you go home and sleep a little? You'll feel better. You want to feel better, don't you?"

I nodded.

"Go home and rest. You'll want to be on your toes when you go to the hospital."

"Yes . . . To the hospital . . ."

"And don't stay there all night. You're falling apart, they might not let you out. We leave for Philly next week. Think you can make it?"

I nodded, and carefully searched for the floor with my feet.

Chapter Thirty-four

The phone was ringing insistently. I opened my eyes and stared at the white tile walls. What is this place? I closed my eyes—there was something I was supposed to do, but first I would rest. The smooth coolness felt good on my face, soothing. There was something I had to do. . . . I couldn't think, the bell kept ringing. The bell . . . the phone. I had to answer the phone.

My hands were numb, I couldn't get a purchase on the floor. My elbows ached. I sat up and looked around stupidly. Why was I on the bathroom floor? Why wasn't I at rehearsal? The phone kept ringing. Whoever it is will probably hang up just as I get there—that always happens. My legs were dead. I wondered if anyone knew where I was. Would I starve or dehydrate while waiting for my legs to awaken? Of course not, idiot. Answer the phone.

"There you are!" It was my stepfather's voice. "I was just about to hang up."

"I'm sorry," I whispered. "I was in the bathroom."

"If you were getting ready to go up to the hospital, no need to. She's still unconscious and will be for the rest of the night. Dr. Hughes says he's pleased with the operation. There was no tumor, just a lot of fluid, which they've drained. No mass either. You can go see her first thing in the morning."

"The operation was a success?"

"Yes. A success, no sign of a tumor. You can see her in the morning. I'm running up to Connecticut now—I'll see you tomorrow?"

"Tomorrow. Thank you." I hung up the receiver and slid to the living-room floor.

My body was stiff from sleeping on the floor and I dreamed I had to fight swallowing my tongue. I tentatively felt my throat; it seemed to be all right. My head ached, but at least my legs were working again. I made my way to the kitchen and filled the kettle. A nice hot cup of coffee and a shower. There was something about the bathroom . . . somewhere I was supposed to go. I'll remember in a minute, as soon as I wake up, as soon as I stop shaking.

It was six o'clock in the morning, the forecast was for fair and seasonable temperatures. I shampooed my hair in the shower, hoping that my head would feel better. Then I remembered. The operation had been a success—it was all over with. Thank God.

I didn't know what to expect as I approached the room. She would probably be a mess, hooked up to more machines than last time. Last time had only been a test; this would probably be worse. But that was all right, the operation had been a success.

Mummy was sitting up; the pillows behind her had been neatly fluffed. She was smiling, a lopsided wonderful smile. Big messy stitches ran from the top of her head to just above her right ear. Her face was swollen and bruised, but she was looking at me with both eyes; they were beautiful. She was alive.

I buried my head in her arms. "There, there, my pet," she crooned as she patted my back.

I rose and wiped the tears from my eyes with my hands. I never remembered to carry any Kleenex. "How do you feel?" My voice was quavering.

She smoothed the sheets with her elegant hands. "Well, it's painful, of course, but the doctor says I may be able to go home next week. Isn't that wonderful?"

I nodded.

"Naturally I won't be able to do too much for a while."

"The rest will do you good. I meant what I said, I'll come home and take care of you."

"No, don't be silly. I'll be fine. I don't want you to leave your job."

"Can you see all right?"

"Yes. I still need my glasses, of course, but no more double vision. I must really look like something the cat dragged in." She gestured lightly toward her face.

"You've had better days," I smiled. Sweat was running down my body, yet I seemed to be shuddering with cold. "Excuse me, I have to use the bathroom."

I tried to retch quietly. The water in the bowl was tinged with red. It can't be me, I thought. It can't be blood. I flushed and turned to the sink; my hands were palsied as I turned the cold water on. I groped in my bag for the bottle. It wasn't there. I had forgotten to put it in. You don't need it now— it's going to be all right. I dabbed cold water on my face and began to vomit convulsively into the sink. It was blood. It was mine. I turned the water on full-force. Wash it away, wash it away. Everything will be all right.

"Are you feeling all right?" She was sitting behind her breakfast tray, her napkin spread across her lap. The ridiculous-looking stitches were furrowed with worry.

"I'm all right. Must have been something I ate."

"I asked them for an extra cup of coffee. Maybe you'd rather have tea?"

"No, coffee will be fine." I held the cup with both hands

and took a sip. It felt like battery acid going down my esophagus.

"Now, tell me about the play."

"We'll be out of town for twelve weeks—four weeks in Washington, Philadelphia, and Boston. Then back here for previews, and then the opening."

"Is that usual, to be out of town for so long?"

"Not really, but all the theaters did well with advance sales when they announced the production. Clive decided to make hay while he could."

"Well, I'd hate for you to miss that after you've worked so hard. You are going to go, aren't you?"

"Clive wants me to come, but I'd rather be with you."

"I'm going to be fine, really I am. I want you to go."

"Are you sure?"

"Absolutely."

"If they let you go home, I'll come up this weekend."

"That would be wonderful. Bring your laundry—you can do it in the machine and hang it on the line to dry. Everything always smells cleaner when it's been hung out to dry."

"I'd like that."

Clive was lumbering up the aisle, scowling. He and Saunders had apparently just had another go-around. The director was sitting tenth row center, his head buried in his hands. "Stinking little faggot," Clive hissed.

"Now what?" I whispered.

"Don't ask. I just told him if he didn't stop the crap I was going to beat him to a pulp. He'll shape up now. How's your mother?"

"She looks horrible, but the operation was a success. She'll be going home soon."

"You coming out of town?"

"Yes, if it's still all right."

"It's all right. Maybe now you can get some sleep. You scared the shit out of me yesterday. I thought you'd gone over the edge."

"You did?"

"All that ranting and raving—for a minute I thought we were going to have to take you to Bellevue. Christ, what would I have told your mother? I'm sorry, Mrs. Muir, your daughter can't be there because she's in a rubber room."

I had ranted and raved? What was he talking about? The last thing I remembered were the bugs swarming in Sardi's bar. "What happened?"

"You serious? You don't remember?"

I shook my head slowly; it still hurt.

"Better it be forgotten, you really don't want to know. I think you'd better lay off the pills, at least for a while."

When we took our position in the corner at the bar, the bartender started to say something, but Clive silenced him. "Forget it, it was just a bad day—her mother was having major surgery. She's okay now. Two double vodkas on the rocks. You want a twist, kid?"

"Yes, please."

The bartender didn't look happy. "I told you, she's okay." Clive's voice was firm.

"Yes, Mr. Weymouth. Two double vodkas, one with a twist."

The glasses sparkled like diamonds. Clive handed me mine and held his glass toward me. "To better times, for all of us."

My blood raced and sang with anticipation. "To no more hospitals! To big box-office receipts and lots of theater-party bookings!"

"Now you're talking!"

I rested my arm comfortably on the backrest of the stool, suddenly aware that we were surrounded by the crème de la crème of New York theater people, many of whom were clapping Clive on the back familiarly and were being introduced to me. "Larry, I want you to meet my good right hand. Mark my words, one day she will be someone to reckon with." On and on it went.

The bartender held the phone to me: "Call for you, Miss Muir." I plugged one ear and heard Tom telling me to stay put, he'd be right along.

"Cavendish?" Clive asked, smiling.

"He's on his way over."

"Good, time for another round." He nodded to the bartender, who smiled this time.

Whatever had happened yesterday, Clive was right: I didn't want to know. This was today and everything was right with the world. It didn't matter why or how I came to be on the bathroom floor. What mattered was that I was safe at last, surrounded by laughter and dreamers.

"We open October twenty-fifth at the Billy Rose," I heard myself say to a reporter from the *Herald Tribune*. And my mother would be there.

Chapter Thirty-five

Dress rehearsal in Washington was catastrophic. The costumes had been shipped to Philadelphia by mistake. Even so, Saunders had given a surprising performance in a raw-silk sports jacket and Dacron slacks.

"We can always do it in modern dress, I suppose," Clive muttered as we slumped into his suite. He poured two stiff vodkas into dirty glasses that were on the coffee table. "Sorry, kid, there's no ice. You can call room service if you want some."

"This is all right." I reached for the glass, it was stuck to the veneer.

"Order some anyway. We'll need it for the meeting. Get some more glasses, too."

I pried up the glass and carried it with me to the telephone.

"Remind me to get more booze tomorrow. We're going through this stuff like crazy and I have a feeling we're really going to need it." He popped some Dexedrine tablets into his mouth and finished his drink. "Want some?" he asked as he dropped the bottle on the table.

"Just one. Is it going to be a long night?"

"Very."

The opening went smoothly. The house was packed with VIPs from government and New York. Perle Mesta was hosting a cast party on a yacht anchored in the Potomac. The press agent would bring the reviews directly to the yacht, the moment they came off the press. I assumed that I had not been invited and I hung in the shadows backstage as the New York people swarmed to Saunders's dressing room.

"Come on, kid, we're riding over to the boat in grand style. Billy Rose is giving us a lift in his Rolls." Clive was breathless. His oily hair looked as if he had been tearing at it. The seat of his tuxedo pants was shiny, like the ones the conductors on the New Haven Railroad wore.

"I'm not going, am I?"

"Sure you are. This will be something to tell the folks about at home."

"But I'm not dressed properly." I had on a simple cotton shirtdress; the director had burned a hole in it with his cigar ash during the intermission.

"No one's going to be looking at you. Come on, we don't want to keep the man waiting."

A small orchestra was playing Cole Porter tunes. I sat next to the stern rail watching the glittering, shiny people. Saunders was relaxed and smiling for the first time since rehearsals had begun. Everyone was saying the production was brilliant. Clive was regaling a small crowd with Hamlet's soliloquy in perfect meter and a Yiddish accent. This would be something to tell mummy about. Courtney, too. Everyone who was anyone in Washington was milling about the yacht; champagne flowed like water. With the exception of Clive's baggy old tuxedo and my dress with the yawning hole in the skirt, everyone looked beautiful. Clive was right, no one was paying any attention to me. I relaxed and accepted another drink from a white-coated waiter.

I called home every day to talk with mummy. She sounded weak, but always said she was getting better. It worried me that she always sounded groggy. My stepfather explained that she slept a lot, the trauma of the surgery had been very debilitating. "She's coming along," he always assured me.

When we reached Philadelphia, the play was running smoothly, if a little long. Clive and I spent all of our free time drinking and going over production notes in the Variety Club. The club was always noisy and jammed with people from the other productions playing the other theaters, giving the room a festive atmosphere.

"What's on your mind, kid? You haven't been your usual effusive self lately."

"I've tried to get through to my mother for the last three days. She's always sleeping, or at least that's what they're telling me."

"You don't believe them?"

"I'm not sure."

"What do they say?"

"That she's asleep."

"Well, she probably is."

"No matter what time of day I call?"

"Surgery like that takes a lot out of you. I'm sure they'd tell you if something was wrong. Don't be such a pessimist, relax. We've turned the corner, everything is going to be all right. I'm giving you a raise when we get back to town. You deserve it."

"Thanks, Clive. I appreciate it." Clive was right, I was being overly negative. I had another drink, but I still couldn't shake the feeling that everything wasn't all right.

During the last performance in Boston, I turned to Clive at intermission and told him I was going home.

"Now?"

"Right now if I can get a seat on the shuttle."

"What's the rush? Go down on the train with the rest of us in the morning."

"I have to go now."

He sighed with exasperation. "Why, for God's sake? We have to give the actors their notes."

"I can't, I have to go now. My mother is dying."

"Jeez, I'm sorry. You should have said something sooner. When did they call?"

"They didn't."

He looked at me strangely and started to speak, then stopped and dug into his pocket. "Okay. Don't worry about checking out of the hotel—I'll take care of it. Here, you'll probably need some cash." He thrust a wad of damp bills into my hand.

I started to refuse.

"Don't worry about it, we can settle up later. Go on, get your things. I'll see you in New York."

He walked across the darkened stage and I turned and left the theater.

There was a light in the living room. I paid the taxi driver and walked slowly up the driveway. The door would be open; I'd said I'd get in late—but not this late. They were probably all asleep. I sighed, and walked through the door.

Everything in the living room had been rearranged; it confused me for a moment. Then I remembered. Agnes, Jim's mother, had come to stay. She was running the house—making sure meals were made, laundry was done. A dreadful woman, Agnes. She would be in the other bed in the guest room. I carried my bag to the den and set it in the corner. I was exhausted; it had been an ordeal getting home. The shuttle to La Guardia had been delayed, then a long wait for a taxi into the city. I had missed the train and had to wait for the first one out in the morning. I probably should have waited, come down with the company.

I turned the light out in the living room; the sun had come up while I was on the train. There was a bottle in my bag. I tiptoed back to the den and zipped it open.

"You're up?"

I jumped, nearly dropping the bottle on the floor. Jim was standing in the doorway. "No, I just got here."

"You just got here?"

"The plane was late—I missed the last train."

"How did you get here from the station?"

"Taxi."

"You could have called."

"It was so early, I didn't want to disturb anyone."

He nodded. "I'm making some coffee, you want some?"

"That would be nice. I'll be there in a minute, I just want to change."

He turned and walked toward the kitchen. I fumbled for the bottle, wondering if he had seen it. I didn't care if he had. I uncorked it and took a long drink, then another. After I changed, I walked to the kitchen. He was wiping the counter. "It's almost ready. Have some juice."

"No, I'll wait for the coffee."

"Go sit on the porch, I'll bring it."

I did as I was told. I had just lit a cigarette when he arrived with the cups.

"Tell me about it." I could barely speak.

"She's lost a great deal of weight."

"I thought you said she was getting better?"

He was concentrating on stirring his coffee, avoiding my eyes. "She was. She was up, walking around. She looked wonderful, she even played bridge with the Bouchards. Then . . ." He cleared his throat. He's afraid, I thought. He's afraid to tell me. I sat and waited, staring at his downturned face. He sipped his coffee. "Her speech started to go. Not much, just a little slur. At first I thought she was drinking again. That's when I had my mother come up. I took all the liquor out of the house, but I couldn't watch her while I was at work. I had to go to work."

"Was she drinking?"

"I don't know. My mother never let her out of her sight. She says she wasn't, unless she had some hidden somewhere. I did find a bottle in a bucket hanging on one of the rafters in the garage. Some scotch, but I think it was an old one."

"What's wrong? Didn't you call the doctor?"

"Yes, of course I did. He had me drive her down. She was so weak she couldn't sit up, she had to lie on the back seat."

"What did the doctor say it was?"

"He said there was more pressure, that when she got stronger he would have to do another craniotomy."

"Did he say that in front of her?"

He nodded.

"What did she do?"

"She cried, she didn't want to go through it again. He insisted we put her in the hospital immediately."

"When was this?"

"Three weeks ago."

"And you didn't *tell* me?" I was furious.

"There was nothing you could do. She made me promise not to tell you."

"Did they operate again?"

"No, she still isn't strong enough. As soon as she's stronger, he'll do it. He thought she might be happier at home. She really hates the hospital."

"Is her eye . . ." I couldn't go on.

"Her eye is fine. This time the pressure is affecting her speech."

"Does she still slur?"

He cleared his throat again. "She can't speak at all. She can make sounds, she can be understood if you listen closely."

She can't speak, That was why they stopped putting her on the phone when I called.

He knew what I was thinking. "She always listened on the extension when you called. She would write out questions for me to ask you. Your calls meant a lot to her, but I couldn't tell you, because I knew she was listening."

"Where is she now?"

"Upstairs. She had a bad night, she's sleeping now. She knew you were coming home—I told her. I had to."

"Yes." I said it dully.

"My mother is up—she just went to the kitchen. Do you want me to have her make you something to eat?"

The idea of food repelled me. I told him so.

"You look exhausted. Have you had any sleep?"

"Not really."

"Why don't you lie down? It's still early—she won't be up for a while. If she wakes up, I'll tell you."

"I'd like a bath, I'm filthy. Traveling always makes you dirty."

"How about some more coffee?"

"Okay." I lit another cigarette and stared out at the flower beds, the ones mummy had planted just before the hospital. Yes, a hot bath would be nice. I'll do that—wash my hiar, too.

"Where's Kirsty?"

"She spent the night at Betsy's. This has been very hard on her. I know she must hear your mother at night."

I was afraid to ask what she heard.

"For the last week"—he hadn't waited for me to ask—"she's been having hallucinations. She wakes up the whole house."

"I'm sure she wouldn't if she could help it. What do you tell Kirsty?"

"I try to calm her down. It's hard."

I filled a glass with scotch and set it on the edge of the tub, then stepped into the water. It was bliss; I let my body sink into the comforting warmth. Every bone, every muscle, ached. When the glass was empty, I lathered myself, then turned on the shower and washed my hair. I wanted to be anywhere but in that house. I didn't want to go upstairs. Maybe if I slept for just a little while . . .

I went to the guest room and lay facedown on the bed. Maybe this was all a dream, maybe when I awakened I'd find mummy gathering flowers in the garden.

Jim and his mother were sitting on the porch. The Sunday *Times* was spread about the flagstone floor. Agnes was reading the financial section. "What time is it?" I asked groggily.

Agnes checked her watch. "A little after noon."

"Is my mother awake yet?"

Agnes rattled the paper as she turned the page. "Not yet."

"May I have some more coffee?"

"It's on the stove."

I walked to the kitchen and poured a cup; my hands were shaking. I walked back to the porch on rubbery legs. I felt light-headed.

"Want the theater section?" Jim asked. "There's a big ad for your play."

"I guess she won't be able to come to the opening," I said, accepting the paper.

"No. I'm sorry. She really was looking forward to it."

I couldn't read the print; my eyes wouldn't focus, I couldn't concentrate. I put the paper down. "Maybe I'll just go up and see her."

"Don't wake her up, she needs her rest."

"I won't, I'll just peek in." My voice was shaking.

"Remember, she's lost a lot of weight."

I climbed the stairs carefully, hanging on to the banister. I'd have to speak to Agnes about the living room—it looked terrible. Mummy wouldn't like having her things moved like that.

The shades were drawn on the bedroom windows, a fly buzzed at the screen. I stood looking down at the bed. Her body was curled, childlike, her thumb holding her teeth apart; she was breathing feebly through her mouth. There was no substance to her at all. She had almost lost the ability to swallow and had been subsisting on eggnogs and malted milks that Agnes made for her. I was shocked by the waxy pallor of her skin. Her hair was growing back, though—thick and dark, peppered with white and streaked handsomely at the widow's peak and temples. I stared at the fine profile and tried to pull myself together. Nothing had prepared me for this. It wouldn't do for her to wake and find me standing over her, shuddering. I cautiously took one deep breath after another until the tremors began to subside.

Carefully, without a sound, I carried the vanity bench to

the side of the bed and sat down next to her and waited. I wouldn't leave, I couldn't leave. I wouldn't shake anymore. I was numb.

Her eyes opened. She simply looked at the pillow, as she must have done a thousand times. What memories faced her in those long, solitary hours as her brain slowly lost its power? Were there childhood images? The porridge bowl with the flowers? The clop-clop of great Clydesdales as they pulled carts through Scotland? Tea before the fire? Her mother in the scullery? Primroses, the taste of her first orange? Oh, mummy.

Then, perhaps sensing a presence, the pale eyes looked right at me. I could feel her surprise and pleasure.

"Hi." I said it softly.

She made a sound, flat in the back of her throat. There was no mistaking she had said "Hi" back.

I touched her cheek lightly with the back of my hand; it was warm and soft. "You're having a hard time, aren't you?" I was amazed at the calm in my voice.

There was just a hint of a smile playing at the corners of the mouth. "An hoh." The sounds translated "And how."

I placed my hands on hers; she laced her fingers through mine and spoke again, making each sound carefully so that I would understand. "I'm so sorry, my pet."

I nodded, my throat constricting. It was ending, everything was ending. Who would help me remember? Who would be there to remind me of all the good, bad, and ordinary things we had together? Worse yet, who would join with me? Who would be there to share the future?

"I can't go on anymore. Can you forgive me?"

I stroked her head gently. Each word had been transmitted without actually being articulated. "It's all right," I whispered. "I understand. Do what you have to do."

She closed her eyes, tears beading the once luxurious dark lashes. She rested her cheek on the palm of my hand, holding my wrist with her hand. Her touch was featherlike; she had no strength, none at all. Oh, God, it wasn't fair. She was too young. I hadn't done anything for her yet.

"Will you be all right?" she asked.

"Yes," I promised. *It's too soon! She's too young, she's only forty-four years old*. I leaned closer. "I love you, mummy."

"I'm so tired. You forgive me then?" The wonderful eyes were searching mine. It was important that she believe me.

"Of course I do." I wanted to say more. But I knew it had to be clean, I had to let go, no strings. "I'll be all right, really I will."

She closed her eyes, satisfied. I stared at my hands helplessly. She still had her fingers curled around my right wrist; I could feel my own pulse pounding against her fingers. There was nothing I could do; the knowledge was unbearable. "Thank you, my pet. I'll sleep now."

I leaned over and kissed her lightly on the forehead. She had released my hand and was settling back. I straightened the sheet and let it rest gently across her thin shoulders. She placed her thumb between her teeth and resumed her shallow breathing. I knew we had said goodbye; it was only a matter of time now.

Chapter Thirty-six

My legs were weak, I inched my way to the hall and made my way down the stairs. Jim helped me to a chair and poured me a generous glass of brandy. My body was jerking involuntarily, the despair and rage locked in a ball in my throat. I took a huge swallow and waited for the amber liquid to burn its way through the ball. "Why? *Why* didn't you tell me?"

"We really thought she was getting better." His mind had denied the truth, he refused to believe what he was seeing, he had really believed that she was going to be all right. "We've been doing everything for her, haven't we?" He looked to Agnes for support. She was sitting at the bridge table, shuffling a deck of cards.

"That's right," she agreed in her steely voice. "Except help her to the bathroom—she insists on walking there on her own. A very stubborn woman, your mother. She always was. I remember telling her once that if she ever called me again when she was drunk, I'd call the police. Do you think that stopped her? No. She kept calling and abusing me. I had to change my number. Last week, when she fell in the bathroom, do you think she would let me help her up? No."

"She fell? You let her fall?"

"In the bathroom, right on the floor, hit her head on the toilet." She was using her serves-her-right tone of voice. "Yes, gave herself quite a crack." She shuffled the deck of cards smugly.

"And you call that taking care of her!" I was rising out of the chair. Jim stood up in alarm; he had read my mind: I was going to kill Agnes in the middle of the living room. She held her ground, glaring at me.

"Calm down, it was an accident. Agnes didn't mean to let her fall."

I sank back into the chair, hoping she could feel the loathing I was directing at her. Jim poured me another brandy and silently handed it to me.

There was nothing to do. I stuffed my belongings back into my bag and Jim drove me to the station.

"The doctor feels she might be up to surgery in another week or two."

I looked at him to see if he was serious. He was. "I don't think there's going to be any more surgery," I said.

The train had wheezed into the station. I grabbed my bag and ran for the platform without saying goodbye.

There weren't any seats—the weekend crowd going home. It didn't matter, I stood in the vestibule listening to the screech of the wheels on the rails and took an occasional drink from the bottle in my bag.

The theater was in darkness. The lighting director was focusing the lamps, speaking to the electrician in the booth backstage through a headset. Clive jumped off the stage and walked up the aisle to where I was sitting. "I'm glad you're here. How is everything?" He was staring ahead at the stage.

"She's dying. I just hope it doesn't take too long."

I felt his eyes on me and could just imagine the Charlie Chan squint. "What a thing to say!"

"It's the truth."

"Maybe it isn't."

"It is."

He rose from the seat and walked up the aisle, away from me. I didn't see him again for the rest of the day.

Tom arrived late in the afternoon and suggested we go to "21" to get away from the Sardi's crowd.

"I can't. Look at this dress—it's a mess." It was the one with the cigar hole in the skirt.

"You look fine. Come on, the walk and the air will do you good."

"I don't want to."

"Well, I want you to. Come on." He took my arm and steered me out to the street. We walked in silence to Fifty-second Street. My mind was spinning with images, questions. Had the craniotomy really been necessary? Had the surgery been botched? Had they damaged her brain further by probing for a nonexistent mass? Was Clive going to fire me?

"Clive, you have to understand, has a horror of death. The idea that none of us is invulnerable is more than he can deal with," Tom said as we approached the familiar wrought-iron gate to "21."

"If he saw her, he might understand."

"Even then I don't think he would. Jinny, not everyone has the ability to see a whole piece from a pattern, to interpret life in general from a knowledge of life in particular."

"I'm not sure I understand what you mean."

"I think you do. It's a painful form of insight and it's at the core of your compassion. You don't want to prolong your mother's agony, because you know that she would rather die than live on in the condition she's in."

"It's taking away all her dignity."

"Yes, I imagine it is."

"Will I be able to call home when I get inside?"

"I have a better idea," he said, hailing a cab. "We'll go to my place. You can call her from there."

"What about your wife?"

"She's out of town."

Tom escorted me through the door of the town house and led me to the living room. It was beautiful; museum-quality antiques were everywhere, a concert grand piano stretched across one wall. The couch was comfortable, though, and magazines and books were scattered across the coffee table. For all its splendor, it was a homey room, at ease with itself.

"What'll you have?" Tom asked from the paneled bar he had opened.

"Anything. Is it all right if I use the phone now?"

"Go ahead, it's there somewhere on the desk. I have to get some ice from the kitchen."

I let the phone ring and ring, afraid someone would answer, afraid someone wouldn't. Agnes finally picked up.

"It's Jinny, I'm calling to see how my mother is."

"She's all right. She wouldn't finish her eggnog, though."

"Tell her that I called. I'll call tomorrow."

"I will." She hung up.

I went back to the couch and sat down to wait for Tom. While I waited, I looked around. Leather-bound volumes glowed richly on the shelves. It was a room filled with things that had been carefully and lovingly collected. I wondered if he and his wife had done it together. The paintings were beautifully framed, some were awfully good. I turned and looked closely at one behind me, above the couch. My God, they're *real*. Degas, Rouault, Pissarro, Cézanne, Chagall. Each hung lovingly, with enormous care, in just the right position to catch the light. None of them were ostentatious, none of them proclaimed the enormous wealth needed to collect them.

Tom smiled as he entered with a silver tray. He had changed into blue jeans and a sweatshirt. I had never seen him in anything but a business suit. He looked younger, and I wondered how old he was. I didn't even know.

"Here you are." He handed me a heavy crystal glass.

I sipped the amber liquid; it was wonderful. "What is it?"

"Jack Daniel's, you like it?"

I loved it.

He sat down beside me and placed his beautiful tanned hands on mine. The nails were immaculate, perfectly shaped. He would have made a fine brain surgeon. I wondered if he was the one who played the piano. There was so much about him I didn't know.

He played beautifully. I sat curled on the couch, my shoes tossed under the coffee table and my feet tucked under me. Mozart, Chopin, Beethoven filled the room. It didn't seem unnatural when he walked to me from the piano and enfolded me in an extraordinary embrace. When he led me up the stairs to the bedroom, I felt as though I were watching a *pas de deux*. Our bodies had become exquisite, fluent with time and space. He wasn't Tom, I wasn't Jinny. We were dancers straining for beauty and perfection in a theater well insulated from the mayhem of the streets.

When I awoke he was sitting on the edge of the bed. His back was smooth and beautiful, tapering to the slim hips. The muscles were long and lithe and rippled as he reached for a cigarette on the night table. He couldn't be very old. Older men don't have backs like that.

"May I have one too?" I asked sleepily.

He turned and smiled. "Did I wake you?"

"No," I lied.

"How do you feel?"

I moved tentatively; my body was stiff. "All right." Wasn't I supposed to feel all right? I wondered if something had happened that I hadn't remembered. "Why?"

"You slept so deeply, it almost frightened me."

I was relieved. Nothing had happened. Or had it? Would he tell me? I was afraid to ask.

"Jinny?"

"Yes?"

"I'm going to be leaving the country for a while. We're

having trouble with the mining operation in South America. A multinational group is trying to take over and it is one of the biggest profit centers for the family. My father isn't well enough to go down and handle it himself and he wants me to go. You know I wouldn't miss your opening if it weren't something important."

"It's all right." It really was. I had crossed a boundary, I was in a zone where nothing would ever affect me again.

"Are you sure?"

"Absolutely."

Tom dropped me at the office at nine o'clock. Clive was already there, rummaging through the file cabinets.

"What did you lose?"

"My mind. I wonder where I put it?"

"What's wrong?"

"I must have been mad to do this play. Whole thing is a mistake—it's going to be the bomb of the season."

"No, it's not, you're just overtired. What were you really looking for?"

"Saunders's contract."

"It's in your briefcase."

The phone rang; he lunged at the receiver and then barked "Hello!" As he was about to hang up, his eyes dilated and he handed the phone to me. "It's for you."

"Hello?"

There was only silence. I closed my eyes. So, it had finally happened. Then, "Jinny?" Jim's voice, and then another long silence. "You had better come right away."

"What is it?" Clive asked, not wanting an answer.

"They're taking her to the hospital."

Clive reached into his pocket and handed me the keys to his car. "Take my car. Go!"

As I turned into the parking lot at the hospital, I could see Jim and Bernard Bouchard standing next to the steps at the entrance. I rushed toward them, knowing why they were waiting outside: No one was in there, there would be no need to ask for a room number at the main desk.

Bernard moved toward me and held out his arms. "Ah, Jinny," he said softly in his still lush French accent, tears in his deep blue eyes. "Your little mummy, she did not make it."

I buried my head in his shoulder. It was all over. "What happened? When did it happen?"

"In the ambulance. She died in the ambulance. Come, we'll get you some coffee." He held the door for me.

"I want to know about it," I said as I sat on the stool at the coffee-shop counter.

Jim spoke slowly, no emotion in his voice. He was dazed. "I was getting dressed for work when your mother sat up in bed and asked me what I was doing. She wanted to know why I was going to work on Election Day. I was about to say it wasn't Election Day, but something made me stop. So I put on my gardening clothes and went down and made her a break-fast. She ate everything—soft-boiled eggs, toast, everything. I couldn't believe my eyes. I took the tray down to the kitchen, and when I came back up, she was unconscious. I called the doctor in Westport and he came right away. She was in a coma. He called for an ambulance, and then I called you."

"Where is she now?" I was shaking very badly. Bernard steadied me with his hands.

"The funeral home will be picking her up in a little while."

"Aren't they going to do an autopsy?"

Jim looked angry. "No!"

"But don't you want to know *why* she died?"

"What good will it do? She's dead."

"But it might help someone else!" I was shouting, making a scene in the coffee shop. Bernard put his arm around me and walked me out while my stepfather paid the cashier.

"Your father doesn't want an autopsy because he cannot deal with her death. Try to understand."

Selfish bastard. "That's too damn bad," I choked. "She's dead because he never could deal with things."

"Jinny," Bernard soothed, "that's not true. You're upset, he's upset. Come, let me take you home."

"Does Kirsty know?"

"Yes, Genevieve is with her. She went and got her at school."

Why couldn't mummy have married someone like Bernard? He was a kind, good man, not afraid to cry, to feel. "I have my boss's car, I can't leave it here."

"Are you sure you want to drive? Let me take you home."

Home? Where is that now? "No, I'll drive myself. It will give me time to think, to pull myself together."

"You are sure?" He didn't look convinced.

"I'm sure."

I took my time and drove the back way. The leaves were magnificent—mummy had always loved the autumn. When I arrived at the house, the driveway was filled with cars. Must be his sisters and their husbands, I thought dully as I parked near the road. I dreaded going into the house.

"Oh, you poor, poor thing!" It was Jim's sister Louise. "Now you have no family."

She sounded just like Agnes. I ignored her and walked through the living room and up the stairs to Kirsty's room. She was sitting on the edge of her bed, her face white. I stretched out my arms and held her for a moment. We walked together to mummy's room. Someone had made the bed; it looked the way it was supposed to. We stood together silently.

"Oh, good, you're both here," Louise said as she burst in and flung open the closet.

"What are you doing?" My voice was harsh.

"We have to get clothes," she said over her shoulder as she yanked a dress off the rack.

"What for?"

"For the funeral home. They just called—they need something to dress her in."

"Put that back," I said evenly, my voice thick with hatred. "We'll take care of it. Kirsty and I will find something."

"But this is a lovely dress." She wasn't going to give up.

I stepped menacingly toward her. "Get out! *Now!*"

She backed away and I snatched the dress from her outstretched hand. "All right," she said, "but don't take too long."

"Get out!" Kirsty screamed. "We don't want you touching her things!"

The frightened woman fled down the stairs.

"All right." I tried to calm my voice. "Let's see what there is." I peered sadly at the sparse collection of clothes. There wasn't a Hattie Carnegie in sight. We settled on a tailored gray dress.

Chapter Thirty-seven

An unctuous man in an appropriate dark suit greeted us at the door. He invited Jim into his private chamber, "for a moment." His voice was purest velvet; I wondered if he had had to have special training. I couldn't help sniggering, which seemed to disconcert our host; I was sure I saw him check to make sure his fly wasn't open. Before stepping behind the door marked Private, he suggested that I might like to enter the "viewing room."

"Thank you, I'll go in later."

"Very well." He ushered Jim into the office—to settle the bill, no doubt. God, how mummy would have hated this! I was convinced that Agnes was somehow behind it.

An assistant—a younger, thinner duplicate of his employer—stood silently near the door next to a podium that held a richly embossed guest book. I wondered if the bereaved were supposed to sign. There hadn't been time to read up on Emily

Post. I approached him and discreetly asked if there was a ladies' room. He pointed to a small door in an alcove under a grand-looking staircase. I was grateful that I had had the foresight to transfer some brandy into two small bottles that were snuggling in my purse.

The "Powder Room" seemed like the interior of a coffin. I didn't imagine people spent too much time in it. I quietly closed the lid on the commode (this was no ordinary toilet, it was indeed a commode), sat down, lifted a bottle out of my bag, unscrewed the cap, and had a drink. I wondered if it was appropriate to smoke at a "viewing" and pulled out a cigarette just in case. This was all right—a little privacy, a little time to meditate and calm down before . . . before what? I wasn't sure. The brandy certainly was a help. I was sorry that I didn't have some of Clive's little beauties with me, too. He had found a bigger, better tranquilizer since the roach episode in Sardi's. One would be very nice right now.

When I emerged, a decorous line of people, most of whom I had never seen before, were waiting their turn at the guest book. Tacky. No two ways about it, this whole thing was tacky. I saw a familiar angular figure in the line. Courtney. *Courtney!* She looked thinner than ever; dark circles ringed her eyes. Organ Muzak was playing "Autumn Leaves" softly through a speaker behind a potted palm. Why not? I rushed to Courtney, tears misting my eyes.

"Jinny—oh, Jinny." She embraced me in bony arms.

"My God, what are you doing here?"

"My mother saw the death notice in the paper. She called me in Cambridge and I came down this morning." She embraced me again. "I'm *so* sorry."

I nodded and wiped my nose. She reached into her purse and handed me a Kleenex. I accepted it and wiped my eyes. "You're so thin, are you all right?"

"Domesticity, make no mistake, is grueling work. And whatever people may tell you, motherhood is even worse. Being a housewife doesn't offer much opportunity to stare off silently into NBC. Is there a bar around?"

"No, unfortunately."

"*Dommage*. It would add something to the ambience, or whatever the effect is they're trying to achieve."

"Awful, isn't it."

She giggled nervously. "Does your mother know about all this?" Her eyes swept the carefully appointed room.

"For her sake, I hope not."

"I sure could use a drink."

I looked around to make sure no one was watching us. "Why don't you pop into the powder room with this?" I patted my purse.

"I think I will. Hold this for me." She handed me her bag and took mine and headed off for the alcove. She didn't look well at all.

I shook hands with people as they filed by murmuring and kept an anxious eye on the ladies' room door. What was she doing in there? I hoped she wasn't drinking all the brandy; this was going to be a long evening and I didn't have much with me.

When Courtney returned to the foyer, the color had come back to her face. "Do we have to go in yet?"

"I don't know, I've never been to one of these before. I was hoping you could help me out."

"Just look somber, that shouldn't be hard. Can we sit over there?" She indicated a settee along the far wall of the room.

"I don't see why not."

"Maybe you should be greeting the people."

"I don't know who half of them are—I think they're from Jim's office. The people I do know won't mind."

She nodded, and lowered herself primly onto the settee. "Maybe we can go somewhere afterward, have a drink?"

"I'd like that."

"You don't have to go back to the house?"

"Not really. I think they'd be more comfortable if I weren't there. I'd rather be with you."

She reached for a Kleenex in her bag and blew her nose. "I am sorry, Jinny. She was your mother and I loved her. She was part of a lot of my life, too."

"I know. It's such a goddamn waste."

"Do they know what it was? You said in your letter that they didn't find a tumor."

"I don't think they really know. She died of neglect, that's what I think."

She nodded, blew her nose again, and stuffed the used Kleenex back in her purse. "I appreciated that little snort in the john. It's creepy in there, isn't it? Like a coffin."

"An expensive one. One of the deluxe jobs."

"I really can imagine how you must be feeling. On the way down in the car, I thought about the time she caught us smoking in your room. Remember? You had shoved the ashtray in the closet, and all the smoke was billowing out under the door?"

"I lied to her, I said we weren't."

"She knew we were. We were throwing the butts out the bedroom window—they must have been dropping right at her feet on the terrace. I was thinking about that and thousands of little things and I started to cry. Now a portion of my memory has nowhere to go."

I put my arm around her and patted her; she was in worse shape than I was. "I know, Courtney. I know."

"Is there anything I can do? I want so badly to do something."

"You already have. You came—you came all the way from Cambridge. Where's Cornelius? Did he come, too?"

"God knows where he is. He's working on his doctorate, and when he's not writing, he's out with the guys. I don't even wait up for him anymore."

"And little Cornelius?"

"Cinq. We call him Cinq because he's the fifth Cornelius. Can you stand it? Isn't it too much? That's my sainted mother-in-law's doing. I wish she were in that room, not your mother. But if she were, I suppose she'd will me all those dreadful tweed suits and stout shoes Boston ladies wear."

I smiled. Courtney would never make a Boston Brahmin, no matter how many tweed suits she was willed.

She looked over my shoulder. "I think that man by the door is trying to get your attention, or else his undershorts are too tight."

I turned around and saw the assistant funeral director signaling me to go into the viewing room. I rose and stepped across the lush carpet; my shoes felt as if they were made of lead. I was grateful that someone had thought to supply a simple black suit for me to wear. In my haste, I had left New York with only the clothes on my back. It must have been Genevieve Bouchard—only she would have thought of something like that. That meant I owed her some money. I had to remember to ask her.

The room was banked with a magnificent display of autumn flowers. There wasn't a gladiolus anywhere. Mummy had never liked gladioli—they always reminded her of funerals or delicatessen openings. Poor gladioli, they weren't really a bad flower. I glanced quickly at Kirsty. She was staring straight ahead, I patted her hand. Everyone else had already been seated; the assistant director ushered me to a gilt chair with a velvet seat, and then with a start I noticed that the casket was open. Dear God! Who was responsible for that? The possibility had never even entered my mind—it was barbaric. Had Kirsty seen? Our mother's corpse was a few feet away. I began to shake uncontrollably. Someone patted my shoulder, someone sitting in the row behind me. I sat rigidly on the chair and stared straight ahead. Courtney and a woman who had tried to get my mother to join AA were sitting on the opposite side of the room; both were looking back at me with sightless eyes.

The minister spoke briefly. Mummy would have appreciated that; she liked everything to be understated and simple. When he had finished, everyone rose and I was propelled by Louise's husband to the casket. I would have to look—everyone was waiting, watching. Probably hoping I'd make a spectacle of myself. I knew that was Agnes's hope. It was why she had lived so long; she wanted the satisfaction of seeing her predictions come true.

I was revolted by the garish makeup. This horrible effigy stretched out in the padded box couldn't be my mother. What the hell had been done to her? I closed my eyes, clenched my fists, and heard Bernard Bouchard's gentle murmurs as he led me away. "Overcome," I heard Agnes whisper in her I-told-you-so way. The stupid bitch. Courtney stepped to my side. "Let's get out of here. Let's go someplace where we can talk."

I couldn't speak.

"I think that's an excellent idea. Do you need a ride?" Bernard asked.

"No, I have my car. I'll bring her back to the house."

"Good, I will tell the others."

"But I should be with Kirsty."

"Kirsty will be all right, I'll see to that. You go with your friend." He walked toward Kirsty and put his arm around her. Courtney steered me out of the funeral home.

"Whew! What a nightmare," she sighed as she unlocked her car. "I don't know how you made it through. Come on, get in. We need to fortify ourselves and put this barbarism behind us."

I climbed into the passenger seat. "Where do you want to go?"

"Someplace where we won't be bothered. Is Buccilini's still open?"

"Yes, and everything still gets stolen out of the cars in the parking lot."

"Who would want that junk?" She indicated a battered shopping bag filled with diapers and some dog-eared paperback books.

"You never know, diapers make great dust rags."

"How about Lally Bujowski's?"

"I have bad memories of that place."

"Oh, really?" She was hanging on to the steering wheel, peering at me in the half-light.

"Last time I was there, I stuck to the floor."

"You stuck to the floor?"

"Lost my shoes. I never did get them back."

"Okay, we won't go there. How about Barney's?"

"You think we might be a little dressy for Barney's?"

She peered at my suit, then at her own attractive black dress. "A little. Who cares? Maybe they'll think we're two suburban tarts on the town. Frankly, my dear, I don't think the sots who hang out there will even notice us, much less give a damn. They're old pros, they're beyond simple lechery."

"Okay, Barney's. No one will bother us there. Want a drink for the road?"

"You bet." She accepted the small bottle of brandy, took a quick nip, handed it back to me, and started the ignition. I removed the pillbox hat from my head and tossed it over the seat into the diaper bag.

We teetered across the irregular flagstone floor in our needle-heel black pumps and slid into the dark rear booth. Courtney ordered two double scotches and a pitcher of beer. "Make it a big one, we've had a hard day."

"No pitcher of beer," the waiter answered wearily.

"Angelo, don't you remember us? You always gave us pitchers of beer."

"What kind?"

"Whatever's on tap will be fine." Courtney fished her cigarettes out of her bag and lit up. She inhaled deeply and looked around. "I love this place. Scene of so many wonderful crimes."

Angelo placed the tall glasses of scotch in front of us and then went back to the bar for the beer. I took a long swallow. "God, that's good."

"We did have good times, didn't we?"

"We sure did."

"We were too young and stupid to know what was out there waiting."

"I wonder why no one told us."

Courtney sighed. "Who the hell knows? They probably figured we wouldn't have listened anyway."

"They were right, we wouldn't have. How are things really?"

"Hell. Absolute hell. If anyone had told me the day would come when I'd be eyeing the living-room couch lasciviously and falling on it at the first opportunity, so fagged that I sink into immediate unconsciousness, I'd have said they were mad. But that's what it has come to. When I sleep, it's with a passion most mortals bestow on other things."

"What about your writing?"

"Who has time to write? It's all I can do to keep up with Cinq, the washing, and cleaning, the formulae. I really didn't intend producing a son and heir quite so promptly. It was that boring cruise and all the champagne."

"Doesn't Cornelius help?"

"He's never around. He can't come to grips with the fact that diapers must be changed, rinsed, and eventually laundered. And we really can't afford a diaper service."

"Maybe once he gets his doctorate, things will be different."

"It doesn't matter. I don't care anymore."

"That's not true and you know it."

She leaned across the table; her eyes were bloodshot, she looked like hell. "It's the truth, so help me. My only solace is in the bottle under the sink. It warms me whenever I need it. It's my only friend, present company excepted; it never lets me down. You never let me down either, but I never see you anymore. How old are you?"

"How old am I?" I was startled by the question. "I'm the same age as you, twenty-five. Why?"

"Seems to me a lot of my heroines in those idiot novels we used to write were twenty-five. Now that I'm there, I find that I'm not heroic at all. All I am is over twenty-one in a big way. Cornelius complained bitterly for about twenty minutes when he hit thirty, but how can I take him seriously? He doesn't have the slightest recollection of being twenty-one,-five,-eight, or -nine. In fact, now that I think of it, he doesn't recall much—people's last names, where he left his raincoat, me. Sound familiar?"

"Why don't you leave him?"

"I can't. What would I do? Besides, it would kill my father. There's never been a divorce in the family. We just don't quit, we stick it through, hell or high water."

"You can't go on this way."

"Sure I can, with a lot of help from my friend under the sink. Besides, there are so many beautiful underclassmen up there, I just may throw caution to the winds and take one on as a lover."

"I thought you abhorred them all."

"Whatever gave you that idea?"

"Something you wrote about hypersensitive, adolescent neurotics in their dreary revolts."

"Well, not all of them are like that."

"Let me know how you do."

"I will, don't worry. Not that you need to know; you can have anyone you want and probably do."

"Not really."

"Well, get on the stick, Jinny. We're not getting any younger, you know."

"I know. I feel as though almost all of my time has run out, that I don't have much longer."

"Really? In what way?"

"I don't know, it's just a feeling, a feeling that I'll never live to see thirty. There's still so much to do and so little time."

"Is something wrong? Is there something you haven't told me about?"

"No, nothing like that. It's hard to explain."

She lit another cigarette and inhaled thoughtfully. "It could be because both your parents have died so young. It could be that. It could just be Percy Shelley's complaint."

"Which one?"

"The one in 'Ode to the West Wind,' where he falls upon the thorns of life and bleeds. You've had more thorns than anyone I know, thorns I may not even know about, and yet you always seem so surprised when you bleed. And why wouldn't you bleed? You were only a child, for God's sake."

"What do you mean?"

"Seeing Jim at the funeral home made me remember the way he used to beat you. Do you know that even after all these years that still haunts me. I sometimes have nightmares about that awful battering about the head he gave you. I still can't believe that he would do something like that in front of anyone. What amazes me, though, is that you survived all that without becoming some sort of monster yourself."

"What makes you think I'm not a monster?"

"Because you always see the best in everything, you're always ready to embrace life and never ever expect it to be cruel. That's how I know you're not a monster. My God, it's a miracle. Look how cynical I've become despite a pretty fine upbringing. You should be the cynic, not me. I don't understand it. I don't understand it any more than I understand why your mother allowed it to happen. Didn't she ever try to stop him?"

"At first she did. But I think we both sensed that he couldn't really help it. All that rage was erupting out of some awful, dark event in his life. I also think mummy thought he would outgrow it when things got better."

"Outgrow it?" Courtney looked around in embarrassment— she hadn't meant to shout. "The man had some sort of deep-seated emotional problem and she thought he would just grow out of it? Just like that?"

"My mother never had the advantage of having had Psych One. You have to remember, her generation was pretty naïve about things like that. They accepted things we don't. Life was different for them, hard."

"You sound like my father telling me about the Depression."

"It did something to them, something we can't begin to understand, something that kept them from questioning life."

"Did you ever wonder why she married him in the first place?"

"Often. I suppose it's easy to understand. He was handsome and she was a young widow, with a child. All the men were going off to war; she was swept away by it all."

"Didn't you ever ask her?"

"I couldn't, it would have hurt her too much. I think in the beginning she really loved him. I think part of the attraction she felt had to do with his pain, the suffering he had gone through."

"Did she tell you that?"

"Not in so many words. I think she wanted to make the world a beautiful place for him and he just couldn't accept that—it terrified him."

"Sounds like he could have used some help. Too bad he didn't consult a psychiatrist."

"It is too bad. Maybe she wouldn't be lying up in that funeral home. Instead she just gave up and anesthetized herself with booze."

"When did she start doing that?"

"I can't tell you the exact moment she went from having cocktails like everyone else. It just happened gradually. She kept trying to get Jim to try for new things, to talk about his feelings, but he just couldn't and she eventually gave up. It wasn't worth all the anger it provoked."

"But why do you suppose he took it out on you?"

"Maybe because I was a reminder of her other life, of the money that was gone, a million things.

"What did happen to the money? Didn't you get any?"

"It just went in poor investments and then that damn house they built. My father's family didn't leave me anything because my name had been changed from Adams to Muir."

"That's ridiculous. Changing your name didn't make you less an Adams."

"In their eyes it did. When my grandfather died, my father's brother got it all as the sole surviving heir."

"That doesn't seem very fair."

"Uncle Chet hated my father. He was the one who stayed behind and ran the farm and the oil business. He felt that it was really his money, that he had earned it."

Courtney took a long swallow of her beer and then thoughtfully licked the foamy moustache off her upper lip. "What about Kirsty? What will happen to her now? Does Jim abuse her too?"

"Not quite in the same way. He scares her to death sometimes, but she has one thing going for her."

"What's that?"

"He's her father and she loves him."

"I believe you now, I really believe you don't hate Jim. I couldn't grasp that for the longest while. I thought you were being a martyr or trying to be noble."

"It isn't being noble. How can you hate someone for being a victim? For being afraid?" I drank my beer glass dry and stared at the white lacework clinging to the sides of the glass. I never really liked beer, but it wasn't so bad with scotch as a chaser. "I do hate whatever it was that crippled him so. That's the part of life I find so hard to bear. I get so sick and tired of all the stupidity and cruelty. Sometimes I wonder where it will all end, what the use of living is."

"Oh my God, Jinny, you aren't planning anything drastic, are you?"

"I'm not planning to end it all—that's not what I mean."

"I hope not, I really do. But I don't want anything to happen to you. You're my only friend. Maybe you should come back to Cambridge with me. What a time we could have!"

"I'd like to, but I can't. I have to go back to work. I don't want to lose my job."

"To hell with Clive Weymouth, he just uses you. Did it ever occur to you that, however esteemed he may be in his own circle, he's somebody the average person has never heard of? Think about it. However good we are, were, or may become, someone, somewhere, has never heard of us."

"That's fine with me."

"What is it you want?"

"I don't know."

"You must want something."

"Another drink would be nice."

She looked around. The bar was empty. "I think they've closed. Look, it's the first time I've ever seen Barney's bar without someone draped over it."

"Have we paid yet?"

"Yes, it's all taken care of."

"What do I owe you?"

"Not a thing. Father gave me some cash for this very thing. God, I think my legs are dead. I can't move them."

"Can you stand up?"

"I'm not sure." She lurched to her feet, then toppled over in a kneeling position on the flagstone. "If the waiter comes, just tell him I'm looking for a contact lens."

I roared with laughter, tears streamed down my cheeks. "Come on, get up. You can't stay down there."

"The floor is cool—I think I'd like to take a nap."

"Get up, Courtney!"

She scrambled to her feet and we put our arms around each other and teetered out to the sidewalk.

"I can't walk another step, I really can't. I simply must sit down." She parked herself on the curb. I sat down beside her and we both began to sob.

"Tell me," she asked as she shakily rose to her feet, "do you ever hear from Evie?"

"Once in a while. She's finally made it into medical school."

"She was always strange. One of those people who is always glad to see one and whom one is always glad to see, but with whom contact grows less and less as time goes on. Do you think it could be us?"

"Maybe. Do you want me to drive?"

"Maybe you'd better"—she handed me the car keys; "I don't feel too terrific."

I fumbled for the ignition and had some difficulty getting the engine to kick over. "Car's cold," I shivered.

"It always does that, even in the heat. Just let it run for a minute. You going to stay at the Slough of Despond for long?" she asked as she poked through the glove compartment.

"You mean the house?"

"Yah. I was sure I stuck some cigs in here before I left."

"I have some." I handed her my pack. "Doubting Castle would be more apt."

"When your stepfather was having those violent rampages, I used to think of it as the Cave of Despair. When I think of the way he used to beat you about the head, it amazes me that you even survived. He doesn't still do that, does he?"

"I'm sure there have been moments these last few days when he would have loved to, but he hasn't since I was seventeen."

"I didn't know that. What happened?"

"I told him that if he ever laid another hand on me, I would kill him."

"Good for you! What made you do it?"

"I had had enough."

"Yes, your house really was the Cave of Despair. What a strange journey it has been."

"I guess I'll get on with it and get back to New York as soon as I can. There's nothing left for me here."

"Do you ever wonder how many of the kids we knew actually read *Pilgrim's Progress* when it was assigned by Miss Mann?"

"They all did."

"It didn't mean anything to them, did it?"

"I don't know."

"I wonder which ones we are. I mean, are you Christiana or am I? Are you Faithful or am I?"

"A little of both, I guess."

"Is New York Delectable Mountain? Is it?"

"I don't know. Sometimes I think so; other times, I don't know."

"We're drunk, aren't we." It wasn't a question, just a statement of fact. I put the car in first and we lurched and sputtered out of the parking lot.

"Jinny?"

I was concentrating on the road. There were two double lines down the center. I put my hand over my eye so I could see the real one.

"Jinny?" Courtney's voice was small.

"Yes?"

"Do you think we'll ever get there?"

"If you open the window, maybe the air will clear my head."

She rolled the window down and turned the heater up. "No, I mean, get to where it is we're supposed to be in life?"

"I don't know." She slumped down in the seat and stared out the window into the blackness. I crept the car around a curve, grateful that we were alone on the road. "Maybe you'd better spend the night. You can drive home in the morning."

"I can't. My mother will worry, and I should be there to give Cinq his early feeding."

"We have to get up early anyway. The funeral is tomorrow."

"You mean you have to go through all that again in the morning?"

A fat raccoon waddled across the road; I slammed on the

brakes and we both were thrown against the dashboard. "Are you all right?"

"Yah, you just startled me. What was it?"

"A raccoon."

"Did you hit it?"

"No." My knees were shaking, but, mercifully, my vision had gone back to normal. "I guess the thing tonight was what they call a wake. The burial is tomorrow."

"Where?"

"I'm not sure—in Westchester somewhere. It's at ten o'clock."

"I don't know if I can come."

"Don't worry about it. Seeing you tonight saved my life. I don't know what I would have done if you hadn't been there."

"I'll try to make it, but you'll forgive me if I don't?"

I nodded.

It was a movie funeral, or maybe the rain was an effect that came with the package. The sun had been shining when the cortege left the funeral home, and, for the first time since the frantic drive up the Merritt Parkway, I noticed that the trees were in full autumn color. And the play had opened. I hadn't even thought about it. It had opened while Courtney and I were sitting in Barney's. After almost two years of preproduction work, I had no idea if it had been a success or a failure.

Only a handful of people attended the graveside services. Genevieve Bouchard, mummy's closest friend, had not appeared at all. Her absence was conspicuous—I couldn't understand it. I knew she attended funerals; not coming to mummy's disturbed me deeply. I staggered slightly as the first clump of earth hit the coffin: Dust to dust and all that, I thought, as I looked at the muddy lump. Two firm hands steadied me at the elbows, and I wondered wildly what they would all think if they knew I was drunk. Agnes would say, "I told you so." She'd love it.

It was all over. I walked alone down the sloping wet lawn to the limousine that would take us back to Connecticut. After today there would really be no reason to ever go back to the house. Kirsty was there, but she was one of them, a Muir; they would take over and finish molding her into whatever image they had for her—whatever image I couldn't fit. Someday I would have to tell her about her mother—how she really was, not what she eventually became.

On the way back to Connecticut I wondered vaguely what to do about all the people who would be coming back to the house. Maybe I could quietly run down to Gold's and pick up some sandwich makings or something while Jim stalled them with coffee or drinks. How awful, no one had thought of them. Mummy always took care of those things. I should have thought of it.

I was the first to reach the house. I entered the kitchen, and a heady, redolent odor filled my nostrils. It was coming from the oven. Through the doorway I could see that the dining-room table had been laid with the best cloth, the silver had been polished, everything had been arranged in a buffet setting. There was an exquisite arrangement of fresh flowers, and new hand-dipped candles had been set in the candelabra.

I approached the table slowly. Even the best linen napkins were out, freshly laundered, without a crease or wrinkle, folded in neat triangles. I turned from the table and looked into the living room. It had been restored. Everything was the way mummy had kept it, even to the little bowls of flowers on the polished tables. Maybe all this had been a macabre nightmare; mummy's touch was everywhere. My eyes filled with tears. I walked back to the kitchen and saw the note:

Casseroles are in the oven, don't forget to heat the rolls, salad will need tossing, dessert in the refrigerator. Coffee is ground and ready to go. Bar is stocked.

Genevieve—

Genevieve. Mummy's best friend. She had thought of the living, of how mummy would have done it.

I leaned on the counter and wept into a freshly pressed tea towel.

Chapter Thirty-eight

The play was a critical triumph and business was perking along at the box office. Clive had an idea for a new play, one that he would write. But first he had to sail to England to talk it over with a director he admired and hoped to seduce into the project. "You're in charge, kid. I know you can handle whatever comes up. Don't let Saunders try to bully you into anything, and if he gets too out-of-hand, call the William Morris office. Worse comes to worst, you can always cable me." He tossed an enormous bottle of pills on my desk.

"What are they?"

"Some new little goodies, in case things get too tense."

It looked like a year's supply. "How long will you be gone?"

"Two, three weeks, maybe a little longer. Don't worry, money's coming in. The accountants will see that you get paid, and that raise I mentioned is in effect, retroactive."

"Thank you. What's the play?"

"Not fully formed in my mind yet, but it will be unlike anything ever done before. I'll work on it while I'm at sea. No one can get at me there, know what I mean? How did everything go up there, in Connecticut?"

"Horrendous. It was just horrendous."

"Death usually is. Well, we'll soon be on our way again."

"Where will you be?"

"Left all the information on my desk, you can't miss it. Well, kid, wish me *bon voyage*—I'm off."

"Right now?"

"Yup, this minute. We sail on the morning tide." He was gone before I could say anything.

I looked around helplessly. The office was a shambles. My desk was piled with heaps of unopened mail, some of it dated before we had left for Washington. Most of it appeared to be bills and unsolicited manuscripts.

I pulled my bottom desk drawer open and lifted out the bottle of Jack Daniel's I'd kept there since first trying it at Tom's. It was a magic bottle, always there and always full. I poured a generous dollop into my coffee mug and walked into Clive's office. His desk was worse than mine—but then, it had always been that way. On top of the pile was a yellow legal pad covered with his unmistakable scrawl.

To whom it may concern: I, Clive V. Clive, of unsound mind, do hereby bequeath Cornell University to my beloved assistant, Virginia Adams Adam. When you find her, please force brandy down her throat. In her reticule you will find the rest of my worldly goods; a bill, past due, from the Hotel Connaught; two used 6¢ stamps, steamed; one hot budget of my unproduced musical *Lady Macbeth Lives It Up at Pickfair*; a picture of Vice President Nixon, smiling; and the keys to petty cash. When you open her reticule, assuming this is possible, you will also find my other shoe. Then turn left at Haverstraw College, which I'd like to leave to the School of Business Administration. I also leave Virginia

Adams Adam Shubert Alley, Rockefeller Plaza, and the Tappan Zee Bridge, both sides.

The scrawl was signed Clive V. Clive. There was no mention of a London address or phone number. I threw the note in the trash, then pulled it out. It would be something to show Tom and maybe it was funnier than I thought. Clive would call or cable when he ran out of pills—he always did.

Tom. Where was Tom?...

When I came to, I was lying facedown on the couch in Clive's office. It smelled awful. I struggled to a sitting position. My God, I had thrown up all over myself. The offices were completely dark. Where had the day gone? My dress was filthy. I walked with difficulty to the bathroom and tried to wash myself in the sink. The water was rusty brown. I turned off the tap and stared at my reflection: I was a mess, I couldn't go out in the street looking like this. I couldn't leave the couch the way it was, either. Somehow I would have to clean everything up.

When I returned to the office I saw that the magic bottle was on the floor, shattered. A pool of liquid surrounded it. I sat down and stuck my finger in the puddle and tasted it. It was bourbon. Someone had broken the magic bottle; its contents were running all over the floor. How would I be able to get home? I needed it, I needed the magic in the bottle. I picked up a shard of glass and began to lick it, then another. *God! Something is wrong, something is terribly wrong. How will I get home? How will I ever get home?*

There was always Houlihan's Bar down the street—if I could just get there and have one drink, then I could manage the walk to the apartment. I didn't know what time it was. What if someone saw me go in there alone? Ladies don't drink in bars. Women who drink alone in bars at night are asking for trouble. *What to do? What to do?* Maybe I could call someone. Maybe someone could come and take me home. I couldn't do it alone. I picked up another piece of glass. Poor magic bottle. *God, you're disgusting!* I wondered whether, if I swallowed some slivers, I would die. Maybe that wouldn't be so bad.

Clive's bottle! Clive had a bottle or two in his desk, at least he usually did. My knees had locked; it was excruciating to stand. I walked back to Clive's desk and began opening the drawers. Eureka! An unopened quart of vodka. My hands were trembling uncontrollably as I tried to get it open. Now I could get home. Now I would feel better. And I had learned something: Never depend on a magic bottle; always have at least one spare, maybe two; that way you'll never have to risk swallowing splinters of glass. Yes, that was the answer; why hadn't I thought of it before?

My body was shuddering, my nerves were shot. Just the thought of going home had done this to me. I remembered the pills. I'll have one and just relax and wait a little while, then I can go home and come back later and deal with the mess in the office. Tomorrow. Tomorrow everything will be better. I saw spots all around me and froze. Not the bugs again—please, God, not the bugs again! I can't deal with them all alone! . . .

"Jesus Christ! You look awful!" It was Dick Phillips, the company manager. Sunlight was streaming through the skylight. I looked down; there was a little bit of vodka in the bottle on the floor at my feet. I wondered if he had noticed it. "Where is your dress?"

I followed his eyes; I was sitting in my slip. Then I remembered. "I got sick, I washed it."

His frown turned immediately to a look of concern. "You should be home in bed. Come on, I'll take you."

I started to cry. "I can't go like this."

He frowned again. "True. Do you have a raincoat or something?"

"Maybe—maybe there's one in the closet."

He opened the door and pulled a black raincoat out. "Is this yours?"

"No."

"Well, it will have to do. Do you think you can get up?"

The coat was enormous; it was one of Clive's. Dick buttoned

it for me, picked up my purse, and helped me to the door.
"You probably have the bug—it's going around, and with what
you've been through, you're really run down. Stay in bed for
a few days. I'll take care of the office."

"I threw up on the couch."

"Don't worry about it. I'll have it cleaned. Maybe you
should see a doctor?"

"I'll be all right. Just a little rest."

"Okay, but if you're not better in a day, I think you should
see a doctor."

I felt ridiculous in the old raincoat. Dick signaled to a cab
and helped me in. I gave the driver the address and we sped
across town.

I had trouble opening the apartment door; my hands were
shaking again. "Do you want to come in for some coffee?"

"No, I'd better get back to the office. You get to bed. I'll
call you later and see if you need anything."

I leaned on the doorjamb, sweat drenching my body. "Thanks,
Dick."

"Feel better. It's a good thing he's gone; you can get yourself
pulled together."

"Who?"

"Clive. You really shouldn't try to keep up with him. He's
crazy. Go on, get to bed, rest!"

I locked the door, slipped the safety chain in place, and
took off the raincoat, letting it lie where it dropped. It didn't
matter, no one was there to see it; I'd pick it up when I felt
better. Dick was absolutely right, I *had* been through a lot.
That's all it was. I was emotionally worn down, exhausted. It
wasn't anything a few days of rest wouldn't cure. I felt better
already. Maybe a soak in a hot tub . . . but first I had to check
and make sure there was something to drink. That would help
me relax, a drink. It never failed.

There were still five bottles of Jack Daniel's. Tom had sent
a case so we would always have a good supply. Right now I
preferred vodka—it didn't smell as much—but there wasn't
any vodka. That was all right, I could get some tomorrow.

Yes, tomorrow. Everything would be better. If it wasn't, I would do as Dick had suggested, I'd see a doctor.

The ambulance wail pierced my skull. God, it was loud. I opened my eyes. Something was terribly wrong, I couldn't move. My arms were pinned to my sides. I closed my eyes; next time I opened them, I would be out of the nightmare, lying in my own bed. But first the boat would have to stop rocking—it was pitching and rolling, and there was a siren; it was stuck—the sound was maddening. I tried to open my eyes again. It was a dream—I was staring into a strange pair of eyes. The siren was loud because I was strapped on a litter in an ambulance. Now what? I tried to speak and gagged. There was a hose down my throat. Oh, God. What is going on?

When I awoke, I was certain it had been a dream. I tried to pull the sheet away from my neck—it was giving me claustrophobia. My arms and hands were tangled in the sheets; I couldn't get them free. My head was pounding, I couldn't breathe. If I didn't get the sheet away from my throat, I would strangle. I stared up at the ceiling. Why is it so high? I must be caught in the sheets on the floor—that must be it. That's why the ceiling seems so much higher. I looked to the right and then to the left. There was mesh on the window. I wasn't in my room. I wasn't in my own bed. I wasn't caught in the sheets. I was tied up. Oh, my God, it's Nizu and Jean-Claude. They've found me. They've come back. They found out about the bugs and they've tied me up so the bugs can walk all over me, eat me alive! Tears were stinging my raw eyes. Tom. Where was Tom?

The doctor looked bored. He stood by as the orderly removed the straitjacket. I rubbed my throat; it was tender.

"Have you had seizures before?"

My voice was scratchy, I sounded like Margaret Sullavan. Tom would like that. "No, never." Seizures? What seizures! I wanted to scream, but instinct told me to keep silent. Just answer the questions.

"Why are you taking Librium?"

I looked at him blankly, then remembered Clive's gift of the pills. "I don't usually take them. My mother just died, they were given to me—" I was about to say by a friend, but stopped.

"Librium and alcohol do not mix well. Didn't your doctor tell you that?"

"No, he didn't." Clive washed the pills down with alcohol. I wondered if his doctor or whoever had given him the pills had told him that.

"Why were you attempting suicide?"

"Suicide!" I was shocked.

"Apparently you were trying to jump out of a sixth-story window. Someone called the police and they brought you here."

"Window? Police?"

He frowned. "You do remember, don't you?"

I didn't know what he was talking about. Should I tell him? "I wasn't trying to jump out the window." That much I knew. I would never jump out of a window; I hated heights. "I was *in* the window," I really could not remember. All I did remember were the bugs again, millions and millions of bugs swarming everywhere—on the floor, the walls, the bed. That was all I could remember. "I was in the window because of the bugs. They were everywhere. I was trying to get away from the bugs."

"What age are you?"

"Twenty-five."

"Do you know what delirium tremens is?"

"You mean dt's?"

He peered at me, his face devoid of any expression. "That's correct. How much do you drink?"

"One or two."

"Just one or two?"

"Yes."

"One or two drinks, or one or two bottles?"

He was the first doctor who had pressed for that information. I didn't know what to tell him. "Sometimes one or two drinks, sometimes one or two bottles."

"Do you know what an alcoholic is?"

I began to cry.

"You will not live another two years if you continue to drink. I don't know any other way to put it. You came in here last night hallucinating, convulsing. If your neighbor had not called the police, you could easily have died, either by falling out the window or of the seizures. You cannot drink again. You may be only twenty-five, but you're in the terminal stages of alcoholism."

I stared back at him. He must be mad. How could I be an alcoholic? I went to work every day, no matter how I felt. Alcoholics couldn't function. I always functioned or almost always functioned. I couldn't be an alcoholic, I was too young.

His voice was tired. He had read my thoughts, he had seen it all before, his eyes said. "If you're smart, you will never drink again. If you're smarter than that, you'll get help."

"You mean I can go home?"

"If you want to. It would be better if you remained here another few days."

"I have to get to work, my boss is away. I'll lose my job if I'm not there."

"I can't force you to stay or to follow my advice, but if you're smart you'll do both."

Thank you. I will stop drinking. Thank you very much.

He closed the chart and looked at me; I knew by his eyes that he didn't believe me. He'd see. I'd do it. I wasn't going to be an alcoholic.

I signed for my purse, wondering how it had gotten into the ambulance with me. There was a twenty-dollar bill in my wallet. I thought I had had more money than that, but I was afraid to say anything. I knew the check I had written would probably bounce if I didn't get some money into the account. I would have to call Clive's accountant when I got back to the office and ask for an advance on my salary.

As soon as I reached the sidewalk, I began to tremble. *Bellevue*. My God, I had been in Bellevue and by some miracle had been allowed to leave. No, I wouldn't ever drink like that again, and certainly would not take the pills if I was drinking. I hailed a taxi and asked if he could break a twenty.

The apartment was a shambles. Some of the tables had been overturned, lamps were on the floor. I wondered who had done it. Maybe a burglar had come in while I was in the hospital. I'd have to report it to the super. I gingerly began picking everything up, set the lamp on the table next to the bed, and then sat down. Was it possible that I had done it?

No one must know. No one must know that I was losing my mind. I lay down on the bed and pulled the covers up around my shoulders.

"Jinny? You there?" Dick Phillips's voice on the phone sounded far away.

"I'm here," I croaked. My throat was parched.

"Clive cabled that he'll be back next Friday. Thought you'd want to know. Feeling any better?"

"Oh, much."

"Nothing like a week in bed to straighten you out."

A week. "I can't believe it's a week."

"Probably wasn't enough for you. Everything's okay here— I got it all cleaned up."

"Thanks, Dick. Thanks, I really appreciate it."

I halfheartedly straightened up the apartment, ran a bath, and put on a pot of coffee. After I'd bathed and dressed, I'd go to the office, get a check to the bank, and come home and rest some more. I wouldn't drink any Jack Daniel's, or take any of Clive's pills.

Clive was raring to get to work, and, most amazing of all, he had bought a new suit. "Savile Row?" I asked as he showed it off.

"I've always wanted one, and since I had a date with Olivier, I figured that was as good an excuse as I'd ever get."

"You had a date with Olivier?"

"Well, not a *date*. We had a meeting to discuss The Project. He likes the idea, but of course won't make a commitment until he sees at least a draft of the script. I made some notes and figure we can start in right away. That is, if you don't have anything planned."

"I have no plans."

"Where's Tom? He been around?"

"No. He's still away on business."

"What is his business anyway?"

"I don't really know. He's always vague the way really rich people are. Maybe managing the money is what he does, I don't know. It's really not any of my business."

"I hear he's a whip-and-chains man, is that true?"

"No! What a thing to say."

"Guess I'll have to wait until you publish your memoirs to find out what that was all about."

"Assuming I ever write them."

"You want to get something to eat? We can order up, if you like."

"Whatever suits you."

"I'm dying for Chinese. Why don't we go to Ho-Ho?"

"Okay, we'll go to Ho-Ho."

"Are we paid up there?"

"Yes, it's safe."

"Good, I hate disguises."

As soon as we were seated, Clive ordered two double martinis. I toyed with the glass, debating whether to drink it.

"What's the matter, kid? Something wrong?"

"No, I'm all right. It's just that I've been trying not to drink while you were gone."

"One won't hurt. Go on, drink up."

Maybe one would be all right. I sipped the martini. My hand was steady. It was delicious—nice and dry.

"You think Olivier will really do the play?"

"If he likes what we write, he will. Want me to order for you?"

"Yes, please."

"And you know what? You're going to get billing on this one." He grinned and spread his hand across the air, indicating a marquee. "The Project, by Clive Weymouth and Virginia Muir. Starring Laurence Olivier. How about that?"

I shivered. A cold fear clenched its fist in my abdomen. I quickly took another sip and let it filter slowly through my stomach. "Is that the title of the play, *The Project*?"

"It is until we come up with something better. Here's to you, kid. Ready for another?"

Two double martinis and a delicious meal. I had never felt so well. Maybe the doctor at Bellevue was wrong. Nothing had happened; in fact, I felt wonderful, better than I had in a long time. I was ready for anything. A lone trumpet sounded in the distance, someone rehearsing somewhere. The notes reached out and touched me, I felt their loneliness. It was a beautiful night, the streets were empty, the theatergoers were in their seats. The night people hadn't started to come out yet. This was my street—I belonged at last, I had a place in the world: I was walking down Broadway with Clive Weymouth and we were on our way to the office to begin a play for Laurence Olivier. Maybe I could do something after all. The trumpet was somewhere above 47th Street, singing its clarion song.

We worked until three in the morning. Clive was pleased with our progress. "What a team," he beamed. "We really work well together. Let's call it a day. We can resume in the morning. I'll drop you in a cab, but first I have to make a call."

I went to the ladies' room, and as I washed my hands, I peeked in the mirror. The face looking back at me didn't look great, but it didn't look terrible either. As I walked back to the office, I wondered whom Clive could be calling at this hour.

"Ready?" he asked.

"Ready."

"I have to make one quick stop—it's on the way. I'm out of Seconals and there's a guy who can help me out. It won't take long."

"I thought you got the pills from the doctor?"

"The old fart cut me off, so I've got a new source. Can't sleep without my goodies. In fact," he leered, "I can't sleep *with* them either. They do keep me nice and even, though, and we need that right now."

As we rode west on 48th Street, Clive chatted happily about the play.

"What if Olivier doesn't like it?"

"Then we'll get somebody else."

In three weeks we had completed a first draft of one hundred and sixty pages. Everyone who read it thought it was marvelous. Clive wanted to take a few days away from it before one last polish, then it would go out for typing and would be on its way to Olivier.

I was tired, but had been able to maintain the discipline of two martinis before dinner, beer only while working, and an occasional amphetamine. No matter how badly I wanted it, I didn't drink in the morning. It was working; I was drinking normally, like other people. The doctor was wrong. He had said I wouldn't be able to do it.

Chapter Thirty-nine

Within a month I was strapped to a table in the emergency room at Bellevue. This time Clive talked them into releasing me within twenty-four hours.

"I'm sorry, kid, it must have been those shitty pills. That's the last time I buy any from a guy in a doorway. Anyway, you stay home and rest for a day or two. Just one more rewrite and then I think we'll be ready to pack the play off to Olivier. Is there anybody you want me to call?"

"No, there's nobody."

"Can you make it?" he asked from the seat of the taxi. I nodded. "I'll be okay, you can go."

"You sure?"

"Yah, I'm sure. I'm just a little weak. I'll come in tomorrow."

"No, not tomorrow. Take the rest of the week. See you Monday. Feel better."

"Thanks, Clive."

* * *

The phone was ringing as I pushed the door open. I walked woodenly to where the sound was coming from, a pile of papers and books on the floor near the bed. I groped through it all for the receiver.

"Jinny! There you are, I was just about to hang up. Where were you, at work?"

"Tom?"

"How have you been?"

"All right." I lay across the bed; my head was spinning. "Where are you?"

"At the airport, between flights. I have a three-hour layover. I can hop a cab and be there in a half an hour, or you can come out here. That might be better—it would give us more time."

"I don't think I can make it."

"Is someone there?"

"No, I just don't think I can physically do it." I took a breath. "I've been ill."

"Are you all right?"

"I will be. I just need rest."

"I'm on my way, see you!" He hung up before I could tell him not to bother.

I rolled over on my back and tried to get my breath. The apartment was a wreck; I hadn't cleaned it in months. My head spun as I sat up. I had better have a drink, something to get me going. My arms and legs wouldn't move. I groped under the bed; sometimes I'd forget and a bottle would roll behind the dust ruffle. My fingers found the familiar smooth contour and I slowly pulled it out and peered over the edge of the mattress at it. It was empty.

The closet—there might be a bottle in there. I struggled to my feet and pulled myself across the room. If there was a bottle, it would be on the floor in the back. Why did I hide bottles? Whom was I hiding them from? There was no one here but me. I'd have to think about that.

I felt around through the shoes and fallen belts until I found what I was looking for. I had to hurry—Tom would be arriving any minute and I had to be on my feet. I was shuddering convulsively as I tried to open the bottle. God, this has got to stop. Something is wrong. I forced myself to swallow. The vodka rose back up my throat; it wouldn't stay down. I began to cry. Tom couldn't find me like this. I swallowed again and held my hand over my mouth. The vodka rose back up through my nose. God, help me. I swallowed again and used both hands—one over my mouth, the other on my nose. The vodka stayed down. I waited a moment, my eyes smarting, and drank again. It stayed down. Another drink and I would be on my feet.

The doorbell buzzed as I sloshed cold water on my face. "I'm coming, I'm coming."

Tom stared at me from the doorway, then stepped in quickly. He caught my elbows in his hands. "My God!" He steered me into the living room, flipping on the light, ignoring the mess, and sat me in a chair. "You should be in a hospital. What are you doing here alone like this?"

"Oh, Tom—" I couldn't control the tears.

He went to the bathroom and came back with a wet facecloth and gently sponged my face. "It's all right, you're going to be all right. How long have you been like this?"

I just looked at him. I couldn't answer, I didn't know. He reached into his inside jacket pocket and pulled out his address book, flipped it open, and picked up the phone. He spoke quickly and softly, then hung up.

"That was a friend of mine, a doctor. He's coming right over. Just relax. I'm going to change my flight, I'll stay here. Don't worry, don't worry."

I wasn't worried, just exhausted. I closed my eyes, aware that he was straightening up the living room. I heard him running water in the kitchen, clattering through the cupboards, then he was standing above me. "Do you have any coffee?"

"Down below. In the cupboard. In the bottom cupboard."

"I'll find it." He was back in the kitchen again.

* * *

The doctor was kind; he examined me and I felt a needle as he injected me with something. I heard him tell Tom that I should be hospitalized and I struggled to speak, but I was too tired, the effort was too great. Something about detox. I needed to be detoxed. Five days at minimum.

"I have to be on the Coast," I heard Tom say. "Everything I have is tied up in this deal—there's no way I can postpone."

"I'll take her in. Call me in the morning and I'll let you know how everything is."

"I feel like I'm running out."

"There isn't anything you can do. Do you know what she's been taking?"

"What do you mean?"

"What drugs has she been using?"

"I don't think she uses drugs. Maybe some amphetamines once in a while—I don't think she took them regularly."

"Any barbiturates? Did you look around?"

"No, I called you as soon as I got here and then made the coffee."

"Okay, check around, especially the bathroom, bring me whatever you find." He turned to me. "What have you taken?"

I indicated my purse; I didn't know what I had taken, but some of Clive's pills were still in there.

Tom returned. "This is all I could find." He was holding the vodka bottle. The doctor had found the bottle of pills and pocketed them.

"Jinny?" Tom's voice was gentle. "This is Henry Shaw—he's a good friend of mine and a doctor. He's going to look after you while I'm gone. Will you do everything he says?"

I nodded. I would do anything anyone said, I couldn't stand it anymore.

The room was quiet, sunny and pleasant. Dr. Shaw stopped in every morning and afternoon. It wasn't Bellevue and I wasn't tied up. "No need for that," he smiled. "You're getting stronger every day. You're very fortunate, you know that?"

"I don't know how I'm going to pay for all this."

"Don't worry about it, it's all taken care of."

"Tom?"

"It's taken care of. Health insurance."

What did he think I was, a moron? I didn't have any health insurance; Clive couldn't keep up with the payments. I told him that.

"Apparently you're covered on the King Lear plan."

I laughed—it sounded ludicrous—but he was serious. "The production company has the coverage, that's the truth."

I knew it wasn't the truth. "How long will I have to be here?"

"Two weeks at least. After that, I'd like it if you could go away, get out of the city, away from everything, and rest and be with people like yourself."

What did that mean? It didn't sound good and I couldn't bring myself to ask. I'd deal with it when the time came.

Tom called every day. "I have an idea," he said through a terrible connection. "Henry says you need a change, a complete change. What do you say you come out here? I have to be here for a bit longer, then we could go to Palm Springs for a few days and come back. Do you think you can make the flight?"

"It sounds wonderful, but I can't afford a trip like that."

"It's a gift. I wish you'd think about it. I'd like you to do it."

"I can't, it's much too extravagant. Besides, Clive would have a fit. He's pissed at me already for being out so long."

"To hell with Clive—he damn near killed you with those goddamn pills of his. You can tell him I said that. Think about it, Jinny. You'll like California."

New York. New York was the problem. So was Clive. Maybe Tom was right, maybe the change would be good. I could get a fresh start and then I could pay him back. I told him I would come only if I could pay him back.

"All right," he relented. "I'll arrange a prepaid ticket. I'll call you back in an hour with the details. And, Jinny?"

"I know, don't drink on the plane."

He laughed nervously. "Do you think you can do that?"

"I think I can."

* * *

Once we were airborne, I settled comfortably against the window and gazed down at the cloud cover. The stewardess brought me a cup of coffee, and it wasn't until much later that I realized all the other passengers in first class had been drinking cocktails and wine for most of the flight. It didn't matter, none of that mattered now. I was leaving New York; that was what had been the problem. In California I could simply be, for a little while anyway. If I like it there, who knows, maybe I'll stay.

Tom was waiting at the gate. He seemed thinner than I had remembered, and for the first time I noticed that his hair was going gray. He collected my bags and we walked to the exit. I squinted painfully in the intense glare of the sun.

"It's so bright here."

"You get used to it. Are you tired? Want to rest a minute before we walk to the car?"

"No, I'm all right."

He loaded my bags into the rear seat and then gently helped me into the front. "I got you a room at the Beverly Wilshire. The Beverly Hills was booked solid, and I didn't think you'd agree to staying with me."

"No, I wouldn't. We have your reputation to consider."

"*My* reputation?"

"Sure. How would it look if people started talking, started telling everyone you were shacked up with Marie Dressler? You'd be ruined forever."

"Marie Dressler?"

"If I looked like Sophia Loren, it wouldn't be a problem. If I looked like Sophia Loren, nothing would be a problem."

"You look wonderful."

"No, I don't, and you know it. If you want to put me on the next plane back to New York, I won't be offended."

"Don't be ridiculous. A few more days away from Clive and you'll be ready to take on the world. Henry says you're making a good recovery. Was he good to you?"

"Apart from his nasty tests, he treated me like a queen."

"Good. We'll check into your room and if you're hungry

go have a bite. I do have to be at a meeting at two. I tried, but I couldn't get out of it."

"That's all right. I'd really rather lie down for a while."

"You sure?"

"I'm sure."

"I'll call before I leave the office. We'll have dinner. Maybe out at the beach?"

"I'd like that."

We dined by candlelight on a terrace overlooking the Pacific. I couldn't see the ocean, but could feel its presence. The night was beautiful. We ate slowly. I sipped a club soda with a lemon twist; it was delicious, refreshing. But Tom seemed distracted. It was evident that his mind was somewhere else.

"Is it anything you want to discuss?" I asked as the coffee was served.

"No, it's nothing too serious. I will have to fly down to Mexico City in the morning, but I can be back in time for dinner. I'm just disappointed—I thought we could spend the day together."

"You don't have to push yourself on my account. Isn't that an awful lot of flying in one day? Will you be able to get everything done?"

"If worse comes to worst, I can fly back the next morning. I had no idea this would happen. I feel terrible, bringing you all this way and then having to work."

"I'd feel worse if you didn't do what you're out here to do because of me. I'll be all right. I can wander around and look in the shops, maybe sit by the pool. I know some people out here. I could call them and visit. Really, I'll be all right."

"That's a thought. Maybe you could call when we get back to the hotel?"

"I will. I'd like to see them."

"Who are they? What do they do?"

"One guy is an agent now. He used to be an actor and came out about six years ago when all the television moved west."

"Do I know him?"

"No, but you'd like him. He's very nice and he won't get me drunk, if that's what you're worried about."

"That's not it. I just don't like leaving you alone in a strange town."

"I've been in strange cities before. I really don't mind."

Tom saw me to my room. His mouth was tense as he scribbled a phone number on the memo pad next to the telephone. "If anything comes up and you need to reach me, this is where I'll be. I'll call you as soon as I know what my schedule is, okay?"

He kissed me lightly on the forehead. "See you soon. Rest well."

"I will." I stood in the doorway and watched him walk down the corridor. He turned and waved before rounding the corner to the elevators.

I had forgotten to put the Do Not Disturb sign on the door and was awakened by a rotund woman who apologized profusely as she backed out through the door. My watch had stopped; I didn't know what time it was. I dressed and went down to the coffee shop. It was almost lunchtime. I'd walk around for a bit, give the maid a chance to make up the room, and then go back up and see if I could reach Dan. It was a beautiful day and I felt well, really well.

"Jinny!" Dan's voice boomed. "Where are you? When did you get in?"

I explained that I would be in town for just a short while and was waiting for Tom to get back from Mexico.

"You've got to come by and have a dinner—I want you to see the house. Pat will be thrilled when I tell her. Let me call you right back."

I hung up and flipped on the television set. Nothing but some mindless game show. I changed the channels until I found an old movie, then sat on the freshly made bed, waiting for the phone to ring.

When it did, I was surprised to hear Tom. "I can't make it back tonight—I'm really sorry. Did you reach your friends?"

"Yes, we'll probably have dinner. I'll probably go to their house."

He was relieved, which for some reason annoyed me. I was beginning to feel like a prisoner, even though I knew he was only trying to help. Why did he have to be such an old woman about it?

Dan called back an hour later. "Sorry it took so long, but I couldn't get hold of Pat. She'll pick you up at five-thirty, is that all right?"

"That's great. Can I bring anything?"

"Nothing, just yourself. Wear something casual, we'll sit out by the pool."

"I don't have anything that isn't casual."

"Still the same old Jinny." He hung up.

It was 1:30. Four hours to kill. I decided to go out and get something to take to them; it wouldn't be right to go empty-handed. I descended to the lobby and walked out the Wilshire Boulevard entrance. Everyone on the sidewalks looked like they had been curried and groomed for a technicolor extravaganza about Beverly Hills. No one was a day over twenty-two. I felt fat, dumpy, and old, and kept walking, too intimidated to enter any of the shops. I passed a liquor store.

What to get? A house gift would be nice—some little thing, a token. But what? I began walking back toward the hotel and entered the liquor store. Wine, a nice bottle of wine. Dan and Pat had no problem with booze; they might like a nice glass of wine. I'll get one of each, white and red. That way something's bound to go with the dinner. I pored over the bottles and finally made my selection.

"Can you gift-wrap them?" I asked the man behind the counter.

"Certainly."

"Oh, and two quarts of Smirnoff."

He packed the bottles into a shopping bag and I stepped back onto the sidewalk. Yes, it would be good to see Dan and Pat. Like old times. Maybe they'd know of a job. Who knows, maybe I'd even be able to earn enough to buy a little house of my own.

I changed into khaki pants, a loose overshirt, and espadrilles. Not exactly Beverly Hills chic, but who cared? I brushed my hair, stuck the brush in my purse, and picked up the shopping bag. It was heavy. I reached in and removed the two quarts of vodka and set them on the floor of the closet next to my only other pair of shoes.

Pat was waiting in a Mustang convertible; she looked tanned and wonderful in oversize sunglasses. I set the shopping bag on the floor behind the passenger seat.

"What's that?" she asked as I slid in beside her.

"Just a little something for you and Dan."

"You shouldn't have."

"I know, but I'm glad I did."

She drove easily through the traffic to Laurel Canyon. I was intrigued by the size and closeness of the houses. There was no land here. It surprised me.

"It's like living in an apartment. We can hear the neighbors when we're in our bedroom. It's all an illusion, but we love it. We have the feeling of country living and Dan can be at his office in fifteen minutes. Not like back east, where you have to hassle with commuting."

The house was smaller than I had expected, but charming and cool. I handed Pat the package with the wine and she set it on the kitchen counter.

"Want a gin and tonic? We can relax until Dan gets here—everything's in the oven. I hope you like rack of lamb." She popped the oven door open; the aroma was magnificent.

Dan arrived a little later, also tanned and Californian in slacks and silk shirt. He wore Gucci loafers without socks. "I thought you said you hadn't gone West Coast," I smiled.

"I haven't. This is conservative compared to some, and it sure beats a three-piece suit. I'm surprised you haven't moved out here. This place is more your style. You could go to work in what you have on."

"I'd love that."

"I haven't worn a girdle for three years," Pat boasted. "And what's more, I don't need one. We play tennis every day of the year."

"How about a martini?" Dan asked, rubbing his hands.

"No, thank you, I'm not drinking."

"Mind if we have one?"

"No, go ahead."

He went to the kitchen and yelled, "Want some iced tea or a soda?"

"Iced tea will be fine."

He returned with a tray, two frosted martini glasses, a glass pitcher, and a large tumbler of iced tea. *"Voilà!* God, it's good to see you. How long have you been on the wagon?" He sat easily in an armchair and poured the martinis. They looked delicious. I tasted the tea. It was good.

"A while."

"I'm glad to hear it. We were worried about you."

"You were? When?" When were they worried? I hadn't seen them in three years.

"That New Year's party when you passed out in the coat closet."

"I didn't pass out, I fell." I didn't remember the episode.

"Then when we got you to the street and you wouldn't get into the cab, that was frightening. A policeman came over to see what the commotion was all about, and Dan and I had to throw you in. Remember that?"

I didn't know what they were talking about. I sipped more tea.

"Anyway, there were some other things—the time you smashed all your perfume bottles and then insisted the next day that someone else had done it. It really worried us, but heaven help anyone who suggested you stop drinking. When did it happen?"

"What?"

"Stopping. When did you stop?"

"A while ago." I was getting annoyed. Why were they drinking so slowly? The ice was melting in the pitcher and they didn't seem to care.

"I hope you don't mind, but we're having some other people in. A client of Dan's, Charlotte Perkins."

"The old dancer?"

"She's an actress now. Man, she had a rough time. She almost died from booze and pills. She doesn't see well at all, but she's got a nice little career for herself with character parts. You'll like her. Dan didn't want to cancel her, she's so hard to pin down for a dinner date. She doesn't go out much."

"If she can't see, how does she get around?"

"She lives with a guy—he drives her everywhere. He was an old fan. He's the one who saved her life—bailed her out of the drunk tank and got her into a hospital."

Just like Tom. I drank down the rest of the iced tea.

"Ready for some more?" Dan asked.

"Yes, thank you."

"It was a mess, in all the papers. No studio would hire her, she was broke, all her money gone. They thought she might lose one of her legs."

"What from?"

"The booze. I mean she was really nearly dead when Ben came along. He's very sweet, he just likes being with her. I don't think they nooky around, but if they do, that's terrific. Gives you hope for the future." Pat smiled and rose from the chair. "Got to check the oven."

I couldn't take my eyes from the nearly full cocktail glass. Why was it people who could drink never knew how? What a waste.

Charlotte Perkins was a nice woman. Ben listened attentively to everything she said and would urge her on when she tried to retire from the conversation. They offered to drop me at the Beverly Wilshire, it was on their way. I kissed Pat and Dan. The wine bottles were still on the counter unopened. I wondered if they would remember who had brought them when they finally did get around to opening them.

As we pulled into the Beverly Wilshire, Charlotte suggested we meet for lunch.

"I'd like that," I said as I stepped out of the car.

Ben scrawled the telephone number on a piece of memo paper and I stuffed it into my purse. "Thank you, I really enjoyed meeting you."

"Don't forget, lunch before you go back."

"All right," I promised, knowing I probably wouldn't call her.

The message light was flashing on the telephone when I let myself into the room. I called the desk.

"Mr. Cavendish called twice. He will not be able to return until Friday. He will call again in the morning."

"Thank you." I hung up. Friday. This was only Wednesday. Maybe I would rent a car and drive around a bit, see if I could find the Pacific Ocean. It would be good to see it in the daylight. Yes, that's what I would do. I might even call Charlotte Perkins.

The bell captain arranged for a car and rang back when it had been delivered. God, everything was so easy when you had money, when your name was Cavendish. It was going to be another nice day; maybe I would sit on a beach somewhere. I took a large bath towel and folded it and put in my bag. Then I picked up the vodka bottles. They couldn't be in the room when Tom came back; if he saw them, he would suspect the worst. I would give them to Charlotte Perkins. I'd call her and take them to her.

As I stood waiting for the elevator, I remembered. Charlotte Perkins didn't drink. Well, maybe her friend would like them. I stepped into the elevator and descended, standing quietly behind the attractive woman in black who operated the lift in absolute silence.

I signed for the car, the bell captain handed me the keys, and I negotiated my way through the Mercedes and Rolls-Royces toward the Pacific Ocean. This was the life! Maybe I could find something out here. To hell with Clive! To hell with New York!

I drove along the Pacific Coast Highway and finally came to a beach. There it was—the Pacific. Through the smog I could make out the line of the continent as it reached an arm into the sea. I wondered if it was Malibu. The bottles were beside me, in the bag. What friends they had been. My bottles had gotten me through everything; they contained the magic I lacked for living. Maybe one small drink wouldn't hurt. I pulled a bottle slowly from the bag. It was clear, refracting light like a diamond. My dear old friend, don't let me down.

It was dark. I was lying under a car and something was prodding me in the ribs. It was a foot, a foot with a shoe on it. A man's foot. I tried to move; the pain in my ribs was excruciating. "Just drag her out," I heard a voice say.

"Is she dead?" another asked.

"No. Just drunk. Come on, give me a hand."

I felt myself being dragged to the grass—it was moist, cool. I tried to get up, run away. I couldn't move, no matter how hard I tried. Hands were on my shoulders, lifting me to my knees. I vomited. The hands released me and I lay facedown in the sour-smelling contents of my stomach. *Oh, God.* Could they hear me? *Oh, God. Let me die. I can't bear it anymore.*

Chapter Forty

The fishermen had opened my purse and found Charlotte's number. I was propped against a tree when she arrived with Ben. I was aware of her kneeling in front of me. "Oh, Jinny." She breathed it softly. I could hear Ben telling the men that it was all right, that they knew me and would get me home.

"Hadn't we better wait for the police? I called them right after I called you."

"We'll wait, you don't have to stay."

"Isn't that Charlotte Perkins?"

"Where?"

"Over there with the drunk. Come on, stop kidding, that's Charlotte Perkins."

"No, I'm afraid you're mistaken."

Car doors slammed and an engine started. I heard one of the men say, "Show business!"

"Thank you for calling," Ben said to the driver of the car.

"Help me get her up—she can't be here when the police

come," Charlotte huffed as she tugged at my arm.

The police! I struggled to my feet and leaned heavily on Ben. I knew I was a filthy, disgusting mess. How would I face these people again? They loaded me into the back seat; I heard the door close and the engine start. *Please, God, let me die now.*

They took me to their place. While Ben and a friend went back to get my car, Charlotte helped me out of my torn shirt. What had happened? The last memory I had was of a golden afternoon, the Pacific and the full bottle.

"Don't try to talk, sleep. You can tell me about it in the morning."

When I saw the dirt and oil stains and torn knees of my khakis, I knew it wasn't a dream. My shirt and bra were gone; I had on a loose-fitting man's shirt. My legs were shaking as I walked from the tiny bedroom toward the sound of running water in the kitchen.

Charlotte was at the sink, filling a coffeepot. She looked up and smiled. She had to be at least sixty if she was a day, but everything about her was perfect; her nails, her hair, her gold watch. It was hard to imagine her in trouble with booze or pills. I sank onto a chair at the kitchen table; my whole body was vibrating.

"Coffee will be ready in a few minutes," she said gently as she turned on the gas on the stove.

"I'm sorry," I blurted.

"I know. Don't worry about it. Thank God they saw you in the dark. They could have driven right over you."

That thought hadn't occurred to me. I was sorry they didn't. "I don't know what to do." The words echoed madly in my head.

"Do you want a drink?"

I did, I desperately wanted a drink. I knew it was the only thing that would stop the pain. Instead, I said, "No!" God only knew what I might do.

She smiled kindly and continued to fuss with dishes in the

sink. "You're having a hard time, aren't you?"

My God, that's what I had said to my mother as she lay dying. Dying of what? Not neglect. Dying of what had been spelled out so clearly on the death certificate. Toxic encephalopathy. And next to that, under the column marked "Interval between onset and death": years. On the line below, headed "Conditions, if any, which give rise to the above cause": chronic alcoholism.

I couldn't stop shaking. I tucked my hands under my legs and tried to keep from shaking off the chair.

Charlotte carried two cups to the table and set them down. "Cream? Sugar?"

I shook my head no and stared into the steaming black liquid. How was I going to get the cup up off the saucer without the coffee going all over the place? "It's not funny," I heard myself say.

"What's not?"

"What happened. It's not funny."

"Did you think I thought it might be?" Her voice was musical.

"Everyone usually thinks I'm pretty funny. Especially when something like that happens. Ha-ha, good old Jinny, isn't she funny?"

"It's anything but funny." She sipped her coffee, her large eyes trying to focus on me. I remembered what Pat had said: She was almost blind. You'd never know it the way she moved about the kitchen. But she really couldn't see me. That made me feel a little better. I liked being invisible—it made everything easier.

"My mother died an alcoholic." There, I had said it. The hated word.

Charlotte didn't flinch, she continued to sip her coffee. I wondered what she saw. She set the cup down on the saucer and leaned across the table; her eyes were looking directly into mine. "I'm an alcoholic. Would you like some help?"

The dam burst, I began to cry, uncontrollable, bottomless tears. Tears for the waste, for my mother, Marcel, Courtney, Evie, Annie, my father, Harry and Max, the vanished pony,

Fred and Alice . . . everyone, everything, I had ever known and loved and lost.

Charlotte was speaking quietly, telling me her story. The more she spoke, the more I wept. Her hands searched across the table for mine; I hung on to them, afraid I would fall back, drown. Over and over again she repeated, "You have a disease, you have alcoholism. You can get well."

"How? How?"

"The way I did, in Alcoholics Anonymous."

"I can't. I can't do it, I can't go there."

"Yes, you can."

"I can't do it, I just can't."

"It's nothing but people, people like you and me. It's nothing to be afraid of."

She didn't *understand*. I couldn't go there. I couldn't stop drinking. I had tried and tried and I couldn't stop. "I can't stop, don't you understand? I can't stop drinking. I've tried everything and I can't stop."

"I felt the same way."

I looked at her. She had never felt this way, I didn't care how many jails she said she had been in.

When Ben returned, they both suggested I take a bath and sleep for a bit. They would run my clothes through the wash. "Perhaps you'd like to go to a meeting with us? There's one near the hotel. We can drop you off afterward."

Anything, anything to get away from them. I had made my decision: I was going back to New York as soon as I could. "Yes, all right. I'll go."

The meeting was held in the basement of a church. An enormous crowd of people, healthy and smiling, were greeting each other. They all knew Charlotte, and welcomed me with too much enthusiasm. The walls were hung with little signs, each and every one a dreadful cliché. The exuberance in the room was more than I could stand; I sat in a chair counting the minutes until I could get out and away from these poor, benighted people. I had never really unpacked my bags. I could be ready to leave the hotel in five minutes and make the eleven o'clock plane to New York. The Red Eye, that's the one Clive always took.

The moment I closed the door to the room, I dashed to the phone and ordered a taxi for the airport and threw my belongings into a bag. I was still wearing Charlotte's blouse; I'd mail it back to her when I got to New York—she would just have to understand. I would think of something to tell Tom. There had been an emergency at home, that's what I would say. I scribbled him a note, sealed it in an envelope, and left it at the desk.

"I don't think we can make that flight," the cabdriver said.

"Try. There's an emergency—I have to be on the plane."

The flight had been delayed an hour because of fog. I sighed happily and joined the other passengers in the waiting room. No, I wouldn't drink again. Not ever. I'd work on the play, get some continuity in my life.

"Christ, kid, you ever do that again, don't bother coming back! How could you disappear like that? Here we have Olivier practically signed and you just take off. It's unprofessional. I mean it, do it one more time and I'll see that you never work in the theater again!"

"Yes, Clive. I know, Clive. I'm sorry, Clive."

"Oh, stop groveling. Call the Stage and order some food so we can get to work."

"Clive?"

"What!" He growled the word.

"Thanks."

"Aaah!" He gave me the Italian salute. "Just call the Stage. Today we're going to make the magic happen. You don't know how to tango, do you?"

"Not that I know of."

"No matter, we'll muddle through." He popped three Dexamil Spantules into his mouth and began scribbling on his pad.

I walked to my desk and called the delicatessen, then slowly returned to Clive's office. He threw *Variety* across the desk at me. "Look at that! Olivier's been signed for something else. Now we'll have to rewrite the thing for someone else. I don't know about you, but I've had it. Come on, let's go have a drink."

"But I just phoned the order in to the Stage."

"Well, call and cancel it. Do you good to get out and mingle with people."

We ambled down Broadway. It was late afternoon, too early for the theatergoing crowd. Broadway had the feeling of a small neighborhood; many of the faces were familiar, a few were well known. Clive stopped occasionally to chat with an out-of-work actor or actress, and on the corner of 46th Street we bumped into Jerry Hartford. He joined us in our march on Sardi's bar; I suspected it was because he could always be relied upon to pick up the check.

My legs began to ache from standing in the crush at the bar. All the stools were taken, and I was sick and tired of ginger ale. Clive was tossing down one martini after another; I resented the fact that he could have them without any ill effect.

"Jerry's the best goddamn stage manager I've ever worked with," Clive roared through the din. "The best!"

"Okay, Clive," Jerry said, "I think it's time we fed the caged animal. Come on, let's go somewhere quiet."

"We take the kid. You know what, Jer?"

"No, what?"

"She doesn't drink. You know why?"

"No, and I don't need to know." He looked apologetically in my direction.

"Because she turns into David O. Sleznik. That's absolute fact. Show him, Jinny. Show him how you turn into David O. Sleznik."

"You mean Selznik?"

"No, Sleznik. He's a crazy cloak-and-suiter I know—has a shop down on Orchard Street. Buy all my clothes there, can't you tell?"

"Come on, Clive, it's time to go. Jinny doesn't feel like doing Sleznik tonight."

"As a matter of fact, I do." I peered through the bodies in front of the bar and took a glass. It looked like a scotch.

My arms ached. The light was on; I didn't know whether it was morning or night. A half-empty bottle was sitting on the bureau. I'd done it again.

I lay back on the bed; the sheets were tangled. I waited for something to happen, anything. My legs twitched. I pulled myself up and slowly clutched my way to the bathroom and knelt over the toilet and waited. When the retching had subsided, I pulled myself up to the sink and turned on the cold water, then raised my head and looked in the mirror. It was time for my you're-disgusting speech.

I was fascinated by the face peering back at me: bloated and old, the hair matted and dirty; two front teeth were missing; one eye was ringed with blue, like a cartoon shiner. "Who the hell are you?" My voice echoed feebly against the tiles. It couldn't be me, it just couldn't. I sloshed icy water on my face and winced; my eye and mouth hurt. I looked again and raised my fingers to my eye. It *was* me. My God, what had happened?

I crept back by the bed. The phone was off the hook. I sat down on the floor and tried to put the receiver back in the cradle. Was it connected? Was the phone still working? I didn't know. I lifted the receiver again and listened for a dial tone. It was there. My hands were trembling; excruciating spasms were seizing my stomach. The bottle was at eye level. I tore my eyes away and tried to place my index finger in the dial. Whom could I call? Who was left? I tried again; my finger hooked in the last circle, "O" for Operator. Zero. Zero for Jinny.

"Operator," I whispered, "can you connect me with AA?"

"One moment, please." I wondered if they had to go to school to learn how to land on the "M" and "N" the way they did. As I waited, I forgot whom I was calling. Oh, well, I'd know as soon as whoever it was answered.

* * *

The phone was ringing, right in my ear. I swung my hand out and knocked it over. I was on the floor, the phone next to my head. Maybe it was Clive—I must be late again. "Hello?"

"This is AA. You left a message last night?"

"I did? I did. Did I?"

"Are you Jinny?"

"Yes."

"I'm Grace. You left your name and this number. Are you in trouble?"

"Oh, yes, I'm in trouble."

"Are you drinking now?"

"What is now?"

"Now, while you're talking to me."

"No, not now. Not yet."

"Good. That's very good. When did you have your last drink?"

"I don't know. I mean, I don't know what day this is—could you tell me that?"

I was beginning to cry. I heard the voice say to someone on the other end, "Hey, Herb, I've got a live one here."

"Jinny?" The voice was back, clear. It had a definite accent, Bronx. "You want someone to come?"

"Here? Now?"

"Yes. If we send someone, will you let them in?"

"Oh, yes, please. Please."

"Okay. Give me your address and the apartment number, I'll try to get someone right away. Don't have a drink now, okay? Don't have a drink yet, I'll call you right back."

"Right back?"

"Right back. Hang up the phone so I can call you back and tell you who's coming."

"Hang up?"

"Just hang up the phone. Stay right next to it, don't move at all, I'll call you right back."

I hung up and cradled the phone in my lap and waited.

"Jinny? This is Grace. I haven't found anyone yet, but I'm still trying. Did you drink?"

"No."

"That's great. I'm going to call you back again. Stay right by the phone, okay?"

"Okay."

I leaned against the bureau. The bottle was behind me, directly above my head. I didn't look up—I couldn't lift my head. I stared at the phone, waiting.

So it went. Every five minutes, Grace called—she was still trying. Don't drink, hang up, I'll call you back.

"Grace?"

"Yeah?"

"What day is this?"

"You want to know what day, really?"

"Really."

"It's Saturday, April fifteenth."

April 15? I had been at work only yesterday, and the calendar on my desk had said March, March something. "Are you sure?"

"Sure I'm sure. I'm going to try somebody else now. I'll call you back."

No one came. Grace called every ten minutes; I hung on to her voice as she assured me that she would find someone. As the day wore on and it became clear that no one in my area was available, she asked: "Do you think you can get to a meeting?"

"A meeting?"

"There's an AA meeting not far from you. Do you think you can get to it?"

"Where is it?"

"Fifty-ninth and Third. Can you get there?"

"I'll try."

"Are you dressed?"

"Not really."

"Go and put some clothes on. I'll call you back. Go ahead, you can do it."

I wasn't so sure she was right. My legs had long since gone dead. I slowly pulled on a turtleneck sweater and a skirt.

"Jinny?"

"Yes, Grace."

"You dressed?"

"Almost."

"Okay, the address is 347. If you leave now, you'll get there in time for the meeting. Better wear a coat, it's supposed to get chilly tonight. I'll call you tomorrow and see how you're doing. Will you go?"

"I'll try."

"You can do it. If you don't drink, you can do it." She sounded exhausted.

"I won't drink."

"Go to the meeting. People will help you there."

"They won't let me die alone?"

"No, Jinny. They won't let you die alone. I promise you that."

Chapter Forty-one

*It's been almost fifteen years, I realize, since that day I hung
on to Grace's voice. She had told the truth—they didn't let
me die alone. I still look for her at meetings. I still listen
intently, hoping to hear her voice.*

My back aches, my hands are cramped. I have been standing
at the foot of Courtney's bed for I don't know how long. I
have been looking at my life through a dusty prism, watching
the moments in time like dust motes floating in the sunlight.
Is it my imagination? Is the pulsebeat in the ankle under my
left hand a little stronger? I lift my hands and slowly flex the
fingers; they are numb. It could have been my own pulse, but
I don't think so. When had I seen her last? Was it the time she
had told Cornelius she was coming to New York to visit me
but had really come down to have the affair? Yes, that was the
last time.

She had sat with the scotch bottle planted squarely in the center of the coffee table, saying we had a lot to tell each other. We had to make the evening count, cram a week's worth of talk into one night. It made her uncomfortable when I told her I didn't drink anymore.

"You? That's ridiculous, you love scotch!"

"I do, but I don't love what it does to me."

"Well, if you don't drink on an empty stomach, or when you're upset, you'll be all right. Just one? For old times' sake?"

"Not even one. I can't have even one."

She stared thirstily at the scotch. "Well, damn it, I'm not going to let you spoil my fun. I'll have one. I'll have *more* than one." Her hand was trembling as she twisted the top from the bottle and poured a generous drink. "Cheers!"

We talked the night through, remember? You got pretty maudlin as the bottle emptied and went on about how I had always been the reflection of your better self. That I had the courage you lacked. That you knew it the day I told you I had sent my manuscript to Random House. You tried to ridicule me because I knew your darkest secret. I knew your fear and said so. I said it because I cared about you, because I saw your talent.

How long has it been since you cried on my coffee table? Twelve years? I heard there had been another child, but no birth announcement ever came. Why didn't you write or call?

I don't need the answer. I know.

I shake my hands again and gingerly stretch my back and walk to the window. It would have been a good morning to sit on the beach, sharing coffee, hearing about it all. I would love to listen, Courtney. But I can't hear you if you don't speak.

I approach the bed again and place my hands on the ankles once again. Yes, the pulse is stronger, and it isn't mine. "Come on, Courtney, it's time to come back. You can't stay out there forever." I look at the fine head; it moves slightly. "Courtney, I know you can hear me. Come back."

It's no use. I can't do it. What arrogance to think that I could. I should go and tell Connie—let them handle it, they're the pros. The eyelids flutter slightly. I hold my breath and wait.

She looks at me, unseeing. I release my hands slowly and let them hang at my sides. "Hello, Courtney." I say it softly. She is looking right at me.

"Jinny?" The voice is weak, pitifully small. "Jinny? Is that you?"

"Yes." I exhale the word, trying to unlock the tightness in my chest. My back is aching again; I've been standing in one position too long.

She tries to sit up slowly and is held by the restraints. Her eyes widen as she realizes the truth of where she is. She lies back and closes her eyes.

"Courtney, look at me." She is starting to slip away again. "Courtney, I want you to open your eyes and look at me. I know you can." I can hear the anger in my voice.

"How did this happen? How did I get here?"

I smile and stroke her damp forehead. "I was hoping you could tell *me*."

"We were at the Lyttons', a cocktail party. I wanted to go home and Cornelius wouldn't take me—he said it was too far. I guess he didn't realize I meant *home*. The old house. I left the party and started walking. I couldn't find it. I kept walking and walking and I couldn't find it. It was gone."

"You were trying to find your old house?"

"Yes. I must have turned the wrong way and gotten lost in the dark. Can you imagine that? I couldn't find my house. You knew that my parents both died?"

"No, I didn't know."

"First father, then my mother two years later. I know the house was sold, but why couldn't I find it? I thought I had lost my mind."

I stroke her head. "Courtney, how long has it been since you've lived in that house?"

"A long time. Twenty years?"

"At least that. Don't you remember why your parents sold it?"

She closes her eyes and sighs, all the tension is slipping out of her body. I take her chin with my fingers and slowly turn her head back toward me. Her eyes are open. "I remember now. They sold it because of the thruway. The thruway is where the house used to be."

"That's right. You did find it."

"I did?"

"Yes. Don't you see? That's where you were found, walking along the thruway."

Her eyes widen. "I was walking along the thruway?"

"That's right. A truck driver brought you in. You were confused, to say the least. They admitted you as a Jane Doe."

"I don't remember any of it. All I remember is wanting to go home and people wouldn't let me. Is that why I'm in this? Because they don't know who I am?"

"Yes."

"But *you're* here. *You* know who I am."

"Yes, I do."

"Jinny?"

"Yes, Courtney?"

"Do you think you can get me out of this?" She tugged gently at the restraints.

I felt the tears beginning to well in my eyes as I touched her cheek. "I'll try, Courtney. I'll try."

About the Author

MARIANNE MACKAY has worked in New York as a publicist in publishing, theater, and advertising. She was born in Port au Prince, Haiti, and has lived in the Dominican Republic, England, and Washington, D.C. She now lives and works in Connecticut.